The Moon Maid

# The Moon Maid

*Complete and Restored*

Edgar Rice Burroughs

INTRODUCTION TO THE BISON BOOKS EDITION BY

## Terry Bisson

AFTERWORD BY RICHARD J. GOLSAN

"RED BLOOD VS. THE RED FLAG" BY PHILLIP R. BURGER

GLOSSARY BY SCOTT TRACY GRIFFIN

FRONTISPIECE BY J. ALLEN ST. JOHN

ILLUSTRATIONS BY THOMAS FLOYD

University of Nebraska Press
Lincoln and London

Publisher's preface, afterword, glossary and alterations to the text © 2002 by the University of
Nebraska Press
Introduction © 2002 by Terry Bisson
"Red Blood vs. the Red Flag" © 2002 by Phillip R. Burger
Illustrations © 2002 by Thomas Floyd
Manufactured in the United States of America

Library of Congress Cataloging-in-Publication Data
Burroughs, Edgar Rice, 1875–1950.
The moon maid / Edgar Rice Burroughs; introduction to the Bison Books edition by Terry Bisson;
afterword by Richard J. Golsan; Red Blood vs. the red flag by Phillip R. Burger; illustrations by
Thomas Floyd.
p. cm.
"Complete and restored."
ISBN 0-8032-6200-0 (pbk.: alk. paper)
1. Human-alien encounters—Fiction.  2. Moon—Fiction.  I. Title.
PS3503.U687 M66  2002
813'.52—dc21
2001055642

# Contents

# Illustrations

# Publisher's Preface

A S EVERY devotee of Edgar Rice Burroughs recognizes, the twenty-first century is the century of *The Moon Maid*, one of the most beloved science fiction epics of all time. Julian 5th, commanding officer of *The Barsoom*, life companion of the fair Nah-ee-lah, and co-originator of the Great Feud between the houses of Julian and Or-tis, was born in 2000. *The Barsoom* departed on its ill-fated voyage in 2025; twenty-five years later Lieutenant Commander Orthis invaded Earth at the head of a formidable force of Kalkars and Va-gas. By the time of Julian 9th's birth at the close of the century, Earth was conquered and suffering under the rule of the Moon Men.

As we slip into an age anticipated by, dreamed of, and perhaps feared by the "Master of Adventure," it is fitting that his masterpiece future history of this era be made available for all readers. You have in your hands the most complete version of *The Moon Maid* that has ever been published. It has long been known and lamented by Burroughs readers that the 1926 book edition of *The Moon Maid* is essentially an abridged version of the original tale that was published serially in *Argosy All-Story Weekly* in 1923 and 1925. As Alan Hanson has noted (*Burroughs Bulletin* 34, spring 1998), Edgar Rice Burroughs cut substantial portions of the tales "The Moon Men" and "The Red Hawk" (parts 2 and 3) when *The Moon Maid* saga was converted into a book.

This edition contains the text of the original serialization of *The Moon Maid*, and thus it encompasses and reflects the scope and depth of the original vision of its creator. But there's more. Guided by Alan Hanson's research and a careful comparison of the magazine and book editions of the epic, we have incorporated numerous passages, sentences, and words that were either excised by the magazine editors or were added later by Burroughs or an editor to the book edition. Spellings, capitalization, and chapter titles and organization have been standardized to follow usage found in the 1926 book version. A list of such alterations to the magazine text is provided at the conclusion to this edition.

At once exciting, moving, and surprisingly melancholic—a monumental and unsurpassed contribution to science fiction—the intergenerational saga of the Julians and their never-ending struggle for freedom at long last can be fully appreciated and enjoyed.

Gary H. Dunham
Editor in Chief
University of Nebraska Press

TERRY BISSON

# Introduction

I T WAS, I believe, Harlan Ellison who pointed out, with not inconsiderable pride, that easily half of the most enduring fictional characters in modern culture have come to us from genre literature. Thus we have strutting across our stage with the likes of Hamlet, Frankenstein, Don Quixote, Superman, Sherlock Holmes, Job, and Edgar Rice Burroughs's immortal creation, Tarzan.

Any author who has made such an indelible mark on the human imagination needs little introduction and less apology. Had he written nothing else, Burroughs's place in cultural (not to say literary) history would be secure. But of course he did. Write much else, that is.

Edgar Rice Burroughs had failed in his ambition to become either a cavalryman or a gold prospector when he picked up the pen in the early decades of the twentieth century and began the astonishing career that was to make him one of the world's most popular, if least respected, authors.

The early success of both *A Princess of Mars* and *Tarzan of the Apes* led to his production of a torrent of tales—some ninety narratives in all—whose settings, all wildly exotic, ranged from unexplored Africa and Mars to the center of the Earth (Pellucidar), from the steaming jungles of Venus to, what then seemed implausible, the hollow core of the Moon.

Many of these books were sequels to and embellishments of Burroughs's earlier successes. All were written at a dead run, and most were serialized in pulp magazines like *Argosy*, *All-Story Weekly*, and *Blue Book*. They are cliffhangers in which "only the cliffs change," as Brian Aldiss has astutely observed: repetitive, picaresque tales of nonstop adventure based on adolescent fantasies of constrained eroticism and unrestrained power.

*The Moon Maid*, *The Moon Men*, and *The Red Hawk* came rather late in the author's career (the mid-1920s), after Mars had been done to death but before he began writing his last series, set on Venus. The themes are familiar: capture and escape, cruelty and honor, virginity and lust. One senses that the plots have begun to lose their appeal even to their persistent creator. Though the action is fast it is less than furious.

Connected strictly by character (one of which is reincarnated from one generation to the next), and loosely by plot, these three novels, combined here in one volume, cover some five hundred years of future history, in which the earth is conquered by humorless invaders from the Moon.

The trilogy's sequence of events begins in *The Moon Maid*, when a ship bound for Mars is crashed on the Moon as a result of the treacheries of an evil officer-engineer, Orthis. The ship's captain, Julian 5th, is captured by the Va-gas, a bestial centaur race, but he escapes with a beautiful fellow captive, Nah-ee-lah, and throws in with her people, the aristocratic but doomed Laytheans.

Alas, their escape is to no avail. Orthis has armed the Laytheans' former subjects, the resentful, vaguely proletarian and half-educated Kalkars ("those who thought that they thought") with weapons that allow them to obliterate Laythe and prepare for an invasion of Earth.

*The Moon Men* cuts to four generations later. A war-weary and disarmed Earth (the book was written in the aftermath of World War I) was easy pickings. Julian 8th, the descendant of Julian 5th and Nah-ee-lah (the Moon Maid) is a slave in a Kalkar-ruled Chicago. Julian 8th rebels and, with a plucky female at his side, begins to organize his fellow "Yanks" to fight back. *The Moon Men* reads like a 1930s labor saga, except the enemy is not management but a naive, leveling collectivism which "would make all women the property of all men." For Burroughs, who thought each man was entitled to his own, this notion was the ultimate infamy.

By the time of *The Red Hawk* the rebels have been fighting for generations, under the leadership of Julian 8th's descendants. Armed with bows and adorned in warpaint, the "desert Yanks" resemble twenty-fifth-century white Indians, except for their flag of stars and stripes. (The real Indians, meanwhile, are docile, dusky slaves.) Under Julian 20th (Red Hawk) the rebels strike west and retake California in a sea of blood. The descendants of both Julian and Orthis (now Or-tis) unite at last against the Kalkars and their "half-breed" progeny. But the world they rule has been reduced to barbarism.

The action of the three-part story is told through a flimsy framing tale, which even includes a scene on the arctic ice à la Frankenstein. It is formulaic stuff and the formula is worn thin. These three are not the author's best books, and even his best rarely rise above the level of pulp.

But it is not my intention to enumerate Burroughs's literary sins or to echo his detractors. He never aspired to critical success; his innumerable readers are the proof of his pudding. I intend only to affirm the particular importance of these three books, which were instrumental in establishing his now-unassailable reputation as the Father of Modern science fiction.

He was not always considered so.

It is difficult for today's reader to understand that in the last century Burroughs was considered a fantasist, not a respectable science fiction author. Though his stories took place on other planets, their settings were seen as fanciful, improbable, and even absurd.

Such a view was commonly held before the recent triumphant return of the Singapore–Philip Morris lunar interior mapping expedition, which overturned two centuries of obfuscatory Eurocentric pseudo-science and confirmed that the Moon actually *is* a hollow sphere filled with bestial half-humans lusting after the Earth and its women.

To say that this startling but now irrefutable discovery revolutionized planetary science is to belabor the obvious; it altered the literary canon as well, placing Edgar Rice Burroughs at the head of that small but precious coterie of speculative geniuses whose imaginary worlds are prescient reflections of real futures.

He alone understood. And he alone had the courage to address, in prophecy thinly disguised as fiction, the tragedy that awaited unsuspecting humankind. That the Kalkars were destined to outgrow the Moon and cast an envious eye upon our planet, one can unfortunately no longer doubt. That they found Earth to their liking we all now know, to our sorrow. It is only in the incidental details of his future history that Burroughs can be faulted. But what he missed, we all missed. Who among us would have guessed that the cruel Kalkars' ultimate goal was not absolute world domination or total human enslavement, but rather, and rather simply, control of the university presses?

# THE MOON MAID

# The Message from Mars

I MET HIM in the Blue Room of the Transoceanic Liner *Harding* the night of Mars Day—June 10, 1967. I had been wandering about the city for several hours prior to the sailing of the flier watching the celebration, dropping in at various places that I might see as much as possible of scenes that doubtless will never again be paralleled—a world gone mad with joy. There was only one vacant chair in the Blue Room and that at a small table at which he was already seated alone. I asked his permission and he graciously invited me to join him, rising as he did so, his face lighting with a smile that compelled my liking from the first.

I had thought that Victory Day, which we had celebrated two months before, could never be eclipsed in point of mad national enthusiasm, but the announcement that had been made this day appeared to have had even a greater effect upon the minds and imaginations of the people.

The more than half-century of war that had continued almost uninterruptedly since 1914 had at last terminated in the absolute domination of the Anglo-Saxon race over all the other races of the World, and practically for the first time since the activities of the human race were preserved for posterity in any enduring form no civilized, or even semi-civilized, nation maintained a battle line upon any portion of the globe. War was at an end—definitely and forever. Arms and ammunition were being dumped into the five oceans; the vast armadas of the air were being scrapped or converted into carriers for purposes of peace and commerce.

The peoples of all nations had celebrated—victors and vanquished alike—for they were tired of war. At least they thought that they were tired of war; but were they? What else did they know? Only the oldest of men could recall even a semblance of world peace, the others knew nothing but war. Men had been born and lived their lives and died with their grandchildren clustered about them—all with the alarms of war ringing constantly in their ears. Perchance the little area of their activities was never actually encroached upon by the iron-shod hoof of baffle; but always somewhere war endured, now receding like the salt tide only to return again; until there arose that great tidal wave of human emotion in 1959 that swept the entire world for eight bloody years, and receding, left peace upon a spent and devastated world.

Two months had passed—two months during which the world appeared to stand still, to mark time, to hold its breath. What now? We have peace, but what shall we do with it? The leaders of thought and of action are trained for but one condition—war. The reaction brought despondency—our nerves, accustomed to the constant stimulus of excitement, cried out against the monotony of peace, and yet no one wanted war again. We did not know what we wanted.

And then came the announcement that I think saved a world from madness, for it directed our minds along a new line to the contemplation of a fact far more engrossing than prosaic wars and equally as stimulating to the imagination and the nerves—intelligible communication had at last been established with Mars!

Generations of wars had done their part to stimulate scientific research to the end that we might kill one another more expeditiously, that we might transport our youth more quickly to their shallow graves in alien soil, that we might transmit more secretly and with greater celerity our orders to slay our fellow men. And always, generation after generation, there had been those few who could detach their minds from the contemplation of massacre and looking forward to a happier era concentrate their talents and their energies upon the utilization of scientific achievement for the betterment of mankind and the rebuilding of civilization.

Among these was that much ridiculed but devoted coterie who had clung tenaciously to the idea that communication could be established with Mars. The hope that had been growing for a hundred years had never been permitted to die, but had been transmitted from teacher to pupil with ever-growing enthusiasm, while the people scoffed as, a hundred years before, we are told, they scoffed at the experimenters with *flying machines,* as they chose to call them.

About 1940 had come the first reward of long years of toil and hope, following the perfection of an instrument which accurately indicated the direction and distance of the focus of any radio-activity with which it might be attuned. For several years prior to this all the more highly sensitive receiving instruments had recorded a series of three dots and three dashes which began at precise intervals of twenty-four hours and thirty-seven minutes and continued for approximately fifteen minutes. The new instrument indicated conclusively that these signals, if they were signals, originated always at the same distance from the Earth and in the same direction as the point in the universe occupied by the planet Mars.

It was five years later before a sending apparatus was evolved that bade fair to transmit its waves from Earth to Mars. At first their own message was repeated—three dots and three dashes. Although the usual interval of time had not elapsed since we had received their daily signal, ours was immediately answered. Then we sent a message consisting of five dots and two dashes, alternating. Immediately they replied with five dots and two dashes and we knew beyond peradventure of a doubt that we were in communication with the Red Planet, but it required twenty-two years of unremitting effort, with the most brilliant intellects of two worlds concentrated upon it, to evolve and perfect an intelligent system of inter-communication between the two planets.

Today, this tenth of June, 1967, there was published broadcast to the world the first message from Mars. It was dated Helium, Barsoom, and merely extended greetings to a sister world and wished us well. But it was the beginning.

The Blue Room of *The Harding* was, I presume, but typical of every other gathering place in the civilized world. Men and women were eating, drinking, laughing, singing and talking. The flier was racing through the air at an altitude of little over a thousand feet. Its engines, motivated wirelessly from power plants thousands of miles distant, drove it noiselessly and swiftly along its overnight pathway between Chicago and Paris.

I had of course crossed many times, but this instance was unique because of the epoch-making occasion which the passengers were celebrating, and so I sat at the table longer than usual, watching my fellow diners, with, I imagine, a slightly indulgent smile upon my lips, since—I mention it in no spirit of egotism—it had been my high privilege to assist in the consummation of a hundred years of effort that had borne fruit that day. I looked around at my fellow diners and then back to my table companion.

He was a fine looking chap, lean and bronzed—one need not have noted the Air Corps overseas service uniform, the Admiral's stars and anchors or the wound stripes to have guessed that he was a fighting man; he looked it, every inch of him, and there were a full seventy-two inches.

We talked a little—about the great victory and the message from Mars, of course, and though he often smiled I noticed an occasional shadow of sadness in his eyes and once, after a particularly mad outburst of pandemonium on the part of the celebrators, he shook his head, remarking: "Poor devils!" and then: "It is just as well—let them enjoy life while they may. I envy them their ignorance."

"What do you mean?" I asked.

He flushed a little and then smiled. "Was I speaking aloud?" he asked.

I repeated what he had said and he looked steadily at me for a long minute before he spoke again. "Oh, what's the use!" he exclaimed, almost petulantly; "you wouldn't understand and of course you wouldn't believe. I do not understand it myself; but I have to believe because I know—I know from personal observation. God! if you could have seen what I have seen."

"Tell me," I begged; but he shook his head dubiously.

"Do you realize that there is no such thing as Time?" he asked suddenly—"That man has invented Time to suit the limitations of his finite mind, just as he has named another thing, that he can neither explain nor understand, Space?"

"I have heard of such a theory," I replied; "but I neither believe nor disbelieve—I simply do not know."

I thought I had him started and so I waited as I have read in fiction stories is the proper way to entice a strange narrative from its possessor. He was looking beyond me and I imagined that the expression of his eyes denoted that he was witnessing again the thrilling scenes of the past. I must have been wrong, though—in fact I was quite sure of it when he next spoke.

"If that girl isn't careful," he said, "the thing will upset and give her a nasty fall—she is much too near the edge."

I turned to see a richly dressed and much dishevelled young lady busily dancing on a table-top while her friends and the surrounding diners cheered her lustily.

My companion arose. "I have enjoyed your company immensely," he said, "and I hope to meet you again. I am going to look for a place to sleep now—they could not give me a stateroom—I don't seem to be able to get enough sleep since they sent me back." He smiled.

"Miss the gas shells and radio bombs, I suppose," I remarked.

"Yes," he replied, "just as a convalescent misses smallpox."

"I have a room with two beds," I said. "At the last minute my secretary was taken ill. I'll be glad to have you share the room with me."

He thanked me and accepted my hospitality for the night—the following morning we would be in Paris.

As we wound our way among the tables filled with laughing, joyous diners, my companion paused beside that at which sat the young woman who had previously attracted his attention. Their eyes met and into hers

Julian 3rd Tells His Story

came a look of puzzlement and half-recognition. He smiled frankly in her face, nodded and passed on.

"You know her, then?" I asked.

"I shall—in two hundred years," was his enigmatical reply.

We found my room, and there we had a bottle of wine and some little cakes and a quiet smoke and became much better acquainted.

It was he who first reverted to the subject of our conversation in the Blue Room.

"I am going to tell you," he said, "what I have never told another; but on the condition that if you retell it you are not to use my name. I have several years of this life ahead of me and I do not care to be pointed out as a lunatic. First let me say that I do not try to explain anything, except that I do not believe prevision to be a proper explanation. I have actually *lived* the experiences I shall tell you of, and that girl we saw dancing on the table tonight lived them with me; but she does not know it. If you care to, you can keep in mind the theory that there is no such thing as Time—just keep it in mind—you cannot understand it, or at least I cannot. Here goes."

# PART I

## The Moon Maid

*Being the Story of Julian 5th*

# ONE

# The Flight of *The Barsoom*

"I HAD intended telling you my story of the days of the twenty-second century, but it seems best, if you are to understand it, to tell first the story of my great-great-grandfather who was born in the year 2000."

I must have looked up at him quizzically, for he smiled and shook his head as one who is puzzled to find an explanation suited to the mental capacity of his auditor.

"My great-great-grandfather was, in reality, the great-great-grandson of my previous incarnation which commenced in 1896. I married in 1916, at the age of twenty. My son Julian was born in 1917. I never saw him. I was killed in France in 1918—on Armistice Day.

"I was again reincarnated in my son's son in 1937. I am thirty years of age. My son was born in 1970—that is the son of my 1937 incarnation—and his son, Julian 5th, in whom I again returned to Earth, in the year 2000. I see you are confused, but please remember my injunction that you are to try to keep in mind the theory that there is no such thing as Time. It is now the year 1967 yet I recall distinctly every event of my life that occurred in four incarnations—the last that I recall being that which had its origin in the year 2100. Whether I actually skipped three generations that time or through some caprice of Fate I am merely unable to visualize an intervening incarnation, I do not know.

"My theory of the matter is that I differ only from my fellows in that I can recall the events of many incarnations, while they can recall none of theirs other than a few important episodes of that particular one they are experiencing; but perhaps I am wrong. It is of no importance. I will tell you the story of Julian 5th who was born in the year 2000, and then, if we have time and you yet are interested, I will tell you of the torments during the harrowing days of the twenty-second century, following the birth of Julian 9th in 2100."

I will try to tell the story in his own words in so far as I can recall them, but for various reasons, not the least of which is that I am lazy, I shall omit superfluous quotation marks—that is, with your permission, of course.

My name is Julian. I am called Julian 5th. I come of an illustrious family—my great-great-grandfather, Julian 1st, a major at twenty-two, was killed in France early in The Great War. My great-grandfather, Julian 2nd, was killed in battle in Turkey in 1938. My grandfather, Julian 3rd, fought continuously from his sixteenth year until peace was declared in his thirtieth year. He died in 1992 and during the last twenty-five years of his life was an Admiral of the Air, being transferred at the close of the war to command of the International Peace Fleet, which patrolled and policed the world. He also was killed in line of duty, as was my father who succeeded him in the service.

At sixteen I graduated from the Air School and was detailed to the International Peace Fleet, being the fifth generation of my line to wear the uniform of my country. That was in 2016, and I recall that it was a matter of pride to me that it rounded out the full century since Julian 1st graduated from West Point, and that during that one hundred years no adult male of my line had ever owned or worn civilian clothes.

Of course there were no more wars, but there still was fighting. We had the pirates of the air to contend with and occasionally some of the uncivilized tribes of Russia, Africa and central Asia required the attention of a punitive expedition. However, life seemed tame and monotonous to us when we read of the heroic deeds of our ancestors from 1914 to 1967, yet none of us wanted war. It had been too well schooled into us that we must not think of war, and the International Peace Fleet so effectively prevented all preparation for war that we all knew there could never be another. There wasn't a firearm in the world other than those with which we were armed, and a few of ancient design that were kept as heirlooms, or in museums, or that were owned by savage tribes who could procure no ammunition for them, since we permitted none to be manufactured. There was not a gas shell nor a radio bomb, nor any engine to discharge or project one; and there wasn't a big gun of any calibre in the world. I veritably believed that a thousand men equipped with the various engines of destruction that had reached their highest efficiency at the close of the war in 1967 could have conquered the world; but there were not a thousand men so armed—there never could be a thousand men so equipped anywhere upon the face of the Earth. The International Peace Fleet was equipped and manned to prevent just such a calamity.

But it seems that Providence never intended that the world should be without calamities. If man prevented those of possible internal origin there still remained undreamed of external sources over which he had no control. It was one of these which was to prove our undoing. Its seed was sown thirty-three years before I was born, upon that historic day, June 10th, 1967, that Earth received her first message from Mars, since which the two planets have remained in constant friendly communication, carrying on a commerce of reciprocal enlightenment. In some branches of the arts and sciences the Martians, or Barsoomians, as they call themselves, were far in advance of us, while in others we had progressed more rapidly than they. Knowledge was thus freely exchanged to the advantage of both worlds. We learned of their history and customs and they of ours, though they had for ages already known much more of us than we of them. Martian news held always a prominent place in our daily papers from the first.

They helped us most, perhaps, in the fields of medicine and aeronautics, giving us in one, the marvelous healing lotions of Barsoom and in the other, knowledge of the Eighth Ray, which is more generally known on Earth as the Barsoomian Ray, which is now stored in the buoyancy tanks of every air craft and has made obsolete those ancient types of plane that depended upon momentum to keep them afloat.

That we ever were able to communicate intelligibly with them is due to the presence upon Mars of that deathless Virginian, John Carter, whose miraculous transportation to Mars occurred March 4th, 1866, as every school child of the twenty-first century knows. Had not the little band of Martian scientists, who sought so long to communicate with Earth, mistakenly formed themselves into a secret organization for political purposes, messages might have been exchanged between the two planets nearly half a century before they were, and it was not until they finally called upon John Carter that the present inter-planetary code was evolved.

Almost from the first the subject which engrossed us all the most was the possibility of an actual exchange of visits between Earth Men and Barsoomians. Each planet hoped to be the first to achieve this, yet neither withheld any information that would aid the other in the consummation of the great fact. It was a generous and friendly rivalry which about the time of my graduation from the Air School seemed, in theory at least, to be almost ripe for successful consummation by one or the other. We had the Eighth Ray, the motors, the oxygenating devices, the insulating processes— everything to insure the safe and certain transit of a specially designed air craft to Mars, were Mars the only other inhabitant of space. But it was not and it was the other planets and the Sun that we feared.

In 2015 Mars had dispatched a ship for Earth with a crew of five men provisioned for ten years. It was hoped that with good luck the trip might be made in something less than five years, as the craft had developed an actual trial speed of one thousand miles per hour. At the time of my graduation the ship was already off its course almost a million miles and generally conceded to he hopelessly lost. Its crew, maintaining constant radio communication with both Earth and Mars, still hoped for success, but the best informed upon both worlds had given them up.

We had had a ship about ready at the time of the sailing of the Martians, but the government at Washington had forbidden the venture when it became apparent that the Barsoomian ship was doomed—a wise decision, since our vessel was no better equipped than theirs. Nearly ten years elapsed before anything further was accomplished in the direction of assuring any greater hope of success for another interplanetary venture into space, and this was directly due to the discovery made by a former classmate of mine, Lieutenant Commander Orthis, one of the most brilliant men I have ever known, and at the same time one of the most unscrupulous, and, to me at least, the most obnoxious.

We had entered the Air School together—he from New York and I from Illinois—and almost from the first day we had seemed to discover a mutual antagonism that, upon his part at least, must have been considerably strengthened by numerous unfortunate occurrences during our four years beneath the same roof. In the first place he was not popular with either the cadets, the instructors, or the officers of the school, while I was most fortunate in this respect. In those various fields of athletics in which he considered himself particularly expert, it was always I, unfortunately, who excelled him and kept him from major honors. In the class room he outshone us all—even the instructors were amazed at the brilliancy of his intellect—and yet as we passed from grade to grade I often topped him in the final examinations. I ranked always as a cadet officer, and upon graduation I took a higher grade among the new ensigns than he—a rank that had many years before been discontinued, but which had recently been revived.

From then on I saw little of him, his services confining him principally to land service, while mine kept me almost constantly on the air in all parts of the world. Occasionally I heard of him—usually something unsavory; he had married a nice girl and abandoned her—there had been talk of an investigation of his accounts—and the last that there was a rumor that he was affiliated with a secret order that sought to overthrow the government. Some things I might believe of Orthis, but not this.

And during these nine years since graduation, as we had drifted apart in interests, so had the breach between us been widened by constantly increasing difference in rank. He was a Lieutenant Commander and I a Captain, when in 2024 he announced the discovery and isolation of the Eighth Solar Ray, and within two months those of the Moon, Mercury, Venus and Jupiter. The Eighth Barsoomian and the Eighth Earthly Rays had already been isolated, and upon Earth the latter erroneously called by the name of the former.

Orthis' discoveries were hailed upon two planets as the key to actual travel between the Earth and Barsoom, since by means of these several rays the attraction of the Sun and the planets, with the exception of Saturn, Uranus and Neptune, could be definitely overcome and a ship steer a direct and unimpeded course through space to Mars. The effect of the pull of the three farther planets was considered negligible, owing to their great distance from both Mars and Earth.

Orthis wanted to equip a ship and start at once, but again government intervened and forbade what it considered an unnecessary risk. Instead Orthis was ordered to design a small radio operated flier, which would carry no one aboard, and which it was believed could be automatically operated for at least half the distance between the two planets. After his designs were completed, you may imagine his chagrin, and mine as well, when I was detailed to supervise construction, yet I will say that Orthis hid his natural emotions well and gave me perfect cooperation in the work we were compelled to undertake together, and which was as distasteful to me as to him. On my part I made it as easy for him as I could, working with him rather than over him.

It required but a short time to complete the experimental ship and during this time I had an opportunity to get a still better insight into the marvelous intellectual ability of Orthis, though I never saw into his mind or heart.

It was late in 2024 that the ship was launched upon its strange voyage, and almost immediately, upon my recommendation, work was started upon the perfection of the larger ship that had been in course of construction in 2015 at the time that the loss of the Martian ship had discouraged our government in making any further attempt until the then seemingly insurmountable obstacles should have been overcome. Orthis was again my assistant, and with the means at our disposal it was a matter of less than eight months before *The Barsoom,* as she was christened, was completely overhauled and thoroughly equipped for the interplanetary voyage. The various eighth rays that would assist us in overcoming the pull of the Sun, Mercury, Venus, Earth, Mars and Jupiter were stored in carefully constructed and well protected tanks within the hull, and there was a smaller tank at the bow containing the Eighth Lunar Ray, which would permit us to pass safely within the zone of the moon's influence without danger of being attracted to her barren surface.

Messages from the original Martian ship had been received from time to time and with diminishing strength for nearly five years after it had left Mars. Its commander in his heroic fight against the pull of the sun had managed to fall within the grip of Jupiter and was, when last heard from far out in the great void between that planet and Mars. During the past four years the fate of the ship could be naught but conjecture—all that we could be certain of was that its unfortunate crew would never again return to Barsoom.

Our own experimental ship had been speeding upon its lonely way now for eight months, and so accurate had Orthis' scientific deductions proven that the most delicate instrument could detect no slightest deviation from its prescribed course. It was then that Orthis began to importune the government to permit him to set out with the new craft that was now completed. The authorities held out, however, until the latter part of 2025 when, the experimental ship having been out a year and still showing no deviation from its course, they felt reasonably assured that the success of the venture was certain and that no useless risk of human life would be involved.

*The Barsoom* required five men properly to handle it, and as had been the custom through many centuries when an undertaking of more than usual risk was to be attempted, volunteers were called for, with the result that fully half the personnel of the International Peace Fleet begged to be permitted to form the crew of five.

The government finally selected their men from the great number of volunteers, with the result that once more was I the innocent cause of disappointment and chagrin to Orthis, as I was placed in command, with Orthis, two lieutenants and an ensign completing the roster.

*The Barsoom* was larger than the craft dispatched by the Martians, with the result that we were able to carry supplies for fifteen years. We were equipped with more powerful motors which would permit us to maintain an average speed of over twelve hundred miles an hour, carrying in addition an engine recently developed by Orthis which generated sufficient power from light to propel the craft at half-speed in the event that our other engine should break down. None of us was married, Orthis' abandoned wife having recently died. Our estates were taken under trusteeship by the government. Our farewells were made at an elaborate ball at the White

House on December 24, 2025, and on Christmas day we rose from the landing stage at which *The Barsoom* had been moored, and amid the blare of bands and the shouting of thousands of our fellow countrymen we arose majestically into the blue.

I shall not bore you with dry, technical descriptions of our motors and equipment. Suffice it to say that the former were of three types—those which propelled the ship through the air and those which propelled it through ether, the latter of course represented our most important equipment, and consisted of powerful multiple-exhaust separators which isolated the true Barsomian Eighth Ray in great quantities, and, by exhausting it rapidly earthward, propelled the vessel toward Mars. These separators were so designed that, with equal facility, they could isolate the Earthly Eighth Ray which would be necessary for our return voyage. The auxiliary engine, which I mentioned previously and which was Orthis' latest invention, could be easily adjusted to isolate the eighth ray of any planet or satellite or of the sun itself, thus insuring us motive power in any part of the universe by the simple expedient of generating and exhausting the eighth ray of the nearest heavenly body. A fourth type of generator drew oxygen from the ether, while another emanated insulating rays which insured us a uniform temperature and external pressure at all times, their action being analogous to that of the atmosphere surrounding the earth. Science had, therefore, permitted us to construct a little world, which moved at will through space—a little world inhabited by five souls.

Had it not been for Orthis' presence I could have looked forward to a reasonably pleasurable voyage, for West and Jay were extremely likeable fellows and sufficiently mature to be companionable, while young Norton, the ensign, though but seventeen years of age, endeared himself to all of us from the very start of the voyage by his pleasant manners, his consideration and his willingness in the performance of his duties. There were three staterooms aboard *The Barsoom,* one of which I occupied alone, while West and Orthis had the second and Jay and Norton the third. West and Jay were lieutenants and had been classmates at the air school. They would of course have preferred to room together, but could not unless I commanded it or Orthis requested it. Not wishing to give Orthis any grounds for offense I hesitated to make the change, while Orthis, never having thought a considerate thought or done a considerate deed in his life, could not, of course, have been expected to suggest it. We all messed together, West, Jay and Norton taking turns at preparing the meals. Only in the actual operation of the ship were the lines of rank drawn strictly.

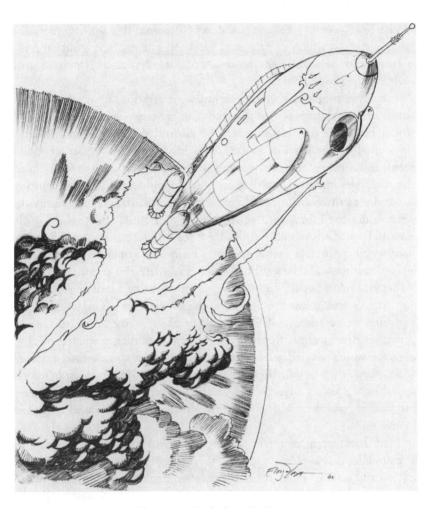

*The Barsoom* Embarks on Its Voyage

Otherwise we associated as equals, nor would any other arrangement have been endurable upon such an undertaking, which required that we five be practically imprisoned together upon a small ship for a period of not less than five years. We had books and writing materials and games, and we were, of course, in constant radio communication with both Earth and Mars, receiving continuously the latest news from both planets. We listened to opera and oratory and heard the music of two worlds, so that we were not lacking for entertainment. There was always a certain constraint in Orthis' manner toward me, yet I must give him credit for behaving outwardly admirably. Unlike the others we never exchanged pleasantries with one another, nor could I, knowing as I did that Orthis hated me, and feeling for him personally the contempt that I felt because of his character. Intellectually he commanded my highest admiration, and upon intellectual grounds we met without constraint or reserve, and many were the profitable discussions we had during the first days of what was to prove a very brief voyage.

It was about the second day that I noticed with some surprise that Orthis was exhibiting a friendly interest in Norton. It had never been Orthis' way to make friends, but I saw that he and Norton were much together and that each seemed to derive a great deal of pleasure from the society of the other. Orthis was a good talker. He knew his profession thoroughly, and was an inventor and scientist of high distinction. Norton, though but a boy, was himself the possessor of a fine mind. He had been honor-man in his graduating class, heading the list of ensigns for that year, and I could not help but notice that he was drinking in every word along scientific lines that Orthis vouchsafed.

We had been out about six days when Orthis came to me and suggested, that inasmuch as West and Jay had been classmates and chums that they be permitted to room together and that he had spoken to Norton who had said that he would be agreeable to the change and would occupy West's bunk in Orthis' stateroom. I was very glad of this for it now meant that my subordinates would be paired off in the most agreeable manner, and as long as they were contented, I knew that the voyage from that standpoint at least would be more successful. I was, of course, a trifle sorry to see a fine boy like Norton brought under the influence of Orthis, yet I felt that what little danger might result would be offset by the influence of West and Jay and myself or counterbalanced by the liberal education which five years' constant companionship with Orthis would be to any man with whom Orthis would discuss freely the subjects of which he was master.

We were beginning to feel the influence of the Moon rather strongly. At the rate we were traveling we would pass closest to it upon the twelfth day, or about the 6th of January, 2026.

Our course would bring us within about twenty thousand miles of the Moon, and as we neared it I believe that the sight of it was the most impressive thing that human eye had ever gazed upon before. To the naked eye it loomed large and magnificent in the heavens, appearing over ten times the size that it does to terrestrial observers, while our powerful glasses brought its weird surface to such startling proximity that one felt that he might reach out and touch the torn rocks of its tortured mountains.

This nearer view enabled us to discover the truth or falsity of the theory that has been long held by some scientists that there is a form of vegetation upon the surface of the Moon. Our eyes were first attracted by what appeared to be movement upon the surface of some of the valleys and in the deeper ravines of the mountains. Norton exclaimed that there were creatures there, moving about, but closer observation revealed the fact of the existence of a weird fungus-like vegetation which grew so rapidly that we could clearly discern the phenomena. From the several days' observation which we had at close range we came to the conclusion that the entire life span of this vegetation is encompassed in a single sidereal month. From the spore it developed in the short period of a trifle over twenty-seven days into a mighty plant that is sometimes hundreds of feet in height. The branches are angular and grotesque, the leaves broad and thick, and in the plants which we discerned the seven primary colors were distinctly represented. As each portion of the Moon passed slowly into shadow the vegetation first drooped, then wilted, then crumbled to the ground, apparently disintegrating almost immediately into a fine, dust-like powder—at least in so far as our glasses revealed, it quite disappeared entirely. The movement which we discerned was purely that of rapid growth, as there is no wind upon the surface of the Moon. Both Jay and Orthis were positive that they discerned some form of animal life, either insect or reptilian. These I did not myself see, though I did perceive many of the broad, flat leaves which seemed to have been partially eaten, which certainly strengthened the theory that there is other than vegetable life upon our satellite.

I presume that one of the greatest thrills that we experienced in this adventure, that was to prove a veritable Pandora's box of thrills, was when we commenced to creep past the edge of the Moon and our eyes beheld for the first time that which no other human eyes had ever rested upon—portions of that two-fifths of the Moon's surface which is invisible from the Earth.

We had looked with awe upon Mare Crisium and Lacus Somniorum,

Sinius Roris, Oceanus Procellarum and the four great mountain ranges. We had viewed at close range the volcanoes of Opollonius, Secchi, Borda, Tycho and their mates, but all these paled into insignificance as there unrolled before us the panorama of the vast unknown.

I cannot say that it differed materially from that portion of the Moon that is visible to us—it was merely the glamour of mystery which had surrounded it since the beginning of time that lent to it its thrill for us. Here we observed other great mountain ranges and wide undulating plains, towering volcanoes and mighty craters and the same vegetation with which we were now become familiar.

We were two days past the Moon when our first trouble developed. Among our stores were one hundred and twenty quarts of spirits per man, enough to allow us each a liberal two ounces per day for a period of five years. Each night, before dinner, we had drunk to the President in a cocktail which contained a single ounce of spirits, the idea being to conserve our supply in the event of our journey being unduly protracted as well as to have enough in the event that it became desirable fittingly to celebrate any particular occasion.

Toward the third meal hour of the thirteenth day of the voyage Orthis entered the messroom noticeably under the influence of liquor.

History narrates that under the regime of prohibition drunkenness was common and that it grew to such proportions as to become a national menace, but with the repeal of the Prohibition Act, nearly a hundred years ago, the habit of drinking to excess abated, so that it became a matter of disgrace for any man to show his liquor, and in the service it was considered as reprehensible as cowardice in action. There was therefore but one thing for me to do. I ordered Orthis to his quarters.

He was drunker than I had thought him, and he turned upon me like a tiger.

"You damned cur," he cried. "All my life you have stolen everything from me; the fruits of all my efforts you have garnered by chicanery and trickery, and even now, were we to reach Mars, it is you who would be lauded as the hero—not I whose labor and intellect have made possible this achievement. But by God we will not reach Mars. Not again shall you profit by my efforts. You have gone too far this time, and now you dare to order me about like a dog and an inferior—I, whose brains have made you what you are."

I held my temper, for I saw that the man was unaccountable for his words. "Go to your quarters, Orthis," I repeated my command. "I will talk with you again in the morning."

West and Jay and Norton were present. They seemed momentarily para-
lyzed by the man's condition and gross insubordination. Norton, however,
was the first to recover. Jumping quickly to Orthis' side he laid his hand
upon his arm. "Come, sir," he said, and to my surprise Orthis accompanied
him quietly to their stateroom.

During the voyage we had continued the fallacy of night and day, gaug-
ing them merely by our chronometers, since we moved always through
utter darkness, surrounded only by a tiny nebula of light, produced by
the sun's rays impinging upon the radiation from our insulating generator.
Before breakfast, therefore, on the following morning I sent for Orthis to
come to my stateroom. He entered with a truculent swagger, and his first
words indicated that if he had not continued drinking, he had at least been
moved to no regrets for his unwarranted attack of the previous evening.

"Well," he said, "what in hell are you going to do about it?"

"I cannot understand your attitude, Orthis," I told him. "I have never
intentionally injured you. When orders from government threw us together
I was as much chagrined as you. Association with you is as distasteful to me
as it is to you. I merely did as you did—obeyed orders. I have no desire to
rob you of anything, but that is not the question now. You have been guilty
of gross insubordination and of drunkenness. I can prevent a repetition of
the latter by confiscating your liquor and keeping it from you during the
balance of the voyage, and an apology from you will atone for the former.
I shall give you twenty-four hours to reach a decision. If you do not see fit
to avail yourself of my clemency, Orthis, you will travel to Mars and back
again in irons. Your decision now and your behavior during the balance
of the voyage will decide your fate upon our return to Earth. And I tell
you, Orthis, that if I possibly can do so I shall use the authority which is
mine upon this expedition and expunge from the log the record of your
transgressions last night and this morning. Now go to your quarters; your
meals will be served there for twenty-four hours and at the end of that time
I shall receive your decision. Meanwhile your liquor will be taken from you."

He gave me an ugly look, turned upon his heel and left my stateroom.

Norton was on watch that night. We were two days past the Moon.
West, Jay and I were asleep in our staterooms, when suddenly Norton
entered mine and shook me violently by the shoulder.

"My God, Captain," he cried, "come quick. Commander Orthis is destroying the engines."

I leaped to my feet and followed Norton amidships to the engine-room,
calling to West and Jay as I passed their stateroom. Through the bull's-eye in
the engine-room door, which he had locked, we could see Orthis working

over the auxiliary generator which was to have proven our salvation in an emergency, since by means of it we could overcome the pull of any planet into the sphere of whose influence we might be carried. I breathed a sigh of relief as my eyes noted that the main battery of engines was functioning properly, since, as a matter of fact, we had not expected to have to rely at all upon the auxiliary generator, having stored sufficient quantities of the Eighth Ray of the various heavenly bodies by which we might be influenced, to carry us safely throughout the entire extent of the long voyage. West and Jay had joined us by this time, and I now called to Orthis, commanding him to open the door. He did something more to the generator and then arose, crossed the engine-room directly to the door, unbolted it and threw the door open. His hair was dishevelled, his face drawn, his eyes shining with a peculiar light, but withal his expression denoted a drunken elation that I did not at the moment understand.

"What have you been doing here, Orthis?" I demanded. "You are under arrest, and supposed to be in your quarters."

"You'll see what I've been doing," he replied truculently, "and it's done—it's done—it can't ever be undone. I've seen to that."

I grabbed him roughly by the shoulder. "What do you mean? Tell me what you have done, or by God I will kill you with my own hands," for I knew, not only from his words but from his expression, that he had accomplished something which he considered very terrible.

The man was a coward and he quailed under my grasp. "You wouldn't dare to kill me," he cried, "and it don't make any difference, for we'll all be dead in a few hours. Go and look at your damned compass."

# TWO

# The Heart of the Moon

NORTON, whose watch it was, had already hurried toward the pilot room where were located the controls and the various instruments. This room, which was just forward of the engine-room, was in effect a circular conning-tower which projected about twelve inches above the upper hull. The entire circumference of this twelve inch superstructure was set with small ports of thick crystal glass.

As I turned to follow Norton I spoke to West. "Mr. West," I said, "you and Mr. Jay will place Lieutenant Commander Orthis in irons immediately. If he resists, kill him."

As I hurried after Norton I heard a volley of oaths from Orthis and a burst of almost maniacal laughter. When I reached the pilot house I found Norton working very quietly with the controls. There was nothing hysterical in his movements, but his face was absolutely ashen.

"What is wrong, Mr. Norton?" I asked. But as I looked at the compass simultaneously I read my answer there before he spoke. We were moving at right angles to our proper course.

"We are falling toward the Moon, sir," he said, "and she does not respond to her control."

"Shut down the engines," I ordered, "they are only accelerating our fall."

"Aye, aye, sir," he replied.

"The Lunar Eighth Ray tank is of sufficient capacity to keep us off the Moon," I said. "If it has not been tampered with, we should be in no danger of falling to the Moon's surface."

"If it has not been tampered with, sir; yes, sir, that is what I have been thinking."

"But the gauge here shows it full to capacity," I reminded him.

"I know, sir," he replied, "but if it were full to capacity, we should not be falling so rapidly."

Immediately I fell to examining the gauge, almost at once discovering that it had been tampered with and the needle set permanently to indicate a maximum supply. I turned to my companion.

"Mr. Norton," I said, "please go forward and investigate the Lunar Eighth Ray tank, and report back to me immediately."

The young man saluted and departed. As he approached the tank it was necessary for him to crawl through a very restricted place beneath the deck.

In about five minutes Norton returned. He was not so pale as he had been, but he looked very haggard.

"Well?" I inquired as he halted before me.

"The exterior intake valve has been opened, sir," he said, "the rays were escaping into space. I have closed it, sir."

The valve to which he referred was used only when the ship was in dry dock, for the purpose of refilling the buoyancy tank, and, because it was so seldom used and as a further precaution against accident, the valve was placed in an inaccessible part of the hull where there was absolutely no likelihood of its being accidentally opened.

Norton glanced at the instrument. "We are not falling quite so rapidly now," he said.

"Yes," I replied, "I had noted that, and I have also been able to adjust the Lunar Eighth Ray gauge—it shows that we have about half the original pressure."

"Not enough to keep us from going aground," he commented.

"No, not here, where there is no atmosphere. If the Moon had an atmosphere we could at least keep off the surface if we wished to. As it is, however, I imagine that we will be able to make a safe landing, though, of course that will do us little good. You understand, I suppose, Mr. Norton, that this is practically the end."

He nodded. "It will be a sad blow to the inhabitants of two worlds," he remarked, his entire forgetfulness of self indicating the true nobility of his character.

"It is a sad report to broadcast," I remarked, "but it must be done, and at once. You will, please, send the following message to the Secretary of Peace:

"U.S.S. *The Barsoom*, January 6, 2026, about twenty thousand miles off the Moon. Lieutenant Commander Orthis, while under the influence of liquor, has destroyed auxiliary engine and opened exterior intake valve Lunar Eighth Ray buoyancy tank. Ship sinking rapidly. Will keep you—"

Norton who had seated himself at the radio desk leaped suddenly to his feet and turned toward me. "My God, sir," he cried, "he has destroyed the radio outfit also. We can neither send nor receive."

A careful examination revealed the fact that Orthis had so cleverly and completely destroyed the instruments that there was no hope of repairing them. I turned to Norton.

"We are not only dead, Norton, but we are buried, as well."

I smiled as I spoke and he answered me with a smile that betokened his utter fearlessness of death.

"I have but one regret, sir," he said, "and that is that the world will never know that our failure was not due to any weakness of our machinery, ship or equipment."

"That is, indeed, too bad," I replied, "for it will retard transportation between the two worlds possibly a hundred years—maybe forever."

I called to West and Jay who by this time had placed Orthis in irons and confined him to his stateroom. When they came I told them what had happened, and they took it as coolly as did Norton. Nor was I surprised, for these were fine types selected from the best of that splendid organization which officered the International Peace Fleet.

Together we immediately made a careful inspection of the ship, which revealed no further damage than that which we had already discovered, but which was sufficient as we well knew, to preclude any possibility of our escaping from the pull of the Moon.

"You gentlemen realize our position as well as I," I told them. "Could we repair the auxiliary generator we might isolate the Lunar Eighth Ray, refill ours tank, and resume our voyage. But the diabolical cleverness with which Lieutenant Commander Orthis has wrecked the machine renders this impossible. We might fight away from the surface of the Moon for a considerable period, but in the end it would avail us nothing. It is my plan, therefore, to make a landing. In so far as the actual lunar conditions are concerned, we are confronted only by a mass of theories, many of which are conflicting. It will, therefore, be at least a matter of consuming interest to us to make a landing upon this dead world where we may observe it closely, but there is also the possibility, remote, I grant you, that we may discover conditions there which may in some manner alleviate our position. At least we can be no worse off. To live for fifteen years cooped in the hull of this dead ship is unthinkable. I may speak only for myself, but to me it would be highly preferable to die immediately than to live on thus, knowing that there was no hope of rescue. Had Orthis not destroyed the radio outfit we could have communicated with Earth and another ship been outfitted and sent to our rescue inside a year. But now we cannot tell them, and they will never know our fate. The emergency that has arisen has, however, so altered conditions that I do not feel warranted in taking this step without consulting you gentlemen. It is a matter now largely of the duration of our lives. I cannot proceed upon the mission upon which I have been dispatched, nor can I return to Earth. I wish, therefore, that you would express yourselves freely concerning the plan which I have outlined."

West, who was the senior among them was naturally the one to reply first. He told me that he was content to go wherever I led, and Jay and Norton in turn signified a similar willingness to abide by whatever decision I might reach. They also assured me that they were as keen to explore the surface of the Moon at close range as I, and that they could think of no better way of spending the remainder of their lives than in the acquisition of new experiences and the observation of new scenes.

"Very well, Mr. Norton," I said, "you will set your course directly toward the Moon."

Aided by lunar gravity our descent was rapid.

As we plunged through space at a terrific speed, the satellite seemed to be leaping madly toward us, and at the end of fifteen hours I gave orders to slack off and brought the ship almost to a stop about nine thousand feet above the summit of the higher lunar peaks. Never before had I gazed upon a more awe-inspiring scene than that presented by those terrific peaks towering five miles above the broad valleys at their feet. Sheer cliffs of three and four thousand feet were nothing uncommon, and all was rendered weirdly beautiful by the variegated colors of the rocks and the strange prismatic hues of the rapidly-growing vegetation upon the valley floors. From our loftly elevation above the peaks we could see many craters of various dimensions, some of which were huge chasms, three and four miles in diameter. As we descended slowly we drifted directly over one of these abysses, into the impenetrable depths of which we sought to strain our eyesight. Some of us believed that we detected a faint luminosity far below, but of that we could not be certain. Jay thought it might be the reflected light from the molten interior. I was confident that had this been the case there would have been a considerable rise of temperature as we passed low across the mouth of the crater.

At this altitude we made an interesting discovery. There is an atmosphere surrounding the Moon. It is extremely tenuous, but yet it was recorded by our barometer at an altitude of about fifteen hundred feet above the highest peak we crossed. Doubtless in the valleys and deep ravines, where the vegetation thrived, it is denser, but that I do not know, since we never landed upon the surface of the Moon. As the ship drifted we presently noted that it was taking a circular course paralleling the rim of the huge volcanic crater above which we were descending. I immediately gave orders to alter our course since, as we were descending constantly, we should presently be below the rim of the crater and, being unable to rise, be hopelessly lost in its huge maw.

It was my plan to drift slowly over one of the larger valleys as we descended, and make a landing amidst the vegetation which we perceived growing in riotous profusion and movement beneath us. But when West, whose watch it now was, attempted to alter the course of the ship, he found that it did not respond. Instead it continued to move slowly in a great circle around the inside rim of the crater. At the moment of this discovery we were not much more than five hundred feet above the summit of the volcano, and we were constantly, though slowly, dropping. West looked up at us, smiled, and shook his head.

"It is no use, sir," he said, addressing me. "It is about all over, sir, and there won't even be any shouting. We seem to be caught in what one might call a lunar whirlpool, for you will have noticed, sir, that our circles are constantly growing smaller."

"Our speed does not seem to be increasing," I remarked, "as would follow were we approaching the vortex of a true whirlpool."

"I think I can explain it, sir," said Norton. "It is merely due to the action of the Lunar Eighth Ray which still remains in the forward buoyancy tank. Its natural tendency is to push itself away from the Moon, which, as far as we are concerned, is represented by the rim of this enormous crater. As each portion of the surface repels us in its turn we are pushed gently along in a lessening circle, because, as we drop nearer the summit of the peak the greater the reaction of the Eighth Lunar Ray. If I am not mistaken in my theory our circle will cease to narrow after we have dropped beneath the rim of the crater."

"I guess you are right, Norton," I said. "At least it is a far more tenable theory than that we are being sucked into the vortex of an enormous whirlpool. There is scarcely enough atmosphere for that, it seems to me."

As we dropped slowly below the rim of the crater the tenability of Norton's theory became more and more apparent, for presently, though our speed increased slightly, the diameter of our circular course remained constant, and, at a little greater depth, our speed as well. We were descending now at the rate of a little over ten miles an hour, the barometer recording a constantly increasing atmospheric pressure, though nothing approximating that necessary to the support of life upon Earth. The temperature rose slightly, but not alarmingly. From a range of twenty-five or thirty below zero, immediately after we had entered the shadow of the crater's interior, it rose gradually to zero at a point some one hundred and twenty-five miles below the summit of the giant extinct volcano that had engulfed us.

During the next ten miles our speed diminished rapidly, until we suddenly realized that we were no longer falling, but that our motion had been reversed and we were rising. Up we went for approximately eight miles, when suddenly we began to fall again. Again we fell, but this time for only six miles, when our motion was reversed and we rose again a distance of about four miles. This see-sawing was continued until we finally came to rest at about what we estimated was a distance of some one hundred and thirty miles below the summit of the crater. It was quite dark, and we had only our instruments to tell us of what was happening to the ship, the interior of which was, of course, brilliantly illuminated and comfortably warm.

Now below us, and now above us, for the ship had rolled completely over each time we had passed the point at which we came finally to rest, we had noted the luminosity that Norton had first observed from above the mouth of the crater. Each of us had been doing considerable thinking, and at last young Norton could contain himself no longer.

"I beg your pardon, sir," he said deferentially, "but won't you tell us what you think of it; what your theory is as to where we are and why we hang here in mid-air, and why the ship rolled over every time we passed this point?"

"I can only account for it," I replied, "upon a single and rather preposterous hypothesis, which is that the Moon is a hollow sphere, with a solid crust some two hundred and fifty miles in thickness. Gravity is preventing us from rising above the point where we now are, while centrifugal force keeps us from falling."

The others nodded. They too had been forced to accept the same apparently ridiculous theory, since there was none other that could explain our predicament. Norton had walked across the room to read the barometer which he had rather neglected while the ship had been performing her eccentric antics far below the surface of the Moon. I saw his brows knit as he glanced at it, and then I saw him studying it carefully, as though to assure himself that he had made no mistake in the reading. Then he turned toward us.

"There must be something wrong with this instrument, sir," he said. "It is registering pressure equivalent to that at the Earth's surface."

I walked over and looked at the instrument. It certainly was registering the pressure that Norton had read, nor did there seem to be anything wrong with the instrument.

"There is a way to find out," I said. "We can shut down the insulating generator and open an air cock momentarily. It won't take five seconds to determine whether the barometer is correct or not. It was, of course, in some respects a risky proceeding, but with West at the generator, Jay at the air cock and Norton at the pump I knew that we would be reasonably safe, even if there proved to be no atmosphere without. The only danger lay in the chance that we were hanging in a poisonous gas of the same density as the earthly atmosphere, but as there was no particular incentive to live in the situation in which we were, we each felt that no matter what chance we might take it would make little difference in the eventual outcome of our expedition.

I tell you that it was a very tense moment as the three men took their posts to await my word of command. If we had indeed discovered a true atmosphere beneath the surface of the Moon, what more might we not discover? If it were an atmosphere, we could propel the ship in it, and we could, if nothing more, go out on deck to breathe fresh air. It was arranged that at my word of command West was to shut off the generator, Jay to open the air cock, and Norton to start the pump. If fresh air failed to enter through the tube Jay was to give the signal, whereupon Norton would reverse the pump, West start the generator, and immediately Jay would close the air cock again.

As Jay was the only man who was to take a greater chance than the others, I walked over and stood beside him, placing my nostrils as close to the air cock as his. Then I gave the word of command. Everything worked perfectly and an instant later a rush of fresh, cold air was pouring into the hull of *The Barsoom*. West and Norton had been watching the effects upon our faces closely, so that they knew almost as soon as we did that the result of our test had been satisfactory. We were all smiles, though just why we were so happy I am sure none of us could have told. Possibly it was just because we had found a condition that was identical with an earthly condition, and though we might never see our world again we could at least breathe air similar to hers.

I had them start the motors again then, and presently we were moving in a great spiral upward toward the interior of the Moon. Our progress was very slow, but as we rose the temperature rose slowly, too, while the barometer showed a very-slightly-decreasing atmospheric pressure. The luminosity, now above us, increased as we ascended, until finally the sides of the great well through which we were passing became slightly illuminated.

All this time Orthis had remained in irons in his stateroom. I had given instructions that he was to be furnished food and water, but no one was to speak to him, and I had taken Norton into my stateroom with me. Knowing Orthis to be a drunkard, a traitor and a potential murderer I had no sympathy whatsoever for him. I had determined to court-martial him and did not intend to spend the few remaining hours or years of my life cooped up in a small ship with him, and I knew that the verdict of any court, whether composed of the remaining crew of *The Barsoom,* or appointed by the Judge Advocate General of the Navy, could result in but one thing, and that was death for Orthis. I had left the matter, however, until we were not pressed with other matters of greater importance, and so he still lived, though he shared neither in our fears, our hopes, nor our joys.

About twenty-six hours after we entered the mouth of the crater at the surface of the Moon we suddenly emerged from its opposite end to look upon a scene that was as marvelous and weird, by comparison with the landscape upon the surface of the Moon, as the latter was in comparison with that of our own Earth. A soft, diffused light revealed to us in turn mountains, valleys and sea, the details of which were more slowly encompassed by our minds. The mountains were as rugged as those upon the surface of the satellite, and appeared equally as lofty. They were, however, clothed with verdure almost to their summits, at least a few that were within our range of vision. And there were forests, too—strange forests, of strange trees, so unearthly in appearance as to suggest the weird phantasmagoria of a dream.

We did not rise much above five hundred feet from the opening of the well through which we had come from outer space when I descried an excellent landing place and determined to descend. This was readily accomplished, and we made a safe landing close to a large forest and near the bank of a small stream. Then we opened the forward hatch and stepped out upon the deck of *The Barsoom,* the first Earth Men to breathe the air of Luna. It was, according to Earth time, eleven a.m., January 8, 2026.

I think that the first thing which engaged our interest and attention was the strange, and then, to us, unaccountable luminosity which pervaded the interior of the Moon. Above us were banks of fleecy clouds, the undersurfaces of which appeared to be lighted from beneath, while, through breaks in the cloud banks we could discern a luminous firmament beyond, though nowhere was there any suggestion of a central incandescent orb radiating light and heat as does our sun. The clouds themselves cast no shadows upon the ground, nor, in fact, were there any well-defined shadows even directly beneath the hull of the ship or surrounding the forest trees which grew close at hand. The shadows were vague and nebulous, blending off into nothingnesses at their edges. We ourselves cast no more shadows upon the deck of *The Barsoom* than would have been true upon a cloudy day on Earth. Yet the general illumination surrounding us approximated that of a very slightly hazy Earth day. This peculiar lunar light interested us profoundly, but it was some time before we discovered the true explanation of its origin. It was of two kinds, emanating from widely different sources, the chief of which was due to the considerable radium content of the internal lunar soil, and principally of the rock forming the loftier mountain ranges, the radium being so combined as to diffuse a gentle perpetual light which pervaded the entire interior of the Moon. The secondary source was sunlight, which penetrated to the interior of the Moon through the hundreds of thousands of huge craters penetrating the lunar crust. It was this sunlight which carried heat to the inner world, maintaining a constant temperature of about eighty degrees Fahrenheit.

Centrifugal force, in combination with the gravity of the Moon's crust, confined the internal lunar atmosphere to a blanket which we estimated at about fifty miles in thickness over the inner surface of this buried world. This atmosphere rarefies rapidly as one ascends the higher peaks, with the result that these are constantly covered with perpetual snow and ice, sending great glaciers down mighty gorges toward the central seas. It is this condition which has probably prevented the atmosphere, confined as it is within an almost solid sphere, from becoming superheated, through the unthinkable ages that this condition must have existed. The Earth seasons are reflected but slightly in the Moon, there being but a few degrees difference between summer and winter. There are, however, periodic windstorms, which recur with greater or less regularity once each sidereal month, due, I imagine, to the unequal distribution of crater openings through the crust of the Moon, a fact which must produce an unequal absorption of heat at various times and in certain localities. The natural circulation of the lunar atmosphere, affected as it is by the constantly-changing volume and direction of the sun's rays, as well as the great range of temperature between the valleys and the ice-clad mountain peaks, produces frequent storms of greater or less violence. High winds are accompanied by violent rains upon the lower levels and blinding snowstorms among the barren heights above the vegetation line. Rains which fall from low-hanging clouds are warm and pleasant; those which come from high clouds are cold and disagreeable, yet however violent or protracted the storm, the illumination remains practically constant—there are never any dark, lowering days within the Moon, nor is there any night.

# THREE

# Human Quadrupeds

O F COURSE we did not reach all these conclusions in a few moments, but I have given them here merely as the outcome of our deductions following a considerable experience within the Moon. Several miles from the ship rose foothills which climbed picturesquely toward the cloudy heights of the loftier mountains behind them, and as we looked in the direction of these latter, and then out across the forest, there was appreciable to us a strangeness that at first we could not explain, but which we later discovered was due to the fact that there was no horizon, the distance that one could see being dependent solely upon one's power of vision. The general effect was of being in the bottom of a tremendous bowl, with sides so high that one might not see the top.

The ground about us was covered with rank vegetation of pale hues—lavenders, violets, pinks and yellows predominating. Pink grasses which became distinctly flesh-color at maturity grew in abundance, and the stalks of most of the flowering plants were of this same peculiar hue. The flowers themselves were often of highly complex form, of pale and delicate shades, of great size and rare beauty. There were low shrubs that bore a berry-like fruit, and many of the trees of the forest carried fruit of considerable size and of a variety of forms and colors. Norton and Jay were debating the possible edibility of some of these, but I gave orders that no one was to taste them until we had had an opportunity to learn by analysis or otherwise those varieties that were nonpoisonous.

There was aboard *The Barsoom* a small laboratory equipped especially for the purpose of analyzing the vegetable and mineral products of Mars according to earthly standards, as well as other means of conducting research work upon our sister planet. As we had sufficient food aboard for a period of fifteen years, there was no immediate necessity for eating any of the lunar fruit, but I was anxious to ascertain the chemical properties of the water since the manufacture of this necessity was slow, laborious and expensive. I therefore instructed West to take a sample from the stream and subject it to laboratory tests, and the others I ordered below for sleep.

They were rather more keen to set out upon a tour of exploration, nor could I blame them, but as none of us had slept for rather better than forty-eight hours I considered it of importance that we recuperate our vital forces against whatever contingency might confront us in this unknown world. Here were air, water and vegetation—the three prime requisites for the support of animal life—and so I judged it only reasonable to assume that animal life existed within the Moon. If it did exist, it might be in some highly predatory form, against which it would tax our resources to the utmost to defend ourselves. I insisted, therefore, upon each of us obtaining his full quota of sleep before venturing from the safety of *The Barsoom.*

We already had seen evidences of life of a low order, both reptile and insect, or perhaps it would be better to describe the latter as flying reptiles, as they later proved to be—toad-like creatures with the wings of bats, that flitted among the fleshy boughs of the forest, emitting plaintive cries. Upon the ground near the ship we had seen but a single creature, though the moving grasses had assured us that there were others there aplenty. The thing that we had seen had been plainly visible to us all and may be best described as a five-foot snake with four frog-like legs, and a flat head with a single eye in the center of the forehead. Its legs were very short, and as it moved along the ground it both wriggled like a true snake and scrambled with its four short legs. We watched it to the edge of the river and saw it dive in and disappear beneath the surface.

"Silly looking beggar," remarked Jay, "and devilish unearthly."

"I don't know about that," I returned. "He possessed nothing visible to us that we are not familiar with on Earth. Possibly he was assembled after a slightly different plan from any Earth creature; but aside from that he is familiar to us, even to his amphibious habits. And these flying toads, too; what of them? I see nothing particularly remarkable about them. We have just as strange forms on Earth, though nothing precisely like these. Mars, too, has forms of animal and vegetable life peculiar to herself, yet nothing the existence of which would be impossible upon Earth, and she has, as well, human forms almost identical with our own. You see what I am trying to suggest?"

"Yes, sir," replied Jay; "that there may be human life similar to our own within the Moon."

"I see no reason to be surprised should we discover human beings here," I said; "nor would I be surprised to find a reasoning creature of some widely divergent form. I would be surprised, however, were we to find no form analogous to the human race of Earth."

"That is, a dominant race with well developed reasoning faculties?" asked Norton.

"Yes, and it is because of this possibility that we must have sleep and keep ourselves fit, since we may not know the disposition of these creatures, provided they exist, nor the reception that they will accord us. And so, Mr. Norton, if you will get a receptacle and fetch some water from the stream we will leave Mr. West on watch to make his analysis and the rest of us will turn in."

Norton went below and returned with a glass jar in which to carry the water and the balance of us lined the rail with our service revolvers ready in the event of an emergency as he went over the side. None of us had walked more than a few steps since coming on deck after our landing. I had noticed a slightly peculiar sensation of buoyancy, but in view of the numerous other distractions had given it no consideration. As Norton reached the bottom of the ladder and set foot on lunar soil I called to him to make haste. Just in front of him was a low bush and beyond it lay the river, about thirty feet distant. In response to my command he gave a slight leap to clear the bush and, to our amazement as well as to his own consternation, rose fully eighteen feet into the air, cleared a space of fully thirty-five feet and lit in the river.

"Come!" I said to the others, wishing them to follow me to Norton's aid, and sprang for the rail; but I was too impetuous. I never touched the rail, but cleared it by many feet, sailed over the intervening strip of land, and disappeared beneath the icy waters of the lunar river. How deep it was I do not know; but at least it was over my head. I found myself in a sluggish, yet powerful current, the water seeming to move much as a heavy oil moves to the gravity of Earth. As I came to the surface I saw Norton swimming strongly for the bank and a second later Jay emerged not far from me. I glanced quickly around for West, whom I immediately perceived was still on the deck of *The Barsoom,* where, of course, it was his duty to remain, since it was his watch.

The moment that I realized that my companions were all safe I could not repress a smile, and then Norton and Jay commenced to laugh, and we were still laughing when we pulled ourselves from the stream a short distance below the ship.

"Get your sample, Norton?" I asked.

"I still have the container, sir," he replied, and indeed he had clung to it throughout his surprising adventure, as Jay and I, fortunately, had clung to our revolvers. Norton removed the cap from the bottle and dipped the latter into the stream. Then he looked up at me and smiled.

"I think we have beaten Mr. West to it, sir," he said. "It seems like very good water, sir, and when I struck it I was so surprised that I must have swallowed at least a quart."

"I tested a bit of it myself," I replied. "As far as we three are concerned, Mr. West's analysis will not interest us if he discovers that lunar water contains poisonous matter, but for his own protection we will let him proceed with his investigation."

"It is strange, sir," remarked Jay, "that none of us thought of the natural effects of the lesser gravity of the Moon. We have discussed the matter upon many occasions, as you will recall, yet when we faced the actual condition we gave it no consideration whatsoever."

"I am glad," remarked Norton, "that I did not attempt to jump the river—I should have been going yet. Probably landed on the top of some mountain."

As we approached the ship I saw West awaiting us with a most serious and dignified mien; but when he saw that we were all laughing he joined us, telling us after we reached the deck, that he had never witnessed a more surprising or ludicrous sight in his life.

We went below then and after closing and securing the hatch, three of us repaired to our bunks, while West with the sample of lunar water went to the laboratory. I was very tired and slept soundly for some ten hours, for it was the middle of Norton's watch before I awoke.

The only important entry upon the log since I had turned in was West's report of the results of his analysis of the water, which showed that it was not only perfectly safe for drinking purposes but unusually pure, with an extremely low saline content.

I had been up about a half an hour when West came to me, saying that Orthis requested permission to speak to me. Twenty-four hours before, I had been fairly well determined to bring Orthis to trial and execute him immediately, but that had been when I had felt that we were all hopelessly doomed to death on his account. Now, however, with a habitable world beneath our feet, surrounded by conditions almost identical with those which existed upon Earth, our future looked less dark, and because of this I found myself in a quandary as to what course of action to pursue in the matter of Orthis' punishment. That he deserved death there was no question, but when men have faced death so closely and escaped, temporarily at least, I believe that they must look upon life as a most sacred thing and be less inclined to deny life to others. Be that as it may, the fact remains that having sent for Orthis in compliance with his request I received him in a mood of less stern and uncompromising justice than would have been the case twenty-four hours previous. When he had been brought to my stateroom and stood before me, I asked him what he wished to say to me. He was entirely sober now and bore himself with a certain dignity that was not untinged with humility.

"I do not know what has occurred since I was put in irons, as you have instructed the others not to speak to me or answer my questions. I know, of course, however, that the ship is at rest and that pure air is circulating through it, and I have heard the hatch raised and footsteps upon the upper deck. From the time that has elapsed since I was placed under arrest I know that the only planet upon which we have had time to make a landing is the Moon, and so I may guess that we are upon the surface of the Moon. I have had ample time to reflect upon my actions. That I was intoxicated is, of course, no valid excuse, and yet it is the only excuse that I have to offer. I beg, sir, that you will accept the assurance of my sincere regret of the unforgivable things that I have done, and that you will permit me to live and atone for my wrongdoings, for if we are indeed upon the surface of the Moon it may be that we can ill spare a single member of our small party. I throw myself, sir, entirely upon your mercy, but beg that you will give me another chance."

Realizing my natural antipathy for the man and wishing most sincerely not to be influenced against him because of it, I let his plea influence me against my better judgement with the result that I promised him that I would give the matter careful consideration, discuss it with the others, and be influenced largely by their decision. I had him returned to his stateroom then and sent for the other members of the party. With what fidelity my memory permitted I repeated to them in Orthis' own words his request for mercy.

"And now, gentlemen," I said, "I would like to have your opinions in the matter. It is of as much moment to you as to me, and under the peculiar circumstances in which we are placed, I prefer in so far as possible to defer wherever I can to the judgment of the majority. Whatever my final action, the responsibility will be mine. I do not seek to divide that, and it may be that I shall act contrary to the wishes of the majority in some matters, but in this one I really wish to abide by your desires because of the personal antagonism that has existed between Lieutenant Commander Orthis and myself since boyhood."

I knew that none of these men liked Orthis, yet I knew, too, that they would approach the matter in a spirit of justice tempered by mercy, and so

I was not at all surprised when one after another they assured me that they would be glad if I would give the man another opportunity.

Again I sent for Orthis, and after explaining to him that inasmuch as he had given me his word to commit no disloyal act in the future I should place him on parole, his eventual fate depending entirely upon his own conduct; then had his irons removed and told him that he was to return to duty. He seemed most grateful and assured us that we would never have cause to regret our decision. Would to God that instead of freeing him I had drawn my revolver and shot him through the heart!

We were all pretty well rested up by this time, and I undertook to do a little exploring in the vicinity of the ship, going out for a few hours each day with a single companion, leaving the other three upon the ship. I never went far afield at first, confining myself to an area some five miles in diameter between the crater and the river. Upon both sides of the latter, below where the ship had landed, was a considerable extent of forest. I ventured into this upon several occasions and once, just about time for us to return to the ship, I came upon a well marked trail in the dust of which were the imprints of three-toed feet. Each day I set the extreme limit of time that I would absent myself from the ship with instructions that two of those remaining aboard should set out in search of me and my companion, should we be absent over the specified number of hours. Therefore, I was unable to follow the trail the day upon which I discovered it since we had scarcely more than enough time to make a brief examination of the tracks if we were to reach the ship within the limit I had allowed.

It chanced that Norton was with me that day and in his quiet way was much excited by our discovery. We were both positive that the tracks had been made by a four-footed animal, something that weighed between two hundred and fifty and three hundred pounds. How recently it had been used we could scarcely estimate, but the trail itself gave every indication of being a very old one. I was sorry that we had no time to pursue the animal which had made the tracks but determined that upon the following day I should do so. We reached the ship and told the others what we had discovered. They were much interested and many and varied were the conjectures as to the nature of the animals whose tracks we had seen.

After Orthis had been released from arrest Norton had asked permission to return to the former's stateroom. I had granted his request and the two had been very much together ever since. I could not understand Norton's apparent friendship for this man, and it almost made me doubt the young ensign. One day I was to learn the secret of this intimacy, but at the time I must confess that it puzzled me considerably and bothered me not a little, for I had taken a great liking to Norton and disliked to see him so much in the company of a man of Orthis' character.

Each of the men had now accompanied me on my short excursions of exploration with the exception of Orthis. Inasmuch as his parole had fully reinstated him among us in theory at least, I could not very well discriminate against him and leave him alone of all the others aboard ship as I pursued my investigations of the surrounding country.

The day following our discovery of the trail, I accordingly invited him to accompany me, and we set out early, each armed with a revolver and a rifle. I advised West, who automatically took command of the ship during my absence, that we might be gone considerably longer than usual and that he was to feel no apprehension and send out no relief party unless we should be gone a full twenty-four hours, as I wished to follow up the spoor we had discovered, learn where the trail led and have a look at the animal that had made it.

I led the way directly to the spot at which we had found the trail, about four miles down river from the ship and apparently in the heart of dense forest.

The flying-toads darted from tree to tree about us, uttering their weird and plaintive cries, while upon several occasions, as in the past, we saw four-legged snakes such as we had seen upon the day of our landing. Neither the toads nor the snakes bothered us, seeming only to wish to avoid us.

Just before we came upon the trail, both Orthis and I thought we heard the sound of footsteps ahead of us—something similar to that made by a galloping animal—and when we came upon the trail a moment later it was apparent to both of us that dust was hanging in the air and slowly settling on the vegetation nearby. Something, therefore, had passed over the trail but a minute or two before we arrived. A brief examination of the spoor revealed the fact that it had been made by a three-toed animal whose direction of travel was to our right and toward the river, at this point some half mile from us.

I could not help but feel considerable inward excitement, and I was sorry that one of the others had not been with me, for I never felt perfectly at ease with Orthis. I had done considerable hunting in various parts of the world where wild game still exists but I had never experienced such a thrill as I did at the moment that I undertook to stalk this unknown beast upon an unknown trail in an unknown world. Where the trail would lead me, what I should find upon it, I never knew from one step to another, and the lure of it because of that was tremendous. The fact that there were almost nine million square miles of this world for me to explore, and that no Earth Man had ever before set foot upon an inch of it, helped a great deal to compensate for the fact that I knew I could never return to my own Earth again.

The trail led to the edge of the river which at this point was very wide and shallow. Upon the opposite shore, I could see the trail again directly opposite and I knew therefore that this was a ford. Without hesitating, I stepped into the river, and as I did so I glanced to my left to see stretching before me as far as my eye could reach a vast expanse of water. Here then I had stumbled upon the mouth of the river and, beyond, a lunar sea.

The land upon the opposite side of the river was rolling and grass-covered, but in so far as I could see, almost treeless. As I turned my eyes from the sea back toward the opposite shore, I saw that which caused me to halt in my tracks, cock my rifle and issue a cautious warning to Orthis for silence, for there before us upon a knoll stood a small horse-like animal.

It would have been a long shot, possibly five hundred yards, and I should have preferred to have come closer but there was no chance to do that now, for we were in the middle of the river in plain view of the animal which stood there watching us intently. I had scarcely raised my rifle, however, ere it wheeled and disappeared over the edge of the knoll upon which it had been standing.

"What did it look like to you, Orthis?" I asked my companion.

"It was a good ways off," he replied, "and I only just got my binoculars on it as it disappeared, but I could have sworn that it wore a harness of some sort. It was about the size of a small pony, I should say, but it didn't have a pony's head."

"It appeared tailless to me," I remarked.

"I saw no tail," said Orthis, "nor any ears or horns. It was a devilish funny looking thing. I don't understand it. There was something about it—" he paused. "My God, sir, there was something about it that looked human."

"It gave me that same impression, too, Orthis, and I doubt if I should have fired had I been able to cover it, for just at the instant that I threw my rifle to my shoulder I felt that same strange impression that you mention. There was something human about the thing."

As we talked, we had been moving on across the ford which we found an excellent one, the water at no time coming to our waists while the current was scarcely appreciable. Finally, we stepped out on the opposite shore and a moment later, far to the left, we caught another glimpse of the creature that we had previously seen. It stood upon a distant knoll, evidently watching us.

Orthis and I raised our binoculars to our eyes almost simultaneously and for a full minute we examined the thing as it stood there, neither of us speaking, and then we dropped our glasses and looked at each other.

"What do you make of it, sir?" he asked.

I shook my head. "I don't know what to make of it, Orthis," I replied; "but I should swear that I was looking straight into a human face, and yet the body was that of a quadruped."

"There can be no doubt of it, sir," he replied, "and this time one could see the harness and the clothing quite plainly. It appears to have some sort of a weapon hanging at its left side. Did you notice it, sir?"

"Yes, I noticed it, but I don't understand it."

A moment longer we stood watching the creature until it turned and galloped off, disappearing behind the knoll on which it had stood. We decided to follow the trail which led in a southerly direction, feeling reasonably assured that we were more likely to come in contact with the creature or others similar to it upon the trail than off of it. We had gone but a short distance when the trail approached the river again, which puzzled me at the time somewhat, as we had gone apparently directly away from the river since we had left the ford, but after we had gone some mile and a half, we found the explanation, since we came again to another ford while on beyond we saw the river emptying into the sea and realized that we had crossed an island lying in the mouth of the river.

I was hesitating as to whether to make the crossing and continue along the trail or to go back and search the island for the strange creature we had discovered. I rather hoped to capture it, but since I had finally descried its human face, I had given up all intention of shooting it unless I found that it would be necessary to do so in self defense. As I stood there, rather undecided, our attention was attracted back to the island by a slight noise, and as we looked in the direction of the disturbance, we saw five of the creatures eyeing us from high land a quarter of a mile away. When they saw they were discovered they galloped boldly toward us. They had come a short distance only, when they stopped again upon a high knoll, and then one of them raised his face toward the sky and emitted a series of piercing howls. They came on again toward us nor did they pause until they were within fifty feet of us, when they came to a sudden halt.

# FOUR

# In the Hands of the Va-gas

OUR FIRST view of the creatures proved beyond a question of a doubt that they were in effect human quadrupeds. The faces were very broad, much broader than any human faces that I have ever seen, but their profiles were singularly like those of the ancient North American Indians. Their bodies were covered with a garment with short legs that ended above the knees, and which was ornamented about the collar and also about the bottom of each leg with a rather fanciful geometric design. About the barrel of each was a surcingle and connected with it by a backstrap was something analogous to a breeching in Earth horse harness. Where the breeching straps crossed on either side, was a small circular ornament, and there was a strap resembling a trace leading from this forward to the collar, passing beneath a quite large, circular ornament, which appeared to be supported by the surcingle. Smaller straps, running from these two ornaments upon the left side, supported a sheath in which was carried what appeared to be a knife of some description. And upon the right side a short spear was carried in a boot, similarly suspended from the two ornaments, much as the carbine of our ancient Earth cavalry was carried. The spear, which was about six feet long, was of peculiar design, having a slender, well-shaped head, from the base of which a crescent-shaped arm curved backward from one side, while upon the side opposite the crescent was a short, sharp point at right angles to the median line of the weapon.

For a moment we stood there eyeing each other, and from their appearance I judged that they were as much interested in us as we were in them. I noticed that they kept looking beyond us, across the river toward the mainland. Presently, I turned for a glance in the same direction, and far away beyond a thin forest I saw a cloud of dust which seemed to be moving rapidly toward us. I called Orthis' attention to it.

"Reinforcements," I said. "That is what that fellow was calling for when he screamed. I think we had better try conclusions with the five before any more arrive. We will try to make friends first, but if we are unsuccessful we must fight our way back toward the ship at once."

Accordingly, I stepped forward toward the five with a smile upon my lips and my hand outstretched. I knew of no other way in which to carry to them an assurance of our friendliness. At the same time, I spoke a few words in English in a pleasant and conciliatory tone. Although I knew that my words would be meaningless to them, I hoped that they would catch their intent from my inflection.

Immediately upon my advance, one of the creatures turned and spoke to another, indicating to us for the first time that they possessed a spoken language. Then he turned and addressed me in a tongue that was, of course, utterly meaningless to me; but if he had misinterpreted my action, I could not misunderstand that which accompanied his words, for he reared up on his hind feet and simultaneously drew his spear and a wicked-looking, short-bladed sword or dagger, his companions at the same time following his example, until I found myself confronted by an array of weapons backed by scowling, malignant faces. Their leader uttered a single word which I interpreted as meaning halt, and so I halted.

I pointed to Orthis and to myself, and then to the trail along which we had come, and then back in the direction of the ship. I was attempting to tell them that we wished to go back whence we had come. Then I turned to Orthis.

"Draw your revolver," I said, "and follow me. If they interfere we shall have to shoot them. We must get out of this before the others arrive."

As we turned to retrace our steps along the trail, the five dropped upon all fours, still holding their weapons in their fore-paws, and galloped quickly to a position blocking our way.

"Stand aside," I yelled, and fired my pistol above their hands. From their actions, I judged that they had never before heard the report of a firearm, for they stood an instant in evident surprise, and then wheeled and galloped off for about a hundred yards, where they turned and halted again, facing us. They were still directly across our trail, and Orthis and I moved forward determinedly toward them. They were talking among themselves and at the same time watching us closely.

When we had arrived at a few yards from them, I again threatened them with my pistol, but they stood their ground, evidently reassured by the fact that the thing that I held in my hand, though it made a loud noise, inflicted no injury. I did not want to shoot one of them if I could possibly avoid it, so I kept on toward them, hoping that they would make way for us; but instead they reared again upon their hind feet and threatened us with their weapons.

Just how formidable their weapons were, I could not, of course, determine; but I conjectured that if they were at all adept in its use, their spear might be a very formidable thing indeed. I was within a few feet of them now, and their attitude was more war-like than ever, convincing me that they had no intention of permitting us to pass peacefully.

Their features, which I could now see distinctly, were hard, fierce, and cruel in the extreme. Their leader seemed to be addressing me, but, of course, I could not understand him; but when, at last, standing there upon his hind feet, with evidently as much ease as I stood upon my two legs, he carried his spear back in a particularly menacing movement, I realized that I must act and act quickly.

I think the fellow was just on the point of launching his spear at me, when I fired. The bullet struck him square between the eyes, and he dropped like a log, without a sound. Instantly, the others wheeled again and galloped away, this time evincing speed that was almost appalling, clearing spaces of a hundred feet in a single bound, even though handicapped, as they must have been, by the weapons which they clutched in their fore-paws.

A glance behind me showed the dust-cloud rapidly approaching the river, upon the mainland, and calling to Orthis to follow me, I ran rapidly along the trail which led back in the direction of the ship.

The four Moon creatures retreated for about half a mile, and then halted and faced us. They were still directly in our line of retreat, and there they stood for a moment, evidently discussing their plans. We were nearing them rapidly, for we had discovered that we, too, could show remarkable speed, when retarded by gravity only one-sixth of that of Earth. To clear forty feet at a jump was nothing, our greatest difficulty lying in a tendency to leap to too great heights, which naturally resulted in cutting down our horizontal distance. As we neared the four, who had taken their stand upon the summit of a knoll, I heard a great splashing in the river behind us, and turning, saw that their reinforcements were crossing the ford, and would soon be upon us. There appeared to be fully a hundred of them, and our case looked hopeless indeed, unless we could manage to pass the four ahead of us, and reach the comparative safety of the forest beyond the first ford.

"Commence firing, Orthis," I said. "Shoot to kill. Take the two at the left as your targets, and I'll fire at the two at the right. We had better halt and take careful aim, as we can't afford to waste ammunition."

We came to a stop about twenty-five yards from the foremost creature, which is a long pistol shot; but they were standing still upon the crest of a knoll, distinctly outlined against the sky, and were such a size as to present a most excellent target. Our shots rang out simultaneously. The creature at the left, at which Orthis had aimed, leaped high into the air, and fell to the ground, where it lay kicking convulsively. The one at the right uttered a piercing shriek, clutched at its breast, and dropped dead. Then Orthis and I charged the remaining two, while behind us we heard loud weird cries and the pounding of galloping feet. The two before us did not retreat this time, but came to meet us, and again we halted and fired. This time they were so close that we could not miss them, and the last of our original lunar foemen lay dead before us.

We ran then, ran as neither of us had imagined human beings ever could run. I know that I covered over fifty feet in many a leap, but by comparison with the speed of the things behind us, we might have been standing still. They fairly flew over the lavender sward, indicating that those, which we had first seen, had at no time extended themselves in an effort to escape us. I venture to say that some of them leaped fully three hundred feet at a time, and now, at every bound, they emitted fierce and terrible yells, which I assumed to be their war cry, intended to intimidate us.

"It's no use, Orthis," I said to my companion. "We might as well make our stand here and fight it out. We cannot reach the ford. They are too fast for us."

We stopped then, and faced them, and when they saw we were going to make a stand, they circled and halted about a hundred yards distant, entirely surrounding us. We had killed five of their fellows, and I knew we could hope for no quarter. We were evidently confronted by a race of fierce and warlike creatures, the appearance of which, at least, gave no indication of the finer characteristics that are so much revered among humankind upon Earth. After a good look at one of them, I could not imagine the creature harboring even the slightest conception of the word mercy, and I knew that if we ever escaped that fierce cordon, it would be by fighting our way through it.

"Come," I said to Orthis, "straight through for the ford" and turning again in that direction, I started blazing away with my pistol as I walked slowly along the trail. Orthis was at my side, and he, too, fired as rapidly as I. Each time our weapons spoke, a Moon Man fell. And now, they commenced to circle us at a run, much as the savage Indians of the western plains circled the parked wagon trains of our long-gone ancestors in North America. They hurled spears at us, but I think the sound of our revolvers and the effect of the shots had to some measure unnerved them, for their aim was poor and we were not, at any time, seriously menaced.

As we advanced slowly, firing, we made many hits, but I was horrified to see that every time one of the creatures fell, the nearest of his companions leaped upon him and cut his throat from ear to ear. Some of them had only to fall to be dispatched by his fellows. A bullet from Orthis' weapon shattered the hind leg of one of them, bringing him to the ground. It was, of course, not a fatal wound, but the creature had scarcely gone down, when the nearest to him sprang forward, and finished him. And thus we walked slowly toward the ford, and I commenced to have hope that we might reach it and make our escape. If our antagonists had been less fearless, I should have been certain of it, but they seemed almost indifferent to their danger, evidently counting upon their speed to give them immunity from our bullets. I can assure you that they presented most difficult targets, moving as they did in great leaps and bounds. It was probably more their number than our accuracy that permitted us the hits we made.

We were almost at the ford when the circle suddenly broke, and then formed a straight line parallel to us, the leader swinging his spear about his head, grasping the handle at its extreme end. The weapon moved at great speed, in an almost horizontal plane. I was wondering at the purpose of his action, when I saw that three or four of those directly in the rear of him had commenced to swing their spears in a similar manner. There was something strangely menacing about it that filled me with alarm. I fired at the leader and missed, and at the report of my pistol, a half dozen of them let go of their swift whirling spears, and an instant later, I realized the purpose of their strange maneuver; for the heavy weapons shot toward us, butts first, with the speed of lightning, the crescent-like hooks catching us around a leg, an arm and the neck, hurling us backward to the ground, and each time we essayed to rise, we were struck again, until we finally lay there, bruised and half stunned, and wholly at the mercy of our antagonists, who galloped forward quickly, stripping our weapons from us. Those who had hurled their H spears at us recovered them, and then they all gathered about, examining us, and jabbering among themselves.

Presently, the leader spoke to me, prodding me with the sharp point of his spear. I took it that he wanted me to arise, and I tried to do so, but I was pretty much all in and fell back each time I essayed to obey. Then he spoke to two of his followers, who lifted me and laid me across the back of a third. There I was fastened in a most uncomfortable position by means of leather straps which were taken from various parts of the harnesses of several of the creatures. Orthis was similarly lashed to another of them, whereupon they moved slowly back in the direction from which they had come, stopping, as they went, to collect the bodies of their dead, which were strapped to the backs of others of their companions. The fellow upon whom I rode had several well-defined gaits, one of which, a square trot, was the acme of torture for me, since I was bruised and hurt and had been placed across him face down, upon my belly; but inasmuch as this gait must have been hard, too, upon him, while thus saddled with a burden, he used it but little, for which I was tremendously thankful. When he changed to a single-foot, which, fortunately for me, he often did, I was much less uncomfortable.

As we crossed the ford toward the mainland, it was with difficulty that I kept from being drowned, since my head dragged in the water for a considerable distance and I was mighty glad when we came out again on shore. The thing that bore me was consistently inconsiderate of me, bumping me against others, and against the bodies of their slain that were strapped to the backs of his fellows. He was apparently quite tireless, as were the others, and we often moved for what seemed many miles at a fast run. Of course, my lunar weight was equivalent to only about thirty pounds on Earth while our captors seemed fully as well-muscled as a small earthly horse, and as we later learned, were capable of carrying heavy burdens.

How long we were on the march, I do not know, for where it is always daylight and there is no sun nor other means of measuring time, one may only guess at its duration, the result being influenced considerably by one's mental and physical sensations during the period. Judged by these considerations, then, we might have been on the trail for many hours, for I was not only most uncomfortable in body, but in mind as well. However that may be, I know only that it was a terrible journey; that we crossed rivers twice after reaching the mainland, and came at last to our destination, amid low hills, where there was a level, park-like space, dotted with weird trees. Here the straps were loosened, and we were dumped upon the ground, more dead than alive, and immediately surrounded by great numbers of creatures who were identical with those who had captured us.

When I was finally able to sit up and look about, I saw that we were at the threshold of a camp or village, consisting of a number of rectangular huts, with high-peaked roofs, thatched or rather shingled, with the broad, round leaves of the trees that grew about.

We saw now for the first time the females and the young. The former were similar to the males, except that they were of lighter build, and they were far more numerous. They had udders, with from four to six teats, and many of them were followed by numerous progeny, several that I saw having as high as six young in a litter. The young were naked, but the females wore a garment similar to that worn by the males, except that it was less ornate, as was their harness and other trappings. From the way the women and children rushed upon us as we were unloaded in camp, I felt that they were going to tear us to pieces, and I really believe they would have had not our captors prevented. Evidently the word was passed that we were not to be injured, for after the first rush they contented themselves with examining us, and sometimes feeling of us or our clothing, the while they discussed us, but with the bodies of those who were slain, it was different, for when they discovered these where they had been unloaded upon the ground, they fell upon them and commenced to devour them, the warriors joining them in the gruesome and terrible feast. Orthis and I understood now that they had cut the throats of their fellows to let the blood, in anticipation of the repast to come.

As we came to understand them and the conditions under which they lived, many things concerning them were explained. For example, at least two-thirds of the young that are born are males, and yet there are only about one-sixth as many adult males, as there are females. They are naturally carnivorous, but with the exception of one other creature upon which they prey, there is no animal in that part of the interior lunar world with which I am familiar, that they may eat with safety. The flying-toad and the walking snake and the other reptilia are poisonous, and they dare not eat them. The time had been, I later learned, possibly, however, ages before, when many other animals roamed the surface of the inner Moon, but all had become extinct except our captors and another creature, of which we, at the time of our capture, knew nothing, and these two preyed upon one another, while the species which was represented by those into whose hands we had fallen, raided the tribes and villages of their own kind for food, and ate their own dead, as we had already seen. As it was the females to whom they must look for the production of animal food, they did not kill these of their own species and never ate the body of one. Enemy women of their own kind, whom they captured, they brought to their villages, each warrior adding to his herd the individuals that he captured. As only the males are warriors, and as no one will eat the flesh of a female, the mortality among the males is, accordingly, extremely high, accounting for the vastly greater number of adult females. The latter are very well treated, as the position of a male in a community is dependent largely upon the size of his herd.

The principal mortality among the females results from three causes— raids by the other flesh-eating species which inhabit the inner lunar world, quarrels arising from jealousy among themselves, and death while bringing forth their young, especially during lean seasons when their warriors have been defeated in battle and have been unable to furnish them with flesh.

These creatures eat fruit and herbs and nuts as well as meat, but they do not thrive well upon these things exclusively. Their existence, therefore, is dependent upon the valor and ferocity of their males whose lives are spent in making raids and forays against neighboring tribes and in defending their own villages against invaders.

As Orthis and I sat watching the disgusting orgy of cannibalism about us, the leader of the party that had captured us came toward us from the center of the village, and speaking a single word, which I later learned meant come, he prodded us with his spear point until finally we staggered to our feet. Repeating the word, then, he started back into the village.

"I guess he wants us to follow him, Orthis," I said. And so we fell in behind the creature, which was evidently what he desired, for he nodded his head, and stepped on in the direction that he had taken, which led toward a very large hut—by far the largest in the village.

In the side of the hut presented to us there seemed to be but a single opening, a large door covered by heavy hangings, which our conductor thrust aside as we entered the interior with him. We found ourselves in a large room, without any other opening whatsoever, save the doorway through which we had entered, and over which the hanging had again been drawn, yet the interior was quite light, though not so much so as outside, but there were no means for artificial lighting apparent. The walls were covered with weapons and with the skulls and other bones of creatures similar to our captors, though Orthis and I both noticed a few skulls much narrower than the others and which, from their appearance, might have been the human skulls of Earth Men, though in discussing it later, we came to the conclusion that they were the skulls of the females and the young of the species, whose faces are not so wide as the adult male.

Lying upon a bed of grasses at the opposite side of the room was a large male whose skin was of so much deeper lavender hue than the others that we had seen, as to almost suggest a purple. The face, though badly disfigured by scars, and grim and ferocious in the extreme, was an intelligent one, and the instant that I looked into those eyes, I knew that we were in the presence of a leader. Nor was I wrong, for this was the chief or king of the tribe into whose clutches Fate had thrown us.

A few words passed between the two, and then the chief arose and came toward us. He examined us very critically, our clothing seeming to interest him tremendously. He tried to talk with us, evidently asking us questions, and seemed very much disgusted when it became apparent to him that we could not understand him, nor he us, for Orthis and I spoke to one another several times, and once or twice addressed him. He gave some instructions to the fellow who had brought us, and we were taken out again, and to another hut, to which there was presently brought a portion of the carcass of one of the creatures we had killed before we were captured. I could not eat any of it, however, and neither could Orthis; and after a while, by signs and gestures, we made them understand that we wished some other kind of food, with the result that a little later, they brought us fruit and vegetables, which were more palatable and, as we were to discover later, sufficiently nutritious to carry us along and maintain our strength.

I had become thirsty, and by simulating drinking, I finally succeeded in making plain to them my desire in that direction, with the result that they led us out to a little stream which ran through the village, and there we quenched our thirst.

We were still very weak and sore from the manhandling we had received, but we were both delighted to discover that we were not seriously injured, nor were any of our bones broken.

# FIVE

# A Lunar Storm

S HORTLY after we arrived at the village, they took away our watches, our pocket-knives, and everything that we possessed of a similar nature, and which they considered as curiosities. The chief wore Orthis' wristwatch above one fore-paw and mine above the other, but as he did not know how to wind them, nor the purpose for which they were intended, they did him or us no good. The result was, however, that it was now entirely impossible for us to measure time in any way, and I do not know, even to this day, how long we were in this strange village. We ate when we were hungry, and slept when we were tired. It was always daylight; and it seemed that there were always raiding parties going out or returning, so that flesh was plentiful, and we became rather reconciled to our fate; in so far as the immediate danger of being eaten was concerned, but why they kept us alive, as we had slain so many of their fellows, I could not understand.

It must have been immediately after we arrived that they made an attempt to teach us their language. Two females were detailed for this duty. We were given unlimited freedom within certain bounds, which were well indicated by the several sentries which constantly watched from the summit of hills surrounding the village. Past these we could not go, nor do I know that we had any particular desire to do so, since we realized only too well that there would be little chance of our regaining the ship should we escape the village, inasmuch as we had not the remotest idea in what direction it lay.

Our one hope lay in learning their language, and then utilizing our knowledge in acquiring some definite information as to the surrounding country and the location of *The Barsoom*.

It did not seem to take us very long to learn their tongue, though, of course, I realize that it may really have been months. Almost before we knew it, we were conversing freely with our captors. When I say freely, it is possible that I exaggerate a trifle, for though we could understand them fairly well, it was with difficulty that we made ourselves understood, yet we managed it some way, handicapped as we were by the peculiarities of the most remarkable language of which I have any knowledge.

It is a very difficult language to speak, and as a written language, would be practically impossible. For example, there is their word *gu-e-ho,* for which Orthis and I discovered twenty-seven separate and distinct meanings, and that there are others I have little or no doubt. Their speech is more aptly described as song, the meaning of each syllable being governed by the note in which it is sung. They speak in five notes, which we may describe as A, B, C, D and E. *Gu* sung in A means something radically different from *gu* sung in E, and again if *gu* is sung in A, followed by *e* in G, it means something other than if *gu* had been sung in D followed by *e* in A.

Fortunately for us, there are no words of over three syllables, and most of them consist of only one or two, or we should have been entirely lost. The resulting speech, however, is extremely beautiful, and Orthis used to say that if he closed his eyes, he could imagine himself living constantly in grand opera.

The chief's name, as we learned, was Ga-va-go; the name of the tribe or village was No-vans, while the race to which they belonged was known as Va-gas.

When I felt that I had mastered the language sufficiently well to make myself at least partially understood, I asked to speak to Ga-va-go, and shortly thereafter, I was taken to him.

"You have learned our speech?" he asked.

I nodded in the affirmative. "I have," I said, "and I have come to ask why we are held captives and what you intend to do with us. We did not come to seek a quarrel with you. We wish only to be friends, and to be allowed to go our way in peace."

"What manner of creature are you," he asked, "and where do you come from?"

I asked him if he had ever heard of the Sun or the stars or the other planets or any worlds outside his own, and he replied that he had not, and that there were no such things.

"But there are, Ga-va-go," I said, "and I and my companion are from another world, far, far outside your own. An accident brought us here. Give us back our weapons, and let us go."

He shook his head negatively.

"Where you come from, do you eat one another?" he asked.

"No," I replied, "we do not."

"Why?" he asked, and I saw his eyes narrow as he awaited my reply.

Was it mental telepathy or just luck that put the right answer in my mouth, for somehow, intuitively, I seemed to grasp what was in the creature's mind.

"Our flesh is poison," I said, "those who eat it die."

He looked at me then for a long time, with an expression upon his face which I could not interpret. It may have been that he doubted my word, or again, it may have been that my reply confirmed his suspicion, I do not know; but presently he asked me another question.

"Are there many like you in the land where you live?"

"Millions upon millions," I replied.

"And what do they eat?"

"They eat fruits and vegetables and the flesh of animals," I answered.

"What animals?" he asked.

"I have seen no animals here like them," I replied, "but there are many kinds unlike us, so that we do not have to eat flesh of our own race."

"Then you have all the flesh that you want?"

"All that we can eat," I replied. "We raise these animals for their flesh."

"Where is your country?" he demanded. "Take me to it."

I smiled. "I cannot take you to it," I said. "It is upon another world."

It was quite evident that he did not believe me, for he scowled at me ferociously.

"Do you wish to die?" he demanded.

I told him that I had no such longing.

"Then you will lead me to your country," he said, "where there is plenty of flesh for everyone. You may think about it until I send for you again. Go!" And thus he dismissed me. Then he sent for Orthis, but what Orthis told him, I never knew exactly, for he would not tell me, and as our relations, even in our captivity, were far from friendly, I did not urge him to any confidences. I had occasion to notice, however, that from that time Ga-va-go indicated a marked preference for Orthis, and the latter was often called to his hut.

I was momentarily expecting to be summoned in to Ga-va-go's presence, and learn my fate, when he discovered that I could not lead him to my country, where flesh was so plentiful. But at about this time we broke camp, and in the press of other matters, he evidently neglected to take any further immediate action in my case, or at least, so I thought, until I later had reason to suspect that he felt that he need no longer depend upon me to lead him to this land of milk and honey.

The Va-gas are a nomadic race, moving hither and thither, either as they are pressed—by some foes, or till their victories have frightened away the other tribes from their vicinity, in either of which events, they march in search of fresh territory. The move that we made now was necessitated by the fact that all the other tribes nearby had fled before the ferocity of the No-vans, whose repeated and successful raids had depleted the villages of their neighbors and filled them with terror.

The breaking of camp was a wonderfully simple operation. All their few belongings, consisting of extra clothing, trappings, weapons, and their treasured skulls and bones of victims, were strapped to the backs of the women. Orthis and I each bestrode a warrior detailed by Ga-va-go for the purpose of transporting us, and we filed out of the village, leaving the huts behind.

Ga-va-go, with a half-dozen warriors, galloped far ahead. Then came a strong detachment of warriors, with the women folks behind them, another detachment of warriors following in the rear of the women and children, while others rode upon either flank. A mile or so in the rear, came three warriors, and there were two or three scattered far out on either flank. Thus we moved, thoroughly protected against surprise, regulating our speed by that of the point with which Ga-va-go traveled.

Because of the women and the children, we moved more slowly than warriors do when on the march alone, when they seldom, if ever, travel slower than a trot, and more generally, at a fast gallop. We moved along a well-worn trail, passing several deserted villages, from which the prey of the No-vans had fled. We crossed many rivers, for the lunar world is well watered. We skirted several lakes, and at one point of high ground, I saw, far at our left, the waters of what appeared to be a great ocean.

There was never a time when Orthis and I were not plentifully supplied with food, for there is an abundance of it growing throughout all the territory we crossed, but the No-vans had been without flesh for several days and were, in consequence, mad with hunger, as the fruits and vegetables which they ate, seemed not to satisfy them at all.

We were moving along at a brisk trot when, without warning, we were struck by a sudden gust of wind that swept, cold and refreshing, down from some icy mountain fastness. The effect upon the No-vans was electrical. I would not have had to understand their language to realize that they were terrified. They looked apprehensively about and increased their speed as though endeavoring to overtake Ga-va-go, who was now far ahead with the point. A moment later a dash of rain struck us, and then it was every man for himself and the devil take the hindmost, as they broke into a wild stampede to place themselves close to their chief. Their hysterical flight was like the terrorized rush of wild cattle. They jostled and tripped one another, and stumbled and fell and were trampled upon, in their haste to escape.

Old Ga-va-go had stopped with his point, and was waiting for us. Those who accompanied him seemed equally terrified with the rest, but evidently they did not dare run until Ga-va-go gave the word. I think, however, that they all felt safer when they were close to him, for they had a great deal of confidence in him, yet they were still pretty badly frightened, and it would not have taken much to have set them off again into another rout. Ga-va-go waited until the last of the rearguard straggled in, and then he set off directly toward the mountains, the entire tribe moving in a compact mass, though they might have fallen easy prey to an ambush or any sudden attack. They knew, however, what I half guessed, that knowing that their enemies were as terrified of the storm as they, there was little danger of their being attacked—none whatever, in fact.

We came at last to a hillside covered with great trees which offered some protection from both the wind and the rain, which had now arisen to the proportion of a hurricane.

As we came to a halt, I slipped from the back of the warrior who had been carrying me, and found myself beside one of the women who had taught Orthis and me the language of the Va-gas.

"Why is everyone so terrified?" I asked her.

"It is Zo-al," she whispered, fearfully. "He is angry."

"Who is Zo-al?" I asked.

She looked at me in wide-eyed astonishment. "Who is Zo-al!" she repeated. "They told me that you said that you came from another world, and I can well believe it, when you ask, who is Zo-al?"

"Well, who is he?" I insisted.

"He is a great beast," she whispered. "He is everywhere. He lives in all the great holes in the ground, and when he is angry, he comes forth and makes the water fall and the air run away. We know that there is no water up there," and she pointed toward the sky. "But when Zo-al is angry, he makes water fall from where there is no water, so mighty is Zo-al, and he makes the air to run away so that the trees fall before it as it rushes past, and huts are knocked flat or carried high above the ground. And then, O terror of terrors, he makes a great noise, before which mighty warriors fall upon the ground and cover up their ears. We have angered Zo-al, and he is punishing us, and I do not dare to ask him not to send the big noise."

It was at that instant that there broke upon my ears the most terrific detonation that I have ever heard. So terrific was it that I thought my ear drums had burst and simultaneously, a great ball of fire seemed to come rolling down from the mountain heights above us.

The woman, covering her ears, shuddered, and when she saw the ball of fire, she voiced a piercing shriek.

"The light that devours!" she cried. "When that comes too, it is the end, for then is Zo-al mad with rage."

The ground shook to the terrifying noise, and though the ball of fire did not pass close to us, still could I feel the heat of it even as it went by at a distance, leaving a trail of blackened and smoking vegetation in its rear. What flames there were, the torrential rain extinguished almost immediately. It must have traveled about ten miles, down toward the sea, across rolling hills and level valleys, when suddenly it burst, the explosion being followed by a report infinitely louder than that which I had first heard. An earthquake could scarce have agitated the ground more terrifyingly than did this peal of lunar thunder.

I had witnessed my first lunar electrical storm, and I did not wonder that the inhabitants of this strange world were terrified by it. They attribute these storms, as they do all their troubles, to Zo-al, a great beast, which is supposed to dwell in the depth of the lunar craters, the lower ends of which open into the interior lunar world. As we cowered there among the trees, I wondered if they were not afraid that the wind would blow the forest down and crush them, and I asked the woman who stood beside me.

"Yes," she said, "that often happens, but more often does it happen that if one is caught in a clearing, the air that runs away picks him up and carries him along to drop him from a great height upon the hard ground. The trees bend before they break, and those who watch are warned and they escape destruction if they are quick. When the wind that runs seizes one, there is no escape."

"It seems to me," I said, "that it would have been safer if Ga-va-go had led us into one of those sheltered ravines," and I indicated a gorge in the hillside at our right.

"No," she said, "Ga-va-go is wise. He led us to the safest spot. We are sheltered from the air that runs away, and perhaps a little from the light that devours, nor can the waters that drown, reach us here, for presently they will fill that ravine full."

Nor was she wrong. Rushing down from the hillside, the water poured in torrents into the ravine, and presently, though it must have been twenty or thirty feet deep, it was filled almost to overflowing. Whoever had sought refuge there, would have been drowned and washed away to the big ocean far below. It was evident that Ga-va-go had not been actuated solely by blind terror, though I came to know that he must have felt terror, for these terrible electrical storms alone can engender it in the breasts of these fearless and ferocious people.

The storm must have lasted for a considerable time; how long, of course, I do not know, but some idea of its duration may be gained by the fact that I became hungry and ate of the fruit of the trees, which sheltered us, at least six times, and slept twice. We were soaked to the skin and very cold, for the rain evidently came from a great altitude. During the entire storm, the No-vans scarcely moved from their positions beneath the trees, with their backs toward the storm, where they stood with lowered heads like cattle. We experienced twelve detonations of the ground-shaking thunder, and witnessed six manifestations of the light that devours. Trees had fallen all about us, and as far as we could see, the grasses lay flat and matted upon the ground. They told me that storms of the severity of this were infrequent, though rain and wind, accompanied by electrical manifestations, might be expected at any season of the year—I use that expression from habit, for one can scarcely say that there are any well-marked seasonal changes within the Moon that could indicate corresponding divisions of time as upon the Earth. From what I was able to gather from observation and from questioning the Va-gas, lunar vegetation reproduces itself entirely independent of any seasonal restrictions, the frequency and temperature of the rains having, seemingly, the greatest influence in the matter. A period of drought and cold rains retards growth and germination, while frequent warm rains have an opposite effect, the result being that you find vegetation of the same variety in all stages of development, growing side by side— blossoms upon one tree, fruit upon another, and the dry seed-pods upon a third. Not even, therefore, by the growth of plant life, might one measure time within the Moon, and the period of gestation among the Va-gas is similarly irregular, being affected by the physical condition of the female as well as by climatic conditions, I imagine. When the tribe is well-fed, and the weather warm, the warriors victorious, and the minds of the women at peace, they bring forth their young in an incredibly short period. On the other hand, a period of cold, or of hunger, and of long marches, following defeat, induces an opposite result. It seems to me that the females nurse their young for a very short period of time, for they grow rapidly, and as soon as their molars are through, and they can commence eating meat, they are weaned. They are devilish little rascals, their youthful exuberance finding its outlet in acts of fiendish cruelty. As they are not strong enough to inflict their tortures on adults they perpetrate them upon one another, with the result that the weaker are often killed, after they are weaned and have left the protection of their savage mothers. Of course, they tried to play some of their fiendish tricks on Orthis and myself, but after we had knocked a few of them down, they left us severely alone.

During the storm, they huddled, shivering and cold, against the adults. Possibly I should be ashamed to say it, but I felt no pity for them, and rather prayed that they would all be chilled to death, so hateful and wantonly cruel were they. As they become adults, they are less wanton in their atrocities, though no less cruel, their energies, however, being intelligently directed upon the two vital interests of their lives—procuring flesh and women.

Shortly after the rain ceased, the wind began to abate, and as I was cold, cramped and uncomfortable, I walked out into the open, in search of exercise that would stimulate my circulation and warm me again. As I walked briskly to and fro, looking here and there at the evidences of the recent storm, my glance chanced to rise toward the sky, and there I saw what appeared at first to be a huge bird, a few hundred feet above the forest in which we had sought shelter. It was flapping its great wings weakly and seemed to be almost upon the verge of exhaustion, and though I could see that it was attempting to fly back in the direction of the mountains, the force of the wind was steadily carrying it in the direction of the lowlands and the sea. Presently it would be directly above me, and as it drew nearer, I knit my brows in puzzlement, for except for its wings, and what appeared to be a large hump upon its back, its form bore a striking resemblance to that of a human being.

Some of the No-vans evidently saw me looking upwards thus interestedly, and prompted by curiosity, joined me. When they saw the creature flying weakly overhead, they set up a great noise, until presently all the tribe had run into the open and were looking up at the thing above us.

The wind was lessening rapidly, but it still was strong enough to carry the creature gently toward us, and at the same time I perceived that whatever it was, it was falling slowly to the ground, or more correctly, sinking slowly.

"What is it?" I asked of the warrior standing beside me.

"It is a U-ga," be replied. "Now shall we eat."

I had seen no birds in the lunar world, and as I knew they would not eat the flying reptiles, I guessed that this must be some species of bird life, but as it dropped closer, I became more and more convinced that it was a winged human being, or at least a winged creature with human form.

As it fluttered toward the ground, the No-vans ran along to meet it, waiting for it to fall within reach. As they did so, Ga-va-go called to them to bring the creature to him alive and unharmed.

I was about a hundred yards from the spot, when the poor thing finally fell into their clutches. They dragged it to the ground roughly, and a moment later I was horrified to see them tear its wings from it and the hump from its back. There was a great deal of grumbling at Ga-va-go's order, as following the storm and their long fast, the tribe was ravenously hungry.

"Flesh, flesh!" they growled. "We are hungry. Give us flesh!" But Ga-va-go paid no attention to them, standing to one side beneath a tree, awaiting the prisoner that they were bringing toward him.

# SIX

# An Exodus and a Battle

O RTHIS, who was becoming the almost constant companion of the chief, was standing beside the latter, while I was twenty-five or thirty yards away, and directly between Ga-va-go and the warriors who were approaching with the prisoner, who would of necessity have to pass close beside me. I remained where I was, therefore, in order to get a better look at it; which was rather difficult because it was almost entirely surrounded by No-vans. However as they came opposite me, there was a little break momentarily in the ranks, and I had my first opportunity, though brief, for a closer observation of the captive; and my comprehension was almost staggered by what my eyes revealed to me, for there before me, was as perfectly formed a human female as I had ever seen. By earthly standards, she appeared a girl of about eighteen, with hair of glossy blackness, that suggested more the raven's wing than aught else and a skin of almost marble whiteness, slightly tinged with a creamy shade. Only in the color of her skin, did she differ from earthly women in appearance, except that she seemed far more beautiful than they. Such perfection of features seemed almost unbelievable. Had I seen her first posed motionless, I could have sworn that she was chiseled from marble, yet there was nothing cold about her appearance. She fairly radiated life and feeling. If my first impression had been startling, it was nothing to the effect that was produced when she turned her eyes full upon me. Her black brows were two thin, penciled arches, beneath which were dark wells of light, vying in blackness with her raven hair. On either cheek was just the faintest suggestion of a deeper cream, and to think that these hideous creatures saw in that form divine only flesh to eat! I shuddered at the thought and then my eyes met hers and I saw an expression of incredulity and surprise registered in those liquid orbs. She half-turned her head as she was dragged past, that she might have a further look at me, for doubtless she was as surprised to see a creature like me as I was to see her.

Involuntarily I started forward. Whether there was an appeal for succor in those eyes I do not know, but at least they aroused within me instantly, that natural instinct of a human male to protect the weak. And so it was that I was a little behind her and to her right, when she was halted before Ga-va-go.

The savage Va-gas' chieftain eyed her coldly, while from all sides there arose cries of "Give us flesh! Give us flesh! We are hungry!" to which Ga-va-go paid not the slightest attention.

"From whence come you, U-ga?" he demanded.

Her head was high, and she eyed him with cold dignity as she replied, "From Laythe."

The No-van raised his brows. "Ah," he breathed, "from Laythe. The flesh of the women from Laythe is good," and he licked his thin lips.

The girl narrowed her eyes, and tilted her chin a bit higher. "Rympth!" she ejaculated, disgustedly.

As rympth is the name of the four-legged snake of Va-nah, the inner lunar world, and considered the lowest and most disgusting of created things, she could not well have applied a more opprobrious epithet to the No-van chieftain, but if it had been her intent to affront him, his expression gave no indication that she had succeeded.

"Your name?" he asked.

"Nah-ee-lah," she replied.

"Nah-ee-lah," he repeated, "Ah, you are the daughter of Sagroth, Jemadar of Laythe."

She nodded in indifferent affirmation, as though aught he might say was a matter of perfect indifference to her.

"What do you expect us to do with you?" asked Ga-va-go, a question which suggested a cat playing with a mouse before destroying it.

"What can I expect of the Va-gas, other than that they will kill me and eat me?" she replied.

A roar of savage assent arose from the creatures surrounding her. Ga-va-go flashed a quick look of anger and displeasure at his people.

"Do not be too sure of that," he snapped. "This be little more than a meal for Ga-va-go alone. It would but whet the appetite of the tribe."

"There are two more," suggested a bold warrior, close beside me, pointing at me and at Orthis.

"Silence!" roared Ga-va-go. "Since when did you become chief of the No-vans?"

"We can starve without a chief," muttered the warrior who had spoken, and from two or three about him arose grumblings of assent.

Swift, at that, Ga-va-go reared upon his hind feet, and in the same motion, drew and hurled his spear, the sharp point penetrating the breast of the malcontent, piercing his heart. As the creature fell, the warrior closest to him slit his throat, while another withdrew Ga-va-go's spear from the corpse, and returned it to the chief.

"Divide the carcass among you," commanded the chief, "and whosoever thinks that there is not enough, let him speak as that one spoke, and there shall be more flesh to eat."

Thus did Ga-va-go, chief of the No-vans, hold the obedience of his savage tribesmen. There was no more muttering then, but I saw several cast hungry eyes at me—hungry, angry eyes that boded me no good.

In what seemed an incredibly short space of time, the carcass of the slain warrior had been divided and devoured, and once again we set out upon the march, in search of new fields to conquer, and fresh flesh to eat.

Now Ga-va-go sent scouts far in advance of the point, for we were entering territory which he had not invaded for a long time, a truth which was evidenced by the fact that there were only about twenty warriors in the tribe, besides Ga-va-go, who were at all familiar with the territory. Naturally quarrelsome and disagreeable, the No-vans were far from pleasant companions upon that memorable march, since they had not recovered from the fright and discomforts of the storm and, in addition, were ravenously hungry. I imagine that none, other than Ga-va-go, could have held them. What his purpose was in preserving the three prisoners, that would have made such excellent food for the tribe, I did not know. However, we were not slain, though I judged the fellow who carried me, would much sooner have eaten me, and to vent his spite upon me he trotted as much as he could, and I can assure you that he had the most devilishly execrable trot I ever sat. I felt that he was rather running the thing into the ground, for he had an easy rack, which would have made it much more comfortable for both of us, and inasmuch as I knew that I was safe as long as I was under Ga-va-go's protection, I made up my mind to teach the fellow a lesson, which I finally did, although almost as much to my discomfort as his, by making no effort to ease myself upon his back so that at every step I rose high and came down hard upon him, sitting as far back as possible so as to pound his kidneys painfully. It made him very angry and he threatened me with all kinds of things if I didn't desist, but I only answered by suggesting that he take an easier gait, which at last he was forced to do.

Nah-ee-lah and a Va-gas

Orthis was riding ahead with Ga-va-go, who as usual led the point, while the new prisoner astride a No-van warrior was with the main body, as was I.

Once the warriors that we bestrode paced side by side, and I saw the girl eyeing me questioningly. She seemed much interested in the remnants of my uniform, which must have differed greatly from any clothing she had seen in her own world. It seemed that she spoke and understood the same language that Ga-va-go used, and so at last I made bold to address her.

"It is unfortunate," I said, "that you have fallen into the hands of these creatures. I wish, that I might be of service to you, but I also am a prisoner."

She acknowledged my speech with a slight inclination of her head, and at first I thought that she was not going to reply, but finally looking me full in the face she asked, "What are you?"

"I am one of the inhabitants of the planet Earth."

"Where is that, and what is planet?" she asked, for I had had to use the Earth word, since there is no word of similar meaning in the language of the Va-gas.

"You know, of course," I said, "that space outside of Va-nah is filled with other worlds. The closest to Va-nah is Earth, which is many, many times larger than your world. It is from Earth that I come."

She shook her head. "I do not understand," she said. She closed her eyes, and waved her hands with a gesture that might have included the universe. "All, all is rock," she said, "except here in the center of everything, in this space we call Va-nah. All else is rock."

I suppressed a smile at the vast egotism of Va-nah, but yet how little different is it from many worldlings, who conceive that the entire cosmos exists solely for the inhabitants of Earth. I even know men in our own enlightened twenty-first century, who insist that Mars is not inhabited and that the messages that are purported to come from our sister planet, are either the evidences of a great world hoax, or the voice of the devil luring people from belief in the true God.

"Did you ever see my like in Va-nah?" I asked her.

"No," she replied, "I never did, but I have not been to every part of Va-nah. Va-nah is a very great world, and there are many corners of it of which I know nothing."

"I am not of Va-nah," I told her again, "I am from another world far, far away;" and then I tried to explain something of the universe to her—of the sun and the planets and their satellites, but I saw that it was as far beyond her as are the conceptions of eternity and space beyond the finite mind of Earth Men. She simply couldn't get it, that was all. To her, everything was solid rock that we know as space. She thought for a long time, though, and then she said, "Ah, perhaps after all there may be other worlds than Va-nah. The great Hoos, those vast holes that lead into the eternal rock, may open into other worlds like Va-nah. I have heard that theory discussed, but no one in Va-nah believes it. It is true, then!" she exclaimed brightly, "and you come from another world like Va-nah. You came through one of the Hoos, did you not?"

"Yes, I came through one of the Hoos," I replied—the word means hole in the Va-gas tongue—"but I did not come from a world like Va-nah. Here you live upon the inside of a hollow sphere. We Earth Men live upon the outside of a similar though much larger sphere."

"But what holds it up?" she cried, laughing. It was the first time that she had laughed, and it was a very contagious laugh, and altogether delightful. Although I knew that it would probably be useless, I tried to explain the whole thing to her, commencing with the nebular hypothesis, and winding up with the relations that exist between the Moon and the Earth. If I didn't accomplish anything else, I at least gave her something to distract her mind from her grave predicament, and to amuse her temporarily, for she laughed often at some of my statements. I had never seen so gay and vivacious a creature, nor one so entirely beautiful as she. The single, sleeveless, tunic-like garment that she wore, fell scarcely to her knees and as she bestrode the No-van warrior, it often flew back until her thighs, even, were exposed. Her figure was divinely perfect, its graceful contours being rather accentuated than hidden by the diaphanous material of her dainty covering; but when she laughed, she exposed two rows of even white teeth that would be the envy of the most beautiful of Earth Maids.

"Suppose," she said, "that I should take a handful of gravel and throw it up in the air. According to your theory the smaller would all commence to revolve about the larger and they would go flying thus wildly around in the air forever, but that is not what would happen. If I threw a handful of gravel into the air it would fall immediately to the ground again, and if the worlds you tell me of were cast thus into the air, they too would fall, just as the gravel falls."

It was useless, but I had known that from the beginning. What would be more interesting would be to question her, and that I had wished to do for some time, but she always put me off with a pretty gesture and a shake of her head, insisting that I answer some of her questions instead, but this time I insisted.

"Tell me, please," I asked, "how you came to the spot where you were captured, how you flew, and what became of your wings, and why, when they tore them from you, it did not injure you?"

She laughed at that quite merrily.

"The wings do not grow upon us," she explained, "we make them and fasten them upon our arms."

"Then you can support yourself in the air with wings fastened to your arms?" I demanded, incredulously.

"Oh, no," she said, "the wings we use simply for propelling ourselves through the air. In a bag, upon our backs, we carry a gas that is lighter than air. It is this gas which supports us, and we carry it in such quantities as to maintain a perfect equilibrium, so that we may float at any altitude, or with our wings rise or fall gently; but as I hovered over Laythe, came the air that runs, and seizing me with its strong arms bore me off across the surface of Va-nah. Futilely I fought against it until I was spent and weak, and then it dropped me into the clutches of the Va-gas, for the gas in my bag had become depleted. It was not intended to carry me aloft for any great length of time."

She had used a word which, when I questioned her, she explained so that I understood that it meant time, and I asked her what she meant by it and how she could measure it, since I had seen no indication of the Va-gas having any conception of a measurable aspect of duration.

Nah-ee-lah explained to me that the Va-gas, who were a lower order, had no means of measuring time, but that the U-ga, the race to which she belonged, had always been able to compute time through their observation of the fact that during certain periods the bottoms of the hoos, or craters, were illuminated, and for another period they were dark, and so they took as a unit of measure the total period from the beginning of this light in a certain crater to its beginning again, and this they called a *ula*, which corresponds with a sidereal month. By mechanical means they divide this into a hundred parts, called *ola*, the duration of each of which is about six hours and thirty-two minutes earth time. Ten ulas make a *keld*, which one might call the lunar year of about two hundred and seventy-two days earth time.

I asked her many questions and took great pleasure in her answers, for she was a bright, intelligent girl, and although I saw many evidences of regal dignity about her, yet her manner toward me was most natural and unaffected, and I could not help but feel that she occupied a position of importance among her own people.

Our conversation was suddenly interrupted, however, by a messenger from the point, who came racing back at tremendous speed, carrying word from Ga-va-go that the scouts were signaling that they had discovered a large village, and that the warriors were to prepare to fight.

The Moon Maid in Laythe

Immediately we moved up rapidly to Ga-va-go, and then we all advanced toward the scout who could be seen upon a knoll far ahead. We were cautioned to silence, and as we moved at a brisk canter over the soft, pale lavender vegetation of the inner Moon, the feet of the Va-gas giving forth no sound, the picture presented to my earthly eyes was weird and mysterious in the extreme.

When we reached the scout, we learned that the village was situated just beyond a low ridge not far distant, so Ga-va-go gave orders that the women, the children, and the three prisoners should remain under a small guard where we were until they had topped the ridge, when we were to advance to a position where we might overlook the village, and if the battle was against the No-vans we could retreat to a point which he indicated to the warriors left to guard us. This was to be the rendezvous, for following defeat the Va-gas warriors scatter in all directions, thus preventing any considerable body of them being attacked and destroyed by a larger body of the pursuing enemy.

As we stood there upon the knoll, watching Ga-va-go and his savage warriors galloping swiftly toward the distant ridge, I could not but wonder that the inhabitants of the village which they were about to attack had not placed sentinels along the ridge to prevent just such a surprise as this, but when I questioned one of the warriors who had been left to guard us, he said that not all the Va-gas tribes were accustomed to posting sentinels when they felt themselves reasonably safe from attack. It had always been Ga-va-go's custom, however, and to it they attributed his supremacy among the other Va-gas tribes over a large territory.

"After a tribe has made a few successful raids and returned victorious, they are filled with pride," the warrior explained to me, "and presently they begin to think that no one dares to attack them and then they grow careless, and little by little the custom of posting sentinels drops into disuse. The very fact that they have no sentinels indicates that they are a large, powerful and successful tribe. We shall feed well for a long time."

The very idea of the thought that was passing through his mind, was repellent in the extreme, and I fairly shuddered when I contemplated the callousness with which this creature spoke of the coming orgy, in which he hoped to devour flesh of his own kind.

Presently we saw our force disappear beyond the ridge, and then we too, advanced, and as we moved forward there came suddenly to us, from the distance the fierce and savage war cry of the No-vans and a moment later it was answered by another no less terrible, rising from the village beyond the ridge. Our guards hastened us then, to greater speed, until, at a full run, we mounted the steep slope of the ridge and halted upon its crest.

Below us lay a broad valley, and in the center a long, beautiful lake, the opposite shore of which was clothed in forest while that nearest us was open and park-like, dotted here and there with beautiful trees, and in this open space we descried a large village.

The ferocity of the scene below us was almost indescribable. The No-vans warriors were circling the village at a rapid run, attempting to keep the enemy in a compact mass within, where it would present a better target for their spears. Already the ground was dotted with corpses. There were no wounded, for whenever one fell the nearest to him whether friend or foe cut his throat, since the victors would devour them all without partiality. The females and the young had taken refuge in the huts, from the doorways of which they watched the progress of the battle. The defenders attempted repeatedly to break through the circling No-vans. The warrior with whom I had been talking told me that if they were successful the females and the young would follow them through the break scattering in all directions, while their warriors attempted to encircle the No-vans. It was almost immediately evident that the advantage lay with the force that succeeded in placing this swift-moving circle about its enemy, and keeping the enemy within it until they had been dispatched, for those in the racing circle presented a poor target, while the compact mass of warriors milling in the center could scarce be missed.

Following several unsuccessful attempts to break through the ring of savage foemen the defenders suddenly formed another smaller ring within, and moving in the opposite direction to the No-vans, raced in a rapid circle. No longer did they cast spears at the enemy, but contented themselves with leaping and bounding at a rapid gait. At first it seemed to me that they had lost their heads with terror, but at last I realized that they were executing a strategic maneuver which demonstrated both cunning and high discipline. In the earlier stages of the battle each side had depended for its weapons upon those hurled by the opposing force, but now the defenders hurled no weapons, and it became apparent that the No-vans would soon no longer have spears to cast at them. The defenders were also lessening their casualties by moving in a rapid circle in a direction opposite to that taken by the attackers, but it must have required high courage and considerable discipline to achieve this result since it is difficult in the extreme to compel men to present themselves continuously as living targets for a foe while they themselves are permitted to inflict no injury upon the enemy.

Ga-va-go apparently was familiar with the ruse, for suddenly he gave a loud cry which was evidently a command. Instantaneously, his entire force wheeled in their tracks and raced in the opposite direction paralleling the defenders of the village, and immediately thereafter cast their remaining spears at comparatively easy targets.

The defenders, who were of the tribe called Lu-thans, wheeled instantly to reverse the direction of their flight. Those wounded in the sudden on-slaught stumbled and fell, tripping and impeding the others, with the result that for an instant they were a tangled mass, without order or formation. Then it was that Ga-va-go and his No-vans leaped in upon them with their short, wicked sword-daggers. At once the battle resolved itself into a fero-cious and bloody hand-to-hand conflict, in which daggers and teeth and three-toed paws each did their share to inflict injury upon an antagonist. In their efforts to escape a blow, or to place themselves in an advantageous position, many of the combatants leaped high into the air, sometimes be-tween thirty and forty feet. Their shrieks and howls were continuous and piercing. Corpses lay piled so thick as to impede the movements of the war-riors, and the ground was slippery with blood, yet on and on they fought, until it seemed that not a single one would be left alive.

"It is almost over," remarked the warrior at my side. "See, there are two or three No-vans now attacking each Lu-than."

It was true, and I saw that the battle could last but a short time. As a matter of fact it ended almost immediately, the remaining Lu-thans suddenly attempting to break away and scatter in different directions. Some of them succeeded in escaping, possibly twenty but I am sure that there were not more than that, and the rest fell.

Ga-va-go and his warriors did not pursue the few who had escaped, evidently considering that it was not worth the effort, since there were not enough of them to menace the village, and there was already plenty of meat lying fresh and warm upon the ground.

We were summoned now, and as we filed down into the village, great was the rejoicing of our females and young.

Guards were placed over the women and children of the defeated Lu-thans, and then at a signal from Ga-va-go, the No-vans fell upon the spoils of war. It was a revolting spectacle, as mothers devoured their sons, and wives, their husbands. I do not care to dwell upon it.

When the victors had eaten their fill, the prisoners were brought forth under heavy guard, and divided by the Va-gas between the surviving No-vans warriors. There was no favoritism shown in the distribution of the prisoners, except that Ga-va-go was given first choice, and received also those that remained after as nearly equal a distribution as possible had been made. I had expected that the male children would be killed, but they were not, being inducted into the tribe upon an equal footing with those that had been born into it.

Being capable of no sentiments of either affection or loyalty, it is immaterial to these creatures to what tribe they belong, but once inducted into a tribe, the instinct of self-preservation holds them to it, since they would be immediately slain by the members of any other tribe.

I learned shortly after this engagement that Ga-va-go had lost fully half his warriors, and that this was one of the most important battles that the tribe had ever fought. The spoils, however, had been rich, for they had taken over ten thousand women and fully fifty thousand young, and great quantities of weapons, harness, and apparel.

The flesh that they could not eat was wrapped up and buried, and I was told that it would remain in excellent condition almost indefinitely.

# SEVEN

# The Moon Maid Escapes

AFTER occupying the new village, Orthis and I were separated, he being assigned a hut close to Ga-va-go, while I was placed in another section of the village. If I could have been said to have been on good terms with any of the terrible creatures of the tribe, it was with the woman who had taught me the language of the Va-gas, and it was from her that I learned why Orthis was treated with such marked distinction by Ga-va-go, whom, it seemed, he had promised to lead to the land of our origin, where, he had assured the savage chieftain, he would find flesh in abundance.

Nah-ee-lah was confined in still another part of the village, and I only saw her occasionally, for it was evident that Ga-va-go wished to keep the prisoners separated. Upon one occasion when I met her at the shore of the lake I asked her why it was that they had not slain and eaten her, and she told me that when Ga-va-go had discovered her identity, and that her father was a Jemadar, a ruler of a great city, he had sent messengers with an offer to return Nah-ee-lah for a ransom of one hundred young women of the city of Laythe.

"Do you think your father will send the ransom?" I asked.

"I do not know," she replied. "I do not see how they are going to get a message to him, for ordinarily, my race kills the Va-gas on sight. They may succeed, however, but even so, it is possible that my father will not send the ransom. I would not wish him to. The daughters of my father's people are as dear to them, as am I to him. It would be wrong to give a hundred of the daughters of Laythe in return for one, even though she be the daughter of the Jemadar."

We had drunk, and were returning toward our huts when, wishing to prolong our conversation and to be with this pleasant companion while I might, I suggested that we walk farther into the woods and gather fruit. Nah-ee-lah signified her willingness, and together we strolled out of the village into the denser woods at its rear, where we found a particularly delicious fruit growing in abundance. I gathered some and offered it to her, but she refused, thanking me, saying that she had but just eaten.

"Do they bring the fruit to you," I asked, "or do you have to come and gather it yourself?"

"What fruit I get I gather," she replied, "but they bring me flesh. It is of that which I have just eaten, and so I do not care for fruit now."

"Flesh!" I exclaimed. "What kind of flesh?"

"The flesh of the Va-gas, of course," she replied. "What other flesh might a U-ga eat?"

I fear that I ill-concealed my surprise and disgust at the thought that the beautiful Nah-ee-lah ate of the flesh of the Va-gas.

"You, too, eat of the flesh of these creatures?" I demanded.

"Why not?" she asked. "You eat flesh, do you not, in your own country. You have told me that you raise beasts solely for their flesh."

"Yes," I replied, "that is true, but we eat only the flesh of lower orders; we do not eat the flesh of humans."

"You mean that you do not eat the flesh of your own species," she said.

"Yes," I replied, "that is what I mean."

"Neither do I," she said. "The Va-gas are not of the same species as the U-ga. They are a lower order, just as are the creatures whose flesh you eat in your own country. You have told me of beef, and of mutton, and of pork, which you have described as creatures that run about on four legs, like the Va-gas. What is the difference, then, between the eating of the flesh of pork and beef or mutton, and the eating of Va-gas, who are low creatures also?"

"But they have human faces!" I cried, "and a spoken language."

"You had better learn to eat them," she said, "otherwise you will eat no flesh in Va-nah."

The more I thought about it the more reason I saw in her point of view. She was right. She was no more transgressing any natural law in eating the flesh of the Va-gas than do we, eating the flesh of cattle. To her the Va-gas were less than cattle. They were dangerous and hated enemies. The more I analyzed the thing, the more it seemed to me that we humans of the earth were more surely transgressing a natural law by devouring our domestic animals, many of which we learned to love, than were the U-ga of Va-nah in devouring the flesh of their four-footed foes, the Va-gas. Upon our earthly farms we raise calves and sheep and little pigs, and oftentimes we become greatly attached to individuals and they to us. We gain their confidence, and they have implicit trust in us, and yet, when they are of the right age, we slay and devour them. Presently it did not seem either wrong or unnatural that Nah-ee-lah should eat the flesh of the Va-gas, but as for myself, I could never do it, nor ever did.

We had left the forest, and were returning to the village to our huts when, near the large hut occupied by Ga-va-go, we came suddenly upon Orthis. At the sight of us together he scowled.

"If I were you," he said to me, "I would not associate with her too much. It may arouse the displeasure of Ga-va-go."

It was the first time that Orthis had spoken to me since we had occupied this village. I did not like his tone or his manner.

"You will please to mind your own business, Orthis," I said to him, and continued on with Nah-ee-lah. I saw the man's eyes narrow malignantly, and then he turned, and entered the hut of Ga-va-go, the chief of the No-vans.

Every time I went to the river, I had to pass in the vicinity of Nah-ee-lah's hut. It was a little out of my way, but I always made the slight detour in the hope of meeting her, though I had never entered her hut nor called for her, since she had never invited me and realizing her position, I did not wish to intrude. I was of course ignorant of the social customs of her people, and feared offending her accidentally.

It chanced that the next time that I walked down to the lake shore, following our stroll in the woods, I made my usual detour that I might pass by the hut of Nah-ee-lah. As I came near I heard voices, one of which I recognized as that of Nah-ee-lah, and the other, a man's voice. The girl's tones were angry and imperious.

"Leave my presence, creature!" were the first words that I could distinguish, and then the man's voice.

"Come," he said, ingratiatingly. "Let us be friends. Come to my hut, and you will be safe, for Ga-va-go is my friend." The voice was the voice of Orthis.

"Go!" she ordered him again. "I would as soon lie with Ga-va-go as with you."

"Know then," cried Orthis, angrily, "that you will go, whether you wish it or not, for Ga-va-go has given you to me. Come!" and then he must have seized her, for I heard her cry out, "How dare you lay hands upon me, Nah-ee-lah, princess of Laythe!"

I was close beside the entrance to the hut now, and I did not wait to hear any more, but thrusting the hanging aside entered. There they were, in the center of the single room, Orthis struggling to drag the girl toward the opening while she resisted and struck at him. Orthis' back was toward me and he did not know that there was another in the hut until I had stepped up behind him and grasping him roughly by the shoulder, had jerked him from the girl and swung him about facing me.

"You cad," I said, "get out of here before I kick you out, and don't ever let me hear of you molesting this girl again."

His eyes narrowed, and he looked at me with an ugly light in them. "Since boyhood, you have cheated me out of all that I wished. You ruined my life on Earth, but now, conditions are reversed. The tables are turned. Believe me, then, when I tell you that if you interfere with me you sign your own death warrant. It is only by my favor that you live at all. If I gave the word Ga-va-go would destroy you at once. Go then to your hut and stop your meddling in the affairs of others—a habit that you developed in a most flagrant degree on Earth, but which will avail you nothing here within the Moon. The woman is mine. Ga-va-go has given her to me. Even if her father should fail to send the ransom her life shall be spared as long as I desire her. Your interference then can only result in your death, and do her no good, for provided you are successful in keeping me from her, you would be but condemning her to death in the event that her father does not send the ransom, and Ga-va-go has told me that there is little likelihood of that, since it is scarcely possible that his messengers will be able to deliver Ga-va-go's demands to Sagroth."

"You have heard him," I said, turning to the girl. "What are your wishes in the matter. Perhaps he speaks the truth."

"I have no doubt but that he speaks the truth," she replied, "but know, strangers, that the honor of a princess of Laythe is dearer than her life."

"Very well, Orthis," I said to the man. "You have heard her. Now get out."

He was almost white with anger, and for a moment I thought that he was going to attack me, but he was ever a coward, and contenting himself with giving me a venomous look, he walked from the hut without another word.

I turned to Nah-ee-lah, after the hanging had dropped behind Orthis. "It is too bad," I said, "that with all your suffering at the hands of the Va-gas, you should also be annoyed by one who is practically of your own species."

"Your kindness more than compensates," she replied graciously. "You are a brave man, and I am afraid that you are going to suffer for your protection of me. This man is powerful. He has made wonderful promises to Ga-va-go. He is going to teach him how to use the strange weapons that you brought from your own world. The woman who brings me my meat told me of all this, and that the tribe is much excited by the promises that your friend has made to Ga-va-go. He will teach them to make the weapons, such as you slew their warriors with, so that they will be invincible, and may go abroad in Va-nah slaying all who oppose them and even raiding the cities of the U-ga. He has told them that he will lead them to the strange thing which brought you from your world to Va-nah, and that there they will find other weapons, like those that you carried, and having the noise which they make, and the things with which they kill. All these he says they may have, and that later he will build other things, such as brought you from your world to Va-nah, and he will take Ga-va-go and all the No-vans to what you call Earth."

"If there is any man in the universe who might do it, it is he," I replied, "but there is little likelihood that he can do it. He is merely deceiving Ga-va-go in the hope of prolonging his own life, against the possibility that an opportunity to escape will develop, in which event he will return to our ship and our friends. He is a bad man though, Nah-ee-lah, and you must be careful of him. There is a vacant hut near yours, and I will come and live in it. There is no use in asking Ga-va-go, for if he is friendly with Orthis, he will not permit me to make the change. If you ever need me, call 'Julian' as loud as you can, and I will come."

"You are very good," she said. "You are like the better men of Laythe, the high nobles of the court of the Jemadar, Sagroth, my father. They too are honorable men, to whom a woman may look for protection, but there are no others in all Va-nah since the Kalkars arose thousands of kelds ago, and destroyed the power of the nobles and the Jemadars, and all the civilization that was Va-nah's. Only in Laythe, have we preserved a semblance of the old order. I wish I might take you to Laythe, for there you would be safe and happy. You are a brave man. It is strange that you are not married."

I was upon the point of making some reply, when the hangings at the doorway parted, and a No-van warrior entered. Behind him were three others. They were walking erect, with drawn spears.

"Here he is," said the leader, and then, addressing me, "Come!"

"Why?" I asked. "What do you want of me?"

"Is it for you to question," he demanded, "when Ga-va-go commands?"

"He has sent for me?" I asked.

"Come!" repeated the leader, and an instant later they had hooked their spears about my arms and neck and none too gently they dragged me from the hut. I had something of a presentiment that this was to be the end. At the doorway I half turned to glance back at the girl. She was standing wide-eyed and tense, watching them drag me away.

"Good-bye—Julian," she said. "We shall never meet again for there is none to carry our souls to a new incarnation."

"We are not dead yet," I called back, "and remember if you need me call me," and then the hanging dropped behind us, and she was shut off from my vision.

They did not take me to my own hut, but to another, not far distant from Nah-ee-lah's, and there they bound my hands and feet with strips of leather and threw me upon the ground. Afterwards they left me, dropping the hanging before the entrance. I did not think that they would eat me, for Orthis had joined with me in explaining to Ga-va-go and the others that our flesh was poisonous, and though they may have questioned the veracity of our statements, nevertheless I was quite sure that they would not risk the chance of our having told the truth.

The Va-gas obtain their leather by curing the hides of their dead. The better portions they use for their trappings and harness. The other portions they cut into thin strips, which they use in lieu of rope. Most of this is very strong, but some of it is not, especially that which is improperly cured.

The warriors who had been sent to seize me had scarcely left the hut before I commenced working with my bonds in an attempt to loosen or break them. I exerted all my strength in the effort, until I became sure that those which held my hands were stretching. The effort, however, was very tiring, and I had to stop often and rest. I do not know how long I worked at them, but it must have been a very long time before I became convinced that however much they gave they were not going to break. Just what I intended to do with my freedom I do not know, since, there was little or no chance that I might escape from the village. Perpetual daylight has its disadvantages, and this was one of them, that there was no concealing nocturnal darkness during which I might sneak away from the village unseen.

As I lay resting after my exertions, I suddenly became aware of a strange, moaning sound from without, and then the hut shook, and I realized that another storm had come. Soon after I heard the beat of rain drops on the roof, and then a staggering, deafening peal of lunar thunder. As the storm waxed in violence, I could imagine the terror of the No-vans, nor even in my plight could I resist the desire to smile at their discomfiture. I knew that they must all be hiding in their huts, and again I renewed my efforts to break the bonds at my wrists, but all to no avail; and then suddenly, above the moaning of the wind and the beating of the rain, there came distinctly to my ears in a clear, full voice, a single word: "Julian!"

"Nah-ee-lah," I thought. "She needs me. What are they doing to her?" There flashed quickly before my mental vision a dozen scenes, in each of which I saw the divine figure of the Moon Maid, the victim of some fiendish brutality. Now she was being devoured by Ga-va-go; now some of the females were tearing her to pieces, and again the warriors were piercing that beautiful skin with their cruel spears; or it was Orthis, come to claim Ga-va-go's gift. It was this last thought, I think, which turned me almost mad, giving to my muscles the strength of a dozen men. I have always been accounted a powerful man, but in the instant that that sweet voice came across the storm to find me, and my imagination pictured her in the clutches of Orthis, something within moved me to Herculean efforts far transcending aught that I had previously achieved. As though they had been cotton twine now, the leather bonds at my wrists snapped asunder, and an instant later those at my ankles were torn away, and I was upon my feet. I sprang to the door and into the open, where I found myself in a maelstrom of wind and rain. In two bounds I had cleared the space between the hut in which I had been confined and that occupied by Nah-ee-lah, had torn the hanging aside, and had sprung into the interior; and there I beheld the materialization of my last vision—there was Orthis, one arm about the slender body of the girl pinning her arms close to her side, while his other hand was at her throat, choking her and pressing her slowly backward across his knees toward the ground.

He was facing the door this time, and saw me enter, and as he realized who it was, he hurled the girl roughly from him and rose to meet me. For once in his life he seemed to know no fear, and I think that what with his passion for the girl, and the hatred he felt for me, and the rage that my interference must have engendered, he was momentarily insane, for he suddenly leaped upon me like a madman, and for an instant I came near going down beneath his blows—but only for an instant, and then I caught him heavily upon the chin with my left fist, and again, full in the face with my right, and though he was a splendid boxer, he was helpless in my hands. Neither of us had a weapon, or one of us certainly would have been killed in short order. As it was I tried to kill him with my bare fists, and at last, when he had fallen for the dozenth time, and I had picked him up and held him upon his feet and struck him repeatedly again and again, he no longer moved I was sure that he was dead, and it was with a feeling of relief and of satisfaction in a duty well performed that I looked down upon his lifeless body. Then I turned to Nah-ee-lah.

"Come," I said, "there has been given to us this chance for escape. Never again may such a fortuitous combination of circumstances arise. The Va-gas will be hiding in their huts, crouching in terror of the storm. I do not know whither we may fly, but wherever it be, we can be in no greater danger than we are here."

She shuddered a little at the thought of going out into the terrors of the storm. Though not so fearful of it as the ignorant Va-gas, she still feared the wrath of the elements, as do all the inhabitants of Va-nah, but she did not hesitate, and as I stretched out a hand, she placed one of hers within it, and together we stepped out into the swirling rain and wind.

# EIGHT

# Into the Mouth of the Crater

NAH-EE-LAH and I passed through the village of the No-vans unde-tected, since the people of Ga-va-go were cowering in their huts, terror-stricken by the storm. The girl led me immediately to high ground and upward along a barren ridge toward the high mountains in the dis-tance. I could see that she was afraid though she tried to hide it from me, putting on a brave front that I was sure she was far from feeling. My respect for her increased, as I have always respected courage, and I believe that it requires the highest courage to do that which fills one with fear. The man who performs heroic acts without fear is less brave than he who overcomes his cowardice.

Realizing her fear I retained her hand in mine, that the contact might impart to her a little of the confidence that I felt, now that I was temporarily at least out of the clutches of the Va-gas.

We had reached the ridge above the village when the thought that we were weaponless and without means of protection overwhelmed me. I had been in so much of a hurry to escape the village that I had overlooked this very vital consideration. I spoke to Nah-ee-lah about it, telling her that I had best return to the village and make an effort to regain possession of my own weapons and ammunition. She tried to dissuade me, telling me that such an attempt was foredoomed to failure and prophesying that I would be recaptured.

"But we cannot cross this savage world of yours, Nah-ee-lah, without means of protection," I urged. "We do not know at what minute some fierce creature may confront us—think how helpless we shall be without weapons with which to defend ourselves."

"There are only the Va-gas," she said, "to fear in this part of Va-nah. We know no other dangerous beast, except the tor-ho. They are seldom seen. Against the Va-gas your weapons would be useless, as you already have discovered. The risk of meeting a tor-ho is infinitely less than that which you will incur if you attempt to enter Ga-va-go's hut to secure your weapons. You simply could not do it and escape, for doubtless the dwelling of the Chief is crowded with warriors."

I was compelled, finally, to admit the wisdom of her reasoning and to forego an attempt to secure my rifle and pistol, though I can assure you that I felt lost without them, especially when thus venturing forth into a new world so strange to me as Va-nah, and so savage. As a matter of fact, from what I gleaned from Nah-ee-lah, there was but a single spot upon the entire inner lunar world where she and I could hope to be even reasonably free from danger, and that was her native city of Laythe. Even there I should have enemies, she told me, for her race is ever suspicious of strangers; but the friendship of the princess would be my protection, she assured me with a friendly pressure of the hand.

The rain and wind must have persisted for a considerable time, for when it was finally over and we looked back through a clear atmosphere we found that a low range of mountains lay between us and the distant sea. We had crossed these and were upon a plateau at the foot of the higher peaks. The sea looked very far away indeed, and we could not even guess at the location of the No-vans village from which we had escaped.

"Do you think they will pursue us?" I asked her.

"Yes," she said; "they will try to find us, but it will be like looking for a raindrop in the ocean. They are creatures of the low-lands—I am of the mountains. Down there," and she pointed into the valley, "they might find me easily, but in my own mountains—no."

"We are near Laythe?" I asked.

"I do not know. Laythe is hard to find—it is well hidden. It is for this reason that it exists at all. Its founders were pursued by the Kalkars, and had they not found an almost inaccessible spot they would have been discovered and slain long before they could have constructed an impregnable city."

She led me then straight into the mighty mountains of the Moon, past the mouths of huge craters that reached through the lunar crust to the surface of the satellite, along the edges of yawning chasms that dropped three, four, yes, sometimes five miles, sheer into frightful gorges, and then out upon vast plateaus, but ever upward toward the higher peaks that seemed to topple above us in the distance. The craters, as a rule, lay in the deep gorges, but some we found upon the plateaus, and even a few opened into the summits of mountain peaks as do those upon the outer surface of planets. Those in the low places were, I believe, the openings through which the original molten lunar core was vomitted forth by the surface volcanoes upon the outer crust.

Nah-ee-lah told me that the secret entrance to Laythe lay just below the lip of one of these craters, and it was this she sought. To me the quest seemed hopeless, for as far as the eye could reach lay naught but an indescribable jumble of jagged peaks, terrific gorges and bottomless craters. Yet always the girl seemed to find a way among or about them—instinctively, apparently, she found trails and footholds where there were no trails and where a chamois might have been hard put to it to find secure footing.

In these higher altitudes we found a vegetation that differed materially from that which grew in the lowlands. Edible fruits and berries were, however, still sufficiently plentiful to keep us reasonably well supplied with food. When we were tired we usually managed to find a cave in which we could rest in comparative security, and when it was possible to do so Nah-ee-lah always insisted upon barricading the entrance with rocks, since there was always the danger, she told me, of our being attacked by tor-hos. These blood-thirsty creatures while rare, were nevertheless very much to be feared, since not only were they voracious meat eaters and of such a savage disposition that they attacked nearly everything they saw in wanton ferocity, but even a minor wound inflicted by their fangs or talons often proved fatal, because of the fact that their principal diet was the poisonous flesh of the rymph and the flying toad. I tried to get Nah-ee-lah to describe the creature to me, but inasmuch as there was no creature with which we were both familiar that she might compare it with, I learned little more from her than that it stood between eighteen inches and two feet in height, had long, sharp fangs, four legs and was hairless.

As an aid to climbing, as well as to give me some means of protection, I broke a stout and rather heavy branch from one of the mountain trees, the wood of which was harder than any that I had seen growing in the lowlands. To roam a strange and savage world armed only with a wooden stick seemed to me the height of rashness, but there was no alternative until the time arrived when I might find the materials with which to fashion more formidable weapons. I had in mind a bow and arrows and was constantly on the lookout for wood which I considered adapted to the former, and I also determined to forego my cane for a spear whenever the material for the making of one came to hand. I had little time, however, for such things, as it seemed that when we were not sleeping we were constantly upon the move, Nah-ee-lah becoming more and more impatient to find her native city as the chances for so doing lessened—and it seemed to me that they were constantly lessening. While I was quite sure that she had no more idea where Laythe lay than I, yet we stumbled on and on and on, through the most stupendous mountain ranges that the mind of man can conceive, nor ever, apparently, did Nah-ee-lah discover a single familiar landmark upon which to hang a shred of hope that eventually we might come upon Laythe.

I never saw such a sanguine and hopeful person as Nah-ee-lah. It was her constant belief that Laythe lay just beyond the next mountain, in spite of the fact that she was invariably mistaken—which seemed never to lessen the exuberance of her enthusiasm for the next guess—which I knew beforehand was going to be a wrong guess.

Once just after we had rounded the shoulder of a mountain we came upon a little strip of level land clinging to the side of a mighty peak. I was in the lead—a position which I tried always to take when it was not absolutely necessary for Nah-ee-lah to go ahead in order to find a trail. As I came around the shoulder of the mountain, and in full sight of the little level area, I was positive that I saw a slight movement among some bushes at my right about halfway along one side of the little plain.

As we came abreast of the spot, upon which I kept my eye, there broke upon our ears the most hideous scream that I have ever heard, and simultaneously there leaped from the concealment of the bushes a creature about the size of a North American mountain lion, though quite evidently a reptile and probably a tor-ho, as such it proved to be. There was something about the head and face which suggested the cat family to me, yet there was really no resemblance between it and any of the earthly felines. It came at me with those terrible curved fangs bared and bristling and as it came it emitted the most terrifying sounds—I have called them screams, because that word more nearly describes them than any other, and yet they were a combination of shrieks and moans—the most blood-curdling that I have ever heard.

Nah-ee-lah grasped my arm. "Run!" she cried, "run." But I shook her loose and stood my ground. I wanted to run, that I will admit, but where to? The creature was covering the ground at tremendous speed and our only avenue of escape was the narrow trail over which we had just come, which clung precariously to the side of a perpendicular cliff. And so I stood there waiting, my feeble stick grasped in both hands. Just what I expected to do with it I scarcely knew until the tor-ho was upon me. Then I swung for its head as a batter swings for a pitched ball. I struck it square upon the nose—a terrific blow that not only stopped it, but felled it. I could hear the bones crushing beneath the impact of my crude weapon and I thought that I had done for the thing with that single blow, but I did not know the tremendous vitality of the creature. Almost instantly it was up and at me again, and again I struck it, this time upon the side of the head, and again I heard bones crush and again it fell heavily to the ground.

What appeared to be cold blood was oozing slowly from its wounded face as it came at me for the third time, its eyes glaring hideously, its broken jaws agape to seize me, while its shrieks and moans rose to a perfect frenzy of rage and pain. It reared up and struck at me with its talons now, but I met it again with my bludgeon and this time I broke a fore leg.

How long I fought that awful thing I cannot even guess. Time and time again it charged me furiously and each time, though often by but a miracle of fortune, I managed to keep it from closing, and each blow that I delivered crushed and maimed it a little more, until at last it was nothing but a bleeding wreck of pulp, still trying to crawl toward me upon its broken legs and seize me and drag me down with its broken, toothless jaws. Even then it was with the greatest difficulty that I killed it, that I might put it out of its misery.

Rather exhausted, I turned to look for Nah-ee-lah, and much to my surprise, I found her standing directly behind me.

"I thought you had run away," I said.

"No," she said, "you did not run and so I did not, but I never thought that you would be able to kill it."

"You thought that it would kill me, then?" I asked.

"Certainly," she replied. "Even now I cannot understand how you were able to overcome a tor-ho with that pitiful little stick of wood."

"But if you thought I was going to be killed," I insisted, "why was it that you did not seek safety in flight?"

"If you had been killed I should not have cared to live," she said simply.

I did not exactly understand her attitude and scarcely knew what reply to make.

"It was very foolish of you," I said at last, rather blunderingly, "and if we are attacked again you must run and save yourself."

She looked at me for a moment with a peculiar expression upon her face which I could not interpret and then turned and resumed her way in the direction in which we had been traveling when our journey had been interrupted by the tor-ho. She did not say anything, but I felt that I had offended her and I was sorry. I did not want her falling in love with me, though, and according to earthly standards, her statement that she would rather die than live without me might naturally have been interpreted as a confession of love. The more I thought of it, however, as we moved along in silence, the more possible it seemed to me that her standards might differ widely from mine and that I was only proving myself to be an egotistical ass in assuming that Nah-ee-lah loved me. I wished that I might explain matters to her, but it is one of those things that is rather difficult to explain, and I realized that it might be made much worse if I attempted to do so.

We had been such good friends and our fellowship had been so perfect that the apparently strained silence which existed between us was most depressing. Nah-ee-lah had always been a talkative little person and always gay and cheerful, even under the most trying conditions.

I was rather tired out after my encounter with the tor-ho and should have liked to stop for a rest, but I did not suggest it, neither did Nah-ee-lah, and so we continued on our seemingly interminable way, though, almost exhausted as I was, I dropped some little distance behind my beautiful guide.

She was quite out of sight ahead of me upon the winding trail when suddenly I heard her calling my name aloud. I answered her as, simultaneously, I broke into a run, for I did not know but what she might be in danger, though her voice did not sound at all like it. She was only a short distance ahead and when I came in sight of her I saw her standing at the edge of a mighty crater. She was facing me and she was smiling.

"Oh, Julian," she cried, "I have found it. I am home and we are safe at last."

"I am glad, Nah-ee-lah," I said. "I have been much worried on account of the dangers to which you have been constantly subjected, as well as because of a growing fear that you would never be able to find Laythe."

"Oh, my!" she exclaimed, "I knew that I would find it. If I had to hunt through every mountain range in Va-nah I would have found it."

"You are quite sure that this is the crater where lies the entrance to Laythe?" I asked her.

"There is no doubt of it, Julian," she replied, and she pointed downward over the lip of the crater toward a narrow ledge which lay some twenty feet below and upon which I saw what appeared to be the mouth of a cave opening into the crater.

"But, how are we going to reach it?" I asked.

"It may be difficult," she replied, "but we will find a way."

"I hope so, Nah-ee-lah," I said, "but without a rope or wings I do not see how we are going to accomplish it."

"In the mouth of the tunnel," explained Nah-ee-lah, "there are long poles, each of which has a hook at one end. Ages ago there were no other means of ingress or egress to the city and those who came out to hunt or for any other purpose came through this long tunnel from the city, and from the ledge below they raised their poles and placed the hooked ends over the rim of the crater, after which it was a simple matter to clamber up or down the poles as they wished; but it has been long since these tunnels were used by the people of Va-nah, who had no further need of them after the perfection of the flying wings which you saw me using when I was captured by the Va-gas."

"If they used poles, so may we," I said, "since there are plenty of young trees growing close to the rim of the crater. The only difficulty will be in felling one of them."

"We can do that," said Nah-ee-lah, "if we can find some sharp fragments of stone. It will be slow work, but it can be done," and she started immediately to hunt for a fragment with a cutting edge. I joined her in the search and it was not long before we had discovered several pieces of obsidian with rather sharp edges. We then started to work upon a young tree about four inches in diameter that grew almost straight for a height of some thirty feet.

Cutting the tree down with our bits of lava glass was tedious work, but finally it was accomplished, and we were both much elated when the tree toppled and fell to the ground. Cutting away the branches occupied almost as long a time, but that, too, was finally accomplished. The next problem which confronted us was that of making the top of the pole secure enough to hold while we descended to the ledge before the mouth of the tunnel. We had no rope and nothing with which to fashion one, other than my garments, which I was loath to destroy, inasmuch as in these higher altitudes it was often cold. Presently, however, I hit upon a plan which, if Nah-ee-lah's muscles and my nerves withstood the strain it put upon them, bade fair to assure the success of our undertaking. I lowered the larger end of the pole over the side of the crater until the butt rested upon the ledge before the mouth of the tunnel. Then I turned to Nah-ee-lah.

"Lie down flat at full length, Nah-ee-lah," I directed her, "and hold this pole securely with both hands. You will only have to keep it from toppling to the sides or outward, and to that, I think, your strength is equal. While you hold it, I will descend to the mouth of the tunnel and raise one of the regular hooked poles which you say should be deposited there. If they are not, I believe that I can hold our own pole securely from below while you descend." She looked over into the vast abyss below and shuddered. "I can hold it at the top," she said, "if the bottom does not slip from the ledge."

"That is a chance that I shall have to take," I replied, "but I will descend very carefully and I think there will be little danger upon that score.

I could see, upon a more careful examination of the ledge below, that there was some danger of an accident such as she suggested.

Nah-ee-lah took her position as I had directed and lay grasping the pole securely in both hands at the rim of the crater, which was absolutely perpendicular at this point; and I prepared to make the perilous descent.

I can assure you that my sensations were far from pleasurable as I looked over into that awful abyss. The crater itself was some four or five miles in diameter, and, as I had every reason to suspect, extended fully two hundred and fifty miles through the lunar crust to the surface of the Moon. It was one of the most impressive moments of my life as I clung balancing upon the edge of that huge orifice, gazing into the silent, mysterious depths below. And then I seized the pole very gently and lowered myself over the edge.

"Courage, Julian!" whispered Nah-ee-lah; "I shall hold very tight."

"I shall be quite safe, Nah-ee-lah," I assured her. "I must be safe, for if I am not, how are you to reach the ledge and Laythe?"

As I descended very slowly I tried not to think at all, but to exclude from my mind every consideration of the appalling depths beneath me. I could not have been more than two feet from the ledge when the very thing that we both tried so hard to guard against transpired—a splintered fragment of the pole's butt crumpled beneath my weight and that slight jar was just sufficient to start the base of my precarious ladder sliding toward the edge of the narrow projection upon which I had rested it, and beyond which lay eternity. Above me I heard a slight scream and then the pole slipped from the ledge and I felt myself falling.

It was over in an instant. My feet struck the ledge and I threw myself within the mouth of the tunnel. And then, above me, I heard Nah-ee-lah's voice crying in agonized tones:

"Julian! Julian! I am falling!"

Instantly I sprang to my feet and peered upward from the mouth of the tunnel upon a sight that froze my blood, so horrifying did it seem, for there above me, still clinging to the pole, hung Nah-ee-lah, her body, with the exception of her legs, completely over the edge of the crater. Just as I looked up she dropped the pole and although I made a grab for it I missed it and it fell past me into the maw of the crater.

"Julian! Julian! You are safe!" she cried; "I am glad of that. It terrified me so when I thought you were falling and I tried my best to hold the pole, but your weight dragged me over the edge of the crater. Good-bye, Julian, I cannot hold on much longer."

"You must, Nah-ee-lah!" I cried; "do not forget the hooked poles that

you told me of. I will find one and have you down in no time." And even
as I spoke I turned and dove into the tunnel; but my heart stood still at the
thought that the poles might not be there. My first glance revealed only
the bare rock of walls and floor and ceiling and no hooked poles in sight.
I sprang quickly farther into the tunnel which turned abruptly a few yards
ahead of me and just around the bend my eyes were gladdened by the sight
of a dozen or more of the poles which Nah-ee-lah had described. Seizing
one of them, I ran quickly back to the entrance. I was almost afraid to look
up, but as I did so I was rewarded by the sight of Nah-ee-lah's face smiling
down at me—she could smile even in the face of death, could Nah-ee-lah.

"Just a moment more, Nah-ee-lah!" I cried to her, as I raised the pole
and caught the hook upon the crater's rim. There were small protuberances
on either side of the pole for its entire length, which made climbing it
comparatively simple.

"Make haste, Julian!" she cried, "I am slipping."

It wasn't necessary for her to tell me to make haste. I think that I never
did anything more quickly in my life than I climbed that pole, but I reached
her not an instant too soon, for even as my arm slipped about her, her hold
upon the ledge above gave way, and she came down head foremost upon
me. I had no difficulty in catching her and supporting her weight. My only
fear was that the hook above might not sustain the added weight under the
strain of her falling body. But it held, and I blessed the artisan who had
made it thus strong.

A moment later I had descended to the mouth of the tunnel and drawn
Nah-ee-lah into the safety of its interior. My arm was still around her
and hers about me as she stood there sobbing upon my breast. She was
utterly relaxed and her supple body felt so helpless against me that there
was suddenly aroused within me a feeling such as I had never experienced
before—a rather indescribable feeling, yet one which induced, seemingly,
an irresistible and ridiculous desire to go forth and slay whole armies of
men in protection of this little Moon Maid. It must have been a sudden
mental reversion to some ancient type of crusading ancestor of the Middle
Ages—some knight in armor from whose loins I had sprung, transmitting
to me his own flamboyant, yet none the less admirable, chivalry. The
feeling rather surprised me, for I have always considered myself more or
less practical and hard-headed. But more sober thought finally convinced
me that it was but a nervous reaction from the thrilling moments through
which we had both just passed, coupled with her entire helplessness and
dependence upon me. Be that as it may, I disengaged her arms from about
my neck as gently and as quickly as I could and lowered her carefully to

the floor of the tunnel, so that she sat with her back leaning against one of the walls.

"You are very brave, Julian," she said, "and very strong."

"I am afraid I am not very brave," I told her. "I am almost weak from fright even now—I was so afraid that I would not reach you in time, Nah-ee-lah."

"It is the brave man who is afraid after the danger is past," she said. "He has no time to think of fear until after the happening is all over. You may have been afraid for me, Julian, but you could not have been afraid for yourself, or otherwise you would not have taken the risk of catching me as I fell. Even now I cannot understand how you were able to hold me."

"Perhaps," I reminded her, "I am stronger than the men of Va-nah, for my earthly muscles are accustomed to overcoming a gravity six times as great as that upon your world. Had this same accident happened upon Earth I might not have been able to hold you when you fell."

# NINE

# The Fight with the Kalkars

T HE TUNNEL in which I found myself and along which Nah-ee-lah led me toward the city of Laythe was remarkable in several particulars. It was largely of natural origin, seemingly consisting of a series of caves which may have been formed by bubbles in the cooling lava of the original molten flow and which had later been connected by man to form a continuous subterranean corridor. The caves themselves were usually more or less spherical in shape and the debris from the connecting passageways had been utilized to fill the bottoms of them to the level of the main floor of the passageway. The general trend of the tunnel was upward from the point at which we had entered it, and there was a constant draught of air rushing along it in the same direction in which we were moving, assuring me that it was undoubtedly well ventilated for its full length. The walls and ceiling were coated with a substance of which radium was evidently one of the ingredients, since even after we had lost sight of the entrance the passageway was well illuminated. We had been moving along in silence for quite a little distance when I finally addressed Nah-ee-lah.

"It must seem good," I said, "to travel again this familiar tunnel of your native city. I know how happy I should be were I thus approaching my own birthplace."

"I am glad to be returning to Laythe," she said, "for many reasons, but for one I am sorry, and as for this passageway it is scarcely more familiar to me than to you, since I have traversed it but once before in my life and that when I was a little girl and came here with my father and his court upon the occasion of his periodical inspection of the passageway, which is now practically never used."

"If you are not familiar with the tunnel," I asked, "are you sure that there is no danger of our going astray at some fork or branch?"

"There is but the one passageway," she replied, "which leads from the crater to Laythe."

"And how long is the tunnel?" I asked. "Will we soon enter the city?"

"No," she replied, "it is a great distance from the crater to Laythe."

We had covered some little distance at this time, possibly five or six miles, and she had scarcely ceased speaking when a turn in the passageway led us into a cave of larger proportions than any through which we had previously passed and from the opposite side of which two passageways diverged.

"I thought there were no branches," I remarked.

"I do not understand it," she said. "There is no branch from the tunnel of Laythe."

"Could it be possible that we are in the wrong tunnel?" I asked, "and that this does not lead to Laythe?"

"A moment before I should have been sure that we were in the right tunnel," she replied, "but now, Julian, I do not know, for never had I heard of any branch of our own tunnel."

We had crossed the cave and were standing between the openings of the two divergent passageways.

"Which one shall we take?" I asked, but again she shook her head.

"I do not know," she replied.

"Listen!" I cautioned her. "What was that?" For I was sure that I had heard a sound issuing from one of the tunnels.

We stood peering into an aperture which revealed about a hundred yards of the passageway before an abrupt turn hid the continuation of it from our view. We could hear what now resolved itself into the faint sound of voices approaching us along the corridor, and then quite suddenly the figure of a man appeared around the corner of the turn. Nah-ee-lah leaped to one side out of sight, drawing me with her.

"A Kalkar!" she whispered. "Oh, Julian, if they find us we are lost."

"If there is only one of them I can take care of him," I said.

"There will be more than one," she replied; "there will be many."

"Then, let us return the way we came and make our way to the top of the crater's rim before they discover us. We can throw their hooked poles into the crater, including the one which we use to ascend from the mouth of the tunnel, thus effectually preventing any pursuit."

"We cannot cross this room again to the tunnel upon the opposite side without being apprehended," she replied. "Our only hope is in hiding in this other tunnel until they have passed and trusting to chance that we meet no one within it."

"Come, then," I said. "I dislike the idea of flying like a scared rabbit, but neither would there be any great wisdom in facing armed men without a single weapon of defense."

Even as we had whispered thus briefly together, we found the voices from the other tunnel had increased and I thought that I noted a tone of excitement in them, though the speakers were still too far away for us to understand their words. We moved swiftly up the branch tunnel, Nah-ee-lah in the lead, and after passing the first turn we both felt comparatively safe, for Nah-ee-lah was sure that the men who had interrupted our journey were a party of hunters on their way to the outer world by means of the crater through which we had entered the tunnel and that they would not come up the branch in which we were hiding. Thus believing, we halted after we were safely out of sight and hearing of the large cave we had just left.

"That man was a Kalkar," said Nah-ee-lah, "which means that we are in the wrong tunnel and that we must retrace our steps and continue our search for Laythe upon the surface of the ground." Her voice sounded tired and listless, as though hope had suddenly deserted her brave heart. We were standing shoulder to shoulder in the narrow corridor and I could not resist the impulse to place an arm about her and comfort her.

"Do not despair, Nah-ee-lah," I begged her; "we are no worse off than we have been and much better off than before we escaped the Va-gas of Ga-va-go. Then do you not recall that you mentioned one drawback to your return to Laythe—that you might be as well off here as there? What was the reason, Nah-ee-lah?"

"Ko-tah wants me in marriage," she replied. "Ko-tah is very powerful. He expects one day to be Jemadar of Laythe. This he cannot be while I live unless he marries me."

"Do you wish to marry him?" I asked.

"No," she said; "not now. Before—" she hesitated— "before I left Laythe I did not care so very much; but now I know that I cannot wed with Ko-tah."

"And your father," I continued, "what of him—will he insist that you marry Ko-tah?"

"He cannot do otherwise," replied Nah-ee-lah, "for Ko-tah is very powerful. If my father refuses to permit me to marry him Ko-tah may overthrow him, and when my father is dead, should I still refuse to marry Ko-tah he may slay me, also, and then become Jemadar easily, for the blood of Jemadars flows in his veins."

"It appears to me, Nah-ee-lah, that you will be about as badly off at home as anywhere else in Va-nah. It is too bad that I cannot take you to my own Earth, where you would be quite safe, and I am sure, happy."

"I wish that you might, Julian," she replied simply.

I was about to reply when she placed slim fingers upon my lips. "Hush, Julian!" she whispered, "they are following us up this corridor. Come quickly, we must escape before they overtake us," and so saying, she turned and ran quickly along the corridor which led neither of us knew whither.

But we were soon to find out, for we had gone but a short distance when we came to the tunnel's end in a large circular chamber, at one end of which was a rostrum upon which were a massive, elaborately carved desk and a chair of similar design. Below the rostrum were arranged other chairs in rows, with a broad aisle down the center. The furniture, though of peculiar design and elaborately carved with strange figures of unearthly beasts and reptiles, was not, for all of that, markedly dissimilar to articles of the same purpose fabricated upon Earth. The chairs had four legs, high backs and broad arms, seeming to have been designed equally for durability, service, and comfort.

I glanced quickly around the apartment, as we first entered, only taking in the details later, but I saw that there was no other opening than the one through which we had entered.

"We will have to wait here, Nah-ee-lah," I said. "Perhaps, though, all will be well—the Kalkars may prove friendly."

She shook her head negatively. "No," she said, "they will not be friendly."

"What will they do to us?" I asked.

"They will make slaves of us," she replied, "and we shall spend the balance of our lives working almost continuously until we drop with fatigue under the cruelest of taskmakers, for the Kalkars hate us of Laythe and will hesitate at nothing that will humiliate or injure us."

She had scarcely ceased speaking when there appeared in the entrance of the cave the figure of a man about my own height dressed in a tunic similar to Nah-ee-lah's but evidently made of leather. He carried a knife slung in a scabbard depending from a shoulder belt, and in his right hand he grasped a slender lance. His eyes were close set upon either side of a prominent, hooked nose. They were watery, fishy, blue eyes, and the hair growing profusely above his low forehead was flaxen in color. His physique was admirable, except for a noticeable stoop. His feet were very large and his gait awkward when he moved. Behind him I could see the heads and shoulders of others. They stood there grinning at us for a moment, most malevolently, it seemed to me, and then they entered the cave—a full dozen of them. There were several types, with eyes and hair of different colors, the former ranging from blue to brown, the latter from light blond to almost black.

As they emerged from the mouth of the tunnel they spread out and advanced slowly toward us. We were cornered like rats in a trap. How I longed for the feel of my automatic at my hip! I envied them their slender spears and their daggers. If I could have but these I might have a chance at least to take Nah-ee-lah out of their clutches and save her from the hideous fate of slavery among the Kalkars, for I had guessed what such slavery would mean to her from the little that she had told me, and I had guessed, too, that she would rather die than submit to it. For my own part, life held little for me; I had long since definitely given up any hope of ever returning to my own world, or of finding the ship and being re-united with West and Jay and Norton. There came upon me at that moment, however, a sense of appreciation of the fact that since we had left the village of the No-vans I had been far from unhappy, nor could I attribute this to aught else than the companionship of Nah-ee-lah—a realization that convinced me that I should be utterly miserable were she to be taken from me now. Was I to submit supinely then, to capture and slavery for myself and worse than death for Nah-ee-lah, with the assurance of consequent separation from her? No. I held up my hand as a signal for the advancing Kalkars to halt.

"Stop!" I commanded. "Before you advance farther I wish to know your intentions toward us. We entered this tunnel, mistaking it for that which led to the city of my companion. Permit us to depart in peace and all will be well."

"All will be well, anyway," replied the leader of the Kalkars. "You are a strange creature, such as I have never before seen in Va-nah. Of you we know nothing except that you are not of the Kalkars, and therefore an enemy of the Kalkars, but this other is from Laythe."

"You will not permit us to go in peace, then?" I demanded.

He laughed sneeringly. "Nor in any other way," he said.

I had been standing in the aisle, with my hand upon one of the chairs near the rostrum and now I turned to Nah-ee-lah who was standing close beside me.

"Come," I said to her, "follow me; stay close behind me."

Several of the Kalkars were coming down the main aisle toward us, and as I turned toward them from speaking to Nah-ee-lah, I raised the chair which my hand had been resting upon, and swinging it quickly around my head hurled it full in the face of the leader. As he went down Nah-ee-lah and I ran forward, gaining a little toward the opening of the tunnel, and then without pausing I hurled another chair and a third and a fourth, in rapid succession. The Kalkars tried to bring us down with their lances, but they were so busy dodging chairs that they could not cast their weapons accurately, and even those few which might otherwise have struck us were warded off by my rather remarkable engines of defense.

There had been four Kalkars advancing toward us down the center aisle. The balance of the party had divided, half of it circling the cave to the left and the other half to the right, with the evident intention of coming up the center aisle from behind us. This maneuver had started just before I commenced hurling chairs at the four directly in front of us, and now when those who had intended to take us from the rear discovered that we were likely to make our way through to the tunnel's entrance, some of them sprang toward us along the passageways between the chairs, which necessitated my turning and devoting a moment's attention to them. One huge fellow was in the lead, coming across the backs of the chairs leaping from seat to seat; and being the closest to me, he was naturally my first target. The chairs were rather heavy and the one that I let drive at him caught him full in the chest with an impact that brought a howl from him and toppled him over across the backs of the chairs behind him, where he hung limp and motionless. Then I turned my attention again to those before us, all of whom had fallen before my massive ammunition. Three of them lay still, but one of them had scrambled to his feet and was in the very act of casting his lance as I looked. I stopped the weapon with a chair and as the fellow went down I caught a glimpse of Nah-ee-lah from the corners of my eyes as she snatched the lance from the first Kalkar who had fallen and hurled it at someone behind me. I heard a scream of rage and pain and then I turned in time to see another of the Kalkars fall almost at my feet, the lance imbedded in his heart.

The way before us was temporarily open, while the Kalkars behind us had paused, momentarily, at least, in evident consternation at the havoc I wrought with these unseemly weapons against which they had no defense.

"Get two knives and two lances from those who have fallen," I cried to Nah-ee-lah, "while I hold these others back."

She did as I bade, and slowly we backed toward the mouth of the tunnel. My chairs had accounted for half our enemies when at last we stood in the opening, each armed with a lance and a knife.

"Now run, Nah-ee-lah, as you never ran before," I whispered to my companion. "I can hold them off until you have reached the mouth of the tunnel and clambered to the rim of the crater. If I am lucky, I will follow you."

"I will not leave you, Julian," she replied, "we will go together or not at all."

"But you must, Nah-ee-lah," I insisted, "it is for you that I have been fighting them. What difference can it make in my fate where I am when in Va-nah—all here are my enemies."

She laid her hand gently upon my arm. "I will not leave you, Julian," she repeated, "and that is final."

The Kalkars within the room were now advancing toward us menacingly.

"Halt!" I cried to them, "you see what fate your companions have met, because you would not let us go in peace. That is all we ask. I am armed now and it will be death to any who follow us."

They paused and I saw them whispering together as Nah-ee-lah and I backed along the corridor, a turn in which soon shut them from our view. Then we wheeled and ran like deer along the winding passageway. I did not feel very safe from capture at any time, but at least I breathed a sigh of relief after we had passed the chamber from which the Kalkars had run us into the *cul-de-sac,* and we had seen no sign of any other of their kind. We heard no sound of pursuit, but that in itself meant nothing, since the Kalkars are shod with soft leather sandals, the material for which, like all their other leather trappings, is made of the skins of Va-gas and of the prisoners from Laythe.

As we came to the pile of hooked poles which marked the last turn before the entrance of the tunnel I breathed an inward sigh of relief. Stooping, I gathered them all in my arms, and then we ran on to the opening into the crater, where I cast all but one of the poles into the abyss. That which I retained I hooked over the lip of the crater and then, turning to Nah-ee-lah, I bade her ascend.

"You should have saved two of the poles," she said, "and then we could have ascended together; but I will make haste and you can follow me immediately, for we do not know but that they are pursuing us. I cannot imagine that they will let us escape thus easily."

Even as she spoke I heard the soft patter of sandal shod feet up the corridor.

"Make haste, Nah-ee-lah," I cried; "they come!"

Climbing a pole is slow work at best, but when one is suspended over the brink of a bottomless chasm and is none too sure of the security of the hook that is holding the pole above, one must needs move cautiously. Yet, even so, Nah-ee-lah scrambled upward so rapidly as to fill me with apprehension for her safety. Nor were my fears entirely groundless, for standing in the mouth of the tunnel, where I could keep one eye upon Nah-ee-lah and the other toward the turn around which my pursuers would presently come in view, I saw the girl's hands grasp the rim of the crater at the very instant that the hook came loose and the pole dropped past me into the abyss. I might have caught it as it fell, but my whole mind was fixed upon Nah-ee-lah and her grave danger. Would she be able to draw herself upward, or would she fall? I saw her straining frantically to raise her body above the edge of the volcano, and then from up the corridor behind me came an exultant cry and I turned to face a brawny Kalkar who was racing toward me.

# TEN

# The Kalkar City

N OW, INDEED, did I have reason to curse the stupidity that had permitted me to cast into the abyss all of the hooked poles save one, since even this one was now lost to me and I was utterly without means of escape from the tunnel.

As the fellow approached me at a rapid run I hurled my lance, but being unaccustomed to the weapon, I missed, and then he was upon me, dropping his own lance as he leaped for me, for it was evidently his desire to take me alive and unharmed. I thought that I was going to have him now, for I believed that I was more than a match for him, but there are tricks in every method of attack and this lunar warrior was evidently well schooled in his own methods of offense. He scarcely seemed to touch me, and yet he managed to trip me and push me simultaneously so that I fell heavily backward to the ground and turning a little sideways as I fell, I must have struck my head against the side of the tunnel, for that is the last that I remember until I regained consciousness in the very cave that Nah-ee-lah and I had reached when we saw the first of the Kalkars. I was surrounded by a party of eight of the Kalkars, two of whom were half carrying, half dragging me. I learned later that in the fight before the rostrum I had killed four of their number.

The fellow who had captured me was in very good humor, doubtless because of his success, and when he discovered that I had regained consciousness he started to converse with me.

"You thought that you could escape from Gapth, did you?" he cried, "but never; you might escape from the others, but not from me—no, not from Gapth."

"I did the principal thing that I desired to do," I replied, wishing to learn if Nah-ee-lah had escaped.

"What is that?" demanded Gapth.

"I succeeded in accomplishing the escape of my companion," I replied.

He made a wry face at that. "If Gapth had been there a moment earlier she would not have escaped, either," he said, and by that I knew that she had escaped, unless she had fallen back into the crater; and I was amply repaid for my own capture if it had won freedom for Nah-ee-lah.

"Although I did not escape this time," I said, "I shall next time."

He laughed a nasty laugh. "There will be no next time," he said, "for we are taking you to the city, and once there, there is no escape, for this is the only avenue by which you can reach the outer world and once within the city you never can retrace your steps to the mouth of the tunnel."

I was not so sure of that, myself, for my sense of direction and that of location are very well developed within me. The degree of perfection attained in orientation by many officers of the International Peace Fleet has been described as almost miraculous, and even among such as these my ability in this line was a matter of comment. I was glad, therefore, that the fellow had warned me, since now I should be particularly upon the watch for each slightest scrap of information that would fix in my memory whatever route I might be led over. From the cave in which I regained consciousness there was but a single route to the mouth of the tunnel, but from here on into the city I must watch every turn and fork and crossing and draw upon the tablets of my memory an accurate and detailed map of the entire route.

"We do not even have to confine our prisoners," continued Gapth, "after we have so marked them that their ownership may always be determined."

"How do you mark them?" I asked.

"With heated irons we make the mark of the owner here," and he touched my forehead just above my eyes.

"Pleasant," I thought to myself, and then aloud: "Shall I belong to you?"

"I do not know," he replied, "but you will belong to whomever The Twentyfour allot you."

We moved on after we left the cave for a considerable period of time in silence. I was busy making mental notes of every salient feature that might be useful to me in retracing my steps, but I found nothing other than a winding and gently ascending corridor, without crossings or branches, until we reached the foot of a long flight of stone steps at the summit of which we emerged into a large chamber in the walls of which there must have been at least a dozen doorways, where, to my great disappointment, I was immediately blindfolded. They whirled me around then, but evidently it was done perfunctorily, since it was exactly one full turn and I was halted in my tracks facing precisely in the same direction that I had been before.

This I was positive of, for our powers of orientation are often tested in this way in the air service. Then they marched me straight forward across the room through a doorway directly opposite that at which I had entered the chamber. I could tell when we left the larger chamber and entered the corridor from the different sound which our footsteps made. We advanced along this corridor ninety-seven paces, when we turned abruptly to the right and at the end of thirty-three paces emerged into another chamber, as I could easily tell again from the sound of our footsteps the instant we crossed the threshold. They led me about this chamber a couple of times with the evident intention of bewildering me, but in this they did not succeed, for when they turned again into a corridor I knew that it was the same corridor from which I had just emerged and that I was retracing my steps. This time they took me back thirty-three paces and then turned abruptly to the right. I could not but smile to myself when I realized that we were now continuing directly along the same corridor as that which we had entered immediately after they had first blindfolded me, their little excursion through the short corridor into the second chamber having been but a ruse to bewilder me. A moment later, at the foot of a flight of steps they removed the blind, evidently satisfied that there was now no chance of my being able to retrace my steps and find the main tunnel leading to the crater, while, as a matter of fact, I could easily have retraced every foot of it blindfolded.

From here on we climbed interminable stairways, passed through numerous corridors and chambers, all of which were illuminated by the radium-bearing substance which coated their walls and ceilings, and then we emerged suddenly upon a terrace into the open air, and I obtained my first view of a lunar city. It was built around a crater, and the buildings were terraced back from the rim, the terraces being generally devoted to the raising of garden truck and the principal fruit-bearing trees and shrubs. The city extended upward several hundred feet, the houses, as I learned later, being built one upon another, the great majority of them, therefore, being without windows looking upon the outer world.

I was led along the terrace for a short distance, and during this brief opportunity for observation I deduced that the cultivated terraces lay upon the roofs of the tier of buildings next below. To my right I could see the terraced steps extending downward to the rim of the crater. Nearly all the terraces were covered with vegetation, and in numerous places I saw what appeared to be Va-gas feeding upon the plants, and this I later learned was the fact, and that the Kalkars, when they are able to capture members of the race of Va-gas, keep them in captivity and breed them as we breed cattle, for their flesh. It is necessary, to some extent, to change the diet of the Va-gas almost exclusively to vegetation, though this diet is supplemented by the flesh of the Kalkars, and their Laythean slaves who die, the Va-gas thus being compelled to serve the double purpose of producing flesh for the Kalkars and acting as their scavengers as well.

Upon my left were the faces of buildings, uniformly two stories in height, with an occasional slender tower rising fifteen, twenty or sometimes as high as thirty feet from the terraced roofs above. It was into one of these buildings that my captors led me after we had proceeded a short distance along the terrace, and I found myself in a large apartment in which were a number of male Kalkars, and at a desk facing the entrance a large, entirely bald man who appeared to be of considerable age. To this person I was led by Gapth, who narrated my capture and the escape of Na-ee-lah.

The fellow before whom I had been brought questioned me briefly. He made no comment when I told him that I was from another world, but he examined my garments rather carefully and then after a moment turned to Gapth.

"We will hold him for questioning by The Twentyfour," he said. "If he is not of Va-nah he is neither Kalkar nor Laythean, and consequently, he must be flesh of a lower order and therefore may be eaten." He paused a moment and fell to examining a large book which seemed to be filled with plans upon which strange hieroglyphics appeared. He turned over several leaves, and finally coming evidently to the page he sought, he ran a forefinger slowly over it until it came to rest near the center of the plat. "You may confine him here," he said to Gapth, "in chamber eight of the twenty-fourth section, at the seventh elevation, and you will produce him upon orders from The Twentyfour when next they meet," and then to me: "It is impossible for you to escape from the city, but if you attempt it, it may be difficult for us to find you again immediately and when we do you will be tortured to death as an example to other slaves. Go!"

I went; following Gapth and the others who had conducted me to the presence of this creature. They led me back into the very corridor from which we had emerged upon the terrace and then straight into the heart of that amazing pile for fully half a mile, where they shoved me roughly into an apartment at the right of the corridor with the admonition that I stay there until I was wanted.

I found myself in a dimly lighted, rectangular room, the air of which was very poor, and at the first glance I discovered that I was not alone, for upon a bench against the opposite wall sat a man. He looked up as I entered and I saw that his features were very fine and that he had black hair like Nah-ee-lah. He looked at me for a moment with a puzzled expression in his eyes and then he addressed me.

"You, too, are a slave?" he asked.

"I am not a slave," I replied, "I am a prisoner."

"It is all the same," he said; "but from whence come you? I have never seen your like before in Va-nah."

"I do not come from Va-nah," I replied, and then I briefly explained my origin and how I came to be in his world. He did not understand me, I am sure, for although he seemed to be, and really was, highly intelligent, he could not conceive of any condition concerning which he had had no experience and in this way he did not differ materially from intelligent and highly educated Earth Men.

"And you," I asked, at length—"you are not a Kalkar? From whence come you?"

"I am from Laythe," he replied. "I fell outside the city and was captured by one of their hunting parties."

"Why all this enmity," I asked, "between the men of Laythe and the Kalkars—who are the Kalkars, anyway?"

"You are not of Va-nah," he said, "that I can see, or you would not ask these questions. The Kalkars derive their name from a corruption of a word meaning The Thinkers. Ages ago we were one race, a prosperous people living at peace with all the world of Va-nah. The Va-gas we bred for flesh, as we do today within our own city of Laythe and as the Kalkars do within their city. Our cities, towns and villages covered the slopes of the mountains and stretched downward to the sea. No corner of the three oceans but knew our ships, and our cities were joined together by a network of routes along which passed electrically driven trains"—he did not use the word trains, but an expression which might be liberally translated as ships of the land—"while other great carriers flew through the air. Our means of communication between distant points were simplified by science through the use of electrical energy, with the result that those who lived in one part of Va-nah could talk with those who lived in any other part of Va-nah, though it were to the remotest ends of the world. There were ten great divisions, each ruled by its Jemadar, and each division vied with all the others in the service which it rendered to its people. There were those who held high positions and those who held low; there were those who were rich and those who were poor, but the favors of the state were distributed equally among them, and the children of the poor had the same opportunities for education as the children of the rich, and there it was that our troubles first started. There is a saying among us that no learning is better than a little, and I can well believe this true when I consider the history of my world, where, as the masses became a little educated, there developed among them a small coterie that commenced to find fault with everyone who had achieved greater learning or greater power than they. Finally, they organized themselves into a secret society called The Thinkers, but known more accurately to the rest of Va-nah as those who thought that they thought. It is a long story, for it covers a great period of time, but the result was that, slowly at first, and later rapidly, The Thinkers, who did more talking than thinking, filled the people with dissatisfaction, until at last they arose and took over the government and commerce of the entire world. The Jemadars were overthrown and the ruling class driven from power, the majority of them being murdered, though some managed to escape, and it was these, my ancestors, who founded the city of Laythe. It is believed that there are other similar cities in remote parts of Va-nah inhabited by the descendants of the Jemadar and noble classes, but Laythe is the only one of which we have knowledge. The Thinkers would not work, and the result was that both government and commerce fell into rapid decay. They not only had neither the training nor the intelligence to develop new things, but they could not carry out the old that had been developed for them. The arts and sciences languished and died with commerce and government, and Va-nah fell back into barbarism. The Va-gas saw their chance and threw off the yoke that had held them through countless ages. As the Kalkars had driven the noble class into the lofty mountains, so the Va-gas drove the Kalkars. Practically every vestige of the ancient culture and commercial advancement of Va-nah has been wiped from the face of the world. The Laytheans have held their own for many centuries, but their numbers have not increased.

"Many generations elapsed before the Laytheans found sanctuary in the city of Laythe, and during that period they, too, lost all touch with the science and advancement and the culture of the past. Nor was there any way in which to rebuild what the Kalkars had torn down, since they had destroyed every written record and every book in every library in Va-nah. And so occupied are both races in eking out a precarious existence that there is little likelihood that there will ever again be any advancement made along these lines—it is beyond the intellectual powers of the Kalkars, and the Laytheans are too weak numerically to accomplish aught."

"It does look hopeless," I said, "almost as hopeless as our situation. There is no escape, I imagine, from this Kalkar city, is there?"

"No," he said, "none whatever. There is only one avenue and we are so confused when we are brought into the city that it would be impossible for us to find our way out again through this labyrinth of corridors and chambers."

"And if we did win our way to the outer world we would be as bad off, I presume, for we could never find Laythe, and sooner or later would be recaptured by the Kalkars or taken by the Va-gas. Am I not right?"

"No," he said, "you are not right. If I could reach the rim of the crater beyond this city I could find my way to Laythe. I know the way well, for I am one of Ko-tah's hunters and am thoroughly familiar with the country for great distances in all directions from Laythe."

So this was one of Ko-tah's men. I was glad, indeed, that I had not mentioned Nah-ee-lah or told him of her possible escape, or of my acquaintance with her.

"And who is Ko-tah?" I asked, feigning ignorance.

"Ko-tah is the most powerful noble of Laythe," he replied, "some day he will be Jemadar, for now that Nah-ee-lah, the Princess, is dead, and Sagroth, the Jemadar, grows old, it will not be long before there is a change."

"And if the Princess should return to Laythe," I asked, "would Ko-tah still become Jemadar then, upon the death of Sagroth?"

"He would become Jemadar in any event," replied my companion, "for had the Princess not been carried off by the air that runs away, Ko-tah would have married her, unless she refused, in which event she might have died—people do die, you know."

"You feel no loyalty, then," I asked, "for your old Jemadar, Sagroth, or for his daughter, the Princess?"

"On the contrary, I feel every loyalty toward them, but like many others, I am afraid of Ko-tah, for he is very powerful and we know that sooner or later he will become ruler of Laythe. That is why so many of the high nobles have attached themselves to him—it is not through love of Ko-tah, but through fear that he recruits his ranks."

"But the Princess!" I exclaimed, "would the nobles not rally to her defense?"

"What would be the use?" he asked. "We of Laythe do but exist in the narrow confines of our prison city. There is no great future to which we may look forward in this life, but future incarnations may hold for us a brighter prospect. It is no cruelty, then, to kill those who exist now under the chaotic reign of anarchy which has reduced Va-nah to a wilderness."

I partially caught his rather hopeless point of view and I realized that the fellow was not bad or disloyal at heart, but like all his race, reduced to a state of hopelessness that was the result of ages of retrogression to which they could see no end.

"I can find the way to the mouth of the tunnel where it opens into the crater," I told him. "But how can we reach it unarmed through a city populated with our enemies who would slay us on sight?"

"There are never very many people in the chambers or corridors far removed from the outer terraces, and if we were branded upon the forehead, as accepted slaves are, and your apparel was not so noticeable, we might possibly reach the tunnel without weapons."

"Yes," I said, "my clothes are a handicap. They would immediately call attention to us; yet, it is worth risking, for I know that I can find my way back to the crater and I should rather die than remain a slave of the Kalkars."

The truth of the matter was that I was not prompted so much by abhorrence of the fate that seemed in store for me, as by a desire to learn if Nah-ee-lah had escaped. I was constantly haunted by the horrid fear that her hold upon the rim of the crater had given and that she had fallen into the abyss below. Gapth had thought that she had escaped, but I knew that she might have fallen without either of us having seen her, since the pole up which she had clambered had been fastened a little beyond the opening of the tunnel, so that, had her hold become loosened, she would not have fallen directly past the aperture. The more I thought of it, the more anxious I became to reach Laythe and institute a search for her.

While we were still discussing our chances of escape, two slaves brought us food in the shape of raw vegetables and fruit. I scanned them carefully for weapons, but they had none, a circumstance to which they may owe their lives. I could have used their garments, had they been other than slaves, but I had hit upon a bolder plan than this and must wait patiently for a favorable opportunity to put it into practice.

After eating I became sleepy and was about to stretch out upon the floor of our prison when my companion, whose name was Moh-goh, told me that there was a sleeping apartment adjoining the room in which we were, that had been set apart for us.

The doorway leading to the sleeping chamber was covered by heavy hangings, and as I parted them and stepped into the adjoining chamber, I found myself in almost total darkness, the walls and ceiling of this room not having been treated with the illuminating coating used in the corridors and apartments which they wished to maintain in a lighted condition. I later learned that all their sleeping apartments were thus naturally dark. In one corner of the room was a pile of dried vegetation which I discovered must answer the purpose of mattress and covering, should I require any. However, I was not so particular, as I had been accustomed to only the roughest of fare since I had left my luxurious stateroom aboard *The Barsoom.* How long I slept I do not know, but I was awakened by Moh-goh calling me. He was leaning over me, shaking me by the shoulder.

"You are wanted," he whispered. "They have come to take us before The Twentyfour."

"Tell them to go to the devil," I said, for I was very sleepy and only half awake. Of course, he did not know what devil meant, but evidently he judged from my tone that my reply was disrespectful to the Kalkars.

"Do not anger them," he said, "it will only make your fate the harder. When The Twentyfour command, all must obey."

"Who are The Twentyfour?" I demanded.

"They compose the committee that rules this Kalkar city."

I was thoroughly awakened now and rose to my feet, following him into the adjoining chamber, where I saw two Kalkar warriors standing impatiently awaiting us. As I saw them a phrase leaped to my brain and kept repeating itself: "There are but two, there are but two."

They were across the room from us, standing by the entrance, and Moh-goh was close to me.

"There are but two," I whispered to him in a low voice, "you take one and I will take the other. Do you dare?"

"I will take the one at the right," he replied, and together we advanced across the room slowly toward the unsuspecting warriors. The moment that we were in reach of them we leaped for them simultaneously. I did not see how Moh-goh attacked his man, for I was busy with my own, though it took me but an instant to settle him, for I struck him a single terrific blow upon the chin and as he fell I leaped upon him, wresting his dagger from its scabbard and plunging it into his heart before he could regain his senses from the stunning impact of my fist. Then I turned to assist Moh-goh, only to discover that he needed no assistance, but was already arising from the body of his antagonist, whose throat was cut from ear to ear with his own weapon.

"Quick!" I cried to Moh-goh, "drag them into the sleeping apartment before we are discovered;" and a moment later we had deposited the two corpses in the dimly lighted apartment adjoining.

"We will leave the city as Kalkar warriors," I said, commencing to strip the accoutrements and garments from the man I had slain.

Moh-goh grinned. "Not a bad idea," he said. "If you can find the route to the crater it is possible that we may yet escape."

It took us but a few moments to effect the change, and after we had hidden the bodies beneath the vegetation that had served us as a bed and stepped out into the other chamber, where we could have a good look at one another, we realized that if we were not too closely scrutinized we might pass safely through the corridors beneath the Kalkar city, for the Kalkars are a mongrel breed, comprising many divergent types. My complexion, which differed outrageously from that of either the Kalkars or the Laytheans, constituted our greatest danger, but we must take the chance, and at least we were armed.

"Lead the way," said Moh-goh, "and if you can find the crater I can assure you that I can find Laythe."

"Very good," I said, "come," and stepping into the corridor I moved off confidently in the direction that I knew I should find the passageways and stairs along which I had been conducted from the crater tunnel. I was as confident of success as though I were traversing the most familiar precinct of my native city.

We traveled a considerable distance without meeting anyone, and at last reached the chamber in which I had been blindfolded. As we entered it I saw fully a score of Kalkars lolling upon benches or lying upon vegetation that was piled upon the floor. They looked up as we entered, and at the same time Moh-goh stepped in front of me.

"Who are you and where are you going?" demanded one of the Kalkars.

"By order of The Twentyfour," said Moh-goh, and stepped into the room. Instantly I realized that he did not know in which direction to go, and that by his hesitancy all might be lost.

"Straight ahead, straight across the room," I whispered to him, and he stepped out briskly in the direction of the entrance to the tunnel. Fortunately for us, the chamber was not brilliantly lighted, and the Kalkars were at the far end of it; otherwise they must certainly have discovered my deception, at least, since any sort of close inspection would have revealed the fact that I was not of Va-nah. However, they did not halt us, though I was sure that I saw one of them eyeing me suspiciously, and I venture to say that I took the last twenty steps without drawing a breath.

It was quickly over, however, and we had entered the tunnel which now led without further confusing ramifications directly to the crater.

"We were fortunate," I said to Moh-goh.

"That we were," he replied.

In silence, then, that we might listen for pursuit, or for the sound of Kalkars ahead of us, we hastened rapidly along the descending passageway toward the mouth of the tunnel where it opened into the crater; and at last, as we rounded the last turn and I saw the light of day ahead of me, I breathed a deep sigh of relief, though almost simultaneously my happiness turned to despair at the sudden recollection that there were no hooked poles here to assist us to the summit of the crater wall. What were we to do?

"Moh-goh," I said, turning to my companion as we halted at the end of the tunnel, "there are no poles with which to ascend. I had forgotten it, but in order to prevent the Kalkars from ascending after me, I threw all but one into the abyss, and that one slipped from the rim and was lost also, just as my pursuers were about to seize me."

I had not told Moh-goh that I had had a companion, since it would be difficult to answer any questions he might propound on the subject without revealing the identity of Nah-ee-lah.

"Oh, we can overcome that," replied my companion. "We have these two spears, which are extremely stout, and inasmuch as we shall have plenty of time, we can easily arrange them in some way that will permit us to ascend to the summit of the crater. It is very fortunate that we were not pursued."

The Kalkar's spears had a miniature crescent-shaped hook at the base of their point similar to the larger ones effected by the Va-gas. Moh-goh thought that we could fasten the two spears securely together and then catch the small hook of the upper one upon the rim of the crater, testing its hold thoroughly before either of us attempted to ascend. Beneath his tunic he wore a rope coiled around his waist which he explained to me was a customary part of the equipment of all Laytheans. It was his idea to tie one end of this around the waist of whichever of us ascended first, the other going as far back into the tunnel as possible and bracing himself, so that in the event that the climber fell, he would be saved from death, though I figured that he would get a rather nasty shaking up and some bad bruises, under the best of circumstances.

I volunteered to go first and began fastening one end of the rope securely about my waist while Moh-goh made the two spears fast together with a short length that he had cut from the other end. He worked rapidly, with deft, nimble fingers, and seemed to know pretty well what he was doing. In the event that I reached the summit in safety, I was to pull up the spears and then haul Moh-goh up by the rope.

Having fastened the rope to my satisfaction, I stood as far out upon the ledge before the entrance to the tunnel as I safely could, and with my back toward the crater looked up at the rim twenty feet above me, in a vain attempt to select from below, if possible, a reasonably secure point upon which to hook the spear. As I stood thus upon the edge of eternity, steadying myself with one hand against the tunnel wall, there came down to me from out of the tunnel a noise which I could not mistake. Moh-goh heard it, too, and looked at me, with a rueful shake of his head and a shrug of his shoulders.

"Everything is against us, Earth Man," he said, for this was the name he had given me when I told him what my world was called.

# ELEVEN

# Laythe

THE PURSUERS were not yet in sight, but I knew from the nearness of the sound of approaching footsteps that it would be impossible to complete the splicing of the spears, to find a secure place for the hook above, and for me to scramble upward to the rim of the crater and haul Moh-goh after me before they should be upon us. Our position looked almost hopeless. I could think of no avenue of escape, and yet I tried, and as I stood there with bent head, my eyes cast upon the floor of the tunnel, they fell upon the neatly coiled rope lying at my feet, one end of which was fastened securely about my waist. Instantly there flashed into my mind a mad inspiration. I glanced up at the overhanging rim above me. Could I do it? There was a chance—the lesser gravity of the Moon placed the thing within the realm of possibility, and yet by all earthly standards it was impossible. I did not wait, I could not wait, for had I given the matter any thought I doubt that I would have had the nerve to attempt it. Behind me lay a cavern opening into the depths of space, into which I should be dashed if my mad plan failed; but, what of it? Better death than slavery. I stooped low, then, and concentrating every faculty upon absolute coordination of mind and muscles, I leaped straight upward with all the strength of my legs.

And in that instant during which my life hung in the balance, of what did I think? Of home, of Earth, of the friends of my childhood? No—of a pale and lovely face, with great, dark eyes and a perfect forehead, surmounted by a wealth of raven hair. It was the image of Nah-ee-lah, the Moon Maid, that I would have carried with me into eternity, had I died that instant.

But, I did not die. My leap carried me above the rim of the crater, where I lunged forward and fell sprawling, my arms and upper body upon the surface of the ground. Instantly I turned about and lying upon my belly, seized the rope in both hands.

"Quick, Moh-goh!" I cried to my companion below; "make the rope fast about you, keep hold of the spears and I will drag you up!"

"Pull away," he answered me instantly, "I have no time to make the rope fast about me. They are almost upon me, pull away and be quick about it."

I did as he bade, and a moment later his hands grasped the rim of the crater and with my assistance he gained the top, dragging the spears after him. For a moment he stood there in silence looking at me with a most peculiar expression upon his face; then he shook his head.

"I do not understand, yet," he said, "how you did it, but it was very wonderful."

"I scarcely expected to accomplish it in safety, myself," I replied, "but anything is better than slavery."

From below us came the voices of the Kalkars in angry altercation. Moh-goh picked up a fragment of rock, and leaning over the edge of the crater, threw it down among them. "I got one," he said, turning to me with a laugh, "he tumbled off into nothing; they hate that. They believe that there is no reincarnation for those who fall into a crater."

"Do you think that they will try to follow us?" I asked.

"No," he said, "they will be afraid to use their hooked poles here for a long time, lest we should be in the neighborhood and shove them off into the crater. I will drop another rock down if any of them are in sight and then we will go upon our way. I do not fear them here in the hills, anyway. There is always plenty of broken stone upon the level places, and we of Laythe are trained to use it most effectively—almost as far as I can throw, I can score a hit."

The Kalkars had withdrawn into the tunnel, so Moh-goh lost his opportunity to despatch another, and presently, turned away from the crater and set out into the mountains, I following close behind.

I can assure you that I felt much better, now that I was armed with a spear and a knife, and as we walked I practiced casting stones, at Moh-goh's suggestion and under his instruction, until I became rather proficient in the art.

I shall not weary you with a narration of our journey to Laythe. How long it took, I do not know. It may have consumed a day, a week, a month, for time seemed quite a meaningless term in Va-nah, but at length, after clambering laboriously from the bottom of a deep gorge, we stood upon the edge of a rolling plateau, and at some little distance beheld what at first appeared to be a cone-shaped mountain, rising fully a mile into the air above the surface of the plateau.

"There," cried Moh-goh, "is Laythe! The crater where lies the entrance to the tunnel leading to the city is beyond it."

As we approached the city, the base of which we must skirt order to reach the crater beyond, I was able to obtain a better idea of the dimensions and methods of construction of this great interior lunar city, the base of which was roughly circular and about six miles in diameter, ranging from a few hundred to a thousand feet above the level of the plateau. The base of the city appeared to be the outer wall of an ancient extinct volcano, the entire summit of which had been blown off during some terrific eruption of a bygone age. Upon this base the ancient Laytheans had commenced the construction of their city, the houses of which rose one upon another as did those of the Kalkar city from which we had just escaped. The great age of Laythe was attested by the tremendous height to which these superimposed buildings had arisen, the loftiest wall of Laythe now rising fully a mile above the floor of the plateau. Narrow terraces encircled the periphery of the towering city, and as we approached more closely I saw doors and windows opening upon the terraces and figures moving to and fro, the whole resembling closely an enormous hive of bees. When we had reached a point near the base of the city, I saw that we had been discovered, for directly above us there were people at various points who were unquestionably looking down at us and commenting upon us.

"They have seen us from above," I said to Moh-goh, "why don't you hail them?"

"They take us for Kalkars," he replied. "It is easier for us to enter the city by way of the tunnel, where I shall have no difficulty in establishing my identity."

"If they think we are Kalkars," I said, "will they not attack us?"

"No," he replied, "Kalkars often pass Laythe. If they do not try to enter the city, we do not molest them."

"Your people fear them, then?" I asked.

"It practically amounts to that," he replied. "They greatly outnumber us, perhaps a thousand to one, and as they are without justice, mercy or honor we try not to antagonize them unnecessarily."

We came at length to the mouth of the crater, and here Moh-goh looped his rope about the base of a small tree growing close to the rim and slipped down to the opening of the tunnel directly beneath. I followed his example, and when I was beside him Moh-goh pulled the rope in, coiled it about his waist, and we set off along the passageway leading toward Laythe.

After my long series of adventures with unfriendly people in Va-nah, I had somewhat the sensation of one returning home after a long absence, for Moh-goh had assured me that the people of Laythe would receive me well and that I should be treated as a friend. He even assured me that he would procure for me a good berth in the service of Ko-tah. My greatest regret now was for Nah-ee-lah, and that she was not my companion, instead of Moh-goh. I was quite sure that she was lost, for had she escaped, falling back into the crater outside the Kalkar city, I doubted that she could successfully have found her way to Laythe. My heart had been heavy since we had been separated, and I had come to realize that the friendship of this little Moon Maid had meant a great deal more to me than I had thought. I could scarcely think of her now without a lump coming into my throat, for it seemed cruel, indeed, that one so young and lovely should have met so untimely an end.

The distance between the crater and the city of Laythe is not great, and presently we came directly out upon the lower terrace within the city. This terrace is at the very rim of the crater around which Laythe is built. And here we ran directly into the arms of a force of about fifty warriors.

Moh-goh emerged from the tunnel with his spear grasped in both hands high above his head, the point toward the rear, and I likewise, since he had cautioned me to do so. So surprised were the warriors to see any creatures emerge from this tunnel, which had been so long disused, that we were likely to have been slain before they realized that we had come before them with the signal of peace.

The guard that is maintained at the inner opening of the tunnel is considered by the Laytheans as more or less of an honorary assignment, the duties of which are performed perfunctorily.

"What do you here, Kalkars?" exclaimed the commander of the guard.

"We are not Kalkars," replied my companion. "I am Moh-goh the Paladar, and this be my friend. Can it be that you, Ko-vo the Kamadar, do not know me?"

"Ah!" cried the commander of the guard, "it is, indeed, Moh-goh the Paladar. You have been given up as lost."

"I was lost, indeed, had it not been for this, my friend," replied Moh-goh, nodding his head in my direction. "I was captured by the Kalkars and incarcerated in City No. 337."

"You escaped from a Kalkar city?" exclaimed Ko-vo, in evident incredulity. "That is impossible. It never has been accomplished."

"But we did accomplish it," replied Moh-goh, "thanks to my friend here," and then he narrated briefly to Ko-vo the details of our escape.

"It scarce seems possible," commented the Laythean, when Moh-goh had completed his narrative, "and what may be the name of your friend, Moh-goh, and from what country did you say he came?"

"He calls himself Ju-lan-fit," replied Moh-goh, for that was as near as he could come to the pronunciation of my name. And so it was that as Ju-lan-fit I was known to the Laytheans as long as I remained among them. They thought that fifth, which they pronounced "fit," was a title similar to one of those which always followed the name of its possessor in Laythe, as Sagroth the Jemadar, or Emperor; Ko-vo the Kamadar, a title which corresponds closely to that of the English Duke; and Moh-goh the Paladar, or Count. And so, to humor them, I told them that it meant the same as their Javadar, or Prince. I was thereafter called sometimes Ju-lan-fit, and sometimes Ju-lan Javadar, as the spirit moved him who addressed me.

At Moh-goh's suggestion, Ko-vo the Kamadar detailed a number of his men to accompany us to Moh-goh's dwelling, lest we have difficulty in passing through the city in our Kalkar garb.

As we had stood talking with Ko-vo, my eyes had been taking in the interior sights of this lunar city. The crater about which Laythe is built appeared to be between three and four miles in width, the buildings facing it and rising terrace upon terrace to a height of a mile at least, were much more elaborate of architecture and far richer in carving than those of the Kalkar City No. 337. The terraces were broad and well cultivated, and as we ascended toward Moh-goh's dwelling I saw that much pains had been taken to elaborately landscape many of them, there being pools and rivulets and waterfalls in numerous places. As in the Kalkar city, there were Va-gas fattening for food in little groups upon various terraces. They were sleek and fat and appeared contented, and I learned later that they were perfectly satisfied with their lot, having no more conception of the purpose for which they were bred or the fate that awaited them than have the beef cattle of Earth.

The U-gas of Laythe have induced this mental state in their Va-gas herds by a process of careful selection covering a period of ages, possibly, during which time they have conscientiously selected for breeding purposes the most stupid and unimaginative members of their herds.

At Moh-goh's dwelling we were warmly greeted by the members of his family—his father, mother and two sisters—all of whom, like the other Laytheans I had seen, were of striking appearance. The men were straight and handsome, the women physically perfect and of great beauty.

I could see in the affectionate greetings which they exchanged an indication of a family life and ties similar to those which are most common upon

Earth, while their gracious and hospitable reception of me marked them as people of highly refined sensibilities. First of all they must hear Moh-goh's story, and then, after having congratulated us and praised us, they set about preparing baths and fresh apparel for us, in which they were assisted by a corps of servants, descendants, I was told, of the faithful servitors who had remained loyal to the noble classes and accompanied them in their exile.

We rested for a short time after our baths, and then Moh-goh announced that he must go before Ko-tah, to whom it was necessary that he report, and that he would take me with him. I was appareled now in raiment befitting my supposed rank and carried the weapons of a Laythean gentleman—a short lance, or javelin, a dagger and a sword, but with my relatively darker skin and my blond hair, I could never hope to be aught than an object of remark in any Laythean company. Owing to the color of my hair, some of them thought that I was a Kalkar, but upon this score my complexion set them right.

Ko-tah's dwelling was, indeed, princely, stretching along a broad terrace for fully a quarter of a mile, with its two stories and its numerous towers and minarets. The entire face of the building was elaborately and beautifully carved, the decorations in their entirety recording pictographically the salient features of the lives of Ko-tah's ancestors.

Armed nobles stood on either side of the massive entrance way, and long before we reached this lunar prince I realized that possibly he was more difficult to approach than one of earthly origin, but at last we were ushered into his presence, and Moh-goh, with the utmost deference, presented me to Ko-tah the Javadar. Having assumed a princely title and princely raiment, I chose to assume princely prerogatives as well, believing that my position among the Laytheans would be better assured and all my interests furthered if they thought me of royal blood, and so I acknowledged my introduction to Ko-tah as though we were equals and that he was being presented to me upon the same footing that I was being presented to him.

I found him, like all his fellows, a handsome man, but with a slightly sinister expression which I did not like. Possibly I was prejudiced against him from what Nah-ee-lah had told me, but be that as it may, I conceived a dislike and distrust for him the moment that I laid eyes upon him, and I think, too, that he must have sensed my attitude, for, though he was outwardly gracious and courteous, I believe that Ko-tah the Javadar never liked me.

It is true that he insisted upon allotting me quarters within his palace and that he gave me service high among his followers, but I was at that time a novelty among them, and Ko-tah was not alone among the royalty who would have been glad to have entertained me and showered favors upon me, precisely as do Earth Men when a titled stranger, or famous man from another land, comes to their country.

Although I did not care for him, I was not loth to accept his hospitality, since I felt that because of my friendship for Nah-ee-lah I owed all my loyalty to Sagroth the Jemadar, and if by placing myself in the camp of the enemy I might serve the father of Nah-ee-lah, I was justified in so doing.

I found myself in a rather peculiar position in the palace of Ko-tah, since I was supposed to know little or nothing of internal condition in Laythe, and yet had learned from both Nah-ee-lah and Moh-goh a great deal concerning the intrigues and politics of this lunar city. For example, I was not supposed to know of the existence of Nah-ee-lah. Not even did Moh-goh know that I had heard of her; and so until her name was mentioned, I could ask no questions concerning her, though I was anxious indeed, to discover if by any miracle of chance, she had returned in safety to Laythe, or if aught had been learned concerning her fate.

Ko-tah held me in conversation for a considerable period of time, asking many questions concerning Earth and my voyage from that planet to the Moon. I knew that he was skeptical, and yet he was a man of such intelligence as to realize that there must be something in the Universe beyond his understanding or his knowledge. His eyes told him that I was not a native of Va-nah, and his ears must have corroborated the testimony of his eyes, for try as I would, I never was able to master the Va-nahan language so that I could pass for a native.

At the close of our interview Ko-tah announced that Moh-goh would also remain in quarters in the palace, suggesting that if it was agreeable to me, my companion should share my apartments with me.

"Nothing would give me greater pleasure, Ko-tah the Javadar," I said, "than to have my good friend, Moh-goh the Paladar, always with me."

"Excellent!" exclaimed Ko-tah. "You must both be fatigued. Go, therefore, to your apartments and rest. Presently I will repair to the palace of the Jemadar with my court, and you will be notified in sufficient time to prepare yourselves to accompany me.

The audience was at an end, and we were led by nobles of Ko-tah's palace to our apartments, which lay upon the second floor in pleasant rooms overlooking the terraces down to the brink of the great, yawning crater below.

Until I threw myself upon the soft mattress that served as a bed for me, I had not realized how physically exhausted I had been. Scarcely had I permitted myself to relax in the luxurious ease which precedes sleep ere

I was plunged into profound slumber, which must have endured for a considerable time, since when I awoke I was completely refreshed. Moh-goh was already up and in the bath, a marble affair fed by a continuous supply of icy water which originated among the ice-clad peaks of the higher mountains behind Laythe. The bather had no soap, but used rough fibre gloves with which he rubbed the surface of his skin until it glowed. These baths rather took one's breath away, but amply repaid for the shock by the sensation of exhilaration and well being which resulted from them.

In addition to private baths in each dwelling, each terrace supported a public bath, in which men, women and children disported themselves, re-calling to my mind the ancient Roman baths which earthly history records.

The baths of the Jemadar which I was later to see in the palace of Sagroth were marvels of beauty and luxury. Here, when the Emperor entertains, his guests amuse themselves by swimming and diving, which, from what I have been able to judge, are the national sports of the Laytheans. The Kalkars care less for the water, while the Va-gas only enter it through necessity.

I followed Moh-goh in the bath, in which my first sensation was that I was freezing to death. While we were dressing a messenger from Ko-tah summoned us to his presence, with instructions that we were to be prepared to accompany him to the palace of Sagroth the Jemadar.

# TWELVE

# Ko-tah Threatens the Princess

T HE PALACE of the Emperor stands, a magnificent pile, upon the loftiest terrace of Laythe, extending completely around the enormous crater. There are but three avenues leading to it from the terraces below—three magnificent stairways, each of which may be closed by enormous gates of stone, apparently wrought from huge slabs and intricately chiselled into marvelous designs, so that at a distance they present the appearance of magnificent lacework. Each gate is guarded by a company of fifty warriors, their tunics bearing the imperial design in a large circle over the left breast.

The ceremony of our entrance to the imperial terrace was most gorgeous and impressive. Huge drums and trumpets blared forth a challenge as we reached the foot of the stairway which we were to ascend to the palace. High dignitaries in gorgeous trappings came down the steps to meet us, as if to formally examine the credentials of Ko-tah and give official sanction to his entrance. We were then conducted through the gateway across a broad terrace beautifully landscaped and ornamented by statuary that was most evidently the work of finished artists. These works of art comprised both life size and heroic figures of individuals and groups, and represented for the most part historic or legendary figures and events of the remote past, though there were also likenesses of all the rulers of Laythe, up to and including Sagroth the present Jemadar.

Upon entering the palace we were led to a banquet hail, where we were served with food, evidently purely in accordance with ancient court ceremonial, since there was little to eat and the guests barely tasted of that which was presented to them. This ceremony consumed but a few minutes of Earth time, following which we were conducted through spacious hallways to the throne room of the Jemadar, an apartment of great beauty and considerable size. Its decorations and lines were simple, almost to severity, yet suggesting regal dignity and magnificence. Upon a dais at the far end of the room were three thrones, that in the center being occupied by a man whom I knew at once to be Sagroth, while upon either side sat a woman.

Ko-tah advanced and made his obeisance before his ruler, and after the exchange of a few words betweeen them Ko-tah returned and conducted me to the foot of Sagroth's throne.

I had been instructed that it was in accordance with court etiquette that I keep my eyes upon the ground until I had been presented and Sagroth had spoken to me, and that then I should be introduced to the Jemadav, or Empress, when I might raise my eyes to her, also, and afterward to the occupant of the third throne when I should be formally presented to her.

Sagroth spoke most graciously to me, and as I raised my eyes I saw before me a man of great size and evident strength of character. He was by far the most regal appearing individual my eyes had ever rested upon, while his low, well modulated, yet powerful voice accentuated the majesty of his mien. It was he who presented me to his Jemadav, whom I discovered to be a creature fully as regal in appearance as her imperial mate, and although doubtless well past middle age, still possessing remarkable beauty, in which was to be plainly noted Nah-ee-lah's resemblance to her mother.

Again I lowered my eyes as Sagroth presented me to the occupant of the third throne.

"Ju-lan the Javadar," he repeated the formal words of the presentation, "raise your eyes to the daughter of Laythe, Nah-ee-lah the Nonovar."

As my eyes, filled doubtless with surprise and incredulity, shot to the face of Nah-ee-lah, I was almost upon the verge of an exclamation of the joy and happiness which I felt in seeing her again and in knowing that she was safely returned to her parents and her city once more. But as my eyes met hers the exuberance of my spirit was as effectually and quickly checked by her cold glance and haughty mien as if I had received a blow in the face.

There was no hint of recognition in Nah-ee-lah's expression. She nodded coldly in acknowledgment of the presentation and then let her eyes pass above my head toward the opposite end of the throne room. My pride was hurt, and I was angry, but I would not let her see how badly I was hurt. I have always prided myself upon my control, and so I know that then I hid my emotion and turned once more to Sagroth, as though I had received from his daughter the Nonovar precisely the favor that I had a right to expect. If the Jemadar had noticed aught peculiar in either Nah-ee-lah's manner or mine, he gave no hint of it. He spoke again graciously to me and then dismissed me, with the remark that we should meet again later.

Having withdrawn from the throne room, Ko-tah informed me that following the audience I should have an opportunity to meet Sagroth less formally, since he had commanded that I remain in the palace as his guest during the meal which followed.

"It is a mark of distinction," said Ko-tah, "but remember, Ju-lan the Javadar, that you have accepted the friendship of Ko-tah and are his ally."

"Do not embroil me in the political intrigues of Laythe," I replied. "I am a stranger, with no interest in the internal affairs of your country, for the reason that I have no knowledge of them."

"One is either a friend or an enemy," replied Ko-tah.

"I am not sufficiently well acquainted to be accounted either," I told him; "nor shall I choose my friends in Laythe until I am better acquainted, nor shall another choose them for me."

"You are a stranger here," said Ko-tah. "I speak in your best interests, only. If you would succeed here; aye, if you would live, even, you must choose quickly and you must choose correctly. I, Ko-tah the Javadar, have spoken."

"I choose my own friends," I replied, "according to the dictates of my honor and my heart. I, Ju-lan the Javadar, have spoken."

He bowed low in acquiescence, and when he again raised his eyes to mine I was almost positive from the expression in them that his consideration of me was marked more by respect than resentment.

"We shall see," was all that he said, and withdrew, leaving me to the kindly attention of some of the gentlemen of Sagroth's court who had been standing at a respectful distance out of earshot of Ko-tah and myself. These men chatted pleasantly with me for some time until I was bidden to join Sagroth in another part of the palace.

I found myself now with a man who had evidently thrown off the restraint of a formal audience, though without in the slightest degree relinquishing either his dignity or his majesty. He spoke more freely and his manner was more democratic. He asked me to be seated, nor would he himself sit until I had, a point of Laythean court etiquette which made a vast impression on me, since it indicated that the first gentleman of the city must also be the first in courtesy. He put question after question to me concerning my own world and the means by which I had been transported to Va-nah.

"There are fragmentary, extremely fragmentary, legends handed down from extreme antiquity which suggest that our remote ancestors had some knowledge concerning the other worlds of which you speak," he said, "but these have been considered always the veriest of myths. Can it be possible that, after all, they are based upon truth?"

"The remarkable part of them," I suggested, "is that they exist at all, since it is difficult to understand how any knowledge of the outer Universe could ever reach to the buried depths of Va-nah."

"No, not by any means," he said, "if what you tell me is the truth, for our legends bear out the theory that Va-nah is located in the center of an enormous globe and that our earliest progenitors lived upon the outer surface of this globe, being forced at last by some condition which the legends do not even suggest, to find their way into this inner world."

I shook my head. It did not seem possible.

"And, yet," he said, noting the doubt that my expression evidently betrayed, "you yourself claim to have reached Va-nah from a great world far removed from our globe which you call the Moon. If you reached us from another world, is it then so difficult to believe that those who preceded us reached Va-nah from the outer crust of this Moon? It is almost an historic certainty," he continued, "that our ancestors possessed great ships which navigated the air. As you entered Va-nah by means of a similar conveyance, may not they have done likewise?"

I had to admit that it was within the range of possibilities, and in so doing, to avow that the Moon Men of antiquity had been millions of years in advance of their brethren of the Earth.

But, after all, was it such a difficult conclusion to reach when one considers the fact that the Moon being smaller, must have cooled more rapidly than Earth, and therefore, provided that it had an atmosphere, have been habitable to man ages before man could have lived upon our own planet?

We talked pleasantly upon many subjects for some time, and then, at last, Sagroth arose.

"We will join the others at the tables now," he said, and as he led the way from the apartment in which we had been conversing alone, stone doors opened before us as by magic, indicating that the Jemadar of Laythe was not only well served, but well protected, or possibly well spied upon.

After we emerged from the private audience, guards accompanied us, some preceding the Jemadar and some following, and thus we moved in semi-state through several corridors and apartments until we came out upon a balcony upon the second floor of the palace overlooking the terraces and the crater.

Here, along the rail of the balcony, were numerous small tables, each seating two, all but two of the tables being occupied by royal and noble retainers and their women. As the Jemadar entered, these all arose, facing him respectfully, and simultaneously through another entrance, came the Jemadav and Nah-ee-lah.

They stood just within the room, waiting until Sagroth and I crossed to them. While we were doing so, Sagroth very courteously explained the procedure I was to follow.

"You will place yourself upon the Nonovar's left," he concluded, "and conduct her to her table precisely as I conduct the Jemadav."

Nah-ee-lah's head was high as I approached her and she vouchsafed me only the merest inclination of it in response to my respectful salutation. In silence we followed Sagroth and his Empress to the tables reserved for us. The balance of the company remained standing until, at a signal from Sagroth, we all took our seats. It was necessary for me to watch the others closely, as I knew nothing concerning the social customs of Laythe, but when I saw that conversation had become general I glanced at Nah-ee-lah.

"The Princess of Laythe so soon forgets her friends?" I asked.

"The Princess of Laythe never forgets her friends," she replied.

"I know nothing of your customs here," I said, "but in my world even royalty may greet their friends with cordiality and seeming pleasure."

"And here, too," she retorted.

I saw that something was amiss, that she seemed to be angry with me, but the cause I could not imagine. Perhaps she thought I had deserted her at the entrance to the tunnel leading to the Kalkar city. But no, she must have guessed the truth. What then, could be the cause of her cold aloofness, who, the last that I had seen of her, had been warm with friendship?

"I wonder," I said, trying a new tack, "if you were as surprised to see me alive as I you. I had given you up for lost, Nah-ee-lah, and I had grieved more than I can tell you. When I saw you in the audience chamber I could scarce repress myself, but when I saw that you did not wish to recognize me, I could only respect your desires."

She made no reply, but turned and looked out the window across the terraces and the crater to the opposite side of Laythe. She was ice, who had been almost fire. No longer was she little Nah-ee-lah, the companion of my hardships and dangers. No longer was she friend and confidante, but a cold and haughty Princess, who evidently looked upon me with disfavor. Her attitude outraged all the sacred tenets of friendship, and I was angered.

"Princess," I said, "if it is customary for Laytheans thus to cast aside the sacred bonds of friendship, I should do as well to be among the Va-gas or the Kalkars."

"The way to either is open," she replied haughtily. "You are not a prisoner in Laythe."

Thereafter conversation languished and expired, as far at least, as Nah-ee-lah and I were concerned, and I was more than relieved when the unpleasant function was concluded.

Two young nobles took me in charge, following the meal; as it seemed that I was to remain as a guest in the palace for awhile, and as I expressed a desire to see as much of the imperial residence as I might be permitted to, they graciously conducted me upon a tour of inspection. We went out upon the outer terraces which overlooked the valleys and the mountains, and never in my life have I looked upon a landscape more majestic or inspiring. The crater of Laythe, situated upon a broad plateau entirely surrounded by lofty mountains, titanic peaks that would dwarf our Alps into insignificance and reduce the Himalayas to foothills, lowered far into the distance upon the upper side, the ice-clad summits of those more distant seemed to veritably topple above us, while a thousand feet below us the pinks and lavenders of the weird lunar vegetation lay like a soft carpet upon the gently undulating surface of the plateau.

But my guides seemed less interested in the scenery than in me. They plied me with questions continually, until I was more anxious to be rid of them than aught else that I could think of. They asked me a little concerning my own world and what I thought of Laythe, and if I found the Princess Nah-ee-lah charming, and my opinion of the Emperor Sagroth. My answers must have been satisfactory, for presently they came very close to me and one of them whispered:

"You need not fear to speak in our presence. We, too, are friends and followers of Ko-tah."

"The Devil!" I thought. "They are bound to embroil me in their petty intrigues. What do I care for Sagroth or Ko-tah or"—and then my thoughts reverted to Nah-ee-lah. She had treated me cruelly. Her cold aloofness and her almost studied contempt had wounded me, yet I could not say to myself that Nah-ee-lah was nothing to me. She had been my friend and I had been hers, and I should remain her friend to my dying day. Perhaps, then, if these people were bound to draw me into their political disputes, I might turn their confidences into profit for Nah-ee-lah. I had never told them that I was a creature of Ko-tah's, for I was not, nor had I ever told Ko-tah that I was an enemy to Sagroth; in fact, I had led him to believe the very opposite. And so I gave these two an evasive answer which might have meant anything, and they chose to interpret it as meaning that I was one of them. Well, what could I do? It was not my fault if they insisted upon deceiving themselves, and Nah-ee-lah might yet need the friendship that she had scorned.

"Has Sagroth no loyal followers, then," I asked, "that you are all so sure of the success of the *coup d'etat* that Ko-tah plans?"

"Ah, you know about it then!" cried one of them. "You are in the confidence of the Javadar."

I let them think that I was. It could do no harm, at least.

"Did he tell you when it was to happen?" asked the other.

"Perhaps, already I have said too much," I replied. "The confidences of Ko-tah are not to be lightly spread about."

"You are right," said the last speaker. "It is well to be discreet, but let us assure you, Ju-lan the Javadar, that we are equally in the confidence and favor of Ko-tah with any of those who serve him; otherwise, he would not have entrusted us with a portion of the work which must be done within the very palace of the Jemadar."

"Have you many accomplices here?" I asked.

"Many," he replied, "outside of the Jemadar's guards. They remain loyal to Sagroth. It is one of the traditions of the organization, and they will die for him, to a man and," he added with a shrug, "they shall die, never fear. When the time arrives and the signal is given, each member of the guard will be set upon by two of Ko-tah's faithful followers."

I do not know how long I remained in the City of Laythe. Time passed rapidly, and I was very happy after I returned to the dwelling of Moh-goh. I swam and dived with them and their friends in the baths upon our terrace, and also in those of Ko-tah. I learned to use the flying wings that I had first seen upon Nah-ee-lah the day that she fell exhausted into the clutches of the Va-gas, and many were the lofty and delightful excursions we took into the higher mountains of the Moon, when Moh-goh or his friends organized pleasure parties for the purpose. Constantly surrounded by people of culture and refinement, by brave men and beautiful women, my time was so filled with pleasurable activities that I made no effort to gauge it. I felt that I was to spend the balance of my life here, and I might as well get from it all the pleasure that Laythe could afford.

I did not see Nah-ee-lah during all this time, and though I still heard a great deal concerning the conspiracy against Sagroth, I presently came to attach but little importance to what I did hear, after I learned that the conspiracy had been on foot for over thirteen kelds, or approximately about ten earthly years, and seemed, according to my informers, no nearer consummation than it ever had been in the past.

Time does not trouble these people much, and I was told that it might be twenty kelds before Ko-tah took action, though on the other hand, he might strike within the next ola.

There was an occurrence during this period which aroused my curiosity, but concerning which Moh-goh was extremely reticent. Upon one of the occasions that I was a visitor in Ko-tah's palace, I was passing through a little used corridor in going from one chamber to another, when just ahead of me a door opened and a man stepped out in front of me. When he heard my footsteps behind him he turned and looked at me, and then stepped quickly back into the apartment he had just left and closed the door hurriedly behind him. There would have been nothing particularly remarkable in that, had it not been for the fact that the man was not a Laythean, but unquestionably a Kalkar.

Believing that I had discovered an enemy in the very heart of Laythe, I leaped forward, and throwing open the door, followed into the apartment into which the man had disappeared. To my astonishment, I found myself confronted by six men, three of whom were Kalkars, while the other three were Laytheans, and among the latter I instantly recognized Ko-tah, himself. He flushed angrily as he saw me, but before he could speak I bowed and explained my action.

"I crave your pardon, Javadar," I said. "I thought that I saw an enemy of Laythe in the heart of your palace, and that by apprehending him I should serve you best;" and I started to withdraw from the chamber.

"Wait," he said. "You did right, but lest you misunderstand their presence here, I may tell you that these three are prisoners."

"I realized that at once when I saw you, Javadar," I replied, though I knew perfectly that he had lied to me; and then I backed from the room, closing the door after me.

I spoke to Moh-goh about it the next time that I saw him.

"You saw nothing, my friend," he said. "Remember that—you saw nothing."

"If you mean that it is none of my business, Moh-goh," I replied, "I perfectly agree with you, and you may rest assured that I shall not meddle in affairs that do not concern me."

However, I did considerable thinking upon the matter, and possibly I went out of my way a little more than one should who is attending strictly to his own business, that I might keep a little in touch with the course of the conspiracy, for no matter what I had said to Moh-goh, no matter how I attempted to convince myself that it did not interest me, the truth remained that anything that affected in any way the fate of Nah-ee-lah transcended in interest any event which might transpire within Va-nah, in so far as I was concerned.

The unobtrusive espionage which I practiced bore fruit, to the extent that it permitted me to know that on at least three other occasions delegations of Kalkars visited Ko-tah.

The fact that this ancient palace of the Prince of Laythe was a never-ending source of interest to me aided me in my self-imposed task of spying upon the conspirators, for the retainers of Ko-tah were quite accustomed to see me in out-of-the-way corridors and passages, oftentimes far from the inhabited portions of the building.

Upon the occasion of one of these tours I had descended to a lower terrace, along an ancient stone stairway which wound spirally downward and had discovered a dimly lighted room in which were stored a number of ancient works of art. I was quietly examining these, when I heard voices in an adjoining chamber.

"Upon no other conditions will he assist you, Javadar," said the speaker, whose voice I first heard.

"His demands are outrageous," replied a second speaker. "I refuse to consider them. Laythe is impregnable. He can never take it." The voice was that of Ko-tah.

"You do not know him, Laythean," replied the other. "He has given us engines of destruction with which we can destroy any city in Va-nah. He will give you Laythe. Is that not enough?"

"But he will be Jemadar of Jemadars and rule us all!" exclaimed Ko-tah. "The Jemadar of Laythe can be subservient to none."

"If you do not accede he will take Laythe in spite of you and reduce you to the status of a slave."

"Enough, Kalkar!" cried Ko-tah, his voice trembling with rage. "Be gone! Tell your master that Ko-tah refuses his base demands."

"You will regret it, Laythean," replied the Kalkar, "for you do not know what this creature has brought from another world in knowledge of war and the science of destruction of human life."

"I do not fear him," snapped Ko-tah, "my swords are many, my spearmen are well trained. Be gone, and do not return until your master is ready to sue with Ko-tah for an alliance."

I heard receding footsteps then, and following that, a silence which I thought indicated that all had left the chamber, but presently I heard Ko-tah's voice again.

"What think you of it?" he asked. And then I heard the voice of a third man, evidently a Laythean, replying:

"I think that if there is any truth in the fellow's assertions, we may not too quickly bring about the fall of Sagroth and place you upon the throne of Laythe, for only thus may we stand united against a common outside enemy.

"You are right," replied the Javadar. "Gather our forces. We shall strike within the ola."

I wanted to hear more, but they passed out of the chamber then, and their voices became only a subdued murmur which quickly trailed off into silence. What should I do? Within six hours Ko-tah would strike at the power of Sagroth, and I well knew what that would mean to Nah-ee-lah; either marriage with the new Jemadar, or death, and I guessed that the proud Princess would choose the latter in preference to Ko-tah.

# THIRTEEN

# Ko-tah Is Killed

A S RAPIDLY as I could I made my way from the palace of Ko-tah, and upward, terrace by terrace, toward the palace of the Jemadar. I had never presented myself at Sagroth's palace since Nah-ee-lah had so grievously offended me. I did not even know the customary procedure to follow to gain an audience with the Emperor, but nevertheless I came boldly to the carven gates and demanded to speak with the officer in command of the guards. When he came I told him that I desired to speak either with Sagroth or the Princess Nah-ee-lah at once, upon a matter of the most urgent importance.

"Wait," he said, "and I will take your message to the Jemadar."

He was gone for what seemed to me a very long time, but at last he returned, saying that Sagroth would see me at once, and I was conducted through the gates and into the palace toward the small audience chamber in which Sagroth had once received me so graciously. As I was ushered into the room I found myself facing both Sagroth and Nah-ee-lah. The attitude of the Jemadar seemed apparently judicial, but that of the Princess was openly hostile.

"What are you doing here, traitor?" she demanded, without waiting for Sagroth to speak, and at the same instant a door upon the opposite side of the room burst open and three warriors leaped into the apartment with bared swords. They wore the livery of Ko-tah, and I knew instantly the purpose for which they had come. Drawing my own sword, I leaped forward.

"I have come to defend the life of the Jemadar and his Princess," I cried, as I sprang between them and the advancing three.

"What means this?" demanded Sagroth. "How dare you enter the presence of your Jemadar with drawn sword?"

"They are the assassins of Ko-tah come to slay you!" I cried. "Defend yourself, Sagroth of Laythe!" And with that, I tried to engage the three until help arrived.

I am no novice with the sword. The art of fencing has been one of my chief diversions since my cadet days in the Air School, and I did not fear the Laytheans, though I knew that, even were they but mediocre swordsmen, I could not for long withstand the assaults of three at once. But upon this point I need not have concerned myself, for no sooner had I spoken than Sagroth's sword leaped from its scabbard, and placing himself at my side, he fought nobly and well in defense of his life and his honor.

One of our antagonists merely tried to engage me while the other two assassinated the Jemadar. And so, seeing that he was playing me, and that I could do with him about as I pleased if I did not push him too hard, I drove him back a few steps until I was close at the side of one of those who engaged Sagroth. Then before any could know my intention I wheeled and lunged my sword through the heart of one of those who opposed the father of Nah-ee-lah. So quickly had I disengaged my former antagonist, so swift my lunge, that I had recovered and was ready to meet the renewed assaults of the first who had engaged me almost before he realized what had happened.

It was man against man, now, and the odds were even. I had no opportunity to watch Sagroth, but from the ring of steel on steel, I knew that the two were bitterly engaged. My own man kept me well occupied. He was a magnificent swordsman, but he was only fighting for his life; I was fighting for more—for my life and for my honor, too, since after the word "traitor" that Nah-ee-lah had hurled at me, I had felt that I must redeem myself in her eyes. I did not give any thought at all to the question as to just why I should care what Nah-ee-lah the Moon Maid thought of me, but something within me reacted mightily to the contempt that she had put into that single word.

I could catch an occasional glimpse of her standing there behind the massive desk at which her father had sat upon the first occasion of my coming to this chamber. She stood there very tense, her wide eyes fixed upon me in evident incredulity.

I had almost worn my man down and we were fighting now so that I was facing Nah-ee-lah, with my back toward the doorway through which the three assassins had entered. Sagroth must have been more than holding his own, too, for I could see his opponent slowly falling back before the older man's assaults. And then there broke above the clang of steel a girl's voice—Nah-ee-lah's—raised in accents of fear.

"Julian, beware! Behind you! Behind you!"

At the instant of her warning the eyes of my antagonist left mine, which, for his own good, they never should have done, and passed in a quick glance over my shoulder at something or someone behind me. His lack of concentration cost him his life. I saw my opening the instant that it was made, and with a quick lunge I passed my blade through his heart. Whipping it out again, I wheeled to face a dozen men springing into the chamber. They paid no attention to me, but leaped toward Sagroth, and before I could prevent he went down with half a dozen blades through his body.

Upon the opposite side of the desk from us was another doorway directly behind Nah-ee-lah, and in the instant that she saw Sagroth fall, she called to me in a low voice: "Come, Julian, quick! Or we, too, are lost."

Realizing that the Jemadar was dead and that it would be folly to remain and attempt to fight this whole roomful of warriors, I leaped the desk and followed Nah-ee-lah through the doorway beyond. There was a cry, then, from someone within the room, to stop us, but Nah-ee-lah wheeled and slammed the door in their faces as they rushed forward, fastened it upon our side and then turned to me.

"Julian," she said, "how can you ever forgive me? You who have risked your life for the Jemadar, my father, in spite of the contemptible treatment that in my ignorance I have accorded you?"

"I could have explained," I said, "but you would not let me. Appearances were against me, and so I cannot blame you for thinking as you did."

"It was wicked of me not to listen to you, Julian, but I thought that Ko-tah had won you over, as he has won over even some of the staunchest friends of Sagroth."

"You might have known, Nah-ee-lah, that, even could I have been disloyal to your father, I never could have been disloyal to his daughter."

"I did not know," she said. "How could I?"

There suddenly came over me a great desire to take her in my arms and cover those lovely lips with kisses. I could not tell why this ridiculous obsession had seized upon me, nor why, of a sudden, I became afraid of little Nah-ee-lah, the Moon Maid. I must have looked very foolish indeed, standing there looking at her, and suddenly I realized how fatuous I must appear, and so I shook myself and laughed.

"Come, Nah-ee-lah," I said, "we must not remain here. Where can I take you, that you will be safe?"

"Upon the outer terrace there may be some of the loyal guards," she replied, "but if Ko-tah has already taken the palace, flight will be useless."

"From what I know of the conspiracy, it will be useless," I replied, "for the service of Sagroth and his palace is rotten with the spies and retainers of the Javadar."

"I feared as much," she said. "The very men who came to assassinate Sagroth wore the imperial livery less than an ola since."

"Are there none, then, loyal to you?" I asked her.

"The Jemadar's guard is always loyal," she said, "but they number scarce a thousand men."

"How may we summon them?" I asked.

"Let us go to the outer terraces and if there are any of them there we can congregate the balance, or as many of them as Ko-tah has left alive."

"Come, then," I said, "let us hasten;" and together, hand in hand, we ran along the corridors of the Jemadar's palace to the outer terraces of the highest tier of Laythe. There we found a hundred men, and when we had told them of what had happened within the palace they drew their swords and, surrounding Nah-ee-lah, they shouted:

"To the death for Nah-ee-lah, Jemadav of Laythe!"

They wanted to remain there and protect her, but I told them that there would be nothing gained by that, that sooner or later they would be overwhelmed by far greater numbers, and the cause of Nah-ee-lah lost.

"Send a dozen men," I said to their commander, "to rally all of the loyal guards that remain alive. Tell them to come to the throne room, ready to lay down their lives for the new Jemadav, and then let the dozen continue on out into the city, rallying the people to the protection of Nah-ee-lah. As for us, we will accompany her immediately to the throne room, and there, place her upon the throne and proclaim her ruler of Laythe. A hundred men may hold the throne room for a long time, if we reach it before Ko-tah reaches it with his forces."

The officer looked at Nah-ee-lah questioningly.

"Your command, Jemadav?" he inquired.

"We will follow the plan of Ju-lan the Javadar," she replied.

Immediately a dozen warriors were dispatched to rally the Imperial Guard and arouse the loyal citizens of the city to the protection, of their new Jemadav, while the balance of us conducted Nah-ee-lah by a short course toward the throne room.

As we entered the great chamber at one end, Ko-tah and a handful of warriors came in at the other, but we had the advantage, in that we entered through a doorway directly behind the throne and upon the dais.

"Throw your men upon the main entrance," I called to the officer of the guard, "and hold it until reinforcements come;" and then, as the hundred raced the length of the throne room toward the surprised and enraged

Ko-tah, I led Nah-ee-lah to the central throne and seated her upon it. Then stepping forward, I raised my hand for silence.

"The Jemadar Sagroth is dead!" I cried. "Behold Nah-ee-lah, the Jemadav of Laythe!"

"Stop!" cried Ko-tah, "she may share the throne with me, but she may not possess it alone."

"Take that traitor!" I called to the loyal guard, and they rushed forward, evidently glad to do my bidding. But Ko-tah did not wait to be taken. He was accompanied by only a handful of men, and when he saw that the guard really intended to seize him and realized that he would be given short shift at the hands of Nah-ee-lah and myself, he turned and fled. But I knew he would come back, and come back he did, though not until after the majority of the Jemadav's guard had gathered within the throne room.

He came with a great concourse of warriors, and the fighting was furious, but he might have brought a million men against our thousand and not immediately have overcome us, since only a limited number could fight at one time in the entrance way to the throne room. Already the corpses lay stacked as high as a man's head, yet no single member of Ko-tah's forces had crossed the threshold.

How long the fight was waged I do not know, but it must have been for a considerable time, since I know that our men fought in relays and rested many times, and that food was brought from other parts of the palace to the doorway behind the throne, and there were times when Ko-tah's forces withdrew and rested and recuperated, but always they came back in greater number, and eventually I realized we must be I worn down by the persistence of their repeated attacks.

And then there arose slowly a deep-toned sound, at first we could not interpret. It rose and fell in increasing volume, until finally we knew that it was the sound of human voices, the voices of a great mob—of a mighty concourse of people and that it was sweeping toward us slowly and resistlessly.

Closer and closer it approached the palace as it rose, terrace upon terrace, toward the lofty pinnacle of Laythe. The fighting at the entrance to the throne room had almost ceased. Both sides were worn down almost to utter exhaustion, and now we but stood upon our arms upon either side of the wall of corpses that lay between us, our attention centered upon the sound of the growling multitude that was sweeping slowly upward toward us.

"They come," cried one of Nah-ee-lah's nobles, "to acclaim the new Jemadav and to tear the minions of Ko-tah the traitor to pieces!"

He spoke in a loud voice that was easily audible to Ko-tah and his retainers in the corridor without.

"They come to drag the spawn of Sagroth from the throne!" cried one of Ko-tah's followers. And then from the throne came the sweet, clear voice of Nah-ee-lah:

"Let the people's will be done," she said, and thus we stood, awaiting the verdict of the populace. Nor had we long to wait, for presently we realized that they had reached the palace terrace and entered the building itself. We could hear the shouting horde moving through the corridors and chambers, and finally the muffled bellowing resolved itself into articulate words:

"Sagroth is no more! Rule, Ko-tah, Jemadar of Laythe!"

I turned in consternation toward Nah-ee-lah. "What does mean?" I cried. "Have the people turned against you?"

"Ko-tah's minions have done their work well during these many kelds," said the commander of the Jemadav's guard, who stood upon the upper steps of the dais, just below the throne. "They have spread lies and sedition among the people which not even Sagroth's just and kindly reign could overcome."

"Let the will of the people be done," repeated Nah-ee-lah.

"It is the will of fools betrayed by a scoundrel," cried the commander of the guard. "While there beats a single heart beneath the tunic of a guardsman of the Jemadav, we shall fight for Nah-ee-lah, Empress of Laythe."

Ko-tah's forces, now augmented by the rabble, were pushing their way over the corpses and into the throne room, so that we were forced to join the defenders, that we might hold them off while life remained to any of us. When the commander of the guard saw me fighting at his side he asked me to return to Nah-ee-lah.

"We must not leave the Jemadav alone," he said. "Return and remain at her side, Ju-lan the Javadar, and when the last of us has fallen, drive your dagger into her heart.

I shuddered and turned back toward Nah-ee-lah. The very thought of plunging my dagger into that tender bosom fairly nauseated me. There must be some other way, and yet, what other means of escape could there be for Nah-ee-lah, who preferred death to the dishonor of surrender to Ko-tah, the murderer of her father? As I reached Nah-ee-lah's side, and turned again to face the entrance to the throne room, I saw that the warriors of Ko-tah were being pushed into the chamber by the mob behind them and that our defenders were being overwhelmed by the great number of their antagonists. Ko-tah, with a half dozen warriors, had been carried forward, practically without volition, by the press of numbers in their rear, and even now, with none to intercept him, was running rapidly up the broad center aisle toward the throne. Some of those in the entrance way saw him, and as he reached the foot of the steps leading to the dais, a snarling cry arose:

"Ko-tah the Jemadar!"

With bared sword, the fellow leaped toward me where I stood alone between Nah-ee-lah and her enemies.

"Surrender, Julian!" she cried. "It is futile to oppose them. You are not of Laythe. Neither duty nor honor impose upon you the necessity of offering your life for one of us. Spare him, Ko-tah!" she cried to the advancing Javadar, "and I will bow to the will of the people and relinquish the throne to you."

"Ko-tah the traitor shall never sit upon the throne of Nah-ee-lah!" I exclaimed, and leaping forward, I engaged the Prince of Laythe.

His warriors were close behind him, and it behooved me to work fast, and so I fought as I had never guessed that it lay within me to fight, and at the instant that the rabble broke through the remaining defenders and poured into the throne room of the Jemadars of Laythe, I slipped my point into the heart of Ko-tah. With a single piercing shriek, he threw his hands above his head and toppled backward down the steps to lie dead at the foot of the throne he had betrayed.

For an instant the silence of death reigned in the great chamber. Friend and foe stood alike in the momentary paralysis of shocked surprise.

That tense, breathless silence had endured for but a moment, when it was shattered by a terrific detonation. We felt the palace tremble and rock. The assembled mob looked wildly about, their eyes filled with fear and questioning. But before they could voice a question, another thunderous report burst upon our startled ears, and then from the city below the palace there arose the shrieks and screams of terrified people. Again the palace trembled, and a great crack opened in one of the walls of the throne room. The people saw it, and in an instant their anger against the dynasty of Sagroth was swallowed in the mortal terror which they felt for their own safety. With shrieks and screams they turned and bolted for the doorway. The weaker were knocked down and trampled upon. They fought with fists and swords and daggers, in their mad efforts to escape the crumbling building. They tore the clothing from one another, as each sought to drag back his fellow, that he might gain further in the race for the outer world.

And as the rabble fought, Nah-ee-lah and I stood before the throne of Laythe, watching them, while below us the few remaining members of the Jemadar's guard stood viewing in silent contempt the terror of the people.

Explosion after explosion followed one another in rapid succession. The people had fled. The palace was empty, except for that handful of us faithful ones who remained within the throne room.

"Let us go," I said to Nah-ee-lah, "and discover the origin of these sounds, and the extent of the damage that is being done."

"Come," she said, "here is a short corridor to the inner terrace, where we may look down upon the entire city of Laythe." And then, turning to the commander of the guard she said: "Proceed, please, to the palace gates, and secure them against the return of our enemies, if they have by this time all fled from the palace grounds."

The officer bowed, and followed by the few heroic survivors of the Jemadar's guard, he left by another corridor for the palace gates, while I followed Nah-ee-lah up a stairway that led to the roof of the palace.

Coming out upon the upper terrace, we made our way quickly to the edge overlooking the city and the crater. Below us a shrieking multitude ran hither and thither from terrace to terrace, while, now here and now there, terrific explosions occurred that shattered age-old structures and carried debris high into the air. Many terraces showed great gaps and tumbled ruins where other explosions had occurred and smoke and flames were rising from a dozen portions of the city.

But an instant it took me to realize that the explosions were caused by something that was being dropped into the city from above, and as I looked up I saw a missile describing an arc above the palace, past which it hurtled to a terrace far below, and at once I realized that the missile had originated outside the city. Turning quickly, I ran across the terrace to the outer side which overlooked the plateau upon which the city stood. I could not repress an exclamation of astonishment at the sight that greeted my eyes, for the surface of the plateau was alive with warriors. Nah-ee-lah had followed me and was standing at my elbow. "The Kalkars," she said. "They have come again to reduce Laythe. It has been long since they attempted it, many generations ago, but what is it, Julian, that causes the great noise and the destruction and the fires within Laythe?"

"It is this which fills me with surprise," I said, "and not the presence of the Kalkar warriors. Look! Nah-ee-lah," and I pointed to a knoll lying at the verge of the plateau, where, unless my eyes deceived me badly, there was mounted a mortar which was hurling shells into the city of Laythe. "And there, and there," I continued, pointing to other similar engines of destruction mounted at intervals. "The city is surrounded with them, Nah-ee-lah. Have your people any knowledge of such engines of warfare or of high explosives?" I demanded.

"Only in our legends are such things mentioned," she replied. "It has been ages since the inhabitants of Va-nah lost the art of manufacturing such things."

As we stood there talking, one of the Jemadar's guards emerged from the palace and approached us.

"Nah-ee-lah, Jemadav," he cried, "there is one here who craves audience with you and who says that if you listen to him you may save your city from destruction."

"Fetch him," replied Nah-ee-lah. "We will receive him here."

We had but a moment to wait when the guardsman returned with one of Ko-tah's captains.

"Nah-ee-lah, Jemadav," he cried, when she had given him permission to speak, "I come to you with a message from one who is Jemadar of Jemadars, ruler of all Va-nah. If you would save your city and your people, listen well."

The girl's eyes narrowed. "You are speaking to your Jemadav, fellow," she said. "Be careful, not only of your words, but of your tone."

"I come but to save you," replied the man sullenly. "The Kalkars have discovered a great leader, and they have joined together from many cities to overthrow Laythe. My master does not wish to destroy this ancient city, and there is but one simple condition upon which he will spare it."

"Name your condition," said Nah-ee-lah.

"If you will wed him, he will make Laythe the capital of Va-nah, and you shall rule with him as Jemadav of Jemadavs."

Nah-ee-lah's lips curled in scorn. "And who is the presumptuous Kalkar that dares aspire to the hand of Nah-ee-lah?" she demanded.

"He is no Kalkar, Jemadav," replied the messenger. "He is one from another world, who says that he knows you well and that he has loved you long."

"His name," snapped Nah-ee-lah impatiently.

"He is called Or-tis, Jemadar of Jemadars."

Nah-ee-lah turned toward me with elevated brows and a smile of comprehension upon her face.

"Or-tis," she repeated.

"Now, I understand, my Jemadav," I said, "and I am commencing to have some slight conception of the time that must have elapsed since I first landed within Va-nah, for even since our escape from the Va-gas, Orthis has had time to discover the Kalkars and ingratiate himself among them, to conspire with them for the overthrow of Laythe, and to manufacture explosives and shells and the guns which are reducing Laythe this moment. Even had I not heard the name, I might have guessed that it was Orthis, for it is all so like him—ingrate, traitor, cur."

"Go back to your master," she said to the messenger, "and tell him that Nah-ee-lah, Jemadav of Laythe, would as leave mate with Ga-va-go the Va-ga as with him, and that Laythe will be happier destroyed and her people wiped from the face of Va-nah than ruled by such a beast. I have spoken. Go."

The fellow turned and left us, being accompanied from Nah-ee-lah's presence by the guardsman who had fetched him, and whom Nah-ee-lah commanded to return as soon as he had conducted the other outside the palace gates. Then the girl turned to me:

"O, Julian, what shall I do? How may I combat those terrible forces that you have brought to Va-nah from another world?"

I shook my head. "We, too, could manufacture both guns and ammunition to combat him, but now we have not the time, since Laythe will be reduced to a mass of ruins before we could even make a start. There is but one way, Nah-ee-lah, and that is to send your people—every fighting man that you can gather, and the women, too, if they can bear arms, out upon the plateau in an effort to overwhelm the Kalkars and destroy the guns."

She stood and thought for a long time, and presently the officer of the guard returned and halted before her, awaiting her commands. Slowly she raised her head and looked at him.

"Go into the city," she said, "and gather every Laythean who can carry a sword, a dagger, or a lance. Tell them to assemble on the inner terraces below the castle, and that I, Nah-ee-lah their Jemadav, will address them. The fate of Laythe rests with you. Go."

# FOURTEEN

# Back to *The Barsoom*

T HE CITY was already in flames in many places, and though the people fought valiantly to extinguish them, it seemed to me that they but spread the more rapidly with each succeeding minute. And then, as suddenly as it had commenced, the bombardment ceased. Nah-ee-lah and I crossed over to the outer edge of the terrace to see if we could note any new movement by the enemy, nor did we have long to wait. We saw a hundred ladders raised as if by magic toward the lowest terrace, which rose but a bare two hundred feet above the base of the city. The men who carried the ladders were not visible to us when they came close to the base of the wall, but I guessed from the distant glimpses that I caught of the ladders as they were rushed forward by running men that here, again, Orthis' earthly knowledge and experience had come to the assistance of the Kalkars, for I was sure that only some form of extension ladder could be successfully used to reach even the lowest terrace.

When I saw their intention I ran quickly down into the palace and out upon the terrace before the gates, where the remainder of the guard were stationed, and there I told them what was happening and urged them to hasten the people to the lowest terrace to repulse the enemy before they had secured a foothold upon the city. Then I returned to Nah-ee-lah, and together we watched the outcome of the struggle, but almost from the first I realized that Laythe was doomed, for before any of her defenders could reach the spot, fully a thousand Kalkars had clambered to the terrace, and there they held their own while other thousands ascended in safety to the city.

We saw the defenders rush forth to attack them, and for a moment, so impetuous was their charge, I thought that I had been wrong and that the Kalkars might yet be driven from Laythe. Fighting upon the lower outer terrace far beneath us was a surging mass of shouting warriors. The Kalkars were falling back before the impetuous onslaught of the Laytheans.

"They have not the blood in their veins," whispered Nah-ee-lah, clinging tightly to my arm. "One noble is worth ten of them. Watch them. Already are they fleeing."

And so it seemed, and the rout of the Kalkars appeared almost assured, as score upon score of them were hurled over the edge of the terrace, to fall mangled and bleeding upon the ground hundreds of feet below.

But suddenly a new force seemed to be injected into the strife. I saw a stream of Kalkars emerging above the edge of the lower terrace—new men clambering up the ladders from the plateau below, and as they came they shouted something which I could not understand, but the other Kalkars seemed to take heart and made once more the semblance of a stand against the noble Laytheans, and I saw one, the leader of the newcomers, force his way into the battling throng. And then I saw him raise his hand above his head and hurl something into the midst of the compact ranks of the Laytheans.

Instantly there was a terrific explosion and a great, bloody gap lay upon the terrace where an instant before a hundred of the flower of the fighting men of Laythe had been so gloriously defending their city and their honor.

"Grenades," I exclaimed. "Hand grenades!"

"What is it, Julian? What is it that they are doing down there?" cried Nah-ee-lah. "They are murdering my people."

"Yes, Nah-ee-lah, they are murdering your people, and well may Va-nah curse the day that Earth Men set foot upon your world."

"I do not understand, Julian," she said.

"This is the work of Orthis," I said, "who has brought from Earth the knowledge of diabolical engines of destruction. He first shelled the city with what must have been nothing more than crude mortars, for it is impossible that he has had the time to construct the machinery to build any but the simplest of guns. Now his troops are hurling hand grenades among your men. There is no chance, Nah-ee-lah, for the Laytheans to successfully pit their primitive weapons against the modern agents of destruction which Orthis has brought to bear against them. Laythe must surrender or be destroyed."

Nah-ee-lah laid her head upon my shoulder and wept softly. "Julian," she said at last, "this is the end, then. Take me to the Jemadav, my mother, please, and then you must go and make your peace with your fellow Earth Man. It is not right that you, a stranger, who have done so much for me, should fall with me and Laythe."

"The only peace I can make with Orthis, Nah-ee-lah," I replied, "is the peace of death. Orthis and I may not live together again in the same world."

She was crying very softly, sobbing upon my shoulder, and I put my arm about her in an effort to quiet her.

"I have brought you only suffering and danger, and now death, Julian," she said, "when you deserve naught but happiness and peace."

I suddenly felt very strange and my heart behaved wretchedly, so that when I attempted to speak it pounded so that I could say nothing and my knees shook beneath me. What had come over me? Could it be possible that already Orthis had loosed his poison gas? Then, at last, I managed to gather myself together.

"Nah-ee-lah," I said, "I do not fear death if you must die, and I do not seek happiness except with you."

She looked up suddenly, her great, tear-dimmed eyes wide and gazing deep into mine.

"You mean—Julian? You mean—?"

"I mean, Nah-ee-lah, that I love you," I replied, though I must have stumbled through the words in a most ridiculous manner, so frightened was I.

"Ah, Julian," she sighed, and put her arms about my neck.

"And you, Nah-ee-lah!" I exclaimed incredulously, as I crushed her to me, "can it be that you return my love?"

"I have loved you always," she replied. "From the very first, almost— way back when we were prisoners together in the No-vans village. You Earth Men must be very blind, my Julian. A Laythean would have known it at once, for it seemed to me that upon a dozen occasions I almost avowed my love openly to you.

"Alas, Nah-ee-lah! I must have been very blind, for I had not guessed until this minute that you loved me.

"Now," she said, "I do not care what happens. We have one another, and if we die together, doubtless we shall live together in a new incarnation."

"I hope so," I said, "but I should much rather be sure of it and live together in this."

"And I, too, Julian, but that is impossible."

We were walking now through the corridors of the palace toward the chamber occupied by her mother, but we did not find her there and Nah-ee-lah became apprehensive as to her safety. Hurriedly we searched through other chambers of the palace, until at last we came to the little audience chamber in which Sagroth had been slain, and as we threw open the door I saw a sight that I tried to hide from Nah-ee-lah's eyes as I drew her around in an effort to force her back into the corridor. Possibly she guessed what impelled my action, for she shook her head and murmured: "No, Julian; whatever it is I must see it." And then she pushed her way gently past me, and we stood together upon the theshold, looking at the harrowing sight which the interior of the room displayed.

There were the bodies of the assassins Sagroth and I had slain, and the dead Jemadar, too, precisely as he had fallen, while across his breast lay the body of Nah-ee-lah's mother, a dagger self-thrust through her heart. For just a moment Nah-ee-lah stood there looking at them in silence, as though in prayer, and then she turned wearily away and left the chamber, closing the door behind her. We walked on in silence for some time, ascending the stairway back to the upper terrace. Upon the inner side, the flames were spreading throughout the city, roaring like a mighty furnace and vomiting up great clouds of smoke, for though the Laythean terraces are supported by tremendous arches of masonry, yet there is much wood used in the interior construction of the buildings, while the hangings and the furniture are all inflammable.

"We had no chance to save the city," said Nah-ee-lah, with a sigh. "Our people, called from their normal duties by the false Ko-tah, were leaderless. The fire fighters, instead of being at their posts, were seeking the life of their Jemadar. Unhappy day! Unhappy day!"

"You think they could have stopped the fire?" I asked.

"The little ponds, the rivulets, the waterfalls, the great public baths and the tiny lakes that you see upon every terrace were all built with fire protection in mind. It is easy to divert their waters and flood any tier of buildings. Had my people been at their posts, this, at least, could not have happened."

As we stood watching the flames we suddenly saw people emerging in great numbers upon several of the lower terraces. They were evidently in terrified flight, and then others appeared upon terraces above them— Kalkars who hurled hand grenades amongst the Laytheans beneath them. Men, women, and children ran hither and thither, shrieking and crying and seeking for shelter, but from the buildings behind them, rushing them outward upon the terraces, came other Kalkars with hand grenades. The fires hemmed the people of Laythe upon either side and the Kalkars attacked them from the rear and from above. The weaker fell and were trodden to death, and I saw scores fall upon their own lances or drive daggers into the hearts of their loved ones.

The Destruction of Laythe

The massacre spread rapidly around the circumference of the city and the Kalkars drove the people from the upper terraces downward between the raging fires which were increasing until the mouth of the great crater was filled with roaring flames and smoke. In the occasional gaps we could catch glimpses of the holocaust beneath us.

A sudden current of air rising from the crater lifted the smoke, pall high for a moment, revealing the entire circumference of the crater, the edge of which was crowded with Laytheans. And then I saw a warrior from the opposite side leap upon the surrounding wall that bordered the lower terrace at the edge of the yawning crater. He turned and called aloud some message to his fellows, and then wheeling, threw his arms above his head and leaped outward into the yawning, bottomless abyss. Instantly the others seemed to be inoculated with the infection of his mad act. A dozen men leaped to the wall and dove head foremost into the crater. The thing spread slowly at first, and then with the rapidity of a prairie fire, it ran around the entire circle of the city. Women hurled their children in and then leaped after them. The multitude fought one with another for a place upon the wall from which they might cast themselves to death. It was a terrible—an awe-inspiring sight.

Nah-ee-lah covered her eyes with her hands. "My poor people!" she cried. "My poor people!" And far below her, by the thousands now, they were hurling themselves into eternity, while above them the screaming Kalkars hurled hand grenades among them and drove the remaining inhabitants of Laythe, terrace by terrace, down toward the crater's rim.

Nah-ee-lah turned away. "Come, Julian," she said, "I cannot look, I cannot look." And together we walked across the terrace to the outer side of the city.

Almost directly beneath us upon the next terrace was a palace gate and as we reached a point where we could see it, I was horrified to see that the Kalkars had made their way up the outer terraces to the very palace walls. The Jemadar's guard was standing there ready to defend the palace against the invaders. The great stone gates would have held indefinitely against spears and swords, but even the guardsmen must have guessed that their doom was already sealed and that these gates, that had stood for ages, an ample protection to the Jemadars of Laythe, were about to fall, as the Kalkars halted fifty yards away, and from their ranks a single individual stepped forth a few paces.

As my eyes alighted upon him I seized Nah-ee-lah's arm. "Orthis!" I cried. "It is Orthis." At the same instant the man's eyes rose above the gates and fell upon us. A nasty leer curled his lips as he recognized us.

"I come to claim my bride," he cried, in a voice that reached us easily, "and to balance my account with you, at last," and he pointed a finger at me.

In his right hand he held a large, cylindrical object, and as he ceased speaking he hurled it at the gates precisely as a baseball pitcher pitches a swift ball.

The missile struck squarely at the bottom of the gates. There was a terrific explosion, and the great stone portals crumbled, shattered into a thousand fragments. The last defense of the Empress of Laythe had fallen, and with it there went down in bloody death at least half the remaining members of her loyal guard.

Instantly the Kalkars rushed forward, hurling hand grenades among the survivors of the guard.

Nah-ee-lah turned toward me and put her arms about my neck.

"Kiss me once more, Julian," she said, "and then the dagger."

"Never, never, Nah-ee-lah!" I cried. "I cannot do it."

"But I can!" she exclaimed, and drew her own from its sheath at her hip.

I seized her wrist. "Not that, Nah-ee-lah!" I cried. "There must be some other way." And then there came to me a mad inspiration. "The wings!" I cried. "Where are they kept? The last of your people have been destroyed. Duty no longer holds you here. Let us escape, even if it is only to frustrate Orthis' plans and deny him the satisfaction of witnessing our death."

"But, where can we go?" she asked.

"We may at least choose our own manner of death," I replied, "far from Laythe and far from the eyes of an enemy who would gloat over our undoing."

"You are right, Julian. We still have a little time, for I doubt if Orthis or his Kalkars can quickly find the stairway leading to this terrace." And then she led me quickly to one of the many towers that rise above the palace. Entering it, we ascended a spiral staircase to a large chamber at the summit of the tower. Here were kept the imperial wings. I fastened Nah-ee-lah's to her and she helped me with mine, and then from the pinnacle of the tower we arose above the burning city of Laythe and flew rapidly toward the distant lowlands and the sea. It was in my mind to search out, if possible, the location of *The Barsoom,* for I still entertained the mad hope that my companions yet lived—if I did, why not they?

The heat above the city was almost unendurable and the smoke suffocating, yet we passed through it, so that almost immediately we were hidden from the view of that portion of the palace from which we had arisen, with the result that when Orthis and his Kalkars finally found their way to the upper terrace, as I have no doubt they did, we had disappeared—whither they could not know.

We flew and drifted with the wind across the mountainous country toward the plains and the sea, it being my intention upon reaching the latter to follow the coast line until I came to a river marked by an island at its mouth. From that point I knew that I could reach the spot where *The Barsoom* had landed.

Our long flight must have covered a considerable period of time, since it was necessary for us to alight and rest many times and to search for food. We met, fortunately, with no mishaps, and upon the several occasions when we were discovered by roving bands of Va-gas we were able to soar far aloft and escape them easily. We came at length, however, to the sea, the coast of which I followed to the left, but though we passed the mouths of many rivers, I discovered none that precisely answered the description of that which I sought.

It was borne in upon me at last that our quest was futile, but where we were to find a haven of safety neither of us could guess. The gas in our bags was losing its buoyancy and we had no means wherewith to replenish it. It would still maintain us for a short time, but how long neither of us knew, other than that it had not nearly the buoyancy that it originally possessed.

Off the coast we had seen islands almost continuously and I suggested to Nah-ee-lah that we try to discover one upon which grew the fruits and nuts and vegetables necessary for our subsistence, and where we might also have a constant supply of fresh water.

I discovered that Nah-ee-lah knew little about these islands, practically nothing in fact, not even as to whether they were inhabited; but we determined to explore one, and to this end we selected an island of considerable extent that lay about ten miles off shore. We reached it without difficulty and circled slowly above it, scrutinizing its entire area carefully. About half of it was quite hilly, but the balance was rolling and comparatively level. We discovered three streams and two small lakes upon it, and an almost riotous profusion of vegetable growth, but nowhere did we discern the slightest indication that it was inhabited. And so at last, feeling secure, we made our landing upon the plain, close to the beach.

It was a beautiful spot, a veritable Garden of Eden, where we two might have passed the remainder of our lives in peace and security, for though we later explored it carefully, we found not the slightest evidence that it had ever known the foot of man.

Together we built a snug shelter agast the storms. Together we hunted for food, and during our long periods of idleness we lay upon the soft sward beside the beach, and to pass the time away, I taught Nah-ee-lah my own language.

It was a lazy, indolent, happy life that we spent upon this enchanted isle, and yet, though we were happy in our love, each of us felt the futility of our existence, where our lives must be spent in useless idleness.

We had, however, given up definitely hope for any other form of existence. And thus we were lying one time, as was our wont after eating, stretched in luxurious ease upon our backs on the soft lunar grasses, I with my eyes closed, when Nah-ee-lah suddenly grasped me by the arm.

"Julian," she cried, "what is it? Look!"

I opened my eyes, to find her sitting up and gazing into the sky toward the mainland, a slim forefinger indicating the direction of the object that had attracted her attention and aroused her surprised interest.

As my eyes rested upon the thing her pointing finger indicated, I leaped to my feet with an exclamation of incredulity, for there, sailing parallel with the coast at an altitude of not more than a thousand feet, was a ship, the lines of which I knew as I had known my mother's face. It was *The Barsoom*.

Grasping Nah-ee-lah by the arm, I dragged her to her feet. "Come, quick, Nah-ee-lah!" I cried, and urged her rapidly toward our hut, where we had stored the wings and the gas bags which we had never thought to use again, yet protected carefully, though why we knew not.

There was still gas in the bags—enough to support us in the air; with the assistance of our wings, but to fly thus for long distances would have been most fatiguing, and there was even a question as to whether we could cross the ten miles of sea that lay between us and the mainland; yet I was determined to attempt it. Hastily we donned the wings and bags, and rising together, flapped slowly in the direction of the mainland.

*The Barsoom* was cruising slowly along a line that would cross ours before we could reach the shore, but I hoped that they would sight us and investigate.

We flew as rapidly as I dared, for I could take no chances upon exhausting Nah-ee-lah, knowing that it would be absolutely impossible for me to support her weight and my own, with our depleted gas bags. There was no way in which I could signal to *The Barsoom*. We must simply fly toward her. That was the best that we could do, and finally, try though we would, I realized that we should be too late to intercept her and that unless they saw us and changed their course, we should not come close enough to hail them. To see my friends passing so near, and yet to be unable to apprise them of my presence filled me with melancholy. Not one of the many vicissitudes and dangers through which I had passed since I left Earth depressed me more than the sight of *The Barsoom* forging slowly past us without speaking. I saw her change her course then and move inland still further from us, and I could not but dwell upon our unhappy condition, since now we might never again be able to reach the safety of our island, there being even a question as to whether the gas bags would support us to the mainland.

They did, however, and there we alighted and rested, while *The Barsoom* sailed out of sight toward the mountains.

"I shall not give it up, Nah-ee-lah," I cried. "I am going to follow *The Barsoom* until we find it, or until we die in the attempt. I doubt if we ever can reach the island again, but we can make short flights here on land, and by so doing, we may overtake my ship and my companions."

After resting for a short time, we arose again, and when we were above the trees I saw *The Barsoom* far in the distance, and again it was circling, this time toward the left, so we altered our course and flew after it. But presently we realized that it was making a great circle and hope renewed within our breasts, giving us the strength to fly on and on, though we were forced to come down often for brief rests. As we neared the ship we saw that the circles were growing smaller, but it was not until we were within about three miles of her that I realized that she was circling the mouth of a great crater, the walls of which rose several hundred feet above the surrounding country. We had been forced to land again to rest, when there flashed upon my mind a sudden realization of the purpose of the maneuvers of *The Barsoom*—she was investigating the crater, preparatory to an attempt to pass through it into outer space and seek to return to Earth again.

As this thought impinged upon my brain, a wave of almost hopeless horror overwhelmed me as I thought of being definitely left forever by my companions and that by but a few brief minutes Nah-ee-lah was to be robbed of life and happiness and peace, for at that instant the hull of *The Barsoom* dropped beneath the rim of the crater and disappeared from our view.

Rising quickly with Nah-ee-lah, I flew as rapidly as my tired muscles and exhausted gas bag would permit toward the rim of the crater. In my heart of hearts I knew that I should be too late, for once they had decided to make the attempt, the ship would drop like a plummet into the depths, and by the time I reached the mouth of the abyss it would be lost to my view forever.

And yet I struggled on, my lungs almost bursting from the exertion of my mad efforts toward speed. Nah-ee-lah trailed far behind, for if either of us could reach *The Barsoom* in time we should both be saved, and I could fly faster than Nah-ee-lah; otherwise, I should never have separated myself from her by so much as a hundred yards.

Though my lungs were pumping like bellows, I venture to say that my heart stood still for several seconds before I topped the crater's rim.

At the same instant that I expected the last vestige of my hopes to be dashed to pieces irrevocably and forever, I crossed the rim and beheld *The Barsoom* not twenty feet below me, just over the edge of the abyss, and upon her deck stood West and Jay and Norton.

As I came into view directly above them, West whipped out his revolver and leveled it at me, but the instant that his finger pressed the trigger Norton sprang forward and struck his hand aside.

"My God, sir!" I heard the boy cry, "it is the Captain." And then they all recognized me, and an instant later I almost collapsed as I fell to the deck of my beloved ship.

My first thought was of Nah-ee-lah, and at my direction *The Barsoom* rose swiftly and moved to meet her.

"Great Scott!" cried my guest, leaping to his feet and looking out of the stateroom window, "I had no idea that I had kept you up all night. Here we are in Paris already."

"But the rest of your story," I cried. "You have not finished it, I know. Last night, as you were watching them celebrating in the Blue Room, you made a remark which led me to believe that some terrible calamity threatened the world."

"It does," he said, "and that was what I meant to tell you about, but this story of the third incarnation of which I am conscious was necessary to an understanding of how the great catastrophe overwhelmed the people of the earth."

"But, did you reach Earth again?" I demanded.

"Yes," he said, "in the year 2036. I had been ten years within Va-nah, but did not know whether it was ten months or a century until we landed upon Earth."

He smiled then. "You notice that I still say I. It is sometimes difficult for me to recall which incarnation I am in Perhaps it will be clearer to you if I say Julian 5th returned to Earth in 2036, and in. the same year his son, Julian 6th, was born to his wife, Nah-ee-lah the Moon Maid."

"But how could he return to Earth in the disabled *Barsoom?*"

"Ah," he said, "that raises a point that was of great interest to Julian 5th. After he regained *The Barsoom,* naturally one of the first questions he asked was as to the condition of the ship and their intentions, and when he learned that they had, in reality, been intending to pass through the crater toward the Earth he questioned them further and discovered that it was the young ensign, Norton, who had repaired the engine, having been able to do it by information that he had gleaned from Orthis, after winning the latter's friendship. Thus was explained the intimacy between the two, which Julian 5th had so deplored, but which he now saw that young Norton had encouraged for a patriotic purpose."

"We are docked now and I must be going. Thank you for your hospitality and for your generous interest," and he held out his hand toward me.

"But the story of Julian 9th," I insisted, "am I never to hear that?"

"If we meet again, yes," he promised, with a smile.

"I shall hold you to it," I told him.

"If we meet again," he repeated, and departed, closing the stateroom door after him.

PART II

The Moon Men

*Being the Story of Julian 9th*

# The Conquest

I T WAS EARLY in March, 1969, that I set out from my bleak camp on the desolate shore some fifty miles southeast of Herschel Island after polar bear. I had come into the Arctic the year before to enjoy the first real vacation that I had ever had. The definite close of the Great War, in April two years before, had left an exhausted world at peace—a condition that had never before existed and with which we did not know how to cope.

I think that we all felt lost without war—I know that I did; but I managed to keep pretty busy with the changes that peace brought to my bureau, the Bureau of Communications, readjusting its activities to the necessities of world trade uninfluenced by war. During my entire official life I had had to combine the two—communications for war and communications for commerce, so the adjustment was really not a Herculean task. It took a little time, that was all, and after it was a fairly well accomplished fact I asked for an indefinite leave, which was granted.

My companions of the hunt were three Eskimos, the youngest of whom, a boy of nineteen, had never before seen a white man, so absolutely had the last twenty years of the Great War annihilated the meager trade that had formerly been carried on between their scattered settlements and the more favored lands of so-called civilization.

But this is not a story of my thrilling experiences in the rediscovery of the Arctic regions. It is, rather, merely in way of explanation as to how I came to meet him again after a lapse of some two years.

We had ventured some little distance from shore when I, who was in the lead, sighted a bear far ahead. I had scaled a hummock of rough and jagged ice when I made the discovery and, motioning to my companion to follow me, I slid and stumbled to the comparatively level stretch of a broad floe beyond, across which I ran toward another icy barrier that shut off my view of the bear. As I reached it I turned to look back for my companions, but they were not yet in sight. As a matter of fact I never saw them again.

The whole mass of ice was in movement, grinding and cracking; but I was so accustomed to this that I gave the matter little heed until I had reached the summit of the second ridge, from which I had another view of the bear which I could see was moving directly toward me, though still at a considerable distance. Then I looked back again for my fellows. They were no where in sight, but I saw something else that filled me with consternation—the floe had split directly at the first hummock and I was now separated from the mainland by an ever widening lane of icy water. What became of the three Eskimos I never knew, unless the floe parted directly beneath their feet and engulfed them. It scarcely seems credible to me, even with my limited experience in the Arctics, but if it was not that which snatched them forever from my sight, what was it?

I now turned my attention once more to the bear. He had evidently seen me and assumed that I was prey for he was coming straight toward me at a rather rapid gait. The ominous cracking and groaning of the ice increased, and to my dismay I saw that it was rapidly breaking up all about me and as far as I could see in all directions great floes and little floes were rising and falling as upon the bosom of a long, rolling swell.

Presently a lane of water opened between the bear and me, but the great fellow never paused. Slipping into the water he swam the gap and clambered out upon the huge floe upon which I tossed. He was over two hundred yards away, but I covered his left shoulder with the top of my sight and fired. I hit him and he let out an awful roar and came for me on a run. Just as I was about to fire again the floe split once more directly in front of him and he went into the water clear out of sight for a moment.

When he reappeared I fired again and missed. Then he started to crawl out on my diminished floe once more. Again I fired. This time I broke his shoulder, yet still he managed to clamber onto my floe and advance toward me. I thought that he- would never die until he had reached me and wreaked his vengeance upon me, for though I pumped bullet after bullet into him he continued to advance, though at last he barely dragged himself forward, growling and grimacing horribly. He wasn't ten feet from me when once more my floe split directly between me and the bear and at the foot of the ridge upon which I stood, which now turned completely over, precipitating me into the water a few feet from the great, growling beast. I turned and tried to scramble back onto the floe from which I had been thrown, but its sides were far too precipitous and there was no other that I could possibly reach, except that upon which the bear lay grimacing at me. I had clung to my rifle and without more ado I struck out for a side of the floe a few yards from the spot where the beast lay apparently waiting for me.

He never moved while I scrambled up on it, except to turn his head so that he was always glaring at me. He did not come toward me and I determined not to fire at him again until he did, for I had discovered that my bullets seemed only to infuriate him. The art of big game hunting had been practically dead for years as only rifles and ammunition for the killing of men had been manufactured. Being in the government service I had found no difficulty in obtaining a permit to bear arms for hunting purposes, but the government owned all the firearms and when they came to issue me what I required, there was nothing to be had but the ordinary service rifle as perfected at the time of the close of the Great War, in 1967. It was a great man-killer, but it was not heavy enough for big game.

The water lanes about us were now opening up at an appalling rate, and there was a decided movement of the ice toward the open sea, and there I was alone, soaked to the skin, in a temperature around zero, bobbing about in the Arctic Ocean marooned on a half acre of ice, with a wounded and infuriated polar bear, which appeared to me at this close range to be about the size of the First Presbyterian church at home.

I don't know how long it was after that that I lost consciousness. When I opened my eyes again I found myself in a nice, white iron cot in the sick bay of a cruiser of the newly formed International Peace Fleet which patroled and policed the world. A hospital steward and a medical officer were standing at one side of my cot looking down at me, while at the foot was a fine looking man in the uniform of an admiral. I recognized him at once.

"Ah," I said, in what could have been little more than a whisper, "you have come to tell me the story of Julian 9th. You promised, you know, and I shall hold you to it."

He smiled. "You have a good memory. When you are out of this I'll keep my promise."

I lapsed immediately into unconsciousness again, they told me afterward, but the next morning I awoke refreshed and except for having been slightly frosted about the nose and cheeks, none the worse for my experience. That evening I was seated in the admiral's cabin, a Scotch highball, the principal ingredients of which were made in Kansas, at my elbow, and the admiral opposite me.

"It was certainly a fortuitous circumstance for me that you chanced to be cruising about over the Arctic just when you were," I had remarked.

"Captain Drake tells me that when the lookout sighted me the bear was crawling toward me; but that when you finally dropped low enough to land a man on the floe the beast was dead less than a foot from me. It was a close shave, and I am mighty thankful to you and to the cause, whatever it may have been, that brought you to the spot."

"That is the first thing that I must speak to you about," he replied. "I was searching for you. Washington knew, of course, about where you expected to camp, for you had explained your plans quite in detail to your secretary before you left, and so when the President wanted you I was dispatched immediately to find you. In fact, I requested the assignment when I received instructions to dispatch a ship, in search of you. In the first place I wished to renew our acquaintance and also to cruise to this part of the world, where I had never before chanced to be."

"The President wanted me!" I repeated.

"Yes, Secretary of Commerce White died on the fifteenth and the President desires that you accept the portfolio."

"Interesting, indeed," I replied; "but not half so interesting as the story of Julian 9th, I am sure."

He laughed good naturedly. "Very well," he exclaimed; "here goes!"

Let me preface this story, as I did the other that I told you on board the liner Harding two years ago, with the urgent request that you attempt to keep constantly in mind the theory that there is no such thing as time— that there is no past and no future—that there is only *now*, there never has been anything but *now* and there never will be anything but *now*. It is a theory analogous to that which stipulates that there is no such thing as space. There may be those who think that they understand it, but I am not one of them. I simply know what I know—I do not try to account for it. As easily as I recall events in this incarnation do I recall events in previous incarnations; but, far more remarkable, similarly do I recall, or should I say *foresee?* events in incarnations of the future. No, I do not foresee them—I have lived them.

I have told you of the attempt made to reach Mars in *The Barsoom* and of how it was thwarted by Lieutenant-Commander Orthis. That was in the year 2026. You will recall that Orthis, through hatred and jealousy of Julian 5th, wrecked the engines of *The Barsoom* necessitating a landing upon the Moon, and of how the ship was drawn into the mouth of a great lunar crater and through the crust of our satellite to the world within.

After being captured by the Va-gas, human quadrupeds of the moon's interior, Julian 5th escaped with Nah-ee-lah, Princess of Laythe, daughter of a race of lunar mortals similar to ourselves, while Orthis made friends of the Kalkars, or Thinkers, another lunar human race. Orthis taught the Kalkars, who were enemies of the people of Laythe, to manufacture gunpowder, shells and cannon, and with these attacked and destroyed Laythe.

Julian 5th and Nah-ee-lah, the Moon Maid, escaped from the burning city and later were picked up by *The Barsoom* which had been repaired by Norton, a young ensign, who with two other officers had remained aboard. Ten years after they had landed upon the inner surface of the Moon Julian 5th and his companions brought *The Barsoom* to dock safely at the city of Washington, leaving Lieutenant-Commander Orthis in the Moon.

Julian 5th and the Princess Nah-ee-lah were married and in that same year, 2036, a son was born to them and was called Julian 6th. He was the great-grandfather of Julian 9th for whose story you have asked me, and in whom I lived again in the twenty-second century.

For some reason no further attempts were made to reach Mars, with whom we had been in radio communication for seventy years. Possibly it was due to the rise of a religious cult which preached against all forms of scientific progress and which by political pressure was able to mold and influence several successive weak administrations of a notoriously weak party that had had its origin nearly a century before in a group of peace-at-any-price men.

It was they who advocated the total disarmament of the world, which would have meant disbanding the International Peace Fleet forces, the scrapping of all arms and ammunition, and the destruction of the few munition plants operated by the governments of the United States and Great Britain, who now jointly ruled the world. It was England's king who saved us from the full disaster of this mad policy, though the weaklings of this country aided and abetted by the weaklings of Great Britain succeeded in cutting the peace fleet in two, one half of it being turned over to the merchant marine, in reducing the number of munition factories and in scrapping half the armament of the world.

And then in the year 2050 the blow fell. Lieutenant-Commander Orthis, after twenty-four years upon the Moon, returned to earth with one hundred thousand Kalkars and a thousand Va-gas. In a thousand great ships they came bearing arms and ammunition and strange, new engines of destruction fashioned by the brilliant mind of the arch villain of the universe.

No one but Orthis could have done it. No one but Orthis would have done it. It had been he who had perfected the engines that had made *The*

*Barsoom* possible. After he had become the dominant force among the Kalkars of the Moon he had aroused their imaginations with tales of the great, rich world lying ready and unarmed within easy striking distance of them. It had been an easy thing to enlist their labor in the building of the ships and the manufacture of the countless accessories necessary to the successful accomplishment of the great adventure.

The Moon furnished all the needed materials, the Kalkars furnished the labor and Orthis the knowledge, the brains and the leadership. Ten years had been devoted to the spreading of his propaganda and the winning over of The Thinkers, and then fourteen years were required to build and outfit the fleet.

Five days before they arrived astronomers detected the fleet as minute specks upon the eyepieces of their telescopes. There was much speculation, but it was Julian 5th alone who guessed the truth. He warned the governments at London and Washington, but though he was then in command of the International Peace Fleet his appeals were treated with levity and ridicule. He knew Orthis and so he knew that it was easily within the man's ability to construct a fleet, and he also knew that only for one purpose would Orthis return to Earth with so great a number of ships. It meant war, and the Earth had nothing but a handful of cruisers wherewith to defend herself—there were not available in the world twenty-five thousand organized fighting men, nor equipment for more than half again that number.

The inevitable occurred. Orthis seized London and Washington simultaneously. His well-armed forces met with practically no resistance. There could be no resistance for there was nothing wherewith to resist. It was a criminal offense to possess firearms. Even edged weapons with blades over six inches long were barred by law. Military training, except for the chosen few of the International Peace Fleet, had been banned for years. And against this pitiable state of disarmament and unpreparedness was brought a force of a hundred thousand well armed, seasoned warriors with engines of destruction that were unknown to Earth Men. A description of one alone will suffice to explain the utter hopelessness of the cause of the Earth Men.

This instrument, of which the invaders brought but one, was mounted upon the deck of their flag ship and operated by Orthis in person. It was an invention of his own which no Kalkar understood or could operate. Briefly, it was a device for the generation of radio-activity at any desired vibratory rate and for the directing of the resultant emanations upon any given object within its effective range. We do not know what Orthis called it, but the Earth Men of that day knew it was an electronic rifle.

The Invasion of the Earth

It was quite evidently a recent invention and, therefore, in some respects crude, but be that as it may its effects were sufficiently deadly to permit Orthis to practically wipe out the entire International Peace Fleet in less than thirty days as rapidly as the various ships came within range of the electronic rifle. To the layman the visual effects induced by this weird weapon were appalling and nerve shattering. A mighty cruiser vibrant with life and power might fly majestically to engage the flagship of the Kalkars, when as by magic every aluminum part of the cruiser would vanish as mist before the sun, and as nearly ninety per cent of a Peace Fleet cruiser, including the hull, was constructed of aluminum, the result may be imagined—one moment there was a great ship forging through the air, her flags and pennants flying in the wind, her band playing, her officers and men at their quarters; the next a mass of engines, polished wood, cordage, flags and human beings hurtling earthward to extinction.

It was Julian 5th who discovered the secret of this deadly weapon and that it accomplished its destruction by projecting upon the ships of the Peace Fleet the vibratory rate of radio-activity identical with that of aluminum, with the result that, thus excited, the electrons of the attacked substance increased their own vibratory rate to a point that they became dissipated again into their elemental and invisible state—in other words aluminum was transmuted into something else that was as invisible and intangible as ether. Perhaps it was ether.

Assured of the correctness of his theory, Julian 5th withdrew in his own flagship to a remote part of the world, taking with him the few remaining cruisers of the Fleet. Orthis searched for them for months, but it was not until the close of the year 2050 that the two fleets met again and for the last time. Julian 5th had, by this time, perfected the plan for which he had gone into hiding, and he now faced the Kalkar fleet and his old enemy, Orthis, with some assurance of success. His flagship moved at the head of the short column that contained the remaining hope of a world and Julian 5th stood upon her deck beside a small and innocent looking box mounted upon a stout tripod.

Orthis moved to meet him—he would destroy the ships one by one as he approached them. He gloated at the easy victory that lay before him. He directed the electronic rifle at the flagship of his enemy and touched a button. Suddenly his brows knitted. What was this? He examined the rifle. He held a piece of aluminum before its muzzle and saw the metal disappear. The mechanism was operating, but the ships of the enemy did not disappear. Then he guessed the truth, for his own ship was now but a short distance from that of Julian 5th and he could see that the hull of the latter was entirely coated with a grayish substance that he sensed at once for what it was—an insulating material that rendered the aluminum parts of the enemy's fleet immune from the invisible fire of his rifle.

Orthis's scowl changed to a grim smile. He turned two dials upon a control box connected with the weapon and again pressed the button. Instantly the bronze propellers of the Earth Man's flagship vanished in thin air together with numerous fittings and parts above decks. Similarly went the exposed bronze parts of the balance of the International Peace Fleet, leaving a squadron of drifting derelicts at the mercy of the foe.

Julian 5th's flagship was at that time but a few fathoms from that of Orthis. The two men could plainly see each other's features. Orthis's expression was savage and gloating, that of Julian 5th sober and dignified.

"You thought to beat me, then!" jeered Orthis. "God, but I have waited and labored and sweated for this day. I have wrecked a world to best you, Julian 5th. To best you and to kill you, but to let you know first that I am going to kill you—to kill you in such a way as man was never before killed, as no other brain than mine could conceive of killing. You insulated your aluminum parts thinking thus to thwart me, but you did not know—your feeble intellect could not know—that as easily as I destroyed aluminum I can, by the simplest of adjustments, attune this weapon to destroy any one of a hundred different substances and among them human flesh or human bone.

"That is what I am going to do now, Julian 5th. First I am going to dissipate the bony structure of your frame. It will be done painlessly—it may not even result in instant death, and I am hoping that it will not. For I want you to know the power of a real intellect—the intellect from which you stole the fruits of its efforts for a lifetime; but not again, Julian 5th, for today you die—first your bones, then your flesh, and after you, your men and after them your spawn, the son that the woman I loved bore you; but she—she shall belong to me! Take that memory to hell with you!" and he turned toward the dials beside his lethal weapon.

But Julian 5th placed a hand upon the little box resting upon the strong tripod before him, and he, it was, who touched a button before Orthis had touched his. Instantly the electronic rifle vanished beneath the very eyes of Orthis and at the same time the two ships touched and Julian 5th had leaped the rail to the enemy deck and was running toward his arch enemy.

Orthis stood gazing, horrified, at the spot where the greatest invention of his giant intellect had stood but an instant before, and then he looked up at Julian 5th approaching him and cried out horribly.

"Stop!" he screamed. "Always all our lives you have robbed me of the fruits of my efforts. Somehow you have stolen the secret of this, my greatest invention, and now you have destroyed it. May God in Heaven—"

"Yes," cried Julian 5th, "and I am going to destroy you, unless you surrender to me with all your force."

"Never!" almost screamed the man, who seemed veritably demented, so hideous was his rage. "Never! This is the end, Julian 5th, for both of us," and even as he uttered the last word he threw a lever mounted upon a controlboard before him. There was a terrific explosion and both ships, bursting into flame, plunged meteorlike into the ocean beneath.

Thus went Julian 5th and Orthis to their deaths, carrying with them the secret of the terrible destructive force that the latter had brought with him from the Moon; but the Earth was already undone. It lay helpless before its conquerors. What the outcome might have been had Orthis lived may only remain conjecture. Possibly he would have brought order out of the chaos he had created and instituted a reign of reason. Earth Men would at least have had the advantage of his wonderful intellect and his power to rule the ignorant Kalkars that he had transported from the Moon.

There might even have been some hope had the Earth Men banded together against the common enemy, but this they did not do. Elements who had been discontented with this or that phase of government joined issues with the invaders. The lazy, the inefficient, the defective, who ever place the blame for their failures upon the shoulders of the successful, swarmed to the banners of the Kalkars, in whom they sensed kindred souls.

Political factions, labor and capital each saw, or thought they saw, an opportunity for advantage to themselves in one way or another that was inimical to the interests of the others. The Kalkar fleets returned to the moon for more Kalkars until it was estimated that seven millions of them were being transported to Earth each year.

Julian 6th, with Nah-ee-lah, his Moon Maid mother, lived, as did Or-tis, the son of Orthis and a Kalkar woman, but my story is not to be of them, but of Julian 9th, who was born just a century after the birth of Julian 5th.

Julian 9th will tell his own story.

# ONE

# The Flag

I WAS BORN in the teivos of Chicago on January 1, 2100, to Julian 8th and Elizabeth James. My father and mother were not married as marriages had long since become illegal. I was called Julian 9th. My parents were of the rapidly diminishing intellectual class and could both read and write. This learning they imparted to me, although it was very useless learning—it was their religion. Printing was a lost art and the last of the public libraries had been destroyed almost a hundred years before I reached maturity, so there was little or nothing to read, while to have a book in one's possession was to brand one as of the hated intellectuals, arousing the scorn and derision of the Kalkar rabble and the suspicion and persecution of the lunar authorities who ruled us.

The first twenty years of my life were uneventful. As a boy I played among the crumbling ruins of what must once have been a magnificent city. Pillaged, looted and burned half a hundred times Chicago still reared the skeletons of some mighty edifices above the ashes of her former greatness. As a youth I regretted the departed romance of the long gone days of my forefathers when the Earth Men still retained sufficient strength to battle for existence. I deplored the quiet stagnation of my own time with only an occasional murder to break the monotony of our bleak existence. Even the Kalkar Guard stationed on the shore of the great lake seldom harassed us, unless there came an urgent call from higher authorities for an additional tax collection, for we fed them well and they had the pick of our women and young girls—almost, but not quite as you shall see.

The commander of the guard had been stationed here for years and we considered ourselves very fortunate in that he was too lazy and indolent to be cruel or oppressive. His tax collectors were always with us on market days; but they did not exact so much that we had nothing left for ourselves as refugees from Milwaukee told us was the case there.

I recall one poor devil from Milwaukee who staggered into our market place of a Saturday. He was nothing more than a bag of bones and he told us that fully ten thousand people had died of starvation the preceding month in his teivos. The word teivos is applied impartially to a district and to the administrative body that misadministers its affairs. No one knows what the word really means, though my mother has told me that her grandfather said that it came from another world, the moon, like Kash Guard, which also means nothing in particular—one soldier is a Kash Guard, ten thousand soldiers are a Kash Guard. If a man comes with a piece of paper upon which something is written that you are not supposed to be able to read and kills your grandmother or carries off your sister you say: "The Kash Guard did it."

That was one of the many inconsistencies of our form of government that aroused my indignation even in youth—I refer to the fact that The TwentyFour issued written proclamations and commands to a people it did not allow to learn to read and write, I said, I believe, that printing was a lost art. This is not quite true except as it refers to the mass of the people, for The TwentyFour still maintained a printing department, where it issued money and manifestos. The money was used in lieu of taxation— that is when we had been so over-burdened by taxation that murmurings were heard even among the Kalkar class the authorities would send agents among us to buy our wares, paying us with money that had no value and which we could not use except to kindle our fires.

Taxes could not be paid in money as The TwentyFour would only accept gold and silver, or produce and manufactures, and as all the gold and silver had disappeared from circulation while my father was in his teens we had to pay with what we raised or manufactured.

Three Saturdays a month the tax collectors were in the market places appraising our wares and on the last Saturday they collected one per cent of all we had bought or sold during the month. Nothing had any fixed value—today you might haggle half an hour in trading a pint of beans for a goat skin and next week if you wanted beans the chances were more than excellent that you would have to give four or five goat skins for a pint, and the tax collectors took advantage of that—they appraised on the basis of the highest market values for the month.

My father had a few long haired goats—they were called Montana goats, but he said they really were Angoras, and Mother used to make cloth from their fleece. With the cloth, the milk and the flesh from our goats we lived very well, having also a small vegetable garden beside our house; but there were some necessities that we must purchase in the market place.

It was against the law to barter in private, as the tax collectors would then have known nothing about a man's income. Well, one winter my mother was ill and we were in sore need of coal to heat the room in which she lay, so Father went to the commander of the Kash Guard and asked permission to purchase some coal before market day. A soldier was sent with him to Hoffmeyer, the agent of the Kalkar, Pthav, who had the coal concession for our district—the Kalkars have everything—and when Hoffmeyer discovered how badly we needed coal he said that for five milk goats father could have half his weight in coal.

My father protested, but it was of no avail and as he knew how badly my mother needed heat he took the five goats to Hoffmeyer and brought back the coal. On the following market day he paid one goat for a sack of beans equal to his weight and when the tax collector came for his tithe he said to Father: "You paid five goats for half your weight in beans, and as everyone knows that beans are worth twenty times as much as coal, the coal you bought must be worth one hundred goats by now, and as beans are worth twenty times as much as coal and you have twice as much beans as coal your beans are now worth two hundred goats, which makes your trades for this month amount to three hundred goats. Bring me, therefore, three of your best goats."

He was a new tax collector—the old one would not have done such a thing; but it was about that time that everything began to change. Father said he would not have thought that things could be much worse; but he found out differently later. The change commenced in 2117, right after Jarth became Jemadar of the United Teivos of America. Of course, it did not all happen at once. Washington is a long way from Chicago and there is no continuous railroad between them. The TwentyFour keeps up a few disconnected lines; but it is hard to operate them as there are no longer any trained mechanics to maintain them. It never takes less than a week to travel from Washington to Gary, the western terminus.

Father said that most of the railways were destroyed during the wars after the Kalkars overran the country and that as workmen were then permitted to labor only four hours a day, when they felt like it, and even then most of them were busy making new laws so much of the time that they had no chance to work, there was not enough labor to operate or maintain the roads that were left, but that was not the worst of it. Practically all the men who understood the technical details of operation and maintenance, of engineering and mechanics belonged to the more intelligent class of Earth Men and were, consequently, immediately thrown out of employment and later killed.

For seventy-five years there had been no new locomotives built and but few repairs made on those in existence. The TwentyFour had sought to delay the inevitable by operating a few trains only for their own require-ments—for government officials and troops; but it could now be but a question of a short time before railroad operation must cease—forever. It didn't mean much to me as I had never ridden on a train—never even seen one, in fact, other than the rusted remnants, twisted and tortured by fire, that lay scattered about various localities of our city; but Father and Mother considered it a calamity—the passing of the last link between the old civilization and the new barbarism.

Airships, automobiles, steamships, and even the telephone had gone before their time; but they had heard their fathers tell of these and other wonders. The telegraph was still in operation, though the service was poor and there were only a few lines between Chicago and the Atlantic seaboard. To the west of us was neither railroad nor telegraph. I saw a man when I was about ten years old who had come on horseback from a teivos in Missouri. He started out with forty others to get in touch with the east and learn what had transpired there in the past fifty years; but between bandits and Kash Guards all had been killed but himself during the long and adventurous journey.

I shall never forget how I hung about picking up every scrap of the exciting narrative that fell from his lips nor how my imagination worked overtime for many weeks thereafter as I tried to picture myself the hero of similar adventures in the mysterious and unknown west. He told us that conditions were pretty bad in all the country he had passed through; but that in the agricultural districts living was easier because the Kash Guard came less often and the people could gain a fair living from the land. He thought our conditions were worse than those in Missouri and he would not remain, preferring to face the dangers of the return trip rather than live so comparatively close to the seat of The TwentyFour.

Father was very angry when he came home from market after the new tax collector had levied a tax of three goats on him. Mother was up again and the cold snap had departed leaving the mildness of spring in the late March air. The ice had gone off the river on the banks of which we lived and I was already looking forward to my first swim of the year. The goat skins were drawn back from the windows of our little home and the fresh, sun-laden air was blowing through our three rooms.

"Bad times are coming, Elizabeth," said Father, after he had told her of the injustice. "They have been bad enough in the past; but now that the swine have put the king of swine in as Jemadar—"

"S-s-sh!" cautioned my mother, nodding her head toward the open window.

Father remained silent, listening. We heard footsteps passing around the house toward the front and a moment later the form of a man darkened the door. Father breathed a sigh of relief.

"Ah!" he exclaimed, "it is only our good brother Johansen. Come in, Brother Peter and tell us the news."

"And there is news enough," exclaimed the visitor. "The old commandant has been replaced by a new one, a fellow by the name of Or-tis—one of Jarth's cronies. What do you think of that?"

Brother Peter was standing between Father and Mother with his back toward the latter, so he did not see Mother place her finger quickly to her lips in a sign to Father to guard his speech. I saw a slight frown cross my father's brow, as though he resented my mother's warning; but when he spoke his words were such as those of our class have learned through suffering are the safest.

"It is not for me to think," he said, "or to question in any way what The TwentyFour does."

"Nor for me," spoke Johansen quickly; "but among friends—a man cannot help but think and sometimes it is good to speak your mind—eh?"

Father shrugged his shoulders and turned away. I could see that he was boiling over with a desire to unburden himself of some of his loathing for the degraded beasts that Fate had placed in power nearly a century before. His childhood had still been close enough to the glorious past of his country's proudest days to have been impressed through the tales of his elders with a poignant realization of all that had been lost and of how it had been lost. This he and Mother had tried to impart to me as others of the dying intellectuals attempted to nurse the spark of a waning culture in the breasts of their offspring against that always hoped for, yet seemingly hopeless, day when the world should start to emerge from the slough of slime and ignorance into which the cruelties of the Kalkars had dragged it.

"Now, Brother Peter," said Father, at last, "I must go and take my three goats to the tax collector, or he will charge me another one for a fine." I saw that he tried to speak naturally; but he could not keep the bitterness out of his voice.

Peter pricked up his ears. "Yes," he said, "I had heard of that piece of business. This new tax collector was laughing about it to Hoffmeyer. He thinks it a fine joke and Hoffmeyer says that now that you got the coal for so much less than it was worth he is going before The TwentyFour and ask that you be compelled to pay him the other ninety-five goats that the tax collector says the coal is really worth."

"Oh!" exclaimed Mother, "they would not really do such a wicked thing—I am sure they would not."

Peter shrugged. "Perhaps they only joked," he said; "these Kalkars are great jokers."

"Yes," said Father, "they are great jokers; but some day I shall have my little joke," and he walked out toward the pens where the goats were kept when not on pasture.

Mother looked after him with a troubled light in her eyes and I saw her shoot a quick glance at Peter, who presently followed Father from the house and went his way.

Father and I took the goats to the tax collector. He was a small man with a mass of red hair, a thin nose and two small, close-set eyes. His name was Soor. As soon as he saw father he commenced to fume.

"What is your name, man?" he demanded insolently.

"Julian 8th," replied Father. "Here are the three goats in payment of my income tax for this month—shall I put them in the pen?"

"What did you say your name is?" snapped the fellow.

"Julian 8th," Father repeated.

"Julian 8th!" shouted Soor. "Julian 8th!" I suppose you are too fine a gentleman to be brother to such as me, eh?"

"Brother Julian 8th," said Father sullenly.

"Go put your goats in the pen and hereafter remember that all men are brothers who are good citizens and loyal to our great Jemadar."

When Father had put the goats away we started for home; but as we were passing Soor he shouted: "Well?"

Father turned a questioning look toward him.

"Well?" repeated the man.

"I do not understand," said Father; "have I not done all that the law requires?"

"What's the matter with you pigs out here?" Soor fairly screamed. "Back in the eastern teivos a tax collector doesn't have to starve to death on his miserable pay—his people bring him little presents."

"Very well," said father quietly, "I will bring you something next time I come to market."

"See that you do," snapped Soor.

Father did not speak all the way home, nor did he say a word until after we had finished our dinner of cheese, goat's milk and corn cakes. I was so angry that I could scarce contain myself; but I had been brought up in an atmosphere of repression and terrorism that early taught me to keep a still tongue in my head.

When Father had finished his meal he rose suddenly—so suddenly that his chair flew across the room to the opposite wall—and squaring his shoulders he struck his chest a terrible blow.

"Coward! Dog!" he cried. "My God! I cannot stand it. I shall go mad if I must submit longer to such humiliation. I am no longer a man. There are no men! We are worms that the swine grind into the earth with their polluted hoofs. And I dared say nothing. I stood there while that offspring of generations of menials and servants insulted me and spat upon me and I dared say nothing but meekly to propitiate him. It is disgusting.

"In a few generations they have sapped the manhood from American men. My ancestors fought at Bunker Hill, at Gettysburg, at San Juan, at Chateau Thierry. And I? I bend the knee to every degraded creature that wears the authority of the beasts at Washington—and not one of them is an American—scarce one of them an Earth Man. To the scum of the Moon I bow my head—I who am one of the few survivors of the most powerful people the world ever knew."

"Julian!" cried my mother, "be careful, dear. Some one may be listening." I could see her tremble.

"And you are an American woman!" he growled.

"Julian, don't!" she pleaded. "It is not on my account—you know that it is not—but for you and our boy. I do not care what becomes of me; but I cannot see you torn from us as we have seen others taken from their families, who dared speak their minds."

"I know, dear heart," he said after a brief silence. "I know—it is the way with each of us. I dare not on your account and Julian's, you dare not on ours, and so it goes. Ah, if there were only more of us: If I could but find a thousand men who dared!"

"S-s-sh!" cautioned Mother. "There are so many spies. One never knows. That is why I cautioned you when Brother Peter was here to-day. One never knows."

"You suspect Peter?" asked Father.

"I know nothing," replied Mother; "I am afraid of every one. It is a frightful existence and though I have lived it thus all my life, and my mother before me and her mother before that, I never became hardened to it."

"The American spirit has been bent, but not broken," said Father. "Let us hope that it will never break."

"If we have the hearts to suffer always it will not break," said Mother, "but it is hard, so hard—when one even hates to bring a child into the world," and she glanced at me, "because of the misery and suffering to which it is doomed for life. I yearned for children, always; but I feared to have them—mostly I feared that they might be girls. To be a girl in this world to-day—Oh, it is frightful!"

After supper Father and I went out and milked the goats and saw that the sheds were secured for the night against the dogs. It seems as though they become more numerous and more bold each year. They run in packs where there were only individuals when I was a little boy and it is scarce safe for a grown man to travel an unfrequented locality at night. We are not permitted to have firearms in our possession, nor even bows and arrows, so we cannot exterminate them and they seem to realize our weakness, coming close in among the houses and pens at night.

They were large brutes—fearless and powerful. There is one pack more formidable than the others which Father says appears to carry a strong strain of collie and Airedale blood—the members of this pack are large, cunning and ferocious and are becoming a terror to the city—we call them the hellhounds.

After we returned to the house with the milk Jim Thompson and his woman, Mollie Sheehan, came over. They live up the river about half a mile, on the next farm, and are our best friends. They are the only people that Father and Mother really trust, so when we are all together alone we speak our minds very freely. It seemed strange to me, even as a boy, that such big strong men as Father and Jim should be afraid to express their real views to anyone, and though I was born and reared in an atmosphere of suspicion and terror I could never quite reconcile myself to the attitude of servility and cowardice which marked us all.

And yet I knew that my father was no coward. He was a fine-looking man, too—tall and wonderfully muscled—and I have seen him fight with men and with dogs and once he defended Mother against a Kash Guard and with his bare hands he killed the armed soldier. He lies in the center of the goat pen now, his rifle, bayonet and ammunition wrapped in many thicknesses of oiled cloth beside him. We left no trace and were never even suspected; but we know where there is a rifle, a bayonet and ammunition.

Jim had had trouble with Soor, the new tax collector, too, and was very angry. Jim was a big man and, like Father, was always smooth shaven as were nearly all Americans, as we called those whose people had lived here long before the Great War. The others—the true Kalkars—grew no beards. Their ancestors had come from the Moon many years before. They had come in strange ships year after year, but finally, one by one, their ships had been lost and as none of them knew how to build others or the engines that operated them the time came when no more Kalkars could come from the Moon to Earth.

That was good for us, but it came too late, for the Kalkars already here bred like flies in a shady stable. The pure Kalkars were the worst, but there were millions of half-breeds and they were bad, too, and I think they really hated us pure bred Earth Men worse than the true Kalkars, or Moon Men, did.

Jim was terribly mad. He said that he couldn't stand it much longer—that he would rather be dead than live in such an awful world; but I was accustomed to such talk—I had heard it since infancy. Life was a hard thing—just work, work, work, for a scant existence over and above the income tax. No pleasures—few conveniences or comforts; absolutely no luxuries—and, worst of all, no hope. It was seldom that any one smiled—anyone in our class—and the grown-ups never laughed. As children we laughed—a little; not much. It is hard to kill the spirit of childhood; but the brotherhood of man had almost done it.

"It's your own fault, Jim," said Father. He was always blaming our troubles on Jim, for Jim's people had been American workmen before the Great War—mechanics and skilled artisans in various trades. "Your people never took a stand against the invaders. They flirted with the new theory of brotherhood the Kalkars brought with them from the Moon. They listened to the emissaries of the malcontents and, afterward, when Kalkars sent their disciples among us they 'first endured, then pitied, then embraced.' They had the numbers and the power to combat successfully the wave of insanity that started with the lunar catastrophe and overran the world—they could have kept it out of America; but they didn't—instead they listened to false prophets and placed their great strength in the hands of the corrupt leaders."

"And how about your class?" countered Jim, "too rich and lazy and indifferent even to vote. They tried to grind us down while they waxed fat off of our labor."

"The ancient sophistry!" snapped Father. "There was never a more prosperous or independent class of human beings in the world than the American laboring man of the twentieth century.

"You talk about us! We were the first to fight it—my people fought and bled and died to keep Old Glory above the capitol at Washington; but we were too few and now the Kash flag of the Kalkars floats in its place and for nearly a century it had been a crime punishable by death to have the Stars and Stripes in your possession."

He walked quickly across the room to the fireplace and removed a stone above the rough, wooden mantel. Reaching his hand into the aperture behind he turned toward us.

"But cowed and degraded as I have become," he cried, "thank God I still have a spark of manhood left—I have had the strength to defy them as my fathers defied them—I have kept this that has been handed down to me—kept it for my son to hand down to his son—and I have taught him to die for it as his forefathers died for it and as I would die for it, gladly."

He drew forth a small bundle of fabric and holding the upper corners between the fingers of his two hands he let it unfold before us—an oblong cloth of alternate red and white striped with a blue square in one corner, upon which were sewn many little white stars.

Jim and Mollie and Mother rose to their feet and I saw Mother cast an apprehensive glance toward the doorway. For a moment they stood thus in silence, looking with wide eyes upon the thing that Father held and then Jim walked slowly toward it and, kneeling, took the edge of it in his great, horny fingers and pressed it to his lips and the candle upon the rough table, sputtering in the spring wind that waved the goat skin at the window, cast its feeble rays upon them.

"It is The Flag, my son," said Father to me. "It is Old Glory—the flag of your fathers—the flag that made the world a decent place to live in. It is death to possess it; but when I am gone take it and guard it as our family has guarded it since the regiment that carried it came back from the Argonne."

I felt tears filling my eyes—why, I could not have told them—and I turned away to hide them—turned toward the window and there, beyond the waving goat skin, I saw a face in the outer darkness. I have always been quick of thought and of action; but I never thought or moved more quickly in my life than I did in the instant following my discovery of the face in the window. With a single movement I swept the candle from the table, plunging the room into utter darkness, and leaping to my father's side I tore The Flag from his hands and thrust it back into the aperture above the mantel. The stone lay upon the mantel itself, nor did it take me but a moment to grope for it and find it in the dark—an instant more and it was replaced in its niche.

So ingrained were apprehension and suspicion in the human mind that the four in the room with me sensed intuitively something of the cause of my act and when I had hunted for the candle, found it and relighted it they were standing, tense and motionless where I had last seen them. They did not ask me a question. Father was the first to speak.

"You were very careless and clumsy, Julian," he said. "If you wanted the candle why did you not pick it up carefully instead of rushing at it so? But that is always your way—you are constantly knocking things over."

He raised his voice a trifle as he spoke; but it was a lame attempt at deception and he knew it, as did we. If the man who owned the face in the dark heard his words he must have known it as well.

As soon as I had relighted the candle I went into the kitchen and out the back door and then, keeping close in the black shadow of the house, I crept around toward the front, for I wanted to learn, if I could, who it was who had looked in upon that scene of high treason. The night was moonless but clear, and I could see quite a distance in every direction, as our house stood in a fair size clearing close to the river. Southeast of us the path wound upward across the approach to an ancient bridge, long since destroyed by raging mobs or rotting away—I do not know which—and presently I saw the figure of a man silhouetted against the starlit sky as he topped the approach. The man carried a laden sack upon his back. This fact was, to some extent, reassuring as it suggested that the eavesdropper was himself upon some illegal mission and that he could ill afford to be too particular of the actions of others. I have seen many men carrying sacks and bundles at night—I have carried them myself. It is the only way, often, in which a man may save enough from the tax collector on which to live and support his family.

This nocturnal traffic is common enough and under our old tax collector and the indolent commandant of former times not so hazardous as it might seem when one realizes that it is punishable by imprisonment for ten years at hard labor in the coal mines and, in aggravated cases, by death. The aggravated cases are those in which a man is discovered trading something by night that the tax collector or the commandant had wanted for himself.

I did not follow the man, being sure that he was one of our own class, but turned back toward the house where I found the four talking in low whispers, nor did any of us raise his voice again that evening.

Father and Jim were talking, as they usually did, of the West. They seemed to feel that somewhere, far away toward the setting sun, there must be a little corner of America where men could live in peace and freedom— where there were no Kash Guards, tax collectors or Kalkars.

It must have been three-quarters of an hour later, as Jim and Mollie were preparing to leave, that there came a knock upon the door which immediately swung open before an invitation to enter could be given. We looked up to see Peter Johansen smiling at us. I never liked Peter. He was a long, lanky man who smiled with his mouth; but never with his eyes. I didn't like the way he used to look at Mother when he thought no one was observing him, nor his habit of changing women every year or two—that was too much like the Kalkars. I always felt toward Peter as I had as a child when, barefooted, I stepped unknowingly upon a snake in the deep grass.

Father greeted the newcomer with a pleasant "Welcome, Brother Johansen;" but Jim only nodded his head and scowled, for Peter had a habit of looking at Mollie as he did at Mother, and both women were beautiful. I think I never saw a more beautiful woman than my mother and as I grew older and learned more of men and the world I marveled that Father had been able to keep her and, too, I understood why she never went abroad; but stayed always closely about the house and farm. I never knew her to go to the market place as did most of the other women. But I was twenty now and worldly wise and so I knew what I had not known as a little child.

"What brings you out so late, Brother Johansen?" I asked. We always used the prescribed "Brother" to those of whom we were not sure. I hate the word—to me a brother meant an enemy as it did to all our class and I guess to every class—even the Kalkars.

"I followed a stray pig," replied Peter to my question. "He went in that direction," and he waved a hand toward the market place. As he did so something tumbled from beneath his coat—something that his arm had held there. It was an empty sack. Immediately I knew who it was who owned the face in the dark beyond our goatskin hanging. Peter snatched the sack from the floor in ill-concealed confusion and then I saw the expression of his cunning face change as he held it toward Father.

"Is this yours, Brother Julian?" he asked. "I found it just before your door and thought that I would stop and ask."

"No," said I, not waiting for Father to speak, "it is not ours—it must belong to the man whom I saw carrying it, full, a short time since. He went by the path beside The Old Bridge." I looked straight into Peter's eyes. He flushed and then went white.

"I did not see him," he said presently; "but if the sack is not yours I will keep it—*at least it is not high treason to have it in my possession.*" Then, without another word, he turned and left the house.

We all knew then that Peter had seen the episode of The Flag. Father said that we need not fear, that Peter was all right; but Jim thought differently and so did Mollie and Mother. I agreed with them. I did not like Peter. Jim and Mollie went home shortly after Peter left and we prepared for bed.

# TWO

# The Hellhounds

MOTHER and Father occupied the one bedroom. I slept on some goat skins in the big room we called the living room. The other room was a kitchen. We ate there also.

Mother had always made me take off my clothes and put on a mohair garment for sleeping. The other young men I knew slept in the same clothes they wore during the day; but Mother was particular about this and insisted that I have my sleeping garments and also that I bathed often—once a week in the winter. In the summer I was in the river so much that I had a bath once or twice a day. Father was also particular about his personal cleanliness. The Kalkars were very different.

My underclothing was of fine mohair, in winter. In summer I wore none: I had a heavy mohair shirt and breeches, tight at waist and knees and baggy between, a goatskin tunic and boots of goatskin. I do not know what we would have done without the goats—they furnished us food and raiment. The boots were loose and fastened just above the calf of the leg with a strap—to keep them from falling down. I wore nothing on my head, summer or winter; but my hair was heavy. I wore it brushed straight back, always, and cut off square behind just below my ears. To keep it from getting in my eyes I always tied a goatskin thong about my head.

I had just slipped off my tunic when I heard the baying of the hellhounds close by. I thought they might be getting into the goat pen, so I waited a moment, listening and then I heard a scream—the scream of a woman in terror. It sounded down by the river near the goat pens, and mingled with it was the vicious growling and barking of the hellhounds. I did not wait to listen longer, but seized my knife and a long staff. We were permitted to have no edged weapon with a blade over six inches long. Such as it was, it was the best weapon I had and much better than none.

I ran out the front door, which was closest, and turned toward the pens in the direction of the hellhounds deep growling and the screams of the woman, which were repeated twice.

As I neared the pens and my eyes became accustomed to the outer darkness I made out what appeared to be a human figure resting partially upon the top of one of the sheds that formed a portion of the pen wall. The legs and lower body dangled over the edge of the roof and I could see three or four hellhounds leaping for it, while another, that had evidently gotten a hold, was hanging to one leg and attempting to drag the figure down.

As I ran forward I shouted at the beasts and those that were leaping for the figure stopped and turned toward me. I knew something of the temper of these animals and that I might expect them to charge, for they were quite fearless of man ordinarily; but I ran forward toward them so swiftly and with such determination that they turned growling and ran off before I reached them; but not far.

The one that had hold of the figure succeeded in dragging it to earth just before I reached them and then it discovered me and turned, standing over its prey, with wide jaws and terrific fangs menacing me. It was a huge beast, almost as large as a full grown goat, and easily a match for several men as poorly armed as I. Under ordinary circumstances I should have given it plenty of room; but what was I to do when the life of a woman was at stake?

I was an American, not a Kalkar—those swine would throw a woman to the hellhounds to save their own skins—and I had been brought up to revere woman in a world that considered her on a par with the cow, the nanny and the sow, only less valuable since the latter were not the common property of the state.

I knew then that death stood very near as I faced that frightful beast and from the corner of an eye I could see its mates creeping closer. There was no time to think, even, and so I rushed in upon the hellhound with my staff and blade. As I did so I saw the wide and terrified eyes of a young girl looking up at me from beneath the beast of prey. I had not thought to desert her to her fate before; but after that single glance I could not have done so had a thousand deaths confronted me.

As I was almost upon the beast it sprang for my throat, rising high upon its hind feet and leaping straight as an arrow. My staff was useless and so I dropped it, meeting the charge with my knife and a bare hand. By luck the fingers of my left hand found the creature's throat at the first clutch; but the impact of his body against mine hurled me to the ground beneath him and there, growling and struggling, he sought to close those snapping fangs upon me. Holding his jaws at arm's length I struck at his breast with

Julian 9th Fights a Hellhound

my blade, nor did I miss him once. The pain of the wounds turned him crazy and yet, to my utter surprise found I still could hold him and not that alone; but that I could also struggle to my knees and then to my feet still holding him at arm's length in my left hand.

I had always known that I was muscular; but until that moment I had never dreamed of the great strength that Nature had given me, for never before had I had occasion to exert the full measure of my powerful thews. It was like a revelation from above and of a sudden I found myself smiling and in the instant a miracle occurred—all fear of these hideous beasts dissolved from my brain like thin air and with it fear of man as well. I, who had been brought out of a womb of fear into a world of terror, who had been suckled and nurtured upon apprehension and timidity—I, Julian 9th, at the age of twenty years, became in the fraction of a second utterly fearless of man or beast. It was the knowledge of my great power that did it—that and, perhaps, those two liquid eyes that I knew to be watching me.

The other hounds were closing in upon me when the creature in my grasp went suddenly limp. My blade must have found its heart. And then the others charged and I saw the girl upon her feet beside me, my staff in her hands, ready to battle with them.

"To the roof!" I shouted to her; but she did not heed. Instead she stood her ground, striking a vicious blow at the leader as he came within range.

Swinging the dead beast above my head I hurled the carcass at the others so that they scattered and retreated again and then I turned to the girl and without more parley lifted her in my arms and tossed her lightly to the roof of the goat shed. I could easily have followed to her side and safety had not something filled my brain with an effect similar to that which I imagined must be produced by the vile concoction brewed by the Kalkars and which they drink to excess, while it would have meant imprisonment for us to be apprehended with it in our possession. At least, I know that I felt a sudden exhilaration—a strange desire to accomplish wonders before the eyes of this stranger, and so I turned upon the four remaining hellhounds who had now bunched to renew the attack and without waiting for them I rushed toward them.

They did not flee; but stood their ground, growling hideously, their hair bristling upon their necks and along their spines, their great fangs bared and slavering; but among them I tore and by the very impetuosity of my attack I overthrew them. The first sprang to meet me and him I seized by the neck and clamping his body between knees I twisted his head entirely around until I heard the vertebrae snap. The other three were upon me then, leaping and tearing; but I felt no fear. One by one I took them in my mighty hands and—lifting them high above my head hurled them violently from me. Two only of the hellhounds returned to the attack and these I vanquished with my bare hands disdaining to use my blade upon such carrion.

It was then that I saw a man running toward me from up the river and another from our house. The first was Jim, who had heard commotion and the girl's screams and the other was my father. Both had seen the last part of the battle and neither could believe that it was I, Julian, who had done this thing. Father was very proud of me and Jim was, too, for he had always said that having no son of his own Father must share me with him.

And then I turned toward the girl who had slipped from the roof and was approaching us. She moved with the same graceful dignity that was Mother's—not at all like the clumsy clods that belonged to the Kalkars, and she came straight to me and laid a hand upon my arm.

"Thank you!" she said; "and God bless you. Only a very brave and powerful man could have done what you have done."

And then, all of a sudden, I did not feel brave at all; but very weak and silly, for all I could do was finger my blade and look at the ground. It was Father who spoke and the interruption helped to dispel my embarrassment.

"Who are you?" he asked, "and from where do you come? It is strange to find a young woman wandering about alone at night; but stranger still to hear one who dares invoke the forbidden Deity."

I had not realized until then that she had used His name; but when I did recall it, I could not but glance apprehensively about to see if any others might be around who could have heard. Father and Jim I knew to be safe; for there was a common tie between our families that lay in the secret religious rites we held once each week. Since that hideous day that had befallen even before my father's birth—that day, which none dared mention above a whisper, when the clergy of every denomination, to the last man, had been murdered by order of The TwentyFour, it had been a capital crime to worship God in any form whatsoever.

Some madman at Washington, filled, doubtless, with the fumes of the awful drink that made them more bestial even than Nature designed them issued the frightful order on the ground that the church was attempting to usurp the functions of the state and that also the clergy were inciting the people to rebellion—nor do I doubt but that the latter was true. Too bad, indeed, that they were not given more time to bring their divine plan to fruition.

We took the girl to the house and when my mother saw her and how young and beautiful she was and took her in her arms, the child broke down and sobbed and clung to Mother, nor could either speak for some time. In the light of the candle I saw that the stranger was of wondrous beauty. I have said that my mother was the most beautiful woman I had ever seen, and such is the truth; but this girl who had come so suddenly among us was the most beautiful girl.

She was about nineteen, delicately molded and yet without weakness. There were strength and vitality apparent in every move she made as well as in the expression of her face, her gestures and her manner of speech. She was girlish and at the same time filled one with an impression of great reserve strength of mind and character. She was very brown, showing exposure to the sun, yet her skin was clear—almost translucent.

Her garb was similar to mine—the common garmenture of people of our class, both men and women. She wore the tunic and breeches and boots just as Mother and Mollie and the rest of us did; but somehow there was a difference—I had never before realized what a really beautiful costume it was. The band about her forehead was wider than was generally worn and upon it were sewn numerous tiny shells, set close together and forming a pattern. It was her only attempt at ornamentation; but even so it was quite noticeable in a world where women strove to make themselves plain rather than beautiful—some going even so far as to permanently disfigure their faces and those of their female offspring while others, many, many others, killed the latter in infancy. Mollie had done so with two. No wonder that grown-ups never laughed and seldom smiled!

When the girl had quieted her sobs on Mother's breast Father renewed his questioning; but Mother said to wait until morning, that the girl was tired and unstrung and needed sleep. Then came the question of where she was to sleep. Father said that he would sleep in the living room with me and that the stranger could sleep with Mother; but Jim suggested that she come home with him as he and Mollie had three rooms, as did we, and no one to occupy his living room. And so it was arranged, although I would rather have had her remain with us.

At first she rather shrank from going, until mother told her that Jim and Mollie were good, kind-hearted people and that she would be as safe with them as with her own father and mother. At mention of her parents the tears came to her eyes and she turned impulsively toward my mother and kissed her, after which she told Jim that she was ready to accompany him.

She started to say good-by to me and to thank me again; but, having found my tongue at last, I told her that I would go with them as far as Jim's house. This appeared to please her and so we set forth. Jim walked ahead and I followed with the girl and on the way I discovered a very strange thing. Father had shown me a piece of iron once that pulled smaller bits of iron to it. He said that it was a magnet.

This slender, stranger girl was certainly no piece of iron, nor was I a smaller bit of anything; but nevertheless I could not keep away from her. I cannot explain it—however wide the way was I was always drawn over close to her, so that our arms touched and once our hands swung together and the strangest and most delicious thrill ran through me that I had ever experienced.

I used to think that Jim's house was a long way from ours—when I had to carry things over there as a boy; but that night it was far too close—just a step or two and we were there.

Mollie heard us coming and was at the door, full of questionings, and when she saw the girl and heard a part of our story she reached out and took the girl to her bosom, just as Mother had. Before they took her in the stranger turned and held out her hand to me.

"Good night!" she said, "and thank you again, and, once more, may God, our Father, bless and preserve you."

And I heard Mollie murmur: "The Saints be praised!" and then they went in and the door closed and I turned homeward, treading on air.

# THREE

# Brother General Or-tis

T HE NEXT day I set out as usual to peddle goat's milk. We were permitted to trade in perishable things on other than market days, though we had to make a strict accounting of all such bartering. I usually left Mollie until the last as Jim had a deep, cold well on his place where I liked to quench my thirst after my morning trip; but that day Mollie got her milk fresh and first and early—about half an hour earlier than I was wont to start out.

When I knocked and she bid me enter she looked surprised at first, for just an instant, and then a strange expression came into her eyes—half amusement, half pity—and she rose and went into the kitchen for the milk jar. I saw her wipe the corners of her eyes with the back of one finger; but I did not understand why—not then.

The stranger girl had been in the kitchen helping Mollie and the latter must have told her I was there, for she came right in and greeted me. It was the first good look I had had of her, for candle light is not brilliant at best. If I had been enthralled the evening before there is no word in my limited vocabulary to express the effect she had on me by daylight. She—but it is useless. I cannot describe her!

It took Mollie a long time to find the milk jar—bless her!—though it seemed short enough to me, and while she was finding it the stranger girl and I were getting acquainted. First she asked after Father and Mother and then she asked our names. When I told her mine she repeated it several times. "Julian 9th," she said; "Julian 9th!" and then she smiled up at me. "It is a nice name, I like it."

"And what is your name?" I asked.

"Juana," she said—she pronounced it Whanna; "Juana St. John."

"I am glad," I said, "that you like my name; but I like yours better." It was a very foolish speech and it made me feel silly; but she did not seem to think it foolish, or if she did she was too nice to let me know it. I have known many girls; but mostly they were homely and stupid. The pretty girls were seldom allowed in the market place—that is, the pretty girls of our class. The Kalkars permitted their girls to go abroad, for they did not care who got them, as long as someone got them; but American fathers and mothers would rather slay their girls than send them to the market place, and the former often was done. The Kalkar girls, even those born of American mothers, were coarse and brutal in appearance—low-browed, vulgar, bovine. No stock can be improved, or even kept to its normal plane, unless high grade males are used.

This girl was so entirely different from any other that I had ever seen that I marvelled that such a glorious creature could exist. I wanted to know all about her. It seemed to me that in some way I had been robbed of my right for many years that she should have lived and breathed and talked and gone her way without my ever knowing it, or her. I wanted to make up for lost time and so I asked her many questions.

She told me that she had been born and raised in the teivos just west of Chicago, which extended along the Desplaines River and embraced a considerable area of unpopulated country and scattered farms.

"My father's home is in a district called Oak Park," she said, "and our house was one of the few that remained from ancient times. It was of solid concrete and stood upon the corner of two roads—once it must have been a very beautiful place, and even time and war have been unable entirely to erase its charm. Three great poplar trees rose to the north of it beside the ruins of what my father said was once a place where motor cars were kept by the long dead owner. To the south of the house were many roses, growing wild and luxuriant, while the concrete walls, from which the plaster had fallen in great patches, were almost entirely concealed by the clinging ivy that reached to the very eaves.

"It was my home and so I loved it; but now it is lost to me forever. The Kash Guard and the tax collector came seldom—we were too far from the station and the market place, which lay southwest of us, on Salt Creek. But recently the new Jemadar, Jarth, appointed another commandant and a new tax collector. They did not like the station at Salt Creek and so they sought for a better location and after inspecting the district they chose Oak Park, and my father's home being the most comfortable and substantial, they ordered him to sell it to The TwentyFour.

"You know what that means. They appraised it at a high figure—fifty thousand dollars it was, and paid him in paper money. There was nothing to do and so we prepared to move. Whenever they had come to look at the house my mother had hidden me in a little cubby-hole on the landing between the second and third floors, placing a pile of rubbish in front of me, but the day that we were leaving to take a place on the banks of the Desplaines, where Father thought that we might live without being disturbed, the new commandant came unexpectedly and saw me.

"How old is the girl?" he asked my mother.

"Fifteen," she replied sullenly.

" 'You lie, you sow!' he cried angrily; 'she is eighteen if she is a day!'

"Father was standing there beside us and when the commandant spoke as he did to Mother I saw Father go very white and then, without a word, he hurled himself upon the swine and before the Kash Guard who accompanied him could prevent, Father had almost killed the commandant with his bare hands.

"You know what happened—I do not need to tell you. They killed my father before my eyes. Then the commandant offered my mother to one of the Kash Guard, but she snatched his bayonet from his belt and ran it through her heart before they could prevent her. I tried to follow her example, but they seized me.

"I was carried to my own bedroom on the second floor of my father's house and locked there. The commandant said that he would come and see me in the evening and that everything would be all right with me. I knew what he meant and I made up my mind that he would find me dead.

"My heart was breaking for the loss of my father and mother, and yet the desire to live was strong within me. I did not want to die—something urged me to live, and in addition there was the teaching of my father and mother. They were both from Quaker stock and very religious. They educated me to fear God and to do no wrong by thought or violence to another, and yet I had seen my father attempt to kill a man, and I had seen my mother slay herself. My world was all upset. I was almost crazed by grief and fear and uncertainty as to what was right for me to do.

"And then darkness came and I heard some one ascending the stairway. The windows of the second story are too far from the ground for one to risk a leap; but the ivy is old and strong. The commandant was not sufficiently familiar with the place to have taken the ivy into consideration and before the footsteps reached my door I had swung out of the window and, clinging to the ivy, made my way to the ground down the rough and strong old stem.

"That was three days ago. I hid and wandered—I did not know in what direction I went. Once an old woman took me in overnight and fed me and gave me food to carry for the next day. I think that I must have been almost mad, for mostly the happenings of the past three days are only indistinct and jumbled fragments of memory in my mind. And then the hellhounds! Oh, how frightened I was! And then—you!"

I don't know what there was about the way she said it; but it seemed to me as though it meant a great deal more than she knew herself. Almost like a prayer of thanksgiving, it was, that she had at last found a safe haven of refuge—safe and permanent. Anyway, I liked the idea.

And then Mollie came in, and as I was leaving she asked me if I would come that evening, and Juana cried: "Oh, yes, do!" and I said that I would.

When I had finished delivering the goats' milk I started for home, and on the way I met old Moses Samuels, the Jew. He made his living, and a scant one it was, by tanning hides. He was a most excellent tanner, but as nearly every one else knew how to tan there was not many customers; but some of the Kalkars used to bring him hides to tan. They knew nothing of how to do any useful thing, for they were descended from a long line of the most ignorant and illiterate people in the Moon and the moment they obtained a little power they would not even work at what small trades their fathers once had learned, so that after a generation or two they were able to live only off the labor of others. They created nothing, they produced nothing, they became the most burdensome class of parasites the world ever has endured.

The rich nonproducers of olden times were a blessing to the world by comparison with these, for the former at least had intelligence and imagination—they could direct others and they could transmit to their offspring the qualities of mind that are essential to any culture, progress or happiness that the world ever may hope to attain.

So the Kalkars patronized Samuels for their tanned hides, and if they had paid him for them the old Jew would have waxed rich; but they either did not pay him at all or else mostly in paper money. That did not even burn well, as Samuels used to say.

"Good morning, Julian," he called as we met. "I shall be needing some hides soon, for the new commander of the Kash Guard has heard of old Samuels and has sent for me and ordered five hides tanned the finest that can be. Have you seen this Or-tis, Julian?" He lowered his voice.

I shook my head negatively.

"Heaven help us!" whispered the old man. "Heaven help us!"

"Is he as bad as that, Moses?" I asked.

The old man wrung his hands. "Bad times are ahead, my son," he said. "Old Samuels knows his kind. He is not lazy like the last one and he is more cruel and more lustful; but about the hides. I have not paid you for the last—they paid me in paper money; but that I would not offer to a friend in payment for a last year's bird's nest. May be that I shall not be able to pay you for these new hides for a long time—it depends upon how Or-tis pays me. Sometimes they are liberal—as they can afford to be with the property of others; but if he is a half-breed, as I hear he is, he will hate a Jew, and I shall get nothing. However, if he is pure Kalkar it may be different—the pure Kalkars do not hate a Jew more than they hate other Earth Men, though there is one Jew who hates a Kalkar."

That night we had our first introduction to Or-tis. He came in person; but I will tell how it all happened. After supper I went over to Jim's. Juana was standing in the little doorway as I came up the path. She looked rested now and almost happy. The hunted expression had left her eyes and she smiled as I approached. It was almost dusk, for the spring evenings were still short; but the air was balmy, and so we stood on the outside talking.

I recited the little gossip of our district that I had picked up during my day's work—The TwentyFour had raised the local tax on farm products—Andrew Wright's woman had given birth to twins, a boy and a girl; but the girl had died; no need of comment here as most girl babies die—Soor had said that he would tax this district until we all died of starvation—pleasant fellow, Soor—one of the Kash Guard had taken Nellie Levy—Hoffmeyer had said that next winter we would have to pay more for coal—Dennis Corrigan had been sent to the mines for ten years because he had been caught trading at night. It was all alike, this gossip of ours—all sordid, or sad, or tragic; but then life was a tragedy with us.

"How stupid of them to raise the tax on farm products," remarked Juana; "their fathers stamped out manufactures and commerce and now they will stamp out what little agriculture is left."

"The sooner they do it the better it will be for the world," I replied. "When they have starved all the farmers to death they themselves will starve."

And then, suddenly, she reverted to Dennis Corrigan. "It would have been kinder to have killed him," she said.

"That is why they did not do so," I replied.

"Do you ever trade at night?" she asked, and then before I could reply: "Do not tell me. I should not have asked; but I hope that you do not—it is so dangerous; nearly always are they caught."

I laughed. "Not nearly always," I said, "or most of us would have been in the mines long since. We could not live otherwise. The accursed income tax is unfair—it has always been unfair, for it falls hardest on those least able to support it."

"But the mines are so terrible!" she exclaimed, shuddering.

"Yes," I replied, "the mines are terrible, I would rather die than go there."

After a while I took Juana over to our house to see my mother. She liked the house very much. My father's father built it with his own hands. It is constructed of stone taken from the ruins of the old city—stone and brick. Father says that he thinks the bricks are from an old pavement, as we still see patches of these ancient bricks in various localities. Nearly all our houses are of this construction, for timber is scarce. The foundation and the walls above the ground for about three feet are of rough stones of various sizes and above this are the bricks. The stones are laid so that some project farther than others and the effect is odd and rather nice. The eaves are low and over-hanging and the roof is thatched. It is a nice house and Mother keeps it scrupulously clean within.

We had been talking for perhaps an hour, sitting in our living room— Father, Mother, Juana, and I—when the door was suddenly thrust open without warning and we looked up to see a man in the uniform of a Kash Guard confronting us. Behind him were others. We all rose and stood in silence. Two entered and took posts on either side of the doorway and then a third came in—a tall, dark man in the uniform of a commander, and we knew at once that it was Or-tis. At his heels were six more.

Or-tis looked at each of us and then, singling out Father, he said: "You are Brother Julian 8th."

Father nodded. Or-tis eyed him for a moment and then his gaze wandered to Mother and Juana, and I saw a new expression lessen the fierce scowl that had clouded his face from the moment of his entry. He was a large man; but not of the heavy type which is most common among his class. His nose was thin and rather fine, his eyes cold, gray, and piercing. He was very different from the fat swine that had preceded him—very different and more dangerous; even I could see that. I could see a thin, cruel upper lip and a full and sensuous lower. If the other had been a pig this one was a wolf and he had the nervous restlessness of the wolf—and the vitality to carry out any wolfish designs he might entertain.

This visit to our home was typical of the man. The former commander had never accompanied his men on any excursion of the sort; but the teivos was to see much of Or-tis. He trusted no one—he must see to everything himself and he was not lazy, which was bad for us.

"So you are Brother Julian 8th!" he repeated. "I do not have good reports of you. I have come for two reasons to-night. One is to warn you that the Kash Guard is commanded by a different sort of man from him whom I relieved. I will stand no trifling and no treason. There must be unquestioned loyalty to the Jemadar at Washington—every national and local law will be enforced. Trouble makers and traitors will get short shrift. A manifesto will be read in each market place Saturday—a manifesto that I have just received from Washington. Our great Jemadar has conferred greater powers upon the commanders of the Kash Guard. You will come to me with all your grievances. Where justice miscarries I shall be the court of last resort. The judgment of any court may be appealed to me.

"On the other hand, let wrongdoers beware as under the new law any cause may be tried before a summary military court over which the commander of the Kash Guard must preside."

We saw what it meant—it didn't require much intelligence to see the infamy and horror of it. It meant nothing more nor less than that our lives and liberty were in the hands of a single man and that Jarth had struck the greatest blow of all at human happiness in a land where we had thought such a state no longer existed—taken from us the last mocking remnant of our already lost freedom, that he might build for his own aggrandizement a powerful political military machine.

"And," continued Or-tis, "I have come for another reason—a reason that looks bad for you, Brother Julian; but we shall see what we shall see," and turning to the men behind him he issued a curt command: "Search the place!" That was all; but I saw, in memory, another man standing in this same living room—a man from beneath whose coat fell an empty sack when he raised an arm.

For an hour they searched that little three room house. For an hour they tumbled our few belongings over and over; but mostly they searched the living room and especially about the fireplace did they hunt for a hidden nook. A dozen times my heart stood still as I saw them feeling of the stones above the mantel.

We all knew what they sought—all but Juana—and we knew what it would mean if they found it. Death for Father and for me, too, perhaps, and worse for Mother and the girl. And to think that Johansen had done this awful thing to curry favor for himself with the new commander! I knew it was he—I knew it as surely as though Or-tis had told me. To curry favor with the commander! I thought that that was the reason then. God, had I but known his real reason!

And while they searched, Or-tis talked with us. Mostly he talked with mother and Juana. I hated the way that he looked at them, especially Juana; but his words were fair enough. He seemed to be trying to get an expression from them of their political ideas—he, who was of the class that had ruthlessly stolen from women the recognition they had won in the twentieth century after ages of slavery and trials, attempting to sound them on their political faiths! They had none—no women have any—they only know that they hate and loathe the oppressors who have hurled them back into virtual slavery. That is their politics; that is their religion. Hate. But then the world is all hate—hate and misery.

Father says that it was not always so; but that once the world was happy—at least, our part of the world; but the people didn't know when they were well off. They came from all other parts of the world to share our happiness and when they had won it they sought to overthrow it, and when the Kalkars came they helped them.

Well, they searched for an hour and found nothing; but I knew that Or-tis was not satisfied that the thing he sought was not there and toward the end of the search I could see that he was losing patience. He took direct charge at last and then when they had no better success under his direction he became very angry.

"Yankee swine!" he cried suddenly, turning upon Father. "You will find that you cannot fool a descendant of the great Jemadar Orthis as you have fooled the others—not for long. I have a nose for traitors—I can smell a Yank farther than most men can see one. Take a warning, take a warning to your kind. It will be death or the mines for every traitor in the teivos."

He stood then in silence for a moment, glaring at Father and then his gaze moved to Juana, where she stood just behind my shoulder at the far side of the room.

"Who are you, girl?" he demanded. "Where do you live and what do you do that adds to the prosperity of the community?"

"Adds to the prosperity of the community!" It was a phrase often on their lips and it was always directed at us—a meaningless phrase, as there was no prosperity. We supported the Kalkars and that was their idea of prosperity. I suppose ours was to get barely sufficient to sustain life and strength to enable us to continue slaving for them.

"I live with Mollie Sheehan," replied Juana, "and help her care for the chickens and the little pigs; also I help with the housework."

"Mm-m," ejaculated Or-tis. Housework! That is good—I shall be needing some one to keep my quarters tidy. How about it, my girl? It will be easy work, and I will pay you well—no pigs or chickens to slave for. Eh?"

"But I love the little pigs and chickens," she pleaded, "and I am happy with Mollie—I do not wish to change."

"Do not wish to change, eh?" he mimicked her. She had drawn farther behind me now, as though for protection, and closer—I could feel her body touching mine. "Mollie can doubtless take care of her own pigs and chickens without help. If she has so many she cannot do it alone, then she has too many, and we will see why it is that she is more prosperous than the rest of us—probably she should pay a larger income tax—we shall see."

"Oh, no!" cried Juana, frightened now on Mollie's account. "Please, she has only a few, scarcely enough that she and her man may live after the taxes are paid."

"Then she does not need you to help her," said Or-tis with finality, a nasty sneer upon his lip. "You will come and work for me, girl!"

And then Juana surprised me—she surprised us all, and particularly Or-tis. Before she had been rather pleading and seemingly a little frightened; but now she drew herself to her full height and with her chin in air looked Or-tis straight in the eye.

"I will not come," she said, haughtily; "I do not wish to." That was all.

Or-tis looked surprised; his soldiers, shocked. For a moment no one spoke. I glanced at Mother. She was not trembling as I had expected. Her head was up, too, and she was openly looking her scorn of the man. Father stood as he usually did before them, with his head bowed; but I saw that he was watching Or-tis out of the corners of his eyes and that his fingers were moving as might the fingers of hands fixed upon a hated throat.

"You will come," said Or-tis, a little red in the face now at this defiance. "There are ways," and he looked straight at me—and then he turned upon his heel and, followed by his Kash Guard, left the house.

# FOUR

# A Fight on Market Day

W HEN THE DOOR had closed upon them Juana buried her face in her hands.

"Oh, what misery I bring everywhere," she sobbed. "To my father and mother I brought death, and now to you all and to Jim and Mollie I am bringing ruin and perhaps death also. But it shall not be—you shall not suffer for me! He looked straight at you, Julian, when he made his threat. What could he mean to do? You have done nothing. But you need not fear. I know how I may undo the harm I have so innocently done."

We tried to assure her that we did not care—that we would protect her as best we could and that she must not feel that she had brought any greater burden upon us than we already carried; but she only shook her head and at last asked me to take her home to Mollie's.

She was very quiet all the way back, though I did my best to cheer her up.

"He cannot make you work for him," I insisted. "Even The TwentyFour, rotten as it is, would never dare enforce such an order. We are not yet entirely slaves."

"But I am afraid that he will find a way," she replied, "through you, my friend. I saw him look at you and it was a very ugly look."

"I do not fear," I said.

"I fear for you. No, it shall not be!" She spoke with such vehement finality that she almost startled me and then she bade me good night and went into Mollie's house and closed the door.

All the way back home I was much worried about her, for I did not like to see her unhappy. I felt that her fears were exaggerated, for even such a powerful man as the commandant could not make her work for him if she did not wish to. Later he might take her as his woman if she had no man, but even then she had some choice in the matter—a month in which to choose some one else if she did not care to bear his children. That was the law.

Of course, they found ways to circumvent the law when they wanted a girl badly enough—the man of her choice might be apprehended upon some trumped-up charge, or even be found some morning mysteriously murdered. It must be a heroic woman who stood out against them for long, and a man must love a girl very deeply to sacrifice his life for her—and then not save her. There was but one way and by the time I reached my cot I was almost frantic with fear lest she might seize upon it.

For a few minutes I paced the floor and with every minute the conviction grew that the worst was about to happen. It became an obsession. I could see her even as plainly as with my physical eyesight and then I could stand it no longer.

Bolting for the doorway I ran as fast as my legs would carry me in the direction of Jim's house. Just before I reached it I saw a shadowy figure moving in the direction of the river. I could not make out who it was; but I knew and redoubled my speed.

A low bluff overhands the stream at this point and upon its edge I saw the figure pause for a moment and then disappear. There was a splash in the water below just as I reached the rim of the bluff—a splash and circling rings spreading outward on the surface of the river in the starlight.

I saw these things—the whole picture—in the fraction of a moment, for I scarcely paused upon the bluff's edge; but dove headlong into the rippling water close to the center of those diverging circles.

We came up together, side by side, and I reached out and seized her tunic, and thus, holding her at arm's length, I swam ashore with her, keeping her chin above water. She did not struggle and when at last we stood upon the bank she turned upon me, tearless, yet sobbing.

"Why did you do it?" she moaned. "Oh, why did you do it? It was the only way—the only way."

She looked so forlorn and unhappy and so altogether beautiful that I could scarcely keep from taking her in my arms, for then, quite unexpectedly, I realized what I had been too stupid to realize before—that I loved her.

But I only took her hands in mine and pressed them very tightly and begged her to promise me that she would not attempt this thing again. I told her that she might never hear from Or-tis again and that it was wicked to destroy herself until there was no other way.

"It is not that I fear myself," she said. "I can always find this way out at the last minute; but I fear for you who have been kind to me. If I go now you will no longer be in danger."

"I would rather be in danger than have you go," I said simply. "I do not fear."

And she promised me before I left her that she would not try it again until there was no other way.

As I walked slowly homeward my thoughts were filled with bitterness and sorrow. My soul was in revolt against this cruel social order that even robbed youth of happiness and love. Although I had seen but little of either something within me—some inherent instinct I suspect—cried aloud that these were my birthright and that I was being robbed of them by the spawn of lunar interlopers. My Americanism was very strong in me—stronger, perhaps, because of the century old effort of our oppressors to crush it and because always we must suppress any outward evidence of it. They called us Yanks in contempt; but the appellation was our pride. And we, in turn, often spoke of them as kaisers; but not to their faces. Father says that in ancient times the word had the loftiest of meanings; but now it has the lowest.

As I approached the house I saw that the candle was still burning in the living room. I had left so hurriedly that I had given it no thought, and as I came closer I saw something else; too. I was walking very slowly and in the soft dust of the pathway my soft boots made no sound, or I might not have seen what I did see—two figures, close in the shadow of the wall, peering through one of our little windows into the living room.

I crept stealthily forward until I was close enough to see that one was in the uniform of a Kash Guard while the other was clothed as are those of my class. In the latter I recognized the stoop-shouldered, lanky figure of Peter Johansen. I was not at all surprised at this confirmation of my suspicions.

I knew what they were there for—hoping to learn the secret hiding place of The Flag—but I also knew that unless they already knew it there was no danger of their discovering it from the outside, since The Flag had been removed from its hiding place but once in my lifetime that I knew of and might never again be, especially since we knew that we were suspected. So I hid and watched them for a while and then circled the house and entered from the front as though I did not know that they were there, for it would never do to let them know that they had been discovered.

Taking off my clothes I went to bed, after putting out the candle. I do not know how long they remained—it was enough to know that we were being watched, and though it was not pleasant I was glad that we were forewarned. In the morning I told Father and Mother what I had seen. Mother sighed and shook her head.

"It is coming," she said. "I always knew that sooner or later it would come. One by one they get us—now it is our turn."

Father said nothing. He finished his breakfast in silence and when he left the house he walked with his eyes upon the ground, his shoulders stooped and his chin upon his breast—slowly, almost unsteadily, he walked, like a man whose heart and spirit are both broken.

I saw Mother choke back a sob as she watched him go and I went and put my arm about her.

"I fear for him, Julian," she said. "A spirit such as his suffers terribly the stings of injustice and degradation. Some of the others do not seem to take it so to heart as he; but he is a proud man of a proud line. I am afraid—" she paused as though fearing even to voice her fears—"I am afraid that he will do away with himself."

"No," I said, "he is too brave a man for that. This will all blow over—they only suspect—they do not know, and we shall be careful and then all will be right again—as right as anything ever is in this world."

"But Or-tis?" she questioned. "It will not be right until he has his will."

I knew that she meant Juana.

"He will never have his will," I said. "Am I not here?"

She smiled indulgently. "You are very strong, my boy," she said; "but what are two brawny arms against the Kash Guard?"

"They would be enough for Or-tis," I replied.

"You would kill him?" she whispered. "They would tear you to pieces!"

"They can tear me to pieces but once."

It was market day and I went in with a few wethers, some hides and cheese. Father did not come along—in fact, I advised him not to as Soor would be there and also Hoffmeyer. One cheese I took as tribute to Soor. God, how I hated to do it! But both Mother and Father thought it best to propitiate the fellow, and I suppose they were right. A lifetime of suffering does not incline one to seek further trouble.

The market place was full, for I was a little late. There were many Kash Guards in evidence—more than usual. It was a warm day—the first really warm day we had had—and a number of men were sitting beneath a canopy at one side of the market place in front of Hoffmeyer's office. As I approached I saw that Or-tis was there, as well as Pthav, the coal baron, and Hoffmeyer, of course, with several others including some Kalkar women and children.

I recognized Pthav's woman—a renegade Yank who had gone to him willingly—and their little child, a girl of about six. The latter was playing in the dust in front of the canopy some hundred feet from the group, and

I had scarcely recognized her when I saw that which made my heart almost stop beating for an instant.

Two men were driving a small bunch of cattle into the market place upon the other side of the canopy, when suddenly I saw one of the creatures, a great bull, break away from the herd and with lowered head charge toward the tiny figure playing, unconscious of danger in the dust. The men tried to head the beast off, but their efforts were futile. Those under the canopy saw the child's danger at the same time that I did and they rose and cried aloud in warning. Pthav's woman shrieked and Or-tis yelled lustily for the Kash Guard; but none hastened in the path of the infuriated beast to the rescue of the child.

I was the closest to her and the moment that I saw her danger I started forward; but even as I ran there passed through my brain some terrible thoughts. She is Kalkar! She is the spawn of the beast Pthav and of the woman who turned traitor to her kind to win ease and comfort and safety! Many a little life has been snuffed out because of her father and his class! Would they save a sister or a daughter of mine?

I thought all these things as I ran; but I did not stop running— something within impelled me to her aid. It must have been simply that she was a little child and I the descendant of American gentlemen. No, I kept right on in the face of the fact that my sense of justice cried out that I let the child die.

I reached her just a moment before the bull did and when he saw me there between him and the child he stopped and with his head down he pawed the earth, thowing clouds of dust about, and bellowed—and then he came for me; but I met him half way, determined to hold him off until the child escaped if it were humanly possible for me to do so. He was a huge beast and quite evidently a vicious one, which possibly explained the reason for bringing him to market, and altogether it seemed to me that he would make short work of me; but I meant to die fighting.

I called to the little girl to run and then the bull and I came together. I seized his horns as he attempted to toss me, and I exerted all the strength in my young body. I had thought that I had let the hellhounds feel it all that other night; but now I knew that I had yet had more in reserve, for to my astonishment I held that great beast and slowly, very slowly, I commenced to twist his head to the left.

He struggled and fought and bellowed—I could feel the muscles of my back and arms and legs hardening to the strain that was put upon them; but almost from the first instant I knew that I was master. The Kash Guards were coming now on the run, and I could hear Or-tis shouting to them to

Julian 9th Saves the Daughter of Pthav

shoot the bull; but before they reached me I gave the animal a final mighty wrench so that he went first down upon one knee and then over on his side and there I held him until a sergeant came and put a bullet through his head.

When he was quite dead Or-tis and Pthav and the others approached. I saw them coming as I was returning to my wethers, my skins and my cheese. Or-tis called to me and I turned and stood looking at him as I had no mind to have any business with any of them that I could avoid.

"Come here, my man," he called.

I moved sullenly toward him a few paces and stopped again.

"What do you want of me?" I asked.

"Who are you?" He was eying me closely now. "I never saw such strength in any man. You should be in the Kash Guard. How would you like that?"

"I would not like it," I replied. It was about then, I guess, that he recognized me, for his eyes hardened. "No," he said, "we do not want such as you among loyal men." He turned upon his heel; but immediately wheeled toward me again.

"See to it, young man," he snapped, "that you use that strength of yours wisely and in good causes."

"I shall use it wisely," I replied, "and in the best of causes."

I think Pthav's woman had intended to thank me for saving her child, and perhaps Pthav had, too, for they had both come toward me; but when they saw Or-tis's evident hostility toward me they turned away, for which I was thankful. I saw Soor looking on with a sneer on his lips and Hoffmeyer eying me with that cunning expression of his.

I gathered up my produce and proceeded to that part of the market place where we habitually showed that which we had to sell, only to find that a man named Vonbulen was there ahead of me. Now there is an unwritten law that each family has its own place in the market. I was the third generation of Julians who had brought produce to this spot—formerly horses mostly, for we were a family of horsemen; but more recently goats since the government had taken over the horse industry. Though father and I still broke horses occasionally for The TwentyFour, we did not own or raise them any more.

Vonbulen had had a little pen in a far corner, where trade was not so brisk as it usually was in our section, and I could not understand what he was doing in ours, where he had three or four scrub pigs and a few sacks of grain. Approaching, I asked him why he was there.

"This is my pen now," he said. "Tax collector Soor told me to use it."

"You will get out of it," I replied. "You know that it is ours—every one in the teivos knows that it is and has been for many years. My grandfather built it and my family have kept it in repair. You will get out!"

"I will not get out," he replied truculently. He was a very large man and when he was angry he looked quite fierce, as he had large mustaches which he brushed upward on either side of his nose—like the tusks of one of his boars.

"You will get out or be thrown out," I told him; but he put his hand on the gate and attempted to bar my entrance.

Knowing him to be heavy minded and stupid, I thought to take him by surprise, nor did I fail as, with a hand upon the topmost rail, I vaulted the gate full in his face, and letting my knees strike his chest, I sent him tumbling backward into the filth of his swine. So hard I struck him that he turned a complete back somersault and as he scrambled, to his feet, his lips fouled with oaths, I saw murder in his eye. And how he charged me! It was for all the world like the charge of the great bull I had just vanquished, except that I think that Vonbulen was angrier than the bull and not so good looking.

His great fists were flailing about in a most terrifying manner and his mouth was open just as though be intended eating me alive; but for some reason I felt no fear. In fact, I had to smile to see his face and his fierce mustache smeared with soft hog dung.

I parried his first wild blows and then stepping in close struck him lightly in the face—I am sure I did not strike him hard, for I did not mean to—I wanted to play with him; but the result was as astonishing to me as it must have been to him, though not so painful. He rebounded from my fist fully three feet and then went over on his back again, spitting blood and teeth from his mouth.

And then I picked him up by the scruff of his neck and the seat of his breeches, and lifting him high above my head, I hurled him out of the pen into the market place where, for the first time, I saw a large crowd of interested spectators.

Vonbulen was not a popular character in the teivos, and many were the broad smiles I saw on the faces of those of my class; but there were others who did not smile. They were Kalkars and half breeds.

I saw all this in a single glance and then I returned to my work, for I was not through. Vonbulen lay where he had alighted and after him and onto him, one by one, I threw his sacks of grain and his scrub pigs and then I opened the gate and started out to bring in my own produce, and livestock. As I did so I almost ran into Soor, standing there eying me with a most malignant expression upon his face.

"What does this mean?" he fairly screamed at me.

"It means," I replied, "that no one can steal the place of a Julian as easily as Vonbulen thought."

"He did not steal it," yelled Soor. "I gave it to him. Get out! It is his."

"It is not yours to give," I replied. "I know my rights and no man shall take them from me without a fight. Do you understand me?"

And then I brushed by him without another glance and drove my wethers into the pen. As I did so I saw that no one was smiling any more—my friends looked very glum and very frightened; but a man came up from my right and stood by my side, facing Soor, and when I turned my eyes in his direction I saw that it was Jim.

Then I realized how serious my act must have seemed, and I was sorry that Jim had come and thus silently announced that he stood with me in what I had done. No others came, although there were many who hated the Kalkars fully as much as we.

Soor was furious; but he could not stop me. Only The TwentyFour could take the pen away from me. He called me names and threatened me; but I noticed that he waited until he had walked a short distance away before he did so. It was as food to a starving man to know that even one of our oppressors feared me. So far this had been the happiest day of my life.

I hurriedly got the goats into the pen and then, with one of the cheeses in my hand, I called to Soor. He turned to see what I wanted, showing his teeth like a rat at bay.

"You told my father to bring you a present," I yelled at the top of my lungs, so that all about in every direction heard and turned toward us. "Here it is!" I cried. "Here is your bribe!" and I hurled the cheese with all my strength full in his face.

He went down like a felled ox and the people scattered like frightened rabbits. Then I went back into the pen and started to open and arrange my hides across the fence so that they might be inspected by prospective purchasers.

Jim, whose pen was next to ours, stood looking across the fence at me for several minutes. At last he spoke:

"You have done a very rash thing, Julian," he said, and then: "I envy you."

It was not quite plain what he meant and yet I guessed that he, too, would have been willing to die for the satisfaction of having defied them. I had not done this thing merely in the heat of anger or the pride of strength; but from the memory of my father's bowed head and my mother's tears—in the realization that we were better dead than alive unless we could hold our heads aloft as men should. Yes, I still saw my father's chin upon his breast and his unsteady gait and I was ashamed for him and for myself; but I had partially washed away the stain and there had finally crystalized in my brain something that must have been forming long in solution there—the determination to walk through the balance of my life with my head up and my fists ready—a man—however short my walk might be.

# FIVE

# The Court Martial

T HAT AFTERNOON I saw a small detachment of the Kash Guard crossing the market place. They came directly toward my pen and stopped
before it. The sergeant in charge addressed me: "You are Brother Julian
9th?" he asked.

"I am Julian 9th," I replied.

"You had better be Brother Julian 9th when you are addressed by Brother
General Or-tis," he snapped back. "You are under arrest—come with me!"

"What for?" I asked.

"Brother Or-tis will tell you if you do not know—you are to be taken
to him."

So! It had come and it had come quickly. I felt sorry for Mother; but,
in a way, I was glad. If only there had been no such person in the world
as Juana St. John I should have been almost happy, for I knew Mother
and Father would come soon and, as she always taught me, we would be
reunited in a happy world on the other side—a world in which there were
no Kalkars or taxes—but then there was a Juana St. John and I was very
sure of this world, while not quite so sure of the other, which I had never
seen, nor any one who had.

There seemed no particular reason for refusing to accompany the Kash
Guard. They would simply have killed me with their bullets and if I went
I might have an opportunity to wipe out some more important swine than
they before I was killed—if they intended killing me. One never knows
what they will do—other than that it will be the wrong thing.

Well, they took me to the headquarters of the teivos, way down on the
shore of the lake; but as they took me in a large wagon drawn by horses it
was not a tiresome trip and, as I was not worrying, I enjoyed it. We passed
through many market places, for numerous districts lie between ours and
headquarters, and always the people stared at me, just as I had stared at

other prisoners being carted away to no one knew what fate. Sometimes they came back—sometimes their did not. I wondered which I would do.

At last we arrived at headquarters after passing through miles of lofty ruins where I had played and explored as a child. I was taken immediately into Or-tis's presence. He sat in a large room at the head of a long table, and I saw that there were other men sitting along the sides of the table, the local representatives of that hated authority known as The TwentyFour, the form of government that the Kalkars had brought with them from the Moon a century before. The TwentyFour originally consisted of a committee of that number. Now, however, it was but a name that stood for power, for government and for tyranny. Jarth the Jemadar was, in reality, what his lunar title indicated—emperor. Surrounding him was a committee of twenty-four Kalkars; but as they had been appointed by him and could be removed by him at will, they were nothing more than his tools. And this body before which I had been haled had in our teivos the same power as The TwentyFour which gave it birth, and so we spoke of it, too, as The TwentyFour, or as the Teivos, as I at first thought it to be.

Many of these men I recognized as members of the teivos. Pthav and Hoffmeyer were there, representing our district, or misrepresenting it, as Father always put it, yet I was presently sure that this could not be a meeting of the teivos proper, as these were held in another building father south—a magnificent pillared pile of olden times that the Govemment had partially restored as they had the headquarters, which also had been a beautiful building in a past age, its great lions still standing on either side of its broad entranceway, facing toward the west.

No, it was not the teivos; but what could it be, and then it dawned upon me that it must be an arm of the new law that Or-tis had announced, and such it proved to be—a special military tribunal for special offenders. This was the first session and it chanced to be my luck that I committed my indiscretion just in time to be haled before it when it needed someone to experiment on.

I was made to stand, under guard, at the foot of the table and as I looked up and down the rows of faces on either side I saw not a friendly eye—no person of my class or race—just swine, swine, swine. Low-browed, brute-faced men, slouching in their chairs, slovely in their dress, uncouth, unwashed, unwholesome looking—this was the personnel of the court that was to try me—for what?

I was soon to find out. Or-tis asked who appeared against me and what was the charge. Then I saw Soor for the first time. He should have been in his district collecting his taxes; but he wasn't. No, he was there on more pleasant business. He eyed me malevolently and stated the charge: resisting an officer of the law in the discharge of his duty and assaulting same with a deadly weapon with intent to commit murder.

They all looked ferociously at me, expecting, no doubt, that I would tremble with terror, as most of my class did before them; but I couldn't tremble—the charge struck me as so ridiculous. As a matter of fact, I am afraid that I grinned. I know I did.

"'What is it," asked Or-tis, "that amuses you so?"

"The charge," I replied.

"What is there funny about that?" he asked again. "Men have been shot for less—men who were not suspected of treasonable acts."

"I did not resist an officer in the discharge of his duty," I said. "It is not one of a tax collector's duties to put a family out of its pen at the market place, is it?—a pen they have occupied for three generations. I ask you, Or-tis, is it?"

Or-tis half rose from his chair. "How dare you address me thus?" he cried.

The others turned scowling faces upon me and, beating the table with their dirty fists, they all shouted and bellowed at me at once; but I kept my chin up as I had sworn to do until I died, and I laughed in their faces.

Finally they quieted down and again I put my question to Or-tis and I'll give him credit for answering it fairly. "No," he said, "only the teivos may do that—the teivos or the commandant."

"Then I did not resist an officer in the discharge of his duty," I shot back at them, "for I only refused to leave the pen that is mine. And now another question: Is a cheese a deadly weapon?"

They had to admit that it was not. "He demanded a present from my father," I explained, "and I brought him a cheese. He had no right under the law to demand it, and so I threw it at him and it hit him in the face. I shall deliver thus every such illegal tithe that is demanded of us. I have my rights under the law and I intend to see that they are respected."

They had never been talked to thus before and suddenly I realized that by merest chance I had stumbled upon the only way in which to meet these creatures. They were moral as well as physical cowards. They could not face an honest, fearless man—already they were showing signs of embarrassment. They knew that I was right and while they could have condemned me had I bowed the knee to them they hadn't the courage to do it in my presence.

The natural outcome was that they sought a scapegoat, and Or-tis was not long in finding one—his baleful eye alighted upon Soor.

"Does this man speak the truth?" he cried at the tax collector. "Did you turn him out of his pen? Did he do no more than throw a cheese at you?"

Soor, a coward before those in authority over him, flushed and stammered.

"He tried to kill me," he mumbled lamely, "and he did almost kill Brother Vonbulen."

Then I told them of that—and always I spoke in a tone of authority and I held my ground. I did not fear them and they knew it. Sometimes I think they attributed it to some knowledge I had of something that might be menacing them—for they were always afraid of revolution. That is why they ground us down so.

The outcome of it was that I was let go with a warning—a warning that if I did not address my fellows as Brother I would be punished, and even then I gave the parting shot, for I told them I would call no man Brother unless he was.

The whole affair was a farce; but all trials were farces, only, as a rule, the joke was on the accused. They were not conducted in a dignified or proper manner as I imagine trials in ancient times to have been. There was neither order nor system.

I had to walk all the way home—another manifestation of justice—and I arrived there an hour or two after supper time. I found Jim and Mollie and Juana at the house, and I could see that Mother had been crying. She started again when she saw me. Poor Mother! I wonder if it has always been such a terrible thing to be a mother; but, no, it cannot have been, else the human race would long since have been extinct—as the Kalkars will rapidly make it, anyway.

Jim had told them of the happenings in the market place—the episode of the bull, the encounter with Vonbulen and the matter of Soor. For the first time in my life, and the only time, I heard my Father laugh aloud. Juana laughed, too; but there was still an undercurrent of terror that I could feel and which Mollie finally voiced.

"They will get us yet, Julian," she said; "but what you have done is worth dying for."

"Yes!" cried my father. "I can go to The Butcher with a smile on my lips after this. He has done what I always wanted to do; but dared not. If I am a coward I can at least thank God that there sprang from my loins a brave and fearless man.

"You are not a coward!" I cried, and Mother looked at me and smiled. I was glad that I said that, then.

You may not understand what Father meant by "going to The Butcher," but it is simple. The manufacture of ammunition is a lost art—that is, the high-powered ammunition that the Kash Guard likes to use—and so they conserve all the vast stores of ammunition that were handed down from ancient times—millions upon millions of rounds—or they would not be able to use the rifles that were handed down with the ammunition. They use this ammunition only in cases of dire necessity, a fact which long ago placed the firing squad of old in the same class with flying machines and automobiles. Now they cut our throats when they kill us and the man who does it is known as The Butcher.

I walked home with Jim and Mollie and Juana; but more especially Juana. Again I noticed that strange magnetic force which drew me to her, so that I kept bumping into her every step or two, and, intentionally, I swung my arm that was nearest to her in the hope that my hand might touch hers, nor was I doomed to disappointment and at every touch I thrilled. I could not but notice that Juana made no mention of my clumsiness, nor did she appear to attempt to prevent our contact; but yet I was afraid of her—afraid that she would notice and afraid that she would not. I am good with horses and goats and hellhounds; but I am not much good with girls.

We had talked upon many subjects and I knew her views and beliefs and she knew mine, so when we parted and I asked her if she would go with me on the morrow, which was the first Sunday of the month, she knew what I meant. She said that she would, and I went home very happy, for I knew that she and I were going to defy the common enemy side by side—that hand in hand we would face the Grim Reaper for the sake of the greatest cause on earth.

On the way home I overtook Peter Johansen going in the direction of our home. I could see that he had no mind to meet me and he immediately fell to explaining lengthily why he was out at night, for the first thing I did was to ask him what strange business took him abroad so often lately after the sun had set.

I could see him flush even in the dark.

"Why," he exclaimed, "this is the first time in months that I have gone out after supper," and then something about the man made me lose my temper and I blurted out what was in my heart.

"You lie!" I cried. "You lie, you damned spy!"

And then Peter Johansen went white and, suddenly whipping a knife from his clothes, he leaped at me, striking wildly for any part of me that the blade might reach. At first he almost got me, so unexpected and so venomous was the attack; but though I was struck twice on the arm and cut a little I managed to ward the point from any vital part, and in a moment I had seized his knife wrist. That was the end—I just twisted it a little—I did not mean to twist hard—and something snapped inside his wrist.

Peter let out an awful scream, his knife dropped from his fingers, and I pushed him from me and gave him a good kick as he was leaving—a kick that I think he will remember for some time. Then I picked up his knife and hurled it as far as I could in the direction of the river, where I think it landed, and went on my way toward home—whistling.

When I entered the house Mother came out of her room and, putting her arms about my neck, she clung closely to me.

"Dear boy," she murmured, "I am so happy, because you are happy. She is a dear girl, and I love her as much as you do."

"What is the matter?" I asked. "What are you talking about?"

"I heard you whistling," she said, "and I knew what it meant—grown men whistle but once in their lives."

I picked her up in my arms and tossed her to the ceiling.

"Oh, Mother, dear!" I cried. "I wish it were true and maybe it will be some day—if I am not too much of a coward; but not yet."

"Then why were you whistling?" she asked, surprised and a bit skeptical, too, I imagine.

"I whistled," I explained, "because I just broke the wrist of a spy and kicked him across the road."

"Peter?" she asked, trembling.

"Yes, Mother, Peter. I called him a spy and he tried to knife me."

"Oh, my son!" she cried. "You did not know. It is my fault, I should have told you. Now he will fight no more in the dark; but will come out in the open and when he does that I am lost."

"What do you mean?" I asked.

"I do not mind dying," she said; "but they will take your father first, because of me."

"What do you mean? I can understand nothing of what you are driving at."

"Then listen," she said. "Peter wants me. That is the reason he is spying on your father. If he can prove something against him and Father is taken to the mines or killed, Peter will claim me."

"How do you know this?" I asked.

"Peter himself has told me that he wants me. He tried to make me leave your dear father and go with him, and when I refused he bragged that he was in the favor of the Kalkars and that he would get me in the end. He has tried to buy my honor with your father's life. That is why I have been so afraid and so unhappy; but I knew that you and father would rather die than have me do that thing, and so I have withstood him."

"Did you tell Father?" I asked.

"I dared not. He would have killed Peter and that would have been the end of us, for Peter stands high in the graces of the authorities."

"I will kill him!" I said.

She tried to dissuade me, and finally I had to promise her that I would wait until I had provocation that the authorities might recognize. God knows I had provocation enough, though.

After breakfast the next day we set out singly and in different directions, as was always our custom on the first Sunday in each month. I went to Jim's first to get Juana, as she did not know the way, having never been with us. I found her ready and waiting and alone, as Jim and Mollie had started a few minutes before, and she was seemingly very glad to see me.

I told her nothing of Peter, as there is enough trouble in the world without burdening people with any that does not directly threaten them— each has plenty of his own. I led her up the river for a mile and all the while we watched to see if we were followed. Then we found a skiff, where I had hidden it, and crossed the—river. After hiding it again we continued on up for half a mile. Here was a raft that I had made myself, and on this we poled again to the opposite shore—if any followed us they must have swum, for there were no other boats on this part of the river.

I had come this way for several years—in fact, ever since I was fifteen years old—and no one had ever suspected or followed me, yet I never relaxed my vigilance, which may account for the fact that I was not apprehended. No one ever saw me take to either the skiff or the raft and no one could even have guessed my destination, so circuitous was the way.

A mile west of the river is a thick forest of very old trees and toward this I led Juana. At its verge we sat down, ostensibly to rest; but really to see if anyone was near who might have followed us or who could accidentally discover our next move. There was no one in sight, and so, with light hearts, we arose and entered the forest.

For a quarter of a mile we made our way along a winding path and then I turned to the left at a right angle and entered thick brush where there was no trail. Always we did this, never covering the last quarter of a mile over the same route, lest we make a path that might be marked and followed.

Presently we came to a pile of brush wood, beneath one edge of which was an opening into which, by stooping low, one might enter. It was screened from view by a fallen tree, over which had been heaped broken branches. Even in winter time and early spring the opening in the brush beyond was invisible to the passers-by, if there had been any passers-by, which except upon rare occasions there were not. A man trailing lost stock might come this way; but no others, for it was a lonely and unfrequented spot. During the summer, the season of the year when there was the greatest danger of discovery, the entire brush pile and its tangled screen were hidden completely beneath a mass of wild vines, so that it was with difficulty that we found it ourselves.

Into this opening I led Juana—taking her by the hand as one might a blind person, although it was not so dark within that she could not see perfectly every step she took. However, I took her by the hand, a poor excuse being better than none. The winding tunnel beneath the brush was a hundred yards long, perhaps—I wished then that it had been a hundred miles. It ended abruptly before a rough stone wall in which was a heavy door. Its oaken panels were black with age and streaked with green from the massive hinges that ran across its entire width in three places, while from the great lag screws that fastened them to the door brownish streaks of rust ran down to mingle with the green and the black. In patches moss grew upon it, so that all in all it had the appearance of great antiquity, though even the oldest among those who knew of it at all could only guess at its age—it had been there longer than they could recall. Above the door, carved in the stone, was a shepherd's crook and the words, *Dieu et mon droit.*

Halting before this massive portal I struck the panels once with my knuckles, counted five and struck again, once; then I counted three and, in the same cadence, struck three times. It was the signal for the day—never twice was it the same. Should one come with the wrong signal and later force the door he would find only an empty room beyond.

Now the door opened a crack and an eye peered forth, it swung outward and we entered a long, low room lighted by burning wicks floating in oil. Across the width of a room were rough wooden benches and at the far end a raised platform upon which stood Orrin Colby, the blacksmith, behind an altar which was the sawn off trunk of a tree, the roots of which, legend has it, still run down into the ground beneath the church, which is supposed to have been built around it.

# SIX

# Betrayed

T HERE WERE twelve people sitting on the benches when we entered, so that with Orrin Colby, ourselves and the man at the door we were sixteen in all. Colby is the head of our church; his great-grandfather having been a Methodist minister. Father and mother were there, sitting next to Jim and Mollie, and there were Samuels the Jew, Betty Worth, who was Dennis Corrigan's woman, and all the other familiar faces.

They had been waiting for us and as soon as we were seated the services commenced with a prayer, everyone standing with bowed head. Orrin Colby always delivered this same short prayer at the opening of services each first Sunday of every month. It ran something like this:

"God of our fathers, through generations of persecution and cruelty in a world of hate that has turned against You, we stand at Your right hand, loyal to You and to our Flag. To us Your name stands for justice, humanity, love, happiness and right and The Flag is Your emblem. Once each month we risk our lives that Your name may not perish from the Earth. Amen!"

From behind the altar he took a shepherd's crook to which was attached a flag like that in my father's possession and held it aloft, wherat we all knelt in silence for a few seconds. Then he replaced it and we arose. Then we sang a song—it was an old, old song that started like this: "Onward, Christian Soldiers." It was my favorite song. Mollie Sheehan played a violin while we sang.

Following the song Orrin Colby talked to us—he always talked about the practical things that affected our lives and our future. It was a homely talk, but it was full of hope for better times. I think that at these meetings, once each month, we heard the only suggestions of hope that ever came into our lives. There was something about Orrin Colby that inspired confidence and hope. These days were the bright spots in our drab existence that helped to make life bearable.

After the talk we sang again and then Samuels the Jew prayed and the regular service was over, after which we had short talks by various members of our church. These talks were mostly on the subject which dominated the minds of all—a revolution; but we never got any further than talking. How could we? We were probably the most thoroughly subjugated people the world ever had known—we feared our masters and we feared our neighbors. We did not know whom we might trust, outside that little coterie of ours, and so we dared not seek recruits for our cause, although we knew that there must be thousands who would sympathize with us. Spies and informers were everywhere—they, the Kash Guard and The Butcher, were the agencies by which they controlled us; but of all we feared most the spies and informers. For a woman, for a neighbor's house, and in one instance of which I know, for a setting of eggs, men have been known to inform on their friends—sending them to the mines or The Butcher.

Following the talks we just visited together and gossiped for an hour or two, enjoying the rare treat of being able to speak our minds freely and fearlessly. I had to re-tell several times my experiences before Or-tis's new court-martial and I know that it was with difficulty that they believed that I had said the things I had to our masters and come away free and alive. They simply could not understand it.

All were warned of Peter Johansen and the names of others under suspicion of being informers were passed around that we might all be on our guard against them. We did not sing again, for even on these days that our hearts were lightest they were too heavy for song. About two o'clock the pass signal for the next meeting was given out and then we started away singly or in pairs. I volunteered to go last, with Juana, and see that the door was locked. An hour later, after the rest had gone, we started out, about five minutes behind Samuels the Jew.

Juana's mother had passed down to her by word of mouth an unusually complete religious training for those days and she, in turn, had transmitted it to Juana. It seemed that they, too, had had a church in their district; but that a short time before it had been discovered by the authorities and destroyed, though none of the members of the organization had been apprehended. So close a watch was kept thereafter that they had never dared seek another meeting place.

She told me that their congregation was much like ours in personnel and with the knowledge she had of ancient religious customs it always seemed odd to her to see so different creeds worshiping under one roof in even greater harmony than many denominations of the same church knew in ancient times. Among us were descendants of Methodist, Presbyterian, Baptist, Roman Catholic and Jew that I knew of and how many more I did not know, nor did any of us care.

We worshiped an ideal and a great hope, both of which were all goodness, and we called these God. We did not care what our great-grandfathers thought about it or what some one a thousand years before had thought or done or what name they had given the Supreme Being, for we knew that there could be but one and whether we called Him one thing or another would not alter Him in any way. This much good, at least, the Kalkars had accomplished in the world; but it had come too late. Those who worshiped any god were becoming fewer and fewer. Our own congregation had fallen from twenty-two a year or so before to fifteen—until Juana made us sixteen.

Some had died natural deaths and some had gone to the mines or The Butcher; but the principal reason of our decadence was the fact that there were too few children to take the place of the adults who died—that and our fear to seek converts. We were dying out, there was no doubt of it, and with us was dying all religion. That was what the lunar theory was doing for the world; but it was only what any one might have expected. Intelligent men and women realized it from almost the instant that this lunar theory stuck its ugly head above our horizon—a political faith that would make all women the common property of all men could not by any remote possibility have respect, or even aught but fear, for any religion of ancient times, and the Kalkars did, just what any one might have known they would do—they deliberately and openly crushed all churches.

Juana and I had emerged from the wood when we noticed a man walking cautiously in the shade of the trees ahead of us. He seemed to be following some one and immediately there sprang to my thoughts the ever-near suspicion—spy.

The moment that he turned a bend in the pathway and was out of our sight Juana and I ran forward as rapidly as we could go that we might get a closer view of him, nor were we disappointed. We saw him and recognized him and we also saw whom he shadowed. It was Peter Johansen, carrying one arm in a sling, sneaking along behind Samuels.

I knew that if Peter was permitted to shadow Samuels home he would discover the devious way the old man followed and immediately, even though he had suspicioned nothing in particular before, he would know that Moses had been upon some errand that he didn't wish the authorities to learn of. That would mean suspicion for old Samuels and suspicion usually ended in conviction upon one charge or another. How far he had followed him we could not guess, but already we knew that it was much too near the church for safety. I was much perturbed.

Casting about in my mind for some plan to throw Peter off the track I finally hit upon a scheme which I immediately put into execution. I knew the way that the old man followed to and from church and that presently he would make a wide detour that would bring him back to the river about a quarter of a mile below. Juana and I could walk straight to the spot and arrive long before Samuels did. And this we proceeded to do.

About half an hour after we reached the point at which we knew he would strike the river, we heard him coming and withdrew into some bushes. On he came all oblivious of the creature on his trail and a moment later we saw Peter come into view and halt at the edge of the trees. Then Juana and I stepped out and hailed Samuels.

"Did you see nothing of them?" I asked in a tone of voice loud enough to be distinctly heard by Peter, and then before Samuels could reply I added: "We have searched far up the river and never a sign of a goat about—I do not believe that they came this way after all; but if they did the hellhounds will get them after dark. Come, now, we might as well start for home and give the search up as a bad job."

I had talked so much and so rapidly that Samuels had guessed that I must have some reason for it, and so he held his peace, other than to say that he had seen nothing of any goats. Not once had Juana or I let our glances betray that we knew of Peter's presence, though I could not help but seeing him dodge behind a tree the moment that he saw us.

The three of us then continued on toward home in the shortest direction and on the way I whispered to Samuels what we had seen. The old man chuckled, for he thought as I did that my ruse must have effectually baffled Johansen—unless he had followed Moses farther than we guessed. We each turned a little white as the consequences of such a possibility were borne home upon us. We did not want Peter to know that we even guessed that we were followed, and so we never once looked behind us, not even Juana, which was remarkable for a woman, nor did we see him again, though we felt that he was following us. I for one was sure, though, that he was following at a safer distance since I had joined Samuels.

Very cautiously during the ensuing week the word was passed around by means with which we were familiar that Johansen had followed Samuels from church; but as the authorities paid no more attention to Moses than before we finally concluded that we had thrown Peter off the trail.

The Sunday following church we were all seated in Jim's yard under one of his trees that had already put forth its young leaves and afforded shade from the sun. We had been talking of homely things—the coming crops, the newborn kids, Mollie's little pigs. The world seemed unusually kindly. The authorities had not persecuted us of late—rather they had left us alone—a respite of two weeks seemed like heaven to us. We were quite sure by this time that Peter Johansen had discovered nothing and our hearts were freer than for a long time past.

We were sitting thus in quiet and contentment, enjoying a brief rest from our lives of drudgery, when we heard the pounding of horses' hoofs upon the hard earth of the path that leads down the river in the direction of the market place. Suddenly the entire atmosphere changed—relaxed nerves became suddenly taut; peaceful eyes resumed their hunted expression. Why? The Kash Guard rides.

And so they came—fifty of them—and at their head rode Brother General Or-tis. At the gateway of Jim's house they drew rein and Or-tis dismounted and entered the yard. He looked at us as a man might look at carrion; and he gave us no greeting, which suited us perfectly. He walked straight to Juana, who was seated on a little bench beside which I stood leaning against the bole of the tree. None of us moved. He halted before the girl.

"I have come to tell you," he said to her, "that I have done you the honor to choose you as my woman, to bear my children and keep my house in order."

He stood then looking at her and I could feel the hair upon my head rise and the corners of my upper lip twitched—I know not why. I only know that I wanted to fly at his throat and kill him, to tear his flesh with my teeth—to see him die! And then he looked at me and stepped back, after which he beckoned to some of his men to enter. When they had come he again addressed Juana, who had risen and stood swaying to and fro, as might one who has been dealt a heavy blow upon the head and half stunned.

"You may come with me now," he said to her, and then I stepped between them and faced him and again he stepped back a pace.

"She will not come with you now, or ever," I said, and my voice was very low—not above a whisper. "She is my woman—I have taken her!"

It was a lie—the last part, but what is a lie to a man who would commit murder in the same cause. He was among his men now—they were close around him and I suppose they gave him courage, for he addressed me threateningly.

"I do not care whose she is," he cried, "I want her and I shall have her.

I speak for her now and I speak for her when she is a widow. After you are dead I have first choice of her and traitors do not live long."

"I am not dead yet," I reminded him. He turned to Juana.

"You shall have thirty days as the law requires; but you can save your friends trouble if you come now—they will not be molested then and I will see that their taxes are lowered."

Juana gave a little gasp and looked around at us and then she straightened her shoulders and came close to me.

"No!" she said to Or-tis. "I will never go. This is my man—he has taken me. Ask him if he will give me up to you. You will never have me—alive."

"Don't be too sure of that," he growled. "I believe that you are both lying to me, for I have had you watched and I know that you do not live under the same roof. And you!" he glared at me. "Tread carefully, for the eyes of the law find traitors where others do not see them." Then he turned and strode from the yard. A minute later they were gone in a cloud of dust.

Now our happiness and peace had fled—it was always thus—and there was no hope. I dared not look at Juana after what I had said; but then, had she not said the same thing? We all talked lamely for a few minutes and then Father and Mother rose to go and a moment later Jim and Mollie went indoors.

I turned to Juana. She stood with her eyes upon the ground and a pretty flush upon her cheek. Something surged up in me—a mighty force, that I had never known, possessed me, and before I realized what it impelled me to do I had seized Juana in my arms and was covering her face and lips with kisses.

She fought to free herself, but I would not let her go.

"You are mine!" I cried. "You are my woman. I have said it—you have said. You are my woman. God, how I love you!"

She lay quiet then and let me kiss her, and presently her arms stole about my neck and her lips sought mine in an interval that I had drawn them away and they moved upon my lips in a gentle caress that was yet palpitant with passion. This was a new Juana—a new and very wonderful Juana.

"You really love me?" she asked at last. "I heard you say it!"

"I have loved you from the moment I saw you looking up at me from beneath the hellhound," I replied.

"You have kept it very much of a secret to yourself then," she teased me. "If you loved me so, why did you not tell me? Were you going to keep it from me all my life, or—were you afraid? Brother Or-tis was not afraid to say that he wanted me. Is my man, my Julian, less brave than he?"

I knew that she was only teasing me, and so I stopped her mouth with kisses and then: "Had you been a hellhound, or Soor, or even Or-tis," I said, "I could have told you what I thought of you, but being Juana and a little girl the words would not come. I am a great coward."

We talked until it was time to go home to supper and I took her hand to lead her to my house. "But first," I said, "you must tell Mollie and Jim what has happened and that you will not be back. For a while we can live under my father's roof, but as soon as may be I will get permission from the teivos to take the adjoining land and work it and then I shall build a house."

She drew back and flushed. "I cannot go with you yet," she said.

"What do you mean?" I asked. "You are mine!"

"We have not been married," she whispered.

"But no one is married," I reminded her. "Marriage is against the law."

"My mother was married," she told me. "You and I can be married. We have a church and a preacher. Why cannot he marry us? He is not ordained because there is none to ordain him; but being the head of the only church that he knows of or that we know of, it is evident that he can be ordained only by God and who knows but that he already has been ordained!"

I tried to argue her out of it as now that heaven was so near I had no mind to wait three weeks to attain it. But she would not argue—she just shook her head and at last I saw that she was right and gave in—as I would have had to do in any event.

The next day I sought Orrin Colby and broached the subject to him. He was quite enthusiastic about it and wondered that they had never thought of it before. Of course, they had not because marriage had been obsolete for so many years that no one considered the ceremony necessary, nor, in fact, was it. Men and women were more often faithful to one another through life than otherwise—no amount of ceremony or ritual could make them more so. But if a woman wants it she should have it. And so it was arranged that at the next meeting Juana and I should be married.

The next three weeks were about the longest of my life and yet they were very, very happy weeks, for Juana and I were much together, as it had finally been decided that in order to carry out our statements to Or-tis she must come and live under our roof. She slept in the living room and I upon a pile of goat skins in the kitchen. If there were any spies watching us, and I know that there were, they saw that we slept every night under the same roof.

Mother worked hard upon a new tunic and breeches for me, while Mollie helped Juana with her outfit. The poor child had come to us with only the clothes she wore upon her back; but even so, most of us had few changes—just enough to keep ourselves decently clean.

I went to Pthav, who was one of our representatives in the teivos, and asked him to procure for me permission to work the vacant land adjoining my father's. The land all belonged to the community, but each man was allowed what he could work as long as there was plenty, and there was more than plenty for us all.

Pthav was very ugly—he seemed to have forgotten that I had saved his child's life—and said that he did not know what he could do for me, that I had acted very badly to General Or-tis and was in disfavor, beside being under suspicion in another matter.

"What has General Or-tis to do with the distribution of land by the teivos?" I asked. "Because he wants my woman will the teivos deny me my rights?"

I was no longer afraid of any of them and I spoke my mind as freely as I wished—almost. Of course, I did not care to give them the chance to bring me to trial as they most assuredly would have done had I really said to them all that was in my heart, but I stood up for my rights and demanded all that their rotten laws allowed me.

Pthav's woman came in while I was talking and recognized me, but she said nothing to me other than to mention that the child had asked for me. Pthav scowled at this and ordered her from the room, just as a man might order a beast around. It was nothing to me, though, as the woman was a renegade anyway.

Finally I demanded of Pthav that he obtain the concession for me unless he could give me some valid reason for refusing.

"I will ask it," he said finally, "but you will not get it—be sure of that."

I saw that it was useless and so I turned and left the room, wondering what I should do. Of course, we could remain under Father's roof, but that did not seem right, as each man should make a home for himself. After Father and Mother died we would return to the old place, as Father had after the death of my grandfather, but a young couple should start their life together alone and in their own way.

As I was leaving the house Pthav's woman stopped me. "I will do what I can for you," she whispered. She must have seen me draw away instinctively as from an unclean thing, for she flushed, and then said: "Please don't! I have suffered enough. I have paid the price of my treachery; but know, Yank," and she put her lips close to my ear, "that at heart I am more Yank than I was when I did this thing. And," she continued, "I have never spoken a word that could harm one of you. Tell them that—please tell them! I do not want them to hate me so, and, God of our Fathers! How I have suffered—the degradation, the humiliation: It has been worse than what you are made to suffer. These creatures are lower than the beasts of the forest. When his friends come he serves them food and drink and—me! Ugh! I could kill him if I were not such a coward. I have seen, and I know how they can make one suffer before death."

I could not but feel sorry for her, and I told her so. The poor creature appeared very grateful, and assured me that she would aid me.

"I know a few things about Pthav that he would not want Or-tis to know," she said, "and even though he beats me for it I will make him get the land for you."

Again I thanked her, and departed, realizing that there were others worse off than we—that the closer one came to the Kalkars the more hideous life became.

At last the day came, and we set out for the church. As before I took Juana, though she tried to order it differently; but I would not trust her to the protection of another. We arrived without mishap—sixteen of us—and after the religious services were over, Juana and I stood before the altar, and were married—much after the fashion of the ancients, I imagine.

Juana was the only one of us who was at all sure about the ceremony, and it had been she who trained Orrin Colby—making him memorize so much that he said his head ached for a week. All I can recall of it is that he asked me if I would take her to be my lawfully wedded wife—I lost my voice, and only squeaked a weak yes—and that he pronounced us man and wife, and then something about not letting anyone put asunder what God had joined together. I felt very much married, and very happy, and then just as it was all nicely over, and everybody was shaking hands with us, there came a loud knocking at the door, and the command: "Open, in the name of the law!"

We looked at one another and gasped. Orrin Colby put a finger to his lips for silence, and led the way toward the back of the church where a rough niche was built in, containing a few shelves upon which stood several rude candlesticks. We knew our parts, and followed him in silence, except one who went quickly about putting out the lights. All the time the pounding on the door became more insistent, and then we could hear the strokes of what must have been an ax beating at the panels. Finally a shot was fired through the heavy wood, and we knew it was the Kash Guard.

Taking hold of the lower shelf Orrin pulled upward with all his strength with the result that all the shelving and woodwork to which it was attached slid upward revealing an opening beyond. Through this we fled, one by one, down a flight of stone steps into a dark tunnel. When the last man

The Wedding of Julian 9th and Juana

had passed I lowered the shelving to its former place, being careful to see that it fitted tightly.

Then I turned, and followed the others, Juana's hand in mine. We groped our way for some little distance in the stygian darkness of the tunnel until Orrin halted, and whispered to me to come to him. I went and stood at his side while he told me what I was to do. He had called upon me because I was the tallest, and the strongest of the men. Above us was a wooden trap. I was to lift this and push it aside.

It had not been moved for generations, and was very heavy with earth, and growing things above; but I put my shoulders to it, and it had to give— either it or the ground beneath my feet, and that could not give. At last I had it off, and in a few minutes I had helped them all out into the midst of a dense wood. Again we knew our parts, for many times had we been coached for just such an emergency, and one by one the men scattered in different directions, each taking his woman with him.

Suiting our movements to a prearranged plan, we reached our homes from different directions, and at different times, some arriving after sun-down; to the end that were we watched none might be sure that we had been upon the same errand or to the same place.

# SEVEN

# The Arrest of Julian 8th

M OTHER HAD supper ready by the time Juana and I arrived. Father said they had seen nothing of the Kash Guard, nor had we; but we could guess at what had happened at the church. The door must finally have given at their blows. We could imagine their rage when they found that their prey had flown, leaving no trace. Even if they found the hidden tunnel, and we doubted that they had, the discovery would profit them but little. We were very sad, though, for we had lost our church. Never again in this generation could it be used. We added another mark to the growing score against Johansen.

The next morning as I was peddling milk to those who live about the market place, Old Samuels came out of his little cottage, and hailed me.

"A little milk this morning, Julian!" he cried, and when I carried my vessel over to him he asked me inside. His cottage was very small, and simply furnished as were all those that made any pretense to furniture of any sort, some having only a pile of rags or skins in one corner for a bed, and perhaps a bench or two which answered the combined purposes of seats and table. In the yard behind his cottage he did his tanning, and there also was a little shed he called his shop where he fashioned various articles from the hides he tanned—belts, head bands, pouches, and the like.

He led me through the cottage, and out to his shed, and when we were there he looked through the windows to see that no one was near.

"I have something here," he said, "that I meant to bring to Juana for a wedding gift yesterday; but I am an old man, and forgetful, and so I left it behind. You can take it to her, though, with the best wishes of Old Samuels the Jew. It has been in my family since the Great War in which my people fought by the side of your people. One of my ancestors was wounded on a battlefield in France, and later nursed back to health by a Roman Catholic nurse, who gave him this token to carry away with him that he might not forget her. The story is that she loved him; but being a nun she could not marry. It has been handed down from father to son—it is my most prized possession, Julian; but being an old man, and the last of my line I wish it to go to those I love most dearly, for I doubt that I have long to live. Again yesterday, I was followed from the church."

He turned to a little cupboard on the wall, and removing a false bottom took from the drawer beneath a small leather bag which he handed to me.

"Look at it," he said, "and then slip it inside your shirt so that none may know that you have it."

Opening the bag I brought forth a tiny image carved from what appeared to be very hard bone—the figure of a man nailed to a cross—a man with a wreath of thorns about his head. It was a very wonderful piece of work—I had never seen anything like it in my life.

"It is very beautiful," I said. "Juana will be thankful, indeed."

"Do you know what it is?" he asked, and I had to admit that I did not.

"It is the figure of the Son of God upon the cross, he explained, "and it is carved from the tusk of an elephant. Juana will—" But he got no farther. "Quick!" he whispered, "hide it. Some one comes!"

I slipped the little figure inside my shirt just as several men crossed from Samuels's cottage to his shop. They came directly to the door, and then we saw that they were Kash Guards. A captain commanded them. He was one of the officers who had come with Or-tis, and I did not know him.

He looked first at me and then at Samuels, finally addressing the latter.

"From the description," he said, "you are the man I want—you are Samuels the Jew?"

Moses nodded affirmatively.

"I have been sent to question you," said the officer, "and if you know when you are well off you will tell me nothing but the truth, and all of that."

Moses made no reply—he just stood there, a little, dried-up old man who seemed to have shrunk to even smaller proportions in the brief moments since the officer had entered. Then the latter turned to me, and looked me over from head to foot.

"Who are you, and what do you here?" he asked.

"I am Julian 9th," I replied. "I was peddling milk when I stopped in to speak with my friend."

"You should be more careful of your friends, young man," he snapped. "I had intended letting you go about your business; but now that you say you are a friend of his we will just keep you, too. Possibly you can help us."

I didn't know what he wanted; but I knew that whatever it was he would get precious little help from Julian 9th. He turned to Moses.

"Do not lie to me! You went to a forbidden meeting yesterday to worship some god, and plot against the teivos. Four weeks ago you went to the same place. Who else was there yesterday?"

Samuels looked the captain straight in the eye, and remained silent.

"Answer me, you dirty Jew!" yelled the officer, "or I will find a way to make you. Who was there with you?"

"I will not answer," said Samuels.

The captain turned to a sergeant standing behind him. "Give him the first reason why he should answer," he directed.

The sergeant, who carried his bayonet fixed to his rifle, lowered the point until it rested against Samuels's leg, and with a sudden jab ran it into the flesh. The old man cried out in pain, and staggered back against his little bench. I sprang forward, white with rage, and seizing the sergeant by the collar of his loose tunic hurled him across the shop. It was all done in less than a second, and then I found myself facing as many loaded rifles as could crowd into the little doorway. The captain had drawn his pistol, and leveled it at my head.

They bound me, and sat me in a corner of the shop, and they were none too gentle in the way they did it, either. The captain was furious, and would have had me shot on the spot had not the sergeant whispered something to him. As it was he ordered the latter to search us both for weapons, and when they did so they discovered the little image on my person. At sight of it a sneer of triumph curled the lip of the officer.

"So-ho!" he exclaimed. "Here is evidence enough. Now we know one at least who worships forbidden gods, and plots against the laws of his land!"

"It is not his," said Samuels. "It is mine. He does not even know what it is. I was showing it to him when we heard you coming, and I told him to hide it in his shirt. It is just a curious relic that I was showing him."

"Then you are the worshiper after all," said the captain.

Old Samuels smiled a crooked smile. "Who ever heard of a Jew worshiping Christ?" he asked.

The officer looked at him sharply. "That is right," he admitted, "you would not worship Christ; but you have been worshiping something—it is all the same—they are all alike. This for all of them," and he hurled the image to the earthern floor, and ground it, in broken fragments, into the dirt with his heel.

Old Samuels went very white then, and his eyes stared wide and round; but he held his tongue. Then they started in on him again, asking him to name those who were with him the day before, and each time they asked him they prodded him with a bayonet until his poor old body streamed blood from a dozen cruel wounds. But he would not give them a single name, and then the officer ordered that a fire be built and a bayonet heated.

"Sometimes hot steel is better than cold," he said. "You had better tell me the truth."

"I will tell you nothing," moaned Samuels in a weak voice. "You may kill me; but you will learn nothing from me."

"But you have never felt red-hot steel before," the captain taunted him. "It has wrung the secrets from stouter hearts than that in the filthy carcass of a dirty old Jew. Come now, save yourself the agony, and tell me who was there, for in the end you will tell."

But the old man would not tell, and then they did the hideous thing that they had threatened—with red-hot steel they burned him after tying him to his bench.

His cries and moans were piteous—it seemed to me that they must have softened stone to compassion; but the hearts of those beasts were harder than stone.

He suffered! God of our Fathers! how he suffered; but they could not force him to tell. At last he lost consciousness and then the brute in the uniform of captain, rageful that he failed, crossed the room, and struck the poor, unconscious old man a heavy blow in the face.

After that it was my turn. He came to me.

"Tell me what you know, pig of a Yank!" he cried.

"As he died, so can I die," I said, for I thought that Samuels was dead.

"You will tell," he shrieked, almost insane with rage. "You will tell or your eyes will be burned from their sockets." He called the fiend with the bayonet—now white hot it seemed, so terrifically it glowed.

As the fellow approached me the horror of the thing they would do to me seared my brain with an anguish almost as poignant as that which the hot iron could inflict on flesh. I had struggled to free myself of my bonds while they tortured Samuels, that I might go to his aid; but I had failed. Yet, now, scarcely without realizing that I exerted myself, I rose, and the cords snapped. I saw them step back in amazement as I stood there confronting them.

"Go," I said to them. "Go before I kill you all. Even the teivos, rotten as it is, will not stand for this usurpation of its authority. You have no right to inflict punishment. You have gone too far."

The sergeant whispered for a moment to his superior, who finally appeared to assent grudgingly to some proposition of the others and then turned, and left the little shop.

"We have no proof against you," said the sergeant to me. "We had no intention of harming you. All that we wanted was to frighten the truth out of you; but as to that," and he jerked a thumb toward Samuels, "we have the proof on him, and what we did we did under orders. Keep a still tongue in your head or it will be the worse for you, and thank the star under which you were born that you did not get worse than he."

Then he left, too, and took the soldiers with him. I saw them pass into the rear doorway of Samuels's cottage, and a moment later I heard their horses' hoofs pounding on the surface of the market place. I could scarcely believe that I had escaped. Then I did not know the reason for it; but that I was to learn later, and that it was not so much of a miracle after all.

I went right to poor old Samuels. He was still breathing, but unconscious—mercifully so. The withered old body was hideously burned, and mutilated, and one eye—but why describe their ghoulish work! I carried him into his cottage, and laid him on his cot, and then I found some flour, and covered his burns with it—that was all I knew to do for him. There were no doctors such as the ancients had, for there were no longer places of learning in which they could be trained. There were those who claimed to be able to heal. They gave herbs and strange concoctions; but as their patients usually died immediately we had little confidence in them.

After I had put the flour on his wounds, I drew up a bench, and sat down beside him so that when he regained consciousness he would find a friend there to wait upon him. As I sat there looking at him he died. Tears came to my eyes in spite of all that I could do, for friends are few, and I had loved this old Jew, as we all did who knew him. He had been a gentle character, loyal to his friends, and inclined to be a little too forgiving to his enemies—even the Kalkars. That he was courageous his death proved.

I put another mark against the score of Peter Johansen.

The following day, Father, Jim, and I buried old Samuels, the authorities came and took all his poor little possessions, and his cottage was turned over to another. But I had one thing, his most prized possession, that they did not get, for before I left him after he died, I went back into his shop, and gathered up the fragments of the man upon the cross, and put them into the little leather bag in which he had kept them.

When I gave them to Juana, and told her the story of them she wept and kissed them, and with some glue such as we make from the hides and tendons of goats we mended it so it was difficult to tell where it had broken. After it was dry Juana wore it in its little bag about her neck, beneath her clothing.

A week after the death of Samuels, Pthav sent for me, and very gruffly told me that the teivos had issued a permit for me to use the land adjoining that allotted to my father. As before, his woman stopped me as I was leaving.

"It was easier than I thought," she told me, "for Or-tis has angered the teivos by attempting to usurp all its powers, and knowing that he hates you they were glad to grant your petition over his objections."

I had heard rumors lately of the growing differences between Or-tis and the teivos, and had learned that it was these that had saved me from the Kash Guard that day—the sergeant having warned his superior that should they maltreat me without good and sufficient reason the teivos could take advantage of the fact to discipline the Guard and they were not yet ready for the test—that was to come later.

During the next two or three months I was busy building our home and getting my place in order. I had decided to raise horses and obtained permission from the teivos to do so—again over Or-tis's objections. Of course, the government controlled the entire horse traffic; but there were a few skilled horsemen permitted to raise them, though at any time their herds could be commandeered by the authorities. I knew that it might not be a very profitable business, but I loved horses and wanted to have just a few—a stallion and two or three mares. These I could use in tilling my fields and in the heavier work of hauling and at the same time I would keep a few goats, pigs and chickens to insure us a living.

Father gave me half his goats and a few chickens and from Jim I bought two young sows and a boar. Later I traded a few goats to the teivos for two old mares that they thought were no longer worth keeping, and that same day I was told of a stallion—a young outlaw—that Hoffmeyer had. The beast was five years old and so vicious that none dared approach him—and they were on the point of destroying him.

I went to Hoffmeyer and asked if I could buy the animal—I offered him a goat for it, which he was glad to accept, and then I took a strong rope and went to get my property. I found a beautiful bay with the temper of a hellhound. When I attempted to enter the pen he rushed at me with ears back and jaws distended, but I knew that I must conquer him now or never, and so I met him with only a rope in my hand, nor did I wait for him. Instead, I ran to meet him and when he was in reach I struck him once across the face with the rope, at which he wheeled and let both hind feet fly out at me. Then I cast the noose that was at one end of the rope and caught him about the neck and for half an hour we had a battle of it.

I never struck him unless he tried to bite or strike me and finally I must have convinced him that I was master, for he let me come close enough to stroke his glossy neck, though he snorted loudly all the while that I did so. When I had quieted him a bit I managed to get a half hitch around his lower jaw, and after that I had no difficulty in leading him from the pen. Once in the open I took the coils of my rope in my left hand and before the creature knew what I was about had vaulted to his back.

He fought fair, I'll say that for him, for he stood on his feet, but for fifteen minutes he brought into play every artifice known to horsekind for unseating a rider. Only my skill and my great strength kept me on his back and at that even the Kalkars who were looking on had to applaud my horsemanship.

After that it was easy. I treated him with kindness, something he had never known before, and as he was an unusually intelligent animal, he soon learned that I was not only his master, but his friend. From being an outlaw he became one of the kindest and most tractable animals I have ever seen, so much so, in fact, that Juana used to ride him bareback.

I love all horses and always have, but I think I never loved any animal as I did Red Lightning, as we named him.

The authorities left us pretty well alone for some time because they were quarreling among themselves. Jim said there was an ancient saying about honest men getting a little peace when thieves fell out and it certainly fitted our case perfectly. But the peace didn't last forever, and when it broke the bolt that fell was the worst calamity that had ever come to us.

One evening Father was arrested for trading at night and taken away by the Kash Guard. They got him as he was returning to the house from the goat pens and would not even permit him to bid good-bye to Mother. Juana and I were eating supper in our own house about three hundred yards away and never knew anything about it until Mother came running over to tell us. She said that it was all done so quickly that they had Father and were gone before she could run from the house to where they arrested him. They had a spare horse and hustled him onto it—then they galloped away toward the lake front. It seems strange that neither Juana nor I heard the hoof beats of the horses, but we did not.

I went immediately to Pthav and demanded to know why Father had been arrested, but he professed ignorance of the whole affair. I had ridden to his place on Red Lightning and from there I started to the Kash Guard barracks where the military prison is. It was contrary to law to approach the barracks after sunset without permission, so I left Red Lightning in the shadow of some ruins a hundred yards away and started on foot toward that part of the post, where I knew the prison to be located. The latter consists of a high stockade around the inside of which are rude shelters. Upon the roofs of these armed guards patrol. The center of the rectangle is an open court where the prisoners exercise, cook their food and wash their clothing—if they care to. There are seldom more than fifty confined here at a time, as it is only a detention camp where they hold those who are awaiting trial and those who have been sentenced to the mines. The latter were usually taken away when there were from twenty-five to forty of them.

They march them in front of mounted guards a distance of about fifty miles to the nearest mines, which lie southwest of our teivos, driving them, like cattle with heavy whips of bullhide. To such great cruelty are they subjected, so escaped convicts tell us, that always at least one out of every ten dies upon the march.

Though men are sometimes sentenced for as short terms as five years in the mines, none ever return, other than the few who escape, so harshly are they treated and so poorly fed. They labor twelve hours a day.

I managed to reach the shadow of the wall of the stockade without being seen, for the Kash Guard was a lazy, inefficient, insubordinate soldier. He did as he pleased, though I understand that under Jarth's régime an effort was made to force discipline as he was attempting to institute a military oligarchy. Since Or-tis came they had been trying to revive the ancient military salute and the use of titles instead of the usual "Brother."

After I reached the stockade I was at a loss to communicate with my father, since any noise I might make would doubtless attract the attention of the guard. Finally through a crack between two boards, I attracted the attention of a prisoner. The man came close to the stockade and I whispered to him that I wished to speak with Julian 8th. By luck I had happened upon a decent fellow, and it was not long before he had brought Father and I was talking with him in low whispers.

He told me that he had been arrested for trading by night and that he was to be tried on the morrow. I asked him if he would like to escape—that I would find the means if he wished me to, but he said that he was innocent of the charge as he had not been off our farm at night for months and that doubtless it was a case of mistaken identity and that he would be freed in the morning.

I had my doubts, but he would not listen to escape as he argued that it would prove his guilt and they would have him for sure.

"Where is there that I may go," he asked, "if I escape? I might hide in the woods, but what a life! I could never return to your mother and so sure am I that they can prove nothing against me that I would rather stand trial than face the future as an outlaw."

I think now that he refused my offer of assistance not because he expected to be released, but because he feared that evil might befall me were I to connive at his escape. At any rate, I did nothing, since he would not let me, and went home again with a heavy heart and dismal forebodings.

Trials before the teivos were public, or at least were supposed to be, though they made it so uncomfortable for spectators that few, if any, had the temerity to attend. But under Jarth's new rule the proceedings of the military courts were secret and Father was tried before such a court.

# EIGHT

# I Horsewhip an Officer

WE PASSED days of mental anguish—hearing nothing, knowing nothing—and then one evening a single Kash Guard rode up to Father's house. Juana and I were there with Mother. The fellow dismounted and knocked at the door—a most unusual courtesy from one of these. He entered at my bidding and stood there a moment looking at mother. He was only a lad—a big, overgrown boy, and there was neither cruelty in his eyes nor the mark of the beast in any of his features. His mother's blood evidently predominated, and he was unquestionably not all Kalkar. Presently he spoke.

"Which is Julian 8th's woman?" he asked; but he looked at Mother as though he already guessed.

"I am," said Mother.

The lad shuffled his feet and caught his breath—it was like a stifled sob.

"I am sorry," he said, "that I bring you such sad news." Then we guessed that the worst had happened.

"The mines?" Mother asked him, and he nodded affirmatively.

"Ten years!" he exclaimed, as one might announce a sentence of death, for such it was. "He never had a chance," he volunteered. "It was a terrible thing. They are beasts!"

I could not but show my surprise that a Kash Guard should speak so of his own kind, and he must have seen it in my face.

"We are not all beasts," he hastened to exclaim.

I commenced to question him then and I found that he had been a sentry at the door during the trial and had heard it all. There had been but one witness—the man who had informed on Father, and Father had been given no chance to make any defense.

I asked him who the informer was.

"I am not sure of the man," he replied; "he was a tall, stoop-shouldered man. I think I heard him called Peter."

But I had known even before I asked. I looked at Mother and saw that she was dry-eyed and that her mouth had suddenly hardened into a firmness of expression such as I had never dreamed it could assume.

"Is that all?" she asked.

"No," replied the youth, "it is not. I am instructed to notify you that you have thirty days to take another man, or vacate these premises," and then he took a step toward Mother.

"I am sorry, madam," he said. "It is very cruel; but what are we to do? It becomes worse each day. Now they are grinding down even the Kash Guard, so that there are many of us who—" but he stopped suddenly as though realizing that he was on the point of speaking treason to strangers, and turning on his heel, he quit the house and a moment later was galloping away.

I expected Mother to break down then; but she did not. She was very brave; but there was a new and terrible expression in her eyes—those eyes that had shone forth always with love. Now they were bitter, hate-filled eyes. She did not weep—I wish to God she had—instead, she did that which I had never known her to do before—she laughed aloud. Upon the slightest pretext, or upon no pretext at all, she laughed. We were afraid for her.

The suggestion dropped by the Kash Guard started in my mind a train of thought of which I spoke to Mother and Juana, and after that Mother seemed more normal for a while, as though I had aroused hope, however feeble, where there had been no hope before. I pointed out that if the Kash Guard was dissatisfied the time was ripe for revolution, for if we could get only a part of them to join us, there would surely be enough of us to overthrow those who remained loyal. Then we would liberate all prisoners and set up a republic of our own such as the ancients had had.

God of our fathers! How many times—how many thousand times had I heard that plan discussed and re-discussed! We would slay all the Kalkars in the world, and we would sell the land again that men might have pride of ownership and an incentive to labor hard and develop it for their children, for well we knew by long experience that no man will develop land that reverts to the government at death, or that government may take away from him at any moment. We would encourage manufactures; we would build schools and churches; we would have music and dancing; once again we would live as our fathers had lived.

We looked for no perfect form of government, for we realized that perfection is beyond the reach of mortal men—merely would we go back to the happy days of our ancestors.

It took time to develop my plan. I talked with everyone I could trust and found them all willing to join me when we had enough. In the meantime, I cared for my own place and Father's as well—I was very busy and time flew rapidly.

About a month after Father was taken away I came home one day with Juana who had accompanied me up river in search of a goat that had strayed. We had found its carcass, or rather its bones, where the hellhounds had left them. Mother was not at our house, where she now spent most of her time, so I went over to Father's to get her. As I approached the door I heard sounds of an altercation and scuffling that made me cover the few remaining yards at a rapid run.

Without waiting to knock, as mother had taught me always to do, I burst into the living room to discover Mother in the clutches of Peter Johansen. She was trying to fight him off; but he was forcing her slowly toward her bedroom, for he was a large and powerful man. He heard me just as I leaped for him and, turning, grappled with me. He tried to hold me off with one hand then while he drew his knife; but I struck him in the face with one fist and knocked him from me, away across the room. He was up again in an instant, bleeding from nose and mouth, and came back at me with his knife in his hand, slashing furiously. Again I struck him and knocked him down and when he arose and came again, I seized his knife hand and tore the weapon from him. He had no slightest chance against me, and he saw it soon, for he commenced to back away and beg for mercy.

"Kill him, Julian," said Mother. "Kill the murderer of your father."

I did not need her appeal to influence me, for the moment that I had seen Peter there I knew my long awaited time had come to kill him. He commenced to cry then—great tears ran down his cheeks and he bolted for the door and tried to escape. It was my pleasure to play with him as a cat plays with a mouse.

I kept him from the door, seizing him and hurling him bodily across the room. Then I let him reach the window, through which he tried to crawl. I permitted him to get so far that he thought he was about to escape and then I seized him again and dragged him back to the floor, and lifting him to his feet I made him fight.

I struck him lightly in the face many times and then I laid him on his back across the table, and kneeling on his chest, I spoke to him softly.

"You had my friend, old Samuels, murdered, and my father, too, and now you come to attack my mother. What did you expect, swine; but this?

Have you no intelligence? You must have known that I would kill you—speak!"

"They said that they would get you today," he whimpered. "They lied to me. They went back on me. They told me that you would be in the pen at the barracks before noon. Damn them, they lied to me!"

So! That was how it was, eh? And the lucky circumstance of the strayed goat had saved me to avenge my father and succor my mother; but they would come yet. I must hurry or they might come before I was through. So I took his head between my hands and bent his neck far back over the edge of the table until I heard his spine part, and that was the end of the vilest traitor who ever lived—one who professed friendship openly and secretly conspired to ruin us. In broad daylight I carried his body to the river and threw it in. I was past caring what they knew. They were coming for me, and they would have their way with me whether they had any pretext or not. But they would have to pay a price for me, that I determined, and I got my knife and strapped it in its scabbard about my waist beneath my shirt. But they did not come—they had lied to Peter just as they lie to everyone.

The next day was market day and tax day, so I went to market with the necessary goats and produce to make my trades and pay my taxes. As Soor passed around the market place making his collections, or rather his levies, for we had to deliver the stuff to his place ourselves, I saw from the excited conversation of those in his wake that he was spreading alarm and consternation among the people of the commune.

I wondered what it might all be about, nor had I long to wait to discover, for he soon reached me. He could neither read nor write; but he had a form furnished by the government upon which were numbers that the agents were taught how to read and which stood for various classes of produce, live-stock and manufactures. In columns beneath these numbers he made marks during the month for the amounts of my trades in each item—it was all crude, of course, and inaccurate; but as they always overcharged us and then added something to make up for any errors they might have made to our credit, the government was satisfied, even if we were not.

Being able to read and write, as well as to figure, I always knew to a dot just what was due from me in tax, and I always had an argument with Soor, from which Government emerged victorious every time.

This month I should have owed him one goat; but he demanded three.

"How is that?" I asked.

"Under the old rate you owed me the equivalent of a goat and a half; but since the tax has been doubled under the new law, you owe me three goats." Then it was I knew the cause of the excitement in other parts of the market place.

"How do you expect us to live if you take everything from us?" I asked.

"The government does not care whether you live or not," he replied, "as long as you pay taxes while you do live."

"I will pay the three goats," I said, "because I have to; but next market day I will bring you a present of the hardest cheese I can find."

He did not say anything, for he was afraid of me unless he was surrounded by Kash Guards, but he looked mighty ugly. After he had passed along to the next victim I walked over to where a number of men were evidently discussing the new tax. There were some fifteen or twenty of them, mostly Yanks, and they were angry—I could see that before I came close enough to hear what they were saying. When I joined them one asked me what I thought of this new outrage.

"Think of it!" I exclaimed. "I think what I have always thought—that as long as we submit without a murmur they will continue to increase our burden, that is already more than we can stagger under."

"They have taken even my seed beans," said one, who raised beans almost exclusively. "As you all know, last year's crop was small and beans brought a high price, so they taxed me on my trades at the high price and then collected the tax in beans at the low price of the previous year. They have been doing that all this year; but I hoped to save enough for seed until now they have doubled the tax I know that I shall have no beans to plant next year."

"What can we do about it?" asked another hopelessly. "What can we do about it?"

"We can refuse to pay the tax," I replied.

They looked at me much as men would look at one who said: "If you do not like it, you may commit suicide."

"The Kash Guard would collect the tax and it would be heavier still, for they would kill us and take our women and all that we possess," said one.

"We outnumber them," said I.

"But we cannot face rifles with our bare hands."

"It has been done," I insisted, "and it is better to die like men, facing the bullets, than by starvation, like spineless worms. We are a hundred, yes, a thousand to their one, and we have our knives, and there are pitchforks and axes, besides the clubs that we can gather. God of our Fathers! I would rather die thus, red with the blood of these swine, than live as they compel us to live!"

I saw some of them looking about to see who might have heard me, for I had raised my voice in excitement; but there were a few who looked steadily at me and nodded their heads in approval.

"If we can get enough to join us, let us do it!" cried one.

"We have only to start," I said, "and they will flock to us."

"How should we start?" asked another.

"I should start on Soor," I replied. "I should kill him and Pthav and Hoffmeyer first, and then make a round of the Kalkar houses where we can find rifles, possibly, and kill them all as we go. By the time the Kash Guard learns of it and can come in force, we shall have a large following. If we can overcome them and take their barracks we shall be too strong for any but a large force, and it will take a month to get many soldiers here from the East. Many of the Kash Guard will join us—they are dissatisfied—one of their number told me so. It will be easy if we are but brave."

They commenced to take a great interest and there was even a cry of "Down with the Kalkars!" but I stopped that in a hurry, as our greatest hope of success lay in a surprise attack.

"When shall we start?" they asked.

"Now," I replied, "if we take them unaware we shall be successful at first, and with success others will join us. Only by numbers, overwhelming numbers, may we succeed."

"Good!" they cried. "Come! Where first?"

Soor," I said. "He is at the far end of the market place. We will kill him first and hang his head on a pole. We will carry it with us and as we kill we will place each head upon a pole and take it with us. Thus we will inspire others to follow us and put fear in the hearts of our enemies."

"Lead on, Julian 9th!" they cried. "We will follow!"

I turned and started in the direction of Soor and we had covered about half the distance when a company of Kash Guard rode into the market place at the very point where Soor was working.

You should have seen my army. Like mist before a hot sun it disappeared from view, leaving me standing all alone in the center of the market place.

The commander of the Kash Guard company must have noticed the crowd and its sudden dispersion, for he rode straight toward me, alone. I would not give him the satisfaction of thinking that I feared him and so I stood there waiting. My thoughts were of the saddest—not for myself, but for the sorry pass to which the Kalkar system had brought Americanism. These men who had deserted me would have been in happier days the flower of American manhood; but generations of oppression and servitude had turned their blood to water. Today they turned tail and fled before a handful of half armed, poorly disciplined soldiers. The terror of the lunar fallacy had entered their hearts and rotted them.

The officer reined in before me and then it was that I recognized him—the beast who had tortured and murdered old Samuels.

"What are you doing here?" he barked.

"Minding my own business, as you had better do," I replied.

"You swine are becoming insufferable," he cried. "Get to your pen, where you belong—I will stand for no mobs and no insolence."

I just stood there looking at him; but there was murder in my heart. He loosened the bull-hide whip that hung at the pommel of his saddle.

"You have to be driven, do you?" He was livid with sudden anger and his voice almost a scream. Then he struck at me—a vicious blow with the heavy whip—struck at my face. I dodged the lash and seized it, wrenching it from his puny grasp. Then I caught his bridle and though his horse plunged and fought I lashed the rider with all my strength a dozen times before he tumbled from the saddle to the trampled earth of the market place.

Then his men were upon me and I went down from a blow on the head. They bound my hands while I was unconscious and then hustled me roughly into a saddle. I was half dazed during the awful ride that ensued—we rode to the military prison at the barracks and all the way that fiend of a captain rode beside me and lashed me with his bull-hide whip.

# NINE

# Revolution

THEN THEY threw me into the pen where the prisoners were kept and after they had left I was surrounded by the other unfortunates incarcerated there. When they learned what I had done they shook their heads and sighed. It would be all over with me in the morning, they said—nothing less than The Butcher for such an offense as mine.

I lay upon the hard ground, bruised and sore, thinking not of my future but of what was to befall Juana and Mother if I, too, were taken from them. The thought gave me new strength and made me forget my hurts, for my mind was busy with plans, mostly impossible plans, for escape—and vengeance. Vengeance was often uppermost in my mind.

Above my head, at intervals, I heard the pacing of the sentry upon the roof. I could tell, of course, each time that he passed and the direction in which he was going. It required about five minutes for him to pass above me, reach the end of his post and return—that was when he went west. Going east he took but a trifle over two minutes. Therefore, when he passed me going west his back was toward me for about two and a half minutes; but when he went east it was only for about a minute that his face was turned from the spot where I lay.

Of course, he could not see me while I lay beneath the shed; but my plan—the one I finally decided upon—did not include remaining in the shed. I had evolved several subtle schemes for escape; but finally cast them all aside and chose, instead, the boldest that occurred to me. I knew that at best the chances were small that I could succeed in any plan and therefore the boldest seemed as likely as any other and it at least had the advantage of speedy results. I would be free or I would be dead in a few brief moments after I essayed it.

I waited, therefore, until the other prisoners had quieted down and comparative silence in the direction of the barracks and the parade assured me that there were few abroad. The sentry came and went and came again upon his monotonous round. Now he was coming toward me from the east and I was ready, standing just outside the shed beneath the low eaves which I could reach by jumping. I heard him pass and gave him a full minute to gain the distance I thought necessary to drown the sounds of my attempt from his ears. Then I leaped for the eaves, caught with my fingers and drew myself quickly to the roof.

I thought that I did it very quietly, but the fellow must have had the ears of a hellhound, for no more had I drawn my feet beneath me for the quick run across the roof than a challenge rang out from the direction of the sentry and almost simultaneously the report of a rifle.

Instantly all was pandemonium. Guards ran, shouting, from all directions, lights flashed in the barracks, rifles spoke from either side of me and from behind me, while from below rose the dismal howlings of the prisoners. It seemed then that a hundred men had known of my plan and been lying in wait for me; but I was launched upon it and even though I had regretted it, there was nothing to do but carry it through to whatever was its allotted end.

It seemed a miracle that none of the bullets struck me; but, of course, it was dark and I was moving rapidly. It takes seconds to tell about it; but it required less than a second for me to dash across the roof and leap to the open ground beyond the prison pen. I saw lights moving west of me and so I ran east toward the lake and presently the firing ceased as they lost sight of me, though I could hear sounds of pursuit. Nevertheless, I felt that I had succeeded and was congratulating myself upon the ease with which I had accomplished the seemingly impossible when there suddenly rose before me out of the black night the figure of a huge soldier pointing a rifle point blank at me. He issued no challenge nor asked any question—just pulled the trigger. I could hear the hammer strike the firing pin; but there was no explosion. I did not know what the reason was, nor did I ever know. All that was apparent was that the rifle misfired and then he brought his bayonet into play while I was springing toward him.

Foolish man! But then he did not know that it was Julian 9th he faced. Pitifully, futilely he thrust at me and with one hand I seized the rifle and tore it from his grasp. In the same movement I swung it behind me and above my head, bringing it down with all the strength of one arm upon his thick skull. Like a felled ox he tumbled to his knees and then sprawled forward upon his face—his head crushed to a pulp. He never new how he died.

Behind me I heard them coming closer and they must have seen me, for they opened fire again and I heard the beat of horses' hoofs upon my right and left. They were surrounding me upon three sides and upon the fourth was the great lake. A moment later I was standing upon the edge of the ancient breakwater while behind me rose the triumphant cries of my pursuers. They had seen me and they knew that I was theirs.

At least, they thought they knew so. I did not wait for them to come closer; but raising my hands above me I dove head foremost into the cool waters of the lake. Swimming rapidly beneath the surface I kept close in the shadows and headed north.

I had spent much of my summer life in the water of the river so that I was as much at home in that liquid element as in air, but this, of course, the Kash Guard did not know, for even had they known that Julian 9th could swim they could not at that time have known which prisoner it was who had escaped and so I think they must have thought what I wanted them to think—that I had chosen self-drowning to recapture.

However, I was sure they would search the shore in both directions and so I kept to the water after I came to the surface. When I was sure that no one was directly above me, I swam farther out until I felt there was little danger of being seen from shore, for it was a dark night. And thus I swam on until I thought I was opposite the mouth of the river when I turned toward the west, searching for it.

Luck was with me. I swam directly into it and a short distance up the sluggish stream before I knew that I was out of the lake; but even then I did not take to the shore, preferring to pass the heart of the ancient city before trusting myself to land.

At last I came out upon the north bank of the river, which is farthest from the Kash Guard barracks, and made my way as swiftly as possible up stream in the direction of my home. Here, hours later, I found an anxious Juana awaiting me, for already she had heard what had transpired in the market place. I had made my plans and had soon explained them to Juana and Mother. There was nothing for them but to acquiesce, as only death could be our lot if we remained in our homes another day. I was astonished, even, that they had not already fallen upon Juana and Mother. As it was they might come any minute. There was no time to lose.

Hastily wrapping up a few belongings I took The Flag from its hiding place above the mantel and tucked it in my shirt—then we were ready. Going to the pens we caught up Red Lightning and the two mares and three of my best milk goats. These latter we tied and after Juana and Mother had mounted the mares I laid one goat in front of each across a mare's withers and the third before myself upon Red Lightning, who did not relish the strange burden and gave me considerable trouble at first.

We rode out upriver, leaving the pens open that the goats might scatter and possibly cover our trail until we could turn off the dusty path beyond Jim's house. We dared not stop to bid Jim and Mollie good-by lest we be apprehended there by our enemies and bring trouble to our good friends. It was a sad occasion for poor Mother, leaving thus her home and those dear neighbors who had been as close to her as her own people; but she was as brave as Juana.

Not once did either of them attempt to dissuade me from the wild scheme I had outlined to them. Instead, they encouraged me and Juana laid her hand upon my arm as I rode beside her, saying: "I would rather that you died thus than that we lived on as downtrodden serfs, without happiness and without hope."

"I shall not die," I said, "until my work is done, at least. Then if die I must I shall be content to know that I leave a happier country for my fellow men to live in."

"Amen!" whispered Juana.

That night I hid them in the ruins of the old church, which we found had been partially burned by the Kalkars. For a moment I held them in my arms—my mother, and my wife—and then I left them to ride toward the southwest and the coal mines. The mines lie about fifty miles away—those to which our people are sent—and west of south according to what I had heard. I had never been to them; but I knew that I must find the bed of an ancient canal and follow it through the district of Joliet and between fifteen and twenty miles beyond, where I must turn south and, after passing a large lake, I would presently come to the mines. I rode the balance of the night and into the morning until I commenced to see people astir in the thinly populated country through which I passed.

Then I hid in a wood through which a stream wound and here, found pasture for Red Lightning and rest for myself. I had brought no food, leaving what little bread and cheese we had brought from the house for Mother and Juana. I did not expect to be gone over a week and I knew that with goat's milk and what they had on hand in addition to what they could find growing wild, there would be no danger of starvation before I returned—after which we expected to live in peace and plenty for the rest of our days.

My journey was less eventful than I had anticipated. I passed through a few ruined villages and towns of greater or less antiquity, the largest of which was ancient Joliet, which was abandoned during the plague fifty years ago, the teivos headquarters and station being removed directly west a few miles to the banks of a little river. Much of the territory I traversed was covered with thick woods, though here and there were the remnants of clearings that must once have been farms which were not yet entirely reclaimed by nature. Now and again I passed those gaunt and lonely towers in which the ancients stored the winter feed for their stock. Those that have endured were of concrete and some showed but little the ravages of time, other than the dense vines that often covered them from base to capital, while several were in the midst of thick forests with old trees almost entwining them, so quickly does nature reclaim her own when man has been displaced.

After I passed Joliet I had to make inquiries. This I did boldly of the few men I saw laboring in the tiny fields scattered along my way. They were poor clods, these descendants of ancient America's rich and powerful farming class—those people of olden times whose selfishness had sought to throw the burden of taxation upon the city dwellers where the ignorant foreign classes were most numerous and had thus added their bit to fomenting the discontent that had worked the downfall of a glorious nation. They themselves suffered much before they died, but nothing by comparison with the humiliation and degradation of their descendants—an illiterate, degraded, starving race.

Early in the second morning I came within sight of the stockade about the mines. Even at a distance I could see that it was a weak, dilapidated thing and that the sentries pacing along its top were all that held the prisoners within. As a matter of fact, many escaped; but they were soon hunted down and killed as the farmers in the neighborhood always informed on them. The commandant at the prison had conceived the fiendish plan of slaying one farmer for every prisoner who escaped and was not recaught.

I hid until night and then, cautiously, I approached the stockade, leaving Red Lightning securely tied in the woods. It was no trick to reach the stockade, so thoroughly was I hidden by the rank vegetation growing upon the outside. From a place of concealment I watched the sentry, a big fellow; but apparently a dull clod who walked with his chin upon his breast and with the appearance of being half asleep.

The stockade was not high and the whole construction was similar to that of the prison pen at Chicago, evidently having been designed by the same commandant in years gone by. I could hear the prisoners conversing in the shed beyond the wall and presently when one came near to where I listened I tried to attract his attention by making a hissing sound.

After what seemed a long time to me, he heard me; but even then it was some time before he appeared to grasp the idea that someone was trying to attract his attention. When he did he moved closer and tried to peer through one of the cracks; but as it was dark out he could see nothing.

"Are you a Yank?" I asked. "If you are I am a friend."

"I am a Yank," he replied. "Did you expect to find a Kalkar working in the mines?"

"Do you know a prisoner called Julian 8th?" I inquired.

He seemed to be thinking for a moment and then he said: "I seem to have heard the name. What do you want of him?"

"I want to speak to him—I am his son."

"Wait!" he whispered. "I think that I heard a man speak that name to-day. I will find out—he is near by."

I waited for perhaps ten minutes when I heard someone approaching from the inside and presently a voice asked if I was still there.

"Yes," I said. "Is that you, Father?" for I thought that the tones were his.

"Julian, my son!" came to me almost as a sob. "What are you doing here?"

Briefly I told him and then of my plan. "Have the convicts the courage to attempt it?" I asked, in conclusion.

"I do not know," he said, and I could not but note the tone of utter hopelessness in his voice. "They would wish to; but here our spirits and our bodies both are broken. I do not know how many would have the courage to attempt it. Wait and I will talk with some of them—all are loyal; but just weak from overwork, starvation and abuse."

I waited for the better part of an hour before he returned. Some will help," he said, "from the first, and others if we are successful. Do you think it worth the risk—they will kill you if you fail—they will kill us all."

"And what is death to that which you are suffering?" I asked.

"I know," he said, "but the worm impaled upon the hook still struggles and hopes for life. Turn back, my son; we can do nothing against them."

"I will not turn back," I whispered. "I will not turn back."

"I will help you; but I cannot speak for the others. They may and they may not."

We had spoken only when the sentry had been at a distance, falling into silence each time he approached the point where we stood. In the intervals of silence I could hear the growing restlessness of the prisoners and I guessed that what I had said to the first man was being passed around from mouth to mouth within until already the whole adjacent shed was seething with something akin to excitement. I wondered if it would arouse their spirit sufficently to carry them through the next ten minutes. If it did success was assured.

Father had told me all that I wanted to know—the location of the guard house and the barracks and the number of Kash Guard posted here—only fifty men to guard five thousand! How much more eloquently than words did this fact bespeak the humiliation of the American people and the utter contempt in which our scurvy masters hold us—fifty men to guard five thousand!

And then I started putting my plan into execution—a mad plan which had only its madness to recommend it. The sentry approached and came opposite where I stood and I leaped for the eaves as I had leaped for the eaves of the prison pen at Chicago, only this time I leaped from the outside where the eaves are closer to the ground and so the task was easier. I leaped for them and caught them, and then I scrambled up behind the sentry and before his dull wits told him that there was someone behind him I was upon his back and the same fingers that threw a mad bull closed upon his windpipe. The struggle was brief—he died quickly and I lowered him to the roof. Then I took his uniform from him and donned it, with his ammunition belt, and I took his bayonetted rifle and started out upon his post, walking with slow tread and with my chin upon my breast as he had walked.

At the end of my post I waited for the sentry I saw coming upon the next and when he was close to me I turned back and he turned back away from me. Then I wheeled and struck him an awful blow upon the head with my rifle. He died more quickly than the other—instantly, I should say.

I took his rifle and ammunition from him and lowered them inside the pen to waiting hands. Then I went on to the next sentry, and the next, until I had slain five more and passed their rifles to the prisoners below. While I was doing this five prisoners who had volunteered to Father climbed to the roof of the shed and stripped the dead men of their uniforms and donned them.

It was all done quietly and in the black night none might see what was going on fifty feet away. I had to stop when I came near to the guard house. There I turned back and presently slid into the pen with my accomplices who had been going among the other prisoners with Father arousing them to mutiny. Now were most of them ready to follow me, for so far my plan had proven successful. With equal quietness we overcame the men at the guard house and then moved on in a silent body toward the barracks.

So sudden and so unexpected was our attack that we met with little resistance. We were almost five thousand to forty now. We swarmed in upon them like wild bees upon a foe and we shot them and bayonetted them until none remained alive. Not one escaped. And now we were flushed with success so that the most spiritless became a veritable lion for courage.

We who had taken the uniforms of the Kash Guard discarded them for our own garb, as we had no mind to go abroad in the hated livery of our oppressors. That very night we saddled their horses with the fifty saddles that were there and fifty men rode the balance of the horses bareback. That made one hundred mounted men and the others were to follow on foot— on to Chicago. "On to Chicago!" was our slogan.

We traveled cautiously, though I had difficulty in making them do so, so intoxicated were they with their first success. I wanted to save the horses and also I wanted to get as many men into Chicago as possible, so we let the weakest ride, while those of us who were strong walked, though I had a time of it getting Red Lightning to permit another on his sleek back.

Some fell out upon the way from exhaustion or from fear, for the nearer Chicago we approached the more their courage ebbed. The very thought of the feared Kalkars and their Kash Guard took the marrow from the bones of many. I do not know that one may blame them, for the spirit of man can endure only so much and when it is broken only a miracle can mend it in the same generation.

We reached the ruined church a week from the day I left Mother and Juana there and we reached it with less than two thousand men, so rapid had been the desertion in the last few miles before we entered the district.

Father and I could scarcely wait to see our loved ones and so we rode on ahead to greet them, and inside the church we found three dead goats and a dying woman—my mother with a knife protruding from her breast. She was still conscious when we entered and I saw a great light of happiness in her eyes as they fell upon Father and upon me. I looked around for Juana and my heart stood still, fearing that I would not find her—and fearing that I would.

Mother could still speak, and as we leaned over her as Father held her in his arms, she breathed a faint story of what had befallen them. They had lived in peace until that very day when the Kash Guard had stumbled upon them—a large detachment under Or-tis himself. They had seized them to take them away; but Mother had had a knife hidden in her clothing and had utilized it as we saw rather than suffer the fate she knew awaited them. That was all, except that Juana had had no knife and Or-tis had carried her off.

I saw Mother die, then, in Father's arms and I helped him bury her after our men came and we had shown them what the beasts had done, though they knew well enough and had suffered themselves enough to know what was to be expected of the swine.

# TEN

# The Butcher

W E WENT on then, Father and I filled with grief and bitterness and hatred even greater than we had known before. We marched toward the market place of our district, and on the way we stopped at Jim's and he joined us. Mollie wept when she heard what had befallen Mother and Juana, but presently she controlled herself and urged us on and Jim with us, though Jim needed no urging. She kissed him good-by with tears and pride mingled in her eyes, and all he said was: "Good-bye, girl. Keep your knife with you always."

And so we rode away with Mollie's "May the Saints be with you!" in our ears. Once again we stopped, at our abandoned goat pens, and there we dug up the rifle, belt and ammunition of the soldier Father had slain years before. These we gave to Jim.

Before we reached the market place our force commenced to dwindle again—most of them could not brave the terrors of the Kash Guard upon which they had been fed in whispered story and in actual experience since infancy. I do not say that these men were cowards—I do not believe that they were cowards and yet they acted like cowards. It may be that a lifetime of training had taught them so thoroughly to flee the Kash Guard that now no amount of urging could make them face it. The terror had become instinctive as is man's natural revulsion for snakes. They could not face the Kash Guard any more than some men can touch a rattler, even though it may be dead.

It was market day and the place was crowded. I had divided my force so that we marched in from two directions in wide fronts, about five hundred men in each party, and surrounded the market place. As there were only a few men from our district among us, I had given orders that there was to be no killing other than that of Kash Guards until we who knew the population could pick out the right men.

When the nearest people first saw us they did not know what to make of it, so complete was the surprise. Never in their lives had they seen men of their own class armed and there were a hundred of us mounted. Across the plaza a handful of Kash Guard were lolling in front of Hoffmeyer's office. They saw my party first, as the other was coming up from behind them, and they mounted and came toward us. At the same moment I drew The Flag from my breast and, waving it above my head, urged Red Lightning forward, shouting, as I rode: "Death to the Kash Guard! Death to the Kalkars!"

And then, of a sudden, the Kash Guard seemed to realize that they were confronted by an actual force of armed men and their true color became apparent—all yellow. They turned to flee, only to see another force behind them. The people had now caught the idea and the spirit of our purpose and they flocked around us shouting, screaming, laughing, crying.

"Death to the Kash Guard!" "Death to the Kalkars!" "The Flag!" I heard more than once, and "Old Glory!" from some who, like myself, had not been permitted to forget. A dozen men rushed to my side and grasping the streaming banner pressed it to their lips, while tears coursed down their cheeks. "The Flag! The Flag!" they cried. "The Flag of our fathers!"

It was then, before a shot had been fired, that one of the Kash Guard rode toward me with a white cloth above his head. I recognized him immediately as the youth who had brought the cruel order to Mother and who had shown sorrow for the acts of his superiors.

"Do not kill us," he said, "and we will join with you. Many of the Kash Guard at the barracks will join, too."

And so the dozen soldiers in the market place joined us, and a woman ran from her house carrying the head of a man stuck upon a short pole and she screamed forth her hatred against the Kalkars—the hatred that was the common bond between us all. As she came closer I saw that it was Pthav's woman and the head upon the short pole was the head of Pthav. That was the beginning—that was the little spark that was needed. Like maniacs, laughing horribly, the people charged the houses of the Kalkars and dragged them forth to death.

Above the shrieking and the groans and the din could be heard shouts for The Flag and the names of loved ones who were being avenged. More than once I heard the name of Samuels the Jew. Never was a man more thoroughly avenged than he that day.

Dennis Corrigan was with us, freed from the mines, and Betty Worth, his woman, found him there, his arms red to the elbows with the blood of our oppressors. She had never thought to see him alive, and when she heard his story, and of how they had escaped, she ran to me and nearly pulled me from Red Lightning's back trying to hug and kiss me.

It was she who started the people shouting for me until a mad, swirling mob of joy-crazed people surrounded me. I tried to quiet them, for I knew that this was no way in which to forward our cause, and finally I succeeded in winning a partial silence. Then I told them that this madness must cease, that we had not yet succeeded, that we had won only a single small district and that we must go forward quietly and in accordance with a sensible plan if we were to be victorious.

"Remember," I admonished them, "that there are still thousands of armed men in the city and that we must overthrow them all, and then there are other thousands that The TwentyFour will throw in upon us, for they will not surrender this territory until they are hopelessly defeated from here to Washington—and that will require months and maybe years."

They quieted down a little then and we formed plans for marching immediately upon the barracks that we might take the Kash Guard by surprise. It was about this time that father found Soor and killed him.

"I told you," said Father, just before he ran a bayonet through the tax collector, "that some day I would have my little joke, and this is the day."

Then a man dragged Hoffmeyer from some hiding place and the people literally tore him to pieces, and that started the pandemonium all over again. There were cries of "On to the barracks!" and "Kill the Kash Guard!" followed by a concerted movement toward the lake front. On the way our numbers were increased by volunteers from every house—either fighting men and women from the houses of our class, or bloody heads from the houses of the Kalkars, for we carried them all with us, waving above us upon the ends of poles and at the head of all I rode with Old Glory, now waving from a tall staff.

I tried to maintain some semblance of order, but it was impossible, and so we streamed along, screaming and killing, laughing and crying, each as the mood claimed him. The women seemed the maddest, possibly because they had suffered most, and Pthav's woman led them. I saw others there with one hand clutching a suckling baby to a bare breast while the other held aloft the dripping head of a Kalkar, an informer, or a spy. One could not blame them who knew the lives of terror and hopelessness they had led—they and their mothers before them.

We had just crossed the new bridge over the river into the heart of the great, ruined city, when the Kash Guard fell upon us from ambush with their full strength. They were poorly disciplined; but they were armed, while we were not disciplined at all nor scarcely armed. We were nothing but an angry mob into which they poured volley after volley at close range.

Men, women and babies went down and many turned and fled; but there were others who rushed forward and grappled hand to hand with the Kash Guard, tearing their rifles from them. We who were mounted rode among them. I could not carry The Flag and fight, so I took it from the staff and replaced it inside my shirt and then I clubbed my rifle and guiding Red Lightning with my knees I drove into them.

God of our fathers! But it was a pretty fight. If I had known that I was to die the next minute I would have died gladly for the joy I had in those few minutes. Down they went before me, to right and to left, reeling from their saddles with crushed skulls and broken bodies, for wherever I hit them made no difference in the result—they died if they came within reach of my rifle, which was soon only a bent and twisted tube of bloody metal.

And so I rode completely through them with a handful of men behind me. We turned then to ride back over the crumbling ruins that were in this spot only mounds of debris and from the elevation of one of these hillocks of the dead past I saw the battle down by the river and a great lump came into my throat. It was all over—all but the bloody massacre. My poor mob had turned at last to flee. They were jammed and stuck upon the narrow bridge and the Kash Guard were firing volleys into that wedged mass of human flesh. Hundreds were leaping into the river only to be shot from the banks by the soldiers.

Twenty-five mounted men surrounded me—all that was left of my fighting force—and at least two thousand Kash Guard lay between us and the river. Even could we have fought our way back we could have done nothing to save the day or our own people. We were doomed to die, but we decided to inflict more punishment before we died.

I had in mind Juana in the clutches of Or-tis—not once had the frightful thought left my consciousness—and so I told them that I would ride to headquarters and search for her and they said that they would ride with me and that we would slay whom we could before the soldiers returned.

Our dream had vanished, our hopes were dead. In silence we rode through the streets toward the barracks. The Kash Guard had not come over to our side as we had hoped—possibly they would have come had we some measure of success in the city; but there could be no success against armed troops for a mob of men, women and children.

I realized too late that we had not planned sufficiently, yet we might have won had not someone escaped and ridden ahead to notify the Kash Guard. Could we have taken them by surprise in the barracks the outcome might have been what it had been in the market places through which we had passed. I had realized our weakness and the fact that if we took time to plan and arrange some spy or informer would have divulged all to the authorities long before we could have put our plans into execution. Really, there had been no other way than to trust to a surprise attack and the impetuosity of our first blow.

I looked about among my followers as we rode along. Jim was there, but not Father—I never saw him again. He probably fell in the battle at the new bridge. Orrin Colby, blacksmith and preacher, rode at my side, covered with blood—his own and Kash Guard. Dennis Corrigan was there, too.

We rode right into the barrack yard, for with their lack of discipline and military efficiency they had sent their whole force against us with the exception of a few men who remained to guard the prisoners and a handful at headquarters building. The latter was overcome with scarcely a struggle and from one whom I took prisoner I learned where the sleeping quarters of Or-tis were located.

Telling my men that our work was done I ordered them to scatter and escape as best they might, but they said that they would remain with me. I told them that the business I was on was such that I must handle it alone and asked them to go and free the prisoners while I searched for Juana. They said that they would wait for me outside and so we parted.

Or-tis's quarters were on the second floor of the building in the east wing and I had no difficulty in finding them. As I approached the door I heard the sound of voices raised in anger within and of rapid movement as though some one was running hither and thither across the floor. I recognized Or-tis's voice—he was swearing foully, and then I heard a woman's scream and I knew it was Juana.

I tried the door and found it locked. It was a massive door, such as the ancients built in their great public buildings, such as this had originally been, and I doubted my ability to force it. I was mad with apprehension and lust for revenge and if maniacs gain tenfold in strength when the madness is upon them I must have been a maniac that moment, for when, after stepping back a few feet, I hurled myself against the door, the shot bolt tore through the splintering frame and the barrier swung in upon its hinges with a loud bang.

Before me, in the center of the room, stood Or-tis with Juana in his clutches. He had her partially upon a table and with one hairy hand he was choking her. He looked up at the noise of my sudden entry, and when he saw me he went white and dropped Juana, at the same time whipping a pistol from its holster at his side. Juana saw me, too, and springing for his arm dragged it down as he pulled the trigger so that the bullet went harmlessly into the floor.

Before he could shake her off I was upon him and had wrenched the weapon from his grasp. I held him in one hand as one might a little child—he was utterly helpless in my grip—and I asked Juana if he had wronged her.

"Not yet," she said, "he just came in after sending the Kash Guard away. Something has happened. There is going to be a battle; but he sneaked back to the safety of his quarters."

Then she seemed to notice for the first time that I was covered with blood. "There has been a battle!" she cried, "and you have been in it."

I told her that I had and that I would tell her about it after I had finished Or-tis. He commenced to plead and then to whimper. He promised me freedom and immunity from punishment and persecution if I would let him live. He promised never to bother Juana again and to give us his protection and assistance. He would have promised me the Sun and the Moon and all the little stars, had he thought I wished them, but I wished only one thing just then and I told him so—to see him die.

"Had you wronged her," I said, "you would have died a slow and terrible death; but I came in time to save her, and so you are saved that suffering."

When he realized that nothing could save him he began to weep, and his knees shook so that he could not stand, and I had to hold him from the floor with one hand and with my other clenched I dealt him a single terrific blow between the eyes—a blow that broke his neck and crushed his skull. Then I dropped him to the floor and took Juana in my arms.

Quickly, as we walked toward the entrance of the building, I told her of all that had transpired since we parted, and that now she would be left alone in the world for a while, until I could join her. I told her where to go and await me in a forgotten spot I had discovered upon the banks of the old canal on my journey to the mines. She cried and clung to me, begging to remain with me, but I knew it could not be, for already I could hear fighting in the yard below. We would be fortunate indeed if one of us escaped. At last she promised on condition that I would join her immediately, which, of course, I had intended doing as soon as I had the chance.

Red Lightning stood where I had left him before the door. A company of Kash Guard, evidently returning from the battle, were engaged with my little band that was slowly falling back toward the headquarters building. There was no time to be lost if Juana was to escape. I lifted her to Red Lightning's back from where she stooped, and threw her dear arms about my neck, covering my lips with kisses.

"Come back to me soon," she begged, "I need you so—and it will not be long before there will be another to need you, too."

I pressed her close to my breast. "And if I do not come back," I said, "take this and give it to my son to guard as his fathers before him have." I placed The Flag in her hands.

The bullets were singing around us and I made her go, watching her as the noble horse raced swiftly across the parade and disappeared among the ruins to the west. Then I turned to the fighting to find but ten men left to me. Orrin Colby was dead and Dennis Corrigan. Jim was left and nine others. We fought as best we could, but we were cornered now, for other guards were streaming onto the parade from other directions and our ammunition was expended.

They rushed us then—twenty to one—and though we did the best we could they overwhelmed us. Lucky Jim was killed instantly, but I was only stunned by a blow upon the head.

That night they tried me before a court-martial and tortured me in an effort to make me divulge the names of my accomplices. But there were none left alive that I knew of, even had I wished to betray them. As it was, I just refused to speak. I never spoke again after bidding Juana good-bye, other than the few words of encouragement that passed between those of us who remained fighting to the last.

Early the next morning I was led forth to The Butcher.

I recall every detail up to the moment the knife touched my throat—there was a slight stinging sensation followed instantly by—oblivion.

It was broad daylight when he finished—so quickly had the night sped— and I could see by the light from the port hole of the room where we sat that his face looked drawn and pinched and that even then he was suffering the sorrows and disappointments of the bitter, hopeless life he had just described.

I rose to retire. "That is all?" I asked.

"Yes," he replied, "that is all of that incarnation."

"But you recall another?" I insisted. He only smiled as I was closing the door.

# PART III

# THE RED HAWK

*Being the Story of Julian 20th*

# ONE

# The Desert Clans

THE JANUARY sun beat hotly upon me as I reined Red Lightning in upon the summit of a barren hill and looked down toward the rich land of plenty that stretched away below me as far as the eye could see. In that direction was the mighty sea, a day's ride, perhaps, to the westward—the sea that none of us had ever looked upon; the sea that had become as fabulous as a legend of the ancients during the nearly four hundred years since the Moon Men had swept down upon us and overwhelmed the Earth in their mad and bloody carnival of revolution.

In the near distance the green of the orange groves mocked us from below, and great patches that were groves of leafless nut trees, and there were sandy patches toward the south that were vineyards waiting for the hot suns of April and May before they, too, broke into riotous, tantalizing green. And from this garden spot of plenty a curling trail wound up the mountainside to the very level where we sat gazing down upon this last stronghold of our foes.

When the ancients built that trail it must have been wide and beautiful indeed, but in the centuries that elapsed man and the elements have sadly defaced it. The rains have washed it away in places, and the Kalkars have made great gashes in it to deter us, their enemies, from invading their sole remaining lands and driving them into the sea; and upon their side of the gashes they have built forts where they keep warriors always. It is so upon every pass that leads down into their country. And well for them that they do so guard themselves!

Since fell my great ancestor, Julian 9th, in the year 2122, at the end of the first uprising against the Kalkars, we have been driving them slowly back across the world. That was over three hundred years ago. For a hundred years they have held us, here, a day's ride from the ocean. Just how far it is we do not know; but in 2408 my grandfather, Julian 18th, rode alone almost to the sea.

He had won back nearly to safety when he was discovered and pursued almost to the tents of his people. There was a battle, and the Kalkars who had dared invade our country were destroyed, but Julian 18th died of his wounds without being able to tell more than that a wondrously rich country lay between us and the sea, which was not more than a day's ride, distant. A day's ride, for us, might be anything under a hundred miles.

We are desert people. Our herds range a vast territory where feed is scarce, that we may be always near the goal that our ancestors set for us three centuries ago—the shore of the western sea into which it is our destiny to drive the remnants of our former oppressors.

In the forests and mountains of Arizona there is rich pasture, but it is far from the land of the Kalkars where the last of the tribe of Or-tis make their last stand, and so we prefer to live in the desert near our foes, driving our herds great distances to pasture when the need arises, rather than to settle down in a comparative land of plenty, resigning the age old struggle, the ancient feud between the house of Julian and the house of Or-tis.

A light breeze moves the black mane of the bright bay stallion beneath me. It moves my own black mane where it falls loose below the buckskin thong that encircles my head and keeps it from my eyes. It moves the dangling ends of The Great Chief's blanket strapped behind my saddle.

On the twelfth day of the eighth month of the year just gone this Great Chief's blanket covered the shoulders of my father, Julian 19th, from the burning rays of the summer's desert sun. I was twenty on that day, and on that day my father fell before the lance of an Or-tis in the Great Feud, and I became The Chief of Chiefs.

Surrounding me today as I sit looking down upon the land of my enemies are fifty of the fierce chieftains of the hundred clans that swear allegiance to the house of Julian. They are bronzed and, for the most part, beardless men.

The insignias of their clans are painted in various colors upon their foreheads, their cheeks, their breasts. Ocher they use, and blue and white and scarlet. Feathers rise from the head bands that confine their hair—the feathers of the vulture, the hawk, and the eagle. I, Julian 20th, wear a single feather. It is from a red-tailed hawk—the clan-sign of my family.

We are all garbed similarly. Let me describe The Wolf, and in his portrait you will see a composite of us all. He is a sinewy, well built man of fifty, with piercing gray-blue eyes beneath straight brows. His head is well shaped, denoting great intelligence. His features are strong and powerful and of a certain fierce cast that might well strike terror to a foeman's heart—and does, if the Kalkar scalps that fringe his ceremonial blanket stand for aught. His breeches, wide below the hips and skin tight from above the knees down, are of the skin of the buck deer. His soft boots, tied tight about the calf of each leg, are also of buck. Above the waist he wears a sleeveless vest of calfskin tanned with the hair on. The Wolf's is of fawn and white.

Sometimes these vests are ornamented with bits of colored stone or metal sewn to the hide in various manners of design. From The Wolf's headband, just above the right ear, depends the tail of a timber wolf—the clan sign of his family.

An oval shield upon which is painted the head of a wolf hangs about this chief's neck, covering his back from nape to kidneys. It is a stout, light shield—a hardwood frame covered with bullhide. Around its periphery have been fastened the tails of wolves. In such matters each man, with the assistance of his women folk, gives rein to his fancy in the matter of ornamentation.

Clan-signs and chief-signs, however, are sacred. The use of one to which he is not entitled might spell death for any man. I say "might" because we have no inflexible laws. We have few laws.

The Kalkars were forever making laws, so we hate them. We judge each case upon its own merits, and we pay more attention to what a man intended doing than what he did.

The Wolf is armed, as are the rest of us, with a light lance about eight feet in length, a knife, and a straight two-edged sword. A short, stout bow is slung beneath his right stirrup leather, and a quiver of arrows is at his saddlebow.

The blades of his sword and his knife and the metal of his lance tip come from a far place called Kolrado, and are made by a tribe that is famous because of the hardness and the temper of the metal of their blades. The Utaws bring us metal also, but theirs is inferior, and we use it only for the shoes that protect our horses' feet from the cutting sands and the rocks of our hard and barren country.

The Kolrados travel many days to reach us, coming once in two years. They pass, unmolested, through the lands of many tribes because they bring what none might otherwise have, and what we need in our never ending crusade against the Kalkars. That is the only thread that holds together the scattered clans and tribes that spread east and north and south beyond the ken of man. All are animated by the same purpose—to drive the last of the Kalkars into the sea.

From the Kolrados we get meager news of clans beyond them toward the rising sun. Far, far to the east, they say,—so far that in a lifetime no man might reach it—lies another great sea, and that there, as here upon the world's western edge, a few Kalkars are making their last stand. All the rest of the world has been won back by the people of our own blood—by Americans.

We are always glad to see the Kolrados come, for they bring us news of other peoples; and we welcome the Utaws, too, although we are not a friendly people, killing all others who come among us, for fear, chiefly, that they may be spies sent by the Kalkars.

It is handed down from father to son that this was not always so, and that once the people of the world went to and fro safely from place to place, and that then all spoke the same language; but now it is different. The Kalkars brought hatred and suspicion among us until now we trust only the members of our own clans and tribes.

The Kolrados, from coming often among us, we can understand, and they can understand us, by means of a few words and many signs, although when they speak their own language among themselves we cannot understand them, except for an occasional word that is like one of ours. They say that when the last of the Kalkars is driven from the world we must live at peace with one another; but I am afraid that that will never come to pass, for who would go through life without breaking a lance or dipping his sword point now and again into the blood of a stranger? Not The Wolf, I swear; nor no more The Red Hawk.

By The Flag! I take more pleasure in meeting a stranger upon a lonely trail than in meeting a friend, for I cannot set my lance against a friend and feel the swish of the wind as Red Lightning bears me swiftly down upon the prey and I crouch in the saddle, nor thrill to the shock as we strike.

I am The Red Hawk. I am but twenty, yet the fierce chiefs of a hundred fierce clans bow to my will. I am a Julian—the twentieth Julian—and from this year 2430 I can trace my line back five hundred and thirty-four years to Julian 1st, who was born in 1896. From father to son, by word of mouth, has been handed down to me the story of every Julian, and there is no blot upon the shield of one in all that long line, nor shall there be any blot upon the shield of Julian 20th.

From my fifth year to my tenth I learned, word for word, as had my father before me, the deeds of my forbears, and to hate the Kalkars and the tribe of Or-tis. This, with riding, was my schooling. From ten to fifteen I learned to use lance and sword and knife, and on my sixteenth birthday I rode forth with the other men—a warrior.

As I sat there this day looking down upon the lands of the accused

Kalkars, my mind went back to the deeds of the fifteenth Julian, who had driven the Kalkars across the desert and over the edge of these mountains into the valley below just one hundred years before I was born, and I turned to The Wolf and pointed down toward the green groves and the distant hills and off beyond to where the mysterious ocean lay.

"For a hundred years they have held us here," I said. "It is too long."

"It is too long," The Wolf agreed.

"When the rains are over The Red Hawk leads his people into the land of plenty."

The Rock raised his spear and shook it savagely toward the valley far below. The scalp-lock fastened just below its metal-shod tip trembled in the wind. "When the rains are over!" cried The Rock. His fierce eyes glowed with the fire of fanaticism.

"The green of the groves we will dye red with their blood!" cried The Rattlesnake.

"With our swords, not our mouths," I said, and wheeled Red Lightning toward the east.

The Coyote laughed, and the others joined with him as we wound downward out of the hills toward the desert.

On the afternoon of the following day we came within sight of our tents, where they were pitched beside the yellow flood of The River. Five miles before that we had seen a few puffs of smoke rise from the summit of a hill to the north of us. It told the camp that a body of horsemen was approaching from the west. It told us that our sentry was on duty and that doubtless all was well.

At a signal my warriors formed themselves in two straight lines, crossing each other at their centers. A moment later another smoke signal arose, informing the camp that we were friends and us that our signal had been rightly read.

Presently, in a wild charge, whooping and brandishing our spears, we charged down among the tents. Dogs, children, and slaves scampered for safety, the dogs barking, the children and the slaves yelling and laughing. As we swung ourselves from our mounts before our tents, slaves rushed out to seize our bridle reins, the dogs leaped, growling, upon us in exuberant welcome, while the children fell upon their sires, their uncles, or their brothers, demanding the news of the ride or a share in the spoils of conflict or chase. Then we went in to our women.

I had no wife, but there were my mother and my two sisters, and I found them awaiting me in the inner tent, seated upon a low couch that was covered, as was the floor, with the bright blankets that our slaves weave from the wool of sheep. I knelt and took my mother's hand and kissed it, and then I kissed her upon the lips, and in the same fashion I saluted my sisters, the elder first.

It is custom among us; but it is also our pleasure, for we both respect and love our women. Even if we did not, we should appear to, if only for the reason that the Kalkars do otherwise. They are brutes and swine.

We do not permit our women a voice in the councils of the men, but none the less do they influence our councils from the seclusion of their inner tents. It is indeed an unusual mother among us who does not make her voice heard in The Council Ring through her husband or her sons, and she does it through the love and respect in which they hold her, and not by scolding and nagging.

They are wonderful, our women. It is for them and The Flag that we have fought the foe across a world for three hundred years. It is for them that we shall go forth and drive him into the sea.

As the slaves prepared the evening meal I chatted with my mother and my sisters. My two brothers, The Vulture and Rain Cloud, lay also at my mother's feet. The Vulture was eighteen, a splendid warrior, a true Julian.

Rain Cloud was sixteen then, and I think the most beautiful creature I had ever seen. He had just become a warrior, but so sweet and lovable was his disposition that the taking of human life appeared a most incongruous calling for him; yet he was a Julian, and there was no alternative.

Every one loved him, and respected him, too, even though he had never excelled in feats of arms, for which he seemed to have no relish; but they respected him because they knew that he was brave and that he would fight as courageously as any of them, even though he might have no stomach for it. Personally, I considered Rain Cloud braver than I, for I knew that he would do well the thing he hated, while I would be only doing well the thing I loved.

The Vulture resembled me in looks and the love of blood, so we left Rain Cloud at home to help guard the women and the children, which was no disgrace, since it is a most honorable and sacred trust, and we went forth to the fighting when there was likely to be any, and when there wasn't we went forth and searched for it. How often have I ridden the trails leading in across our vast frontiers longing for sight of a strange horseman against whom I might bend my lance!

We asked no questions then when we had come close enough to see the clan-sign of the stranger and to know that he was of another tribe and likely he was as keen for the fray as we, otherwise he would have tried to avoid us. We each drew rein at a little distance and set his lance, and each called aloud his name, and then with a mighty oath each bore down upon the other, and then one rode away with a fresh scalp-lock and a new horse to add to his herd, while the other remained to sustain the vulture and the coyote.

Two or three of our great, shaggy hounds came in and sprawled among us as we lay talking with Mother and the two girls, Nallah and Neeta. Behind my mother and sisters squatted three slave girls, ready to do their bidding, for our women do not labor. They ride and walk and swim and keep their bodies strong and fit that they may bear mighty warriors, but labor is beneath them, as it is beneath us.

We hunt and fight and tend our own herds, for that is not menial, but all other labor the slaves perform. We found them here when we came. They have been here always—a stolid, dark-skinned people, weavers of blankets and baskets, makers of pottery, tillers of the soil. We are kind to them, and they are happy.

The Kalkars, who preceded us, were not kind to them. It has been handed down to them from father to son, for over a hundred years, that the Kalkars were cruel to them, and they hate their memory; yet, were we to be driven away by the Kalkars, these simple people would remain and serve anew their cruel masters, for they will never leave their soil.

They have strange legends of a far time when great horses of iron raced across the desert, dragging iron tents filled with people behind them, and they point to holes in the mountainsides through which these iron monsters made their way to the green valleys by the sea, and they tell of men who flew like birds and as swiftly; but of course we know that such things were never true and are but the stories that the old men and the women among them told to the children for their amusement. However, we like to listen to them.

I told my mother of my plans to move down into the valley of the Kalkars after the rains.

She was silent some time before replying.

"Yes, of course," she said: "you would be no Julian were you not to attempt it. At least twenty times before in a hundred years have our warriors gone down in force into the valley of the Kalkars and been driven back. I wish that you might have taken a wife and left a son to be Julian 21st before you set out upon this expedition from which you may not return. Think well of it, my son, before you set forth. A year or two will make no great difference. But you are The Great Chief, and if you decide to go, we can but wait here for your return and pray that all is well with you."

"But you do not understand, Mother," I replied. "I said that we are going to move down in the valley of the Kalkars after the rains. I did not say that we are coming back again. I did not say that you would remain here and wait for our return. You will accompany us.

"The tribe of Julian moves down into the valley of the Kalkars when the rains are over, and they take with them their women and their children and their tents and all their flocks and herds and every other possession that is movable, and—they do not return to live in the desert ever more."

She did not reply, but only sat in thought.

Presently a man-slave came to bid us warriors to the evening meal. The women and the children eat this meal within their tents, but the warriors gather around a great circular table, called The Council Ring.

There were a hundred of us there that night. Flares in the hands of slaves gave us light and there was light from the cooking fire that burned within the circle formed by the table. The others remained standing until I had taken my seat which was the signal that the eating might begin. Before each warrior was an earthenware vessel containing beer and another filled with wine, and there were slaves whose duty it was to keep these filled, which was no small task, for we are hearty men and great drinkers, though there is no drunkenness among us as there is among the Kalkars.

Other slaves brought meat and vegetables—beef and mutton, both boiled and broiled, potatoes, beans and corn, and there were bowls of figs and dried grapes and dried plums. There were also venison and bear meat and fish.

There was a great deal of talk and a great deal of laughter, loud and boisterous, for the evening meal in the home camp is always a gala event. We ride hard and we ride often and we ride long, often we are fighting, and much of the time away from home. Then we have little to eat and nothing to drink but water, which is often warm and unclean and always scarce in our country.

We sit upon a long bench that encircles the outer periphery of the table, and as I took my seat the slaves, bearing platters of meat, passed along the inner rim of the table. As they came opposite each warrior he rose and leaning far across the board, seized a portion of meat with a thumb and finger and cut it deftly away with his sharp knife. The slaves moved in slow procession without pause, and there was a constant gleam and flash of blades and movement and change of color as the painted warriors arose and leaned across the table, the firelight playing upon their beads and metal ornaments and the gay feathers of their headdresses. And the noise!

Pacing to and fro behind the warriors were two or three score shaggy hounds waiting for the scraps that would presently be tossed them—large, savage beasts bred to protect our flocks from coyote and wolf, hellhound and lion; and quite capable of doing it, too.

As the warriors fell to eating, the din subsided, and at a word from me a youth at my elbow struck a deep note from a drum. Instantly there was silence. Then I spoke:

"For a hundred years we have dwelt beneath the heat of this barren wasteland, while our foes occupied a flowering garden, their cheeks fanned by the cooling breezes of the sea. They live in plenty; their women eat of lucious fruits, fresh from the trees, while ours must be satisfied with the dried and wrinkled semblance of the real.

"Ten slaves they have to do their labor for every one that we possess; their flocks and herds find lush pasture and sparkling water beside their masters' tents, while ours pick a scant existence across forty thousand square miles of sandy, rock-bound desert. But these things gall the soul of The Red Hawk least of all. The wine turns bitter in my mouth when in my mind's eye I look out across the rich valleys of the Kalkars and I recall that here alone in all the world that we know there flies not The Flag."

A great growl rose from the fierce throats.

"Since my youth I have held one thought sacred in my breast against the day that the blanket of The Great Chief should fall upon my shoulders. That day has come, and I but await the time that the rains shall be safely over before making of that thought a deed. Twenty times in a hundred years have the Julian warriors ridden down into the Kalkar country in force, but their women and their children and their flocks remained behind in the desert—an unescapable argument for their return.

"It shall not be so again. In April the tribe of Julian leaves the desert forever. With our tents and our women and all our flocks and herds we shall descend and live among the orange groves. This time there shall be no turning back. I, The Red Hawk, have spoken."

The Wolf leaped to his feet, his naked blade flashing in the torchlight.

"The Flag!" he cried.

A hundred warriors sprang erect, a hundred swords arose, shimmering, above our heads.

"The Flag! The Flag!"

I stepped to the table top and raised a tankard of wine aloft.

"The Flag!" I cried again; and we all drank deep.

And then the women came, my mother carrying The Flag, furled upon a long staff. She halted there, at the foot of the table, the other women massed behind her, and she undid the cords that hold it and let The Flag break out in the desert breeze, and we all kneeled and bent our heads to the faded bit of fabric that has been handed down from father to son through all the vicissitudes and hardships and bloodshed of more than five hundred years since the day that it was carried to victory by Julian 1st in a long forgotten war.

This, The Flag, is known from all other flags as The Flag of Argon, although its origin and the meaning of the word that describes it are lost in the mists of time. It is of alternate red and white stripes, with a blue square in one corner upon which are sewn many white stars. The white is yellow with age, and the blue and the red are faded, and it is torn in places, and there are brown spots upon it—the blood of Julians who have died protecting it, and the blood of their enemies. It fills us with awe, for it has the power of life and death, and it brings the rains and the winds and the thunder. That is why we bow down before it.

# TWO

# Exodus

APRIL ARRIVED, and with it the clans, coming at my bidding. Soon there would be little danger of heavy rains in the coast valleys. To have been caught there in a week of rain with an army would have been fatal, for the mud is deep and sticky and our horses would have mired and the Kalkars fallen upon us and destroyed us.

They greatly outnumber us, and so our only hope must lie in our mobility. We realize that we are reducing this by taking along our women and our flocks; but we believe that so desperate will be our straits that we must conquer, since the only alternative to victory must be death—death for us and worse for our women and children.

The clans have been gathering for two days, and all are here—some fifty thousand souls; and of horses, cattle, and sheep there must be a thousand thousand, for we are rich in livestock. In the last two months, at my orders, all our swine have been slaughtered and smoked, for we could not be hampered by them on the long desert march, even if they could have survived it.

There is water in the desert this time of year and some feed, but it will be a hard, a terrible march. We shall lose a great deal of our stock, one in ten, perhaps; The Wolf thinks it may be as high as five in ten.

We shall start tomorrow an hour before sunset, making a short march of about ten miles to a place where there is a spring along the trail the ancients used. It is strange to see all across the desert evidence of the great work they accomplished. After five hundred years the location of their well graded trail, with its wide, sweeping curves, is plainly discernible. It is a narrow trail, but there are signs of another, much wider, that we discover occasionally. It follows the general line of the other, crossing it and recrossing it, without any apparent reason, time and time again. It is almost obliterated by drifting sand, or washed away by the rains of ages. Only where it is of material like stone has it endured.

The pains those ancients took with things! The time and men and effort they expended! And for what? They have disappeared, and their works with them.

As we rode that first night Rain Cloud was often at my side, and as usual he was gazing at the stars.

"Soon you will know all about them," I said, laughing, "for you are always spying upon them. Tell me some of their secrets."

"I am learning them," he replied seriously.

"Only The Flag, who put them there to light our way at night, knows them all," I reminded him.

He shook his head. "They were there, I think, long before The Flag existed."

"Hush!" I admonished him. "Speak no ill of The Flag."

"I speak no ill of it," he replied. "It stands for all to me. I worship it, even as you; yet still I think the stars are older than The Flag, as the Earth must be older than The Flag."

"The Flag made the Earth," I reminded him.

"Then where did it abide before it made the earth?" he asked.

I scratched my head. "It is not for us to ask," I replied. "It is enough that our fathers told us these things. Why would you question them?"

"I would know the truth."

"What good will it do you?" I asked.

This time it was The Rain Cloud who scratched.

"It is not well to be ignorant," he replied at last. "Beyond the desert, wherever I have ridden, I have seen hills. I know not what lies beyond those hills. I should like to see. To the west is the ocean. In my day, perhaps, we shall reach it. I shall build a canoe and go forth upon the ocean and see what lies beyond."

"You will come to the edge of the world and tumble over it, and that will be the end of your canoe and you."

"I do not know about that," he replied. "You think the Earth is flat."

"And who is there that does not think so? Can we not see that it is flat? Look about you—it is like a large, round, flat cake."

"With land in the center and water all round the land?" he asked.

"Of course."

"What keeps the water from running off the edge?" he wanted to know.

I had never thought about that, and so I returned the only answer that I could think of at the time.

"The Flag, of course," I said.

"Do not be a fool, my brother," said Rain Cloud. "You are a great warrior and a mighty chief; you should be wise, and the wise man knows that nothing, not even The Flag, can keep water from running down hill if it is not confined."

"Then it must be confined," I argued. "There must be land to hold the water from running over the edge of the world."

"And what is beyond that land?"

"Nothing," I replied confidently.

"What do the hills stand on? What does the earth stand on?"

"It floats on a great ocean," I explained.

"With hills around it to keep its water from running over its edge?"

"I suppose so."

"And what upholds that ocean and those hills?" he went on.

"Do not be foolish," I told him. "I suppose there must be another ocean below that one."

"And what holds it up?"

I thought he would never stop. I do not enjoy thinking about such useless things. It is a waste of time, yet now that he had started me thinking, I saw that I should have to go on until I had satisfied him. Somehow I had an idea that dear little Rain Cloud was poking fun at me, and so I bent my mind to the thing and really thought, and when I did think I saw how foolish is the belief that we all hold.

"We know only about the land that we can see and the oceans that we know exist, because others have seen them," I said at last. "These things, then, of which we know, constitute the Earth. What upholds the Earth we do not know, but doubtless it floats about in the air as float the clouds. Are you satisfied?"

"Now I will tell you what I think," he said. "I have been watching the Sun, the Moon, and the stars every night since I was old enough to have a thought beyond my mother's breast. I have seen, as you can see, as every one with eyes can see, that the Sun, the Moon, and the stars are round like oranges. They move always in the same paths through the air, though all do not move upon the same path. Why should the Earth be different? It probably is not. It, too, is round, and it moves upon its path. What keeps them all from falling I do not know."

I laughed at that, and called to Nallah, our sister, who rode near by. "Rain Cloud thinks that the Earth is round like an orange."

"We should slip off if that were true," she said.

"Yes, and all the water would run off it," I added.

"There is something about it that I do not understand," admitted Rain Cloud, "yet still I think that I am right. There is so much that none of us knows. Nallah spoke of the water running off the Earth if it were round. Did you ever think of the fact that all the water of which we know runs down forever from the higher places? How does it get back again?"

"The rains and snows," I replied quickly.

"Where do they come from?"

"I do not know."

"There is so much that we do not know," sighed Rain Cloud; "yet all that we can spare the time for is thoughts of fighting. I shall be glad when we have chased the last of the Kalkars into the sea, so that some of us may sit down in peace and think."

"It is handed down to us that the ancients prided themselves upon their knowledge, but what did it profit them? I think we are happier. They must have had to work all their lives to do the things they did and to know all the things they knew, yet they could eat no more or sleep no more or drink no more in a lifetime than can we. And now they are gone forever from the Earth and all their works with them, and all their knowledge is lost."

"And presently we will be gone," said Rain Cloud.

"And we will have left as much as they to benefit those who follow," I replied.

"Perhaps you are right, Red Hawk," said Rain Cloud; "yet I cannot help wanting to know more than I do know."

The second march was also made at night, and was a little longer than the first. We had a good moon, and the desert night was bright. The third march was about twenty-five miles; and the fourth a short one, only ten miles. And there we left the trail of the ancients and continued in a southwesterly direction to a trail that followed a series of springs that gave us short marches the balance of the way to a lake called Bear by our slaves.

The way, of course, was all well known to us, and so we knew just what was ahead and dreaded the fifth march, which was a terrible one, by far the worst of them all. It lay across a rough and broken area of desert and crossed a range of barren mountains. For forty-five miles it wound its parched way from water hole to water hole.

For horsemen alone it would have been but a hard march, but with cattle and sheep to herd across that waterless waste it became a terrific undertaking. Every beast that was strong enough carried hay, oats or barley, in sacks, for we could not depend entirely upon the sparse feed of the desert for so huge a caravan; but water we could not carry in sufficient quantities for the stock. We transported enough, however on the longer marches to insure a supply for the women and all children under sixteen, and on the short marches enough for nursing mothers and children under ten.

We rested all day before the fifth march began, setting forth about three hours before sundown. From fifty camps in fifty parallel lines we started. Every man, woman and child was mounted. The women carried all children under five, usually seated astride a blanket on the horse's rump behind the mother. The rest rode alone. The bulk of the warriors and all the women and children set out ahead of the herds, which followed slowly behind, each bunch securely hemmed in by outriders and followed by a rear guard of warriors.

A hundred men on swift horses rode at the head of the column, and as the night wore on gradually increased their lead until they were out of sight of the remainder of the caravan. Their duty was to reach the camp site ahead of the others and fill the water tanks that slaves had been preparing for the last two months.

We took but a few slaves with us, only personal attendants for the women and such others as did not wish to be separated from their masters and had chosen to accompany us. For the most part the slaves preferred to remain in their own country, and we were willing to let them, since it made fewer mouths to feed upon the long journey, and we knew that in the Kalkar country we should find plenty to take their places, as we would take those from the Kalkars we defeated.

At the end of five hours we were strung out in a column fully ten miles long, and our outriders on either flank were of ten half a mile apart; but we had nothing to fear from the attacks of human enemies, the desert being our best defense against such. Only we of the desert knew the desert trails and the water holes, only we are innured to the pitiless hardships of its barrenness, its heat, and its cruelties.

But we have other enemies, and on this long march they clung tenaciously to our flanks, almost surrounding the great herds with a cordon of gleaming eyes and flashing fangs—the coyotes, the wolves, and the hellhounds. Woe betide the straggling sheep or cow that they might cut off from the protection of the rear guard or the flankers. A savage chorus, a rush, and the poor creature was literally torn to pieces upon its feet. A woman or child with his mount would have suffered a similar fate, and even a lone warrior might be in great danger. If the brutes knew their own strength, they could, I believe, exterminate us, for their numbers are appalling; there must have been as high as a thousand following us upon that long march at a single time.

But they hold us in great fear because we have waged relentless warfare against them for hundreds of years, and the fear of us must be bred in them. Only when in great numbers and goaded by starvation will they attack a full grown warrior. They kept us busy all during the long nights of this wearisome march, and they kept our shaggy hounds busy, too. The coyotes and the wolves are easy prey for the hounds, but the hellhounds are a match for them, and it is these that we fear most. Our hounds, and with the fifty clans there must have been gathered a full two thousand of them, work with tireless efficiency and a minimum of wasted effort when on the march.

In camp they are constantly fighting among themselves, but on the march, never. From the home camp they indulge in futile chases after rabbits, but on the march they consume no energy uselessly. The dogs of each clan have their pack leader, usually an experienced dog owned by the hound-chief of the clan. The Vulture is our hound-chief, and his hound, old Lonay, is pack leader. He does his work and leads his pack with scarce a word from The Vulture. He has about fifty hounds in his pack, twenty-five of which he posts at intervals about the herd, and with the other twenty-five old Lonay brings up the rear.

A high-pitched yelp from one of his sentries is a signal of attack, and brings Lonay and his fighting dogs to the rescue. Sometimes there will be a sudden rush of coyotes, wolves and hellhounds simultaneously from two or three points, and then the discipline and intelligence of old Lonay and his pack merit the affection and regard in which we hold these great, shaggy beasts.

Whirling rapidly two or three times, Lonay emits a series of deep-throated growls and barks, and instantly the pack splits into two or three or more units, each of which races to a different point of trouble. If at any point they are outnumbered and the safety of the herd imperiled, they set up a great wailing which is the signal that they need the help of warriors, a signal that never goes unheeded. In similar cases, or in the hunt, the hounds of other packs will come to the rescue, and all will work together harmoniously, yet if one of these same hounds should wander into the others' camp a half hour later he would be torn to pieces.

But enough of this, and of the long, tiresome march. It was over at last. The years of thought that I had given it, the two months of preparation that had immediately preceded it, the splendid condition of all our stock, the training and the temper of my people bore profitable fruit, and we came through without the loss of a man, woman or child, and with the loss of less than two hundred of our herds and flocks. The mountain crossing on that memorable fifth march took the heaviest toll, fully ten thousand head, mostly lambs and calves falling by the trail side.

With two days out for rest we came, at the end of the tenth march and the twelfth day, to the lake called Bear and into a rich mountain country, lush with feed and game. Here deer and wild goats and wild sheep abounded, with rabbit and quail and wild chicken, and the beautiful wild cattle that the legends of our slaves say are descended from the domestic stock of the ancients.

It was not my plan to rest here longer than was necessary to restore in full the strength and spirits of the stock. Our horses were not jaded, as we had had sufficient to change often. In fact, we warriors had not ridden our war horses once upon the journey. Red Lightning had trotted into the last camp fat and sleek.

To have remained here long would have been to have apprised the enemy of our plans, for the Kalkars and their slaves hunt in these mountains which adjoin their land, and should a single hunter see this vast concourse of Julians our coming would have been known throughout the valleys in a single day, and our purpose guessed by all.

So, after a day of rest, I sent The Wolf and a thousand warriors westward to the main pass of the ancients with orders to make it appear that we were attempting to enter the valley there in force. For three days he would persist in this false advance, and in that time I felt that I should have drawn all the Kalkar fighting men from the valley lying southwest of the lake of the Bear. My lookouts were posted upon every eminence that gave view of the valleys and the trails between the main pass of the ancients and that through which we should pour down from the Bear out into the fields and groves of the Kalkars.

The third day was spent in preparation. The last of the arrows were finished and distributed. We looked to our saddle leathers and our bridles. We sharpened our swords and knives once more and put keener points upon our lances. Our women mixed the war paint and packed our belongings again for another march. The herds were gathered in and held in close, compact bunches.

Riders reported to me at intervals from the various lookouts and from down the trail to the edge of the Kalkar farms. No enemy had seen us, but that they had seen The Wolf and his warriors we had the most reassuring evidence in the reports from our outposts that every trail from south and west was streaming with Kalkar warriors and that they were converging upon the pass of the ancients.*

During the third day we moved leisurely down the mountain trails and as night fell our vanguard of a thousand warriors debouched into the groves of the Kalkars. Leaving four thousand warriors, mostly youths, to guard the women, the children, the flocks and the herds, I set out rapidly in a northwesterly direction toward the pass of the ancients at the head of full twenty thousand warriors.

Our war horses we had led all day as we came slowly out of the mountains riding other animals, and not until we were ready to start upon the twenty-five-mile march to the pass of the ancients did we saddle and mount the fleet beasts upon which the fate of the Julians might rest this night. In consequence our horses were fresh from a two weeks' rest. Three hours of comparatively easy riding should see us upon the flanks of the enemy.

The Rock, a brave and seasoned warrior, I had left behind to guard the women, the children, and the stock. The Rattlesnake, with five thousand warriors, bore along a more westerly trail, after fifteen miles had been covered, that he might fall upon the rear of the enemy from one point while I fell upon them from another, and at the same time place himself between their main body, lying at the foot of the pass, and the source of their supplies and reënforcements.

With The Wolf, the mountains, and the desert upon one side, and The Rattlesnake and I blocking them upon the south and the southeast, the position of the Kalkars appeared to me to be hopeless.

Toward midnight I called a halt to await the report of scouts who had preceded us, and it was not long before they commenced to come in. From them I learned that the camp fires of the Kalkars were visible from an eminence less than a mile ahead. I gave the signal to advance.

Slowly the great mass of warriors moved forward. The trail dipped down into a little valley and then wound upward to the crest of a low ridge, where, a few minutes later, I brought Red Lightning to a halt.

Before me spread a broad valley bathed in the soft light of Moon and stars. Dark masses in the nearer foreground recognized as orange groves even without the added evidence of the sweet aroma of their blossoms that was heavy on the still night air. Beyond, to the northwest, a great area was dotted with the glowing embers of a thousand dying camp fires.

*Probably Cajon Pass.

I filled my lungs with the cool, sweet air; I felt my nerves tingle; a wave of exultation surged through me; Red Lightning trembled beneath me. After nearly four hundred years a Julian stood at last upon the threshold of complete revenge!

# THREE

# Armageddon

V ERY QUIETLY we crept down among the orange groves, nearer, ever nearer, to the sleeping foe. Somewhere to the west of us, beneath the silvery Moon, The Rattlesnake was creeping stealthily forward to strike. Presently the stillness of the night would be broken by the booming of his war drums and the hoarse war cries of his savage horde. It would be the signal that would send The Wolf down from the mountain heights above them and The Red Hawk from the orange groves below them to sink fang and talon into the flesh of the hated Kalkars, and ever The Rattlesnake would be striking at their heels.

Silently we awaited the signal from The Rattlesnake. A thousand bowmen unslung their bows and loosened arrows in their quivers; swords were readjusted, their hilts ready to the hand; men spat upon their right palm that their lance grip might be the surer. The night dragged on toward dawn.

The success of my plan depended upon a surprise attack while the foe slept. I knew that The Rattlesnake would not fail me, but something must have delayed him. I gave the signal to advance silently. Like shadows we moved through the orange groves and deployed along a front two miles in length, a thousand bowmen in the lead and behind these line after line of lancers and swordsmen.

Slowly we moved forward toward the sleeping camp. How like the lazy, stupid Kalkars that no sentries were posted at their rear! Doubtless there were plenty of them on the front exposed to The Wolf. Where they could see an enemy they could prepare for him, but they have not imagination enough to foresee aught.

Only the desert and their great numbers have saved them from extermination during the past hundred years.

Scarce a mile away now we could catch occasional glimpses of the dying embers of the nearest fires, and then from the east there rolled across the valley the muffled booming of distant war drums. A momentary silence followed, and then, faintly, there broke upon our ears the war-cries of our people. At my signal our own drums shattered the silence that had surrounded us.

It was the signal for the charge. From twenty thousand savage throats rose the awful cries of battle, twenty thousand pairs of reins were loosed, and eighty thousand iron shod hoofs set the earth atremble as they thundered down upon the startled enemy, and from the heights above came the growl of the drums of The Wolf and the eerie howls of his painted horde.

It was dawn as we smote the camp. Our bowmen, guiding their mounts with their knees and the swing of their bodies, raced among the bewildered Kalkars, loosing their barbed shafts into the cursing, shrieking mob that fled before them only to be ridden down and trampled by our horses' feet.

Behind the bowmen came the lancers and the swordsmen, thrusting and cutting at those who survived. From our left came the tumult of The Rattlesnake's assault, and from far ahead and above us the sounds of battle proclaimed that The Wolf had fallen on the foe.

Ahead I could see the tents of the Kalkar leaders, and toward these I spurred Red Lightning. Here would be the representatives of the house of Or-tis, and here would the battle center.

Ahead the Kalkars were forming in some semblance of order to check and repel us. They are huge men and ferocious fighters, but I could see that our surprise attack had unnerved them. They gave before us before their chiefs could organize them for resistance, yet again and again they reformed and faced us.

We were going more slowly now, the battle had become largely a matter of hand-to-hand combats; they were checking us, but they were not stopping us. So great were their numbers that even had they been unarmed it would have been difficult to force our horses through their massed ranks.

Back of their front line they were saddling and mounting their horses, which those who had borne the brunt of our first onslaught had been unable to do. We had cut the lines to which their animals had been tethered, and driven them, terrified, ahead of us to add to the confusion of the enemy. Riderless horses were running wildly everywhere, those of the Kalkars and many of our own, whose riders had fallen in battle.

The tumult was appalling, for to the shrieks of the wounded and the groans of the dying were added the screams of stricken horses and the wild, hoarse war-cries of battle-maddened men, and underlying all, the dull booming of the war drums. Above us waved The Flag, not The Flag of

Argon, but a duplicate of it, and here were the drums and a massed guard of picked men.

The Flag and the drums moved forward as we moved. And near me was the clan flag of my family with the red hawk upon it, and with it were its drums. In all there were a hundred clan flags upon that field this day, and the drums of each rolled out, incessantly, defiance of the enemy.

Their horsemen now were rallied, and the dismounted men were falling back behind them, and presently a Kalkar chief upon a large horse confronted me. Already was my blade red with their blood. I had thrown away my lance long since, for we were fighting in too close quarters for its effective use, but the Kalkar had his spear and there was a little open space between us, and in the instant he crouched and put spurs to his horse and bore down upon me.

He was a large man, as most Kalkars are, for they have bred with that alone in mind for five hundred years, so that many of them are seven feet in height and over. He looked very fierce did this fellow, with his great bulk and his little bloodshot eyes.

He wore a war bonnet of iron to protect his head from sword cuts and a vest of iron covered his chest against the thrusts of sword or lance or the barbed tips of arrows. We Julians, or Americans, disdain such protection, choosing to depend upon our skill and agility, not hampering ourselves and our horses with the weight of all this metal.

My light shield was on my left forearm, and in my right hand I grasped my two-edged sword. A pressure of my knees, an inclination of my body, a word in his pointed ear, were all that was needed to make Red Lightning respond to my every wish, even though the reins hung loose upon his withers.

The fellow bore down upon me with a loud yell, and Red Lightning leaped to meet him. The Kalkar's point was set straight at my chest, and I had only a sword on that side to deflect it, and at that I think I might have done so had I cared to try, even though the Kalkar carries a heavy lance and this one was backed by a heavy man and a heavy horse.

These things make a difference, I can tell you out of wide experience. The weight behind a lance has much to do with the success or failure of many a combat. A heavy lance can be deflected by a light sword, but not as quickly as a light lance, and the point of a lance is usually within three feet of you before your blade parries its thrust—within three feet of you and traveling as fast as a running horse can propel it.

You can see that the blow must be a quick and heavy one if it is to turn the lance point even a few inches in the fraction of a second before it enters your flesh.

I usually accomplish it with a heavy downward and outward cut, but in that cut there is always the danger of striking your horse's head unless you rise in your stirrups and lean well forward before delivering it, so that, in reality, you strike well ahead of your horse's muzzle.

This is best for parrying a lance thrust for the groin or belly, but this chap was all set for my chest, and I would have had to have deflected his point too great a distance in the time at my disposal to have insured the success of my defense. And so I changed my tactics.

With my left hand I grasped Red Lightning's mane and at the instant that the Kalkar thought to see his point tear through my chest I swung from my saddle and lay flat against Red Lightning's near side, while the Kalkar and his spear brushed harmlessly past an empty saddle. Empty for but an instant, though.

Swinging back to my seat in the instant that I wheeled Red Lightning, I was upon the Kalkar from the rear even as the fighting mass before him brought him to a halt. He was swinging to have at me again, but even as he faced me my sword swung down upon his iron bonnet, driving pieces of it through his skull and into his brain. A fellow on foot cut viciously at me at the instant I was recovering from the blow I had dealt the mounted Kalkar, so that I was able only to partially parry with my shield, with the result that his point opened up my right arm at the shoulder—a flesh wound, but one that bled profusely, although it did not stay the force of my return, which drove though his collarbone and opened up his chest to his heart.

Once again I spurred in the direction of the tents of the Or-tis, above which floated the red banners of the Kalkars, and around which were massed the flower of the Kalkar forces; too thickly massed, perhaps, for most effective defense, since we were driving them in from three sides and packing them there as tightly as eggs in the belly of a she-salmon.

But now they surged forward and drove us back by weight of numbers, and now we threw ourselves upon them again until they, in their turn, were forced to give the ground that they had won. Sometimes the force of our attack drove them to one side, while at another point their warriors were pushing out into the very body of the massed clans, so that here and there our turning movements would cut off a detachment of the enemy, or again a score or more of our own men would be swallowed by the milling Kalkar horde until, as the day wore on, the great field became a jumbled mass of broken detachments of Julian and Kalkar warriors surging back and forth over a bloody shambles, the iron shoes of their reeking mounts trampling the corpse of friend and foe alike into the gory mire.

There were lulls in the fighting; when, as though by mutual assent, both sides desisted for brief intervals of rest, for we had fought to the limit of endurance. Then we sat, often stirrup to stirrup with a foeman, our chests heaving from our exertions, our mounts, their heads low, blowing and trembling.

Never before had I realized the extreme of endurance to which a man may go before breaking, and I saw many break that day, mostly Kalkars, though, for we are fit and strong at all times. It was only the very young and the very old among us who succumbed to fatigue, and but a negligible fraction of these, but the Kalkars dropped by hundreds in the heat of the day. Many a time that day as I faced an enemy I would see his sword drop from nerveless fingers and his body crumple in the saddle and slip beneath the trampling feet of the horses before ever I had struck him a blow.

Once, late in the afternoon, during a lull in the battle, I sat looking about the chaos of the field. Red with our own blood from a score of wounds and with the blood of friend and foe, Red Lightning and I stood panting in the midst of the welter. The tents of the Or-tis lay south of us—we had fought halfway around them—but they were scarce a hundred yards nearer for all those bitter hours of battle. Some of the warriors of The Wolf were near me, showing how far that old, gray chieftain had fought his way since dawn, and presently behind a mask of blood I saw the flashing eyes of The Wolf himself, scarce twenty feet away.

"The Wolf!" I cried; and he looked up and smiled in recognition.

"The Red Hawk is red indeed," he bantered; "but his pinions are yet unclipped."

"And the fangs of The Wolf are yet undrawn," I replied.

A great Kalkar, blowing like a spent hound, was sitting his tired horse between us. At our words he raised his head.

"You are The Red Hawk?" he asked.

"I am The Red Hawk," I replied.

"I have been searching for you these two hours," he said.

"I have not been far, Kalkar," I told him. "What would you of The Red Hawk?"

"I bear word from Or-tis, the Jemadar."

"What word has an Or-tis for a Julian?" I demanded.

"The Jemadar would grant you peace," he explained.

I laughed. "There is only one peace which we may share together," I said, "and that is the peace of death—that peace I will grant him and he will come hither and meet me. There is nothing that an Or-tis has the power to *grant* a Julian."

"He would stop the fighting while you and he discuss the terms of peace," insisted the Kalkar. "He would stop this bloody strife that must eventually annihilate both Kalkar and Yank." He used an ancient term which the Kalkars have applied to us for ages in a manner of contempt, but which we have been taught to consider as an appellation of honor, although its very meaning is unknown to us and its derivation lost in antiquity.

"Go back to your Jemadar," I said, "and tell him that the world is not wide enough to support both Kalkar and Yank, Or-tis and Julian; that the Kalkars must slay us to the last man, or be slain."

He wheeled his horse toward the tent of the Or-tis, and The Wolf bade his warriors let him pass. Soon he was swallowed by the close-packed ranks of his own people, and then a Kalkar struck at one of us from behind and the battle raged again.

How many men had fallen one might not even guess, but the corpses of warriors and horses lay so thick that the living mounts could but climb and stumble over them, and sometimes barriers of them nearly man-high lay between me and the nearest foeman, so that I was forced to jump Red Lightning over the gory obstacle to find new flesh for my blade. And then, slowly, night descended until man could not tell foe from friend, but I called to my tribesmen about me to pass along the word that we would not move from our ground that night, staying on for the first streak of dawn that would permit us to tell a Kalkar from a Yank.

Once again the tents of the Or-tis were north of me. I had fought completely around them during the long day, gaining two hundred yards in all, perhaps; but I knew that they had weakened more than we, and that they could not stand even another few hours of what they had passed through this day. We were tired, but not exhausted, and our war horses, after a night's rest, would be good for another day, even without food.

As darkness forced a truce upon us all I began to reform my broken clans, drawing them into a solid ring about the position of the Kalkars. Sometimes we would find a lone Kalkar among us, cut off from his fellows; but these we soon put out of danger, letting them lie where they fell. We had drawn off a short distance, scarce more than twenty yards, from the Kalkars, and there in small detachments we were dismounting and removing saddles for a few minutes to rest and cool our horses' backs, and to dispatch the wounded, giving merciful peace to those who must otherwise have soon died in agony. This favor we did to foe as well as friend.

All through the night we heard a considerable movement of men and horses among the Kalkars, and we judged that they were reforming for the dawn's attack, and then, quite suddenly and without warning of any sort, we saw a black mass moving down upon us. It was the Kalkars—the entire body of them—and they rode straight for us, not swiftly, for the corpse-strewn, slippery ground prevented that, but steadily, overwhelmingly, like a great, slow-moving river of men and horses

They swept into us and over us, or they carried us along with them. Their first line broke upon us in a bloody wave and went down, and those behind passed over the corpses of those that had fallen. We hacked until our tired arms could scarce raise a blade shoulder high. Kalkars went down screaming in agony; but they could not halt, they could not retreat, for the great, ever-moving mass behind them pushed them onward; nor could they turn to right or left, because we hemmed them in on both flanks; nor could they flee ahead, for there, too, were we.

Borne on by this resistless tide, I was carried with it. It surrounded me. It pinioned my arms at my sides. It crushed at my legs. It even tore my sword from my hand. At times, when the force ahead stemmed it for a moment and the force behind continued to push on, it rose in the center until horses were lifted from the ground, and then those behind sought to climb over the backs of those in front, until the latter were borne to earth and the others passed over their struggling forms, or the obstacle before gave way and the flood smoothed out and passed along again between the flashing banks of Julian blades, hewing, ever hewing, at the surging Kalkar stream.

Never have I looked upon such a sight as the Moon revealed that night—never in the memory or the tradition of man has there been such a holocaust. Thousands upon thousands of Kalkars must have fallen upon the edge of that torrent as it swept its slow way between the blades of my painted warriors, who hacked at the living mass until their arms fell numb at their sides from utter exhaustion, and then gave way to the eager thousands pressing from behind.

And ever onward I was borne, helpless to extricate myself from the sullen, irresistible flood that carried me southward down the broadening valley. The Kalkars about me did not seem to realize that I was an enemy, or notice me in any way, so intent were they upon escape. Presently we had passed the field of yesterday's thickest fighting, the ground was no longer strewn with corpses and the speed of the rout increased, and as it did so the massed warriors spread to right and left sufficiently to permit more freedom of individual action, still not enough to permit me to worm my way from the current.

That I was attempting to do so, however, was what attracted attention to me at first, and then the single red hawk feather and my other trappings, so different from those of the Kalkars.

"A Yank!" cried one near me, and another drew his sword and struck at me; but I warded the blow with my shield as I drew my knife, a pitiful weapon wherewith to face a swordsman.

"Hold!" cried a voice of authority near by. "It is he whom they call The Red Hawk, their chief. Take him alive to the Jemadar."

I tried to break through their lines, but they closed in upon me, and although I used my knife to good effect upon several of them, they overbore me with their numbers, and then one of them must have struck me upon the head with the flat of his sword, for of a sudden everything went black, and of that moment I remember only reeling in my saddle.

# FOUR

# The Capital

WHEN I regained consciousness it was night again. I was lying upon the ground, out beneath the stars. For a moment I experienced a sense of utter comfort, but as my tired nerves awoke they spoke to me of pain and stiffness from many wounds, and my head throbbed with pain. I tried to raise a hand to it and it was then that I discovered that my wrists were bound. I could feel the matted stiffness of my scalp and I knew that it was caked with dried blood, doubtless from the blow that had stunned me.

In attempting to move that I might ease my cramped muscles I found that my ankles were fastened together as well as my wrists, but I managed to roll over, and raising my head a little from the ground I looked about and saw that I was surrounded by sleeping Kalkars and that we lay in a barren hollow ringed by hills. There were no fires and from this fact and the barrenness and seclusion of the camp I guessed that we were snatching a brief rest in hiding from a pursuing foe.

I tried to sleep, but could do so only fitfully, and presently I heard men moving about and soon they approached and awakened the warriors sleeping near me. The thongs were removed from my ankles shortly thereafter and Red Lightning was brought and I was helped into the saddle. Immediately after, we resumed the march. A glance at the stars showed me that we were moving west. Our way led through hills and was often rough, evidencing that we were following no beaten trail, but rather that the Kalkars were attempting to escape by a devious route.

I could only guess at the numbers of them, but it was evident that there was not the great horde that had set forth from the battlefield below the pass of the ancients. Whether they had separated into smaller bands, or the balance had been slain I could not even conjecture; but that their losses must have been tremendous I was sure.

We traveled all that day, stopping only occasionally when there was water for the horses and the men. I was given neither food nor water, nor did I ask for either. I would die rather than ask a favor of an Or-tis. In fact, I did not speak all that day, nor did any of the Kalkars address me.

I had seen more Kalkars in the last two days than in all my life before and was now pretty familiar with the appearance of them. They range in height from six to eight feet, the majority of them being midway between these extremes. Many of them are bearded, but some shave the hair from all or portions of their faces. A great many wear beards upon their upper lips only.

There is a great variety of physiognomy among them, for they are a half-caste race, being the result of hundreds of years of inter-breeding between the original Moon Men and the women of the Earth whom they seized for slaves when they overran and conquered the world. Among them there is occasionally an individual who might pass anywhere for a Yank, insofar as external appearances are concerned; but the low, coarse, brutal features of the Kalkar preponderate.

They wear a white blouse and breeches of cotton woven by their slaves and long, woolen cloaks fabricated by the same busy hands. Their women help in this work as well as in the work of the fields, for the Kalkar women are no better than slaves, with the possible exception of those who belong to the families of the Jemadar and his nobles. Their cloaks are of red, with collars of various colors, or with borders or other designs to denote rank.

Their weapons are similar to ours, but heavier. They are but indifferent horsemen. That, I think is because they ride only from necessity and not, as we, from love of it.

That night, after dark, we came to a big Kalkar camp. It was one of the camps of the ancients, the first that I ever had seen. It must have covered a great area and some of the huge stone tents were still standing. It was in these that the Kalkars lived or in dirt huts leaning against them. In some places I saw where the Kalkars had built smaller tents from the building materials salvaged from the ruins of the ancient camp, but as a rule they were satisfied with hovels of dirt, or the half-fallen and never-repaired structures of the ancients.

This camp lies about forty-five or fifty miles west of the battlefield, among beautiful hills and rich groves, upon the banks of what must once have been a mighty river, so deeply has it scoured its pathway into the earth in ages gone. *

I was hustled into a hut where a slave woman gave me food and water.

*The camp described probably occupies the site of present-day Pasadena.

There was a great deal of noise and excitement outside, and through the open doorway I could bear snatches of conversation as Kalkas passed to and fro. From what I heard I gathered that the defeat of the Kalkars had been complete and that they were flying toward the coast and their principal camp, called The Capital, which the slave woman told me lay a few miles southwest. This, she said, was a wonderful camp, with tents reaching so high into the heavens that often the Moon brushed against their tops as she made her way through the sky.

They had released my hands, but my feet were still bound and two Kalkars squatted just outside the door of the hut to see that I did not escape. I asked the slave woman for some warm water to wash my wounds and she prepared it for me. Not only that, the kindly soul saw to my wounds herself, and after they had been cleansed she applied a healing lotion which greatly soothed them, and then she bound them as best she could.

I felt much refreshed by this and with the food and drink in me was quite happy, for had I not accomplished what my people had been striving after for a hundred years—a foothold on the western coast? This first victory had been greater than I had dared to hope and if I could but escape and rejoin my people I felt that I could lead them to the waters of the ocean with scarce a halt while the Kalkars still were suffering the demoralization of defeat.

It was while I was thinking these thoughts that a Kalkar chief entered the hut. Beyond the doorway the score of warriors that had accompanied him, waited.

"Come!" commanded the Kalkar, motioning me to arise.

I pointed to my tethered ankles.

"Cut his bonds," he directed the slave woman.

When I was free I arose and followed the Kalkar without. Here the guard surrounded me and we marched away between avenues of splendid trees such as I never had seen before, to a tent of the ancients, a partly ruined structure of imposing height that spread over a great area of ground. It was lighted upon the inside by many flares and there were guards at the entrance and slaves holding other flares.

They led me into a great chamber that must be much as the ancients left it, although I had seen from the outside that in other places the roof of the tent had fallen in and its walls were crumbling. There were many high Kalkars in this place and at the far end of the room, upon a platform, one sat alone on a huge, carved bench—a bench with a high back and arms. It was just large enough for a single man. It is what we call a small bench.

The Kalkars call it *chair*; but this one, I was to learn, they call *throne*, because it is the small bench upon which their ruler sits. I did not know this at the time.

I was led before this man. He had a thin face and a long, thin nose, and cruel lips and crafty eyes. His features, however, were good. He might have passed in any company as a full-blood Yank. My guard halted me in front of him.

"This is he, Jemadar," said the chief who fetched me.

"Who are you?" demanded the Jemadar, addressing me. His tone did not please me. It was unpleasant and dictatorial. I am not accustomed to that, even from equals, and a Julian has no superiors. I looked upon him as scum. Therefore, I did not reply.

He repeated his question angrily. I turned to the Kalkar chief who stood at my elbow. "Tell this man that he is addressing a Julian," I said, "and that I do not like his manner. Let him ask for it in a more civil tone if he wishes information."

The eyes of the Jemadar narrowed angrily. He half arose from his small bench. "A Julian!" he exclaimed. "You are all Julians—but you are *the* Julian. You are The Great Chief of the Julians. Tell me," his tone became suddenly civil, almost ingratiating, "is it not true that you are *the* Julian, The Red Hawk who led the desert hordes upon us?"

"I am Julian 20th, The Red Hawk," I replied; "and you?"

"I am Or-tis, the Jemadar," he replied.

"It has been long since an Or-tis and a Julian met," I said.

"Heretofore they always have met as enemies," he replied. "I have sent for you to offer peace and friendship. For five hundred years we have fought uselessly and senselessly because two of our forebears hated each other. You are the twentieth Julian I am the sixteenth Or-tis. Never before have we seen each other, yet we must be enemies. How silly!"

"There can be no friendship between a Julian and an Or-tis," I replied coldly.

"There can be peace," he said, "and friendship will come later, maybe long after you and I are dead. There is room in this great, rich country for us all. Go back to your people. I will send an escort with you and rich presents. Tell them that the Kalkars would share their country with the Yanks. You will rule half of it and I will rule the other half. If the power of either is threatened the other will come to his aid with men and horses. We can live in peace and our people will prosper. What say you?"

"I sent you my answer yesterday," I told him. "It is the same today—the only peace that you and I can share is the peace of death. There can be but one ruler for this whole country and he will be a Julian—if not I, the next in line. There is not room in all the world for both Kalkar and Yank. For three hundred years we have been driving you toward the sea. Yesterday we started upon the final drive that will not stop until the last of you has been driven from the world you ruined. That is my answer, Kalkar."

He flushed and then paled. "You do not guess our strength," he said after a moment's silence. "Yesterday you surprised us, but even so you did not defeat us. You do not know how the battle came out. You do not know that after you were captured our forces turned upon your weakened warriors and drove them back into the recesses of the mountains. You do not know that even now they are suing for peace. If you would save their lives and yours as well, you will accept my offer."

"No, I do not know these things nor do you," I replied with a sneer; "but I do know that you lie. That has always been the clan-sign of the Or-tis."

"Take him away!" cried the Jemadar. "Send this message to his people: I offer them peace on these terms—they may have all the country east and southeast of a straight line drawn from the pass of the ancients south to the sea; we will occupy the country to the west and northwest of that line. If they accept I will send back their Great Chief. If they refuse, he will go to The Butcher, and remind them that he will not be the first Julian that an Or-tis has sent to The Butcher. If they accept there are to be no more wars between our people."

They took me back then to the hut of the old slave and there I slept until early morning, when I was awakened by a great commotion without. Men were shouting orders and cursing as they ran hurriedly to and fro. There was the trampling of horses' feet, the clank and clatter of trappings of war. Faintly, as from a great distance, I heard, presently, a familiar sound and my blood leaped in answer. It was the war-cry of my people and beneath it ran the dull booming of their drums.

"They come!" I must have spoken aloud, for the old slave woman, busy with some household duty, turned toward me.

"Let them come," she said. "They cannot be worse than these others, and it is time that we changed masters. It has been long now since the rule of the ancients, who, it is said, were not unkind to us. Before them were other ancients, and before those still others. Always they came from far places, ruled us and went their way, displaced by others. Only we remain, never changing.

"Like the coyote, the deer and the mountains we have been here always. We belong to the land, we are the land—when the last of our rulers has passed away we shall still be here, as we were in the beginning—unchanged.

They come and mix their blood with ours, but in a few generations the last traces of it have disappeared, swallowed up by the slow, unchanging flood of ours. You will come and go, leaving no trace; but after you are forgotten we shall still be here."

I listened to her in surprise for I never had heard a slave speak as this one, and I should have been glad to have questioned her further. Her strange prophesy interested me. But now the Kalkars entered the hovel. They came hurriedly and as hurriedly departed, taking me with them. My wrists were tied again and I was almost thrown upon Red Lightning's back. A moment later we were swallowed up by the torrent of horsemen surging toward the southwest.

Less than two hours later we were entering the greatest camp that man has ever looked upon. For miles we rode through it, our party now reduced to the score of warriors who guarded me. The others had halted at the outskirts of the camp to make a stand against my people and as we rode through the strange trails of the camp we passed thousands upon thousands of Kalkars rushing past us to defend The Capital.

We passed vast areas laid out in squares, as was the custom of the ancients, a trail upon each side of the square, and within the grass-grown mounds that covered the fallen ruins of their tents. Now and again a crumbling wall raised its ruin above the desolation, or some more sturdily constructed structure remained almost intact except for fallen roof and floors. As we advanced we encountered more and more of the latter, built of that strange, rocklike substance the secret of which has vanished with the ancients.

Now these mighty tents of a mighty people became larger. Whole squares of them remained and there were those that reared their weatherworn heads far into the sky. It was easy to believe that at night the Moon might scrape against them. Many were very beautiful, with great carvings upon them and more and more of them, as we advanced, had their roofs and floors intact. These were the habitations of the Kalkars. They arose upon each side of the trails like the sides of sheer mountain canyons, their fronts pierced by a thousand openings.

The trail between the tents was deep with dust and filth. In places the last rains had washed clean the solid stone pavement of the ancients, but elsewhere the debris of ages lay thick, rising above the bottom of the lower opening in the tents in many places and spreading itself inward over the floors of the structures.

Bushes and vines and wild oats grew against the walls and in every niche that was protected from the trampling feet of the inhabitants. Offal of every description polluted the trails until my desert bred nose was distressed at the stench. Coarse Kalkar women, with their dirty brats, leaned from the openings above the level of the trail and when they caught sight of me they screamed vile insults.

As I looked upon these stupendous tents, the miles upon miles of them stretching away in every direction, and sought to conceive of the extent of the incalculable effort, time and resources expended by the ancients in the building of them, and then looked upon the filthy horde to whose vile uses they had unwittingly been dedicated my mind was depressed by contemplation of the utter futility of human effort. How long and at what cost had the ancients striven to the final achievement of their mighty civilization! And for what?

How long and at what cost had we striven to wrest its wreckage from the hands of their despoilers! And for what? There was no answer—only that I knew we should go on and on, and generations after us would go on and on, striving, always striving, for that which was just beyond our grasp—victims of some ancient curse laid upon our earliest progenitor, perhaps.

And I thought of the slave woman and her prophesy. Her people would remain, steadfast, like the hills, aspiring to nothing, achieving nothing, except perhaps that one thing we all crave in common—contentment. And when the end comes, whatever that end shall be, the world will doubtless be as well off because of them as because of us, for in the end there will be nothing.

My guard turned in beneath the high arched entrance of a mighty structure. From the filth of its spacious floor rose mighty columns of polished stone, richly variegated. The tops of the columns were carved and decorated in colors and in gold. The place was filled with horses, tied to long lines that stretched almost the length of the room, from column to column. At one end a broad flight of stone steps led upward.

After we dismounted I was led up these steps. There were many Kalkars coming and going. We passed them as I was conducted along a narrow avenue of polished white stone upon either side of which were openings in the walls leading to other chambers.

Through one of these openings we turned into a large chamber and there I saw again the Or-tis whom I had seen the night before. He was standing before one of the openings overlooking the trail below, talking with several of his nobles. One of the latter glanced up and saw me as I entered, calling the Jemadar's attention to me.

Or-tis faced me. He spoke to one near him who stepped to another opening in the chamber and motioned to someone without. Immediately a Kalkar guard entered bringing a youth of one of my desert clans. At sight of me the young warrior raised his hand to his forehead in salute.

"I give you another opportunity to consider my offer of last night," said the Or-tis, addressing me. "Here is one of your own men who can bear your message to your people if you still choose to condemn them to a futile and bloody struggle, and with it he will bear a message from me—that you go to The Butcher in the morning if your warriors do not retire and your chiefs engage to maintain peace hereafter. In that event you will be restored to your people. If you give me this promise yourself you may carry your own message to the tribes of Julian."

"My answer," I replied, "is the same as it was last night, as it will be tomorrow." Then I turned to the Yank warrior. "If you are permitted to depart, go at once to The Vulture and tell him that my last command is that he carry The Flag onward to the sea. That is all."

The Or-tis was trembling with disappointment and rage. He laid a hand upon the hilt of his sword and took a step toward me; but whatever he intended he thought better of it and stopped. "Take him above," he snapped to my guard; "and to The Butcher in the morning."

"I will be present," he said to me, "to see your head roll into the dust and your carcass fed to the pigs."

They took me from the chamber then and led me up and up along an endless stairway, or at least it seemed endless before we finally reached the highest floor of the great tent. There they pushed me into a chamber the doorway to which was guarded by two giant warriors.

Squatted upon the floor of the chamber, his back leaning against the wall, was a Kalkar. He glanced up at me as I entered, but said nothing. I looked about the bare chamber, its floor littered with the dust and debris of ages, its walls stained by the dirt and grease from the bodies that had leaned against it, to the height of a man.

I approached one of the apertures in the front wall. Far below me, like a narrow buckskin thong, lay the trail filled with tiny people and horses no bigger than rabbits. I could see the pigs rooting in the filth—they and the dogs are the scavengers of the camp.

For a long time I stood looking out over what was to me a strange landscape. The tent in which I was confined was among the highest of the nearer structures of the ancients and from its upper floor I could see a vast expanse of tent roofs, some of the structures apparently in an excellent state of preservation, while here and there a grass-grown mound marked the site of others that had fallen.

Evidences of fire and smoke were numerous, and it was apparent that whatever the ancients had built of other materials than their enduring stone had long since disappeared, while many of the remaining buildings had been gutted by flame and left mere shells, as was attested by hundreds of smoke-blackened apertures within the range of my vision.

As I stood gazing out over the distant hills beyond the limits of the camp I became aware of a presence at my elbow. Turning I saw that it was the Kalkar whom I had seen sitting against the wall as I entered the chamber.

"Look well, Yank," he said, in a not unpleasant voice, "for you have not long to look." He was smiling grimly. "We have a wonderful view from here," he continued; "on a clear day you can see the ocean and the island."

"I should like to see the ocean," I said.

He shook his head. "You are very near," he said, "but you will never see it. I should like to see it again myself, but I shall not."

"Why?" I asked.

"I go with you to The Butcher in the morning," he replied simply.

"You?"

"Yes, I."

"And why?"

"Because I am a true Or-tis," he replied.

"Why should they send an Or-tis to The Butcher?" I demanded. "It is not strange that an Or-tis should send me, *the* Julian, to him; but why should an Or-tis send an Or-tis?"

"He is not a true Or-tis who sends me," replied the man, and then he laughed.

"Why do you laugh?"

"Is it not a strange joke of fate," he cried, "that sees *the* Julian and *the* Or-tis going to The Butcher together? By the blood of my sires! I think our feud be over, Julian, at least so far as you and I are concerned."

"It can never be over, Kalkar," I replied.

He shook his head. "Had my father lived and carried out his plans I think it might have ended," he insisted.

"While an Or-tis and a Julian lived? Never!"

"You are young, and the hate that has been suckled into you and yours from your mothers' breasts for ages runs hot in your veins; but my father was old and he saw things as few of my kind, I imagine, ever have seen them. He was a kindly man and very learned and he came to hate the Kalkars and the horrid wrong the first Or-tis did the world and our people when he brought them hither from the Moon, even as you and yours have hated them always. He knew the wrong and he wished to right it.

"Already he had planned means whereby he might get into communication with the Julians and join with them in undoing the crime that our ancestor committed upon the world. He was Jemadar, but he would have renounced his throne to be with his own kind again. Our blood strain is as clear as yours—we are Americans. There is no Kalkar or half-breed blood in our veins. There are perhaps a thousand others among us who have brought down their birthright unsullied. These he would have brought with him, for they all were tired of the Kalkar beasts.

"But some of the Kalkar nobles learned of the plan and among them was he who calls himself Or-tis and Jemadar. He is the son of a Kalkar woman by a renegade uncle of mine. There is Or-tis blood in his veins, but a drop of Kalkar makes one all Kalkar, therefore he is no Or-tis.

"He assassinated my father and then set out to exterminate every pure-blood Or-tis and all those other uncontaminated Americans who would not swear fealty to him. Some have done so to save their hides, but many have gone to The Butcher. Insofar as I know, I am the last of the Or-tis line. There were two brothers and a sister, all younger than I. We scattered and I have not heard of them since, but I am sure that they are dead. The usurper will not tell me—he only laughed in my face when I asked him.

"Yes, if my father had lived the feud might have been ended; but to-morrow The Butcher will end it. However, the other way would have been better. What think you, Julian?"

I stood meditating in silence for a long time. I wondered if, after all, the dead Jemadar's way would not have been better.

# FIVE

# The Sea

I T SEEMED strange indeed to me that I stood conversing thus amicably with an Or-tis. I should have been at his throat, but there was something about him that disarmed me, and after his speech I felt, I am almost ashamed to say, something of friendliness for him.

He was an American after all, and he hated the common enemy. Was he responsible for the mad act of an ancestor dead now nearly four hundred years? But the hate that was almost a part of my being would not down entirely—he was still an Or-tis. I told him as much. He shrugged his shoulders.

"I do not know that I can blame you," he said; "but what matters it? To-morrow we shall both be dead. Let us at least call a truce until then."

He was a pleasant-faced young fellow, two or three years my senior, perhaps, with a winning way that disarmed malice. It would have been very hard to have hated this Or-tis.

"Agreed!" I said, and held out my hand. He took it and then he laughed.

"Thirty-four ancestors would turn over in their graves if they could see this!" he cried.

We talked there by the opening for a long time, while in the trail below us constant streams of Kalkars moved steadily to the battlefront. Faintly, from a great distance, came the booming of the drums.

"You beat them badly yesterday," he said. "They are filled with terror."

"We will beat them again today and tomorrow and the next day until we have driven them into the sea," I said.

"How many warriors have you?" he asked.

"There were full twenty-five thousand when we rode out of the desert," I replied proudly.

He shook his head dubiously. "They must have ten or twenty times twenty-five thousand," he told me.

"Even though they have forty times twenty-five thousand we shall prevail," I insisted.

"Perhaps you will, for you are better fighters; but they have so many youths growing into the warrior class every day. It will take years to wear them down. They breed like rabbits. Their women are married before they are fifteen, as a rule. If they have no child at twenty they are held up to scorn and if they are still childless at thirty they are killed, and unless they are mighty good workers they are killed at fifty anyhow—their usefulness to the State is over."

Night came on. The Kalkars brought us no food or water. It became very dark. In the trail below and in some of the surrounding tents flares gave a weird, flickering light. The sky was overcast with light clouds. The Kalkars in the avenue beyond our doorway dozed. I touched the Or-tis upon the shoulder where he lay stretched beside me on the hard floor.

"What is it?" he whispered.

"I am going," I said. "Do you wish to come?"

He sat up. "How are you going?" he demanded, still in a low whisper.

"I do not know, nor how far I shall go; but I am going, if only far enough to cheat The Butcher."

He laughed. "Good! I will go with you."

It had taken me a long time to overcome the prejudices of heredity and I had thought long before I could bring myself to ask an Or-tis to share with me this attempt to escape; but now it was done. I hoped I would not regret it.

I arose and moved cautiously toward the doorway. A wick, burning from the nozzle of a clay vessel filled with oil, gave forth a sickly light. It shone upon two hulking Kalkars nodding against the wall as they sat upon the stone floor of the avenue.

My knife, of course, had been taken from me and I was unarmed; but here was a sword within my reach and another for the Or-tis. The hilt of one protruded from beneath the cloak of the nearer Kalkar. My hand, reaching forth, was almost upon it when he moved. I could not wait to learn if he was awaking or but moving in his sleep. I lunged for the hilt, grasped it and the fellow was awake. At the same instant the Or-its sprang upon the other.

He whom I had attacked lumbered to his feet, clawing at the hand that had already half drawn his sword from its scabbard, and at the same time be set up a terrific yelling. I struck him on the jaw with my clenched fist. I struck him as hard as I could strike as he loomed above me his full eight feet.

The Or-tis was having a bad time with his man, who had seized him by the throat and was trying to draw a knife to finish him. The knife must have become stuck in its scabbard for a moment, or his long, red cloak was in the way. I do not know. I saw only a flash of it from the corner of my eye as my man stiffened and then sank to the floor.

Then I wheeled upon the other, a naked blade in my hand. He threw the Or-tis aside when he saw me and whipped out his own sword, but he was too slow. As I ran my point into his heart I heard the sound of running footsteps ascending the stairway and the shouts of men. I handed the sword I carried to the Or-tis and snatched the other from the fellow I had just finished.

Then I kicked the puny flare as far as I could kick it and called to the Or-tis to follow me. The light went out and together we ran along the dark avenue toward the stairway, up which we could hear the warriors coming in response to the cries of our late antagonists.

We reached the head of the stairs but a moment before the Kalkars appeared. There were three of them and one carried a weak, smoking flare that did little but cast large, grotesque, dancing shadows upon wall and stair and reveal our targets to us without revealing us to them.

"Take the last one," I whispered to the Or-tis.

We leaned over the railing and as he smote the head of the last of the three I finished the second. The first, carrying the flare, turned to find himself facing two swords. He gave a shriek and started down the avenue.

That would not do. If he had kept still we might have let him live, for we were in a hurry; but he did not keep still and so we pursued him. He reminded me of a comet as he fled through the dark with his tail of light, only it was such a little tail. He was a fast comet, though, and we could not catch him until the end of the avenue brought him to bay, then, in turning, he slipped and fell.

I was upon him in the same instant, but some fancy stayed my blade when I might have run it through him. Instead I seized him, before he could recover himself, and lifting him from the floor I hurled him through the aperture at the end of the avenue. He still clung to his lamp, and as I leaned out above him he appeared a comet indeed, although he was quickly extinguished when he struck the pavement in the courtyard far below.

The Or-tis chuckled at my elbow. "The stupid clod!" he ejaculated. "He clung to that flare even to death, when, had he thrown it away and dodged into one of these many chambers he could have eluded us and still lived."

"Perhaps he needed it to light his way to Hell," I suggested.

"They need no help in that direction," the Or-tis assured me, "for they will all get there, if there be such a place."

We retraced our steps to the stairway again, but once more we heard men ascending. The Or-tis plucked me by the sleeve. "Come," he whispered; "it is futile to attempt escape in this direction now that the guard is aroused. I am familiar with this place. I have been here many times. If we have the nerve we may yet escape. Will you follow me?"

"Certainly," I replied.

The corpses of two of our recent antagonists lay at our feet at the head of the stairs, where we stood. Or-tis stooped and snatched their cloaks and bonnets from them. "We shall need these if we reach the ground—alive," he said. "Follow me closely."

He turned and continued along the corridor, presently entering a chamber at the left.

Behind us we could hear the Kalkars ascending the stairs. They were calling to their fellows above, from whom they would never receive a reply; but they were evidently coming slowly, for which we were both thankful.

Or-tis crossed the chamber to an aperture in the wall. "Below is the courtyard," he said. "It is a long way down. These walls are laid in uneven courses. An agile man might make his way to the bottom without falling. Shall we try it? We can go down close to these apertures and thus rest often if we wish."

"You go on one side and I will go on the other," I told him.

He rolled the two cloaks and the bonnets into a bundle and dropped them into the dark void beneath, then we slid over the edge of the aperture. Clinging with my hands I found a foothold and then another below the first.

The ledges were about half the width of my hand. Some of them were rounded by time and the weather. These did not afford a very good hold. However, I reached the aperture below without mishap and there, I am free to confess, I was glad to pause for a moment, as I was panting as though I had run a mile.

Or-tis came down in safety, too. "The Butcher appears less terrible," he said.

I laughed. "He would have it over quicker," I replied.

The next stage we descended two floors before we halted. I liked to have slipped and fallen twice in that distance. I was wet with sweat as I took a seat beside my companion.

I do not like to recall that adventure. It sends shivers through me always, even now; but at last it was over—we reached the bottom together and donned the cloaks and the bonnets of the Kalkars. The swords, for which

Julian 20th and the Or-tis Escape

we had no scabbards, we slipped through our own belts, the cloaks hiding the fact that they were scabbardless.

The smell of horses was strong in our nostrils as we crept forward toward a doorway. All was darkness within, as we groped forward to find that we were in a small chamber with a door at the opposite side. Nearly all the doors of the ancients have been destroyed, either by the fires that have gutted most of the buildings, by decay or by the Kalkars that have used them for fuel; but there are some left—they are the metal doors, and this was one.

I pushed it open enough to see if there was a light beyond. There was. It was in the great chamber on the first floor where the horses were tethered. It was not a brilliant light, but a sad, flickering light. Even the lights of the Kalkars are grimy and unclean. It cast a pallid luminescence beneath it, elsewhere were heavy shadows. The horses, when they moved, cast giant shadows upon the walls and floor and upon the great polished stone columns.

A guard loafed before the door that led to the trail in front of the tent. It was composed of five or six men. I suppose there were others in some nearby chamber. The doorway through which we peered was in shadow.

I pushed it open far enough to admit our bodies and we slipped through. In an instant we were hidden from the sight of the guard among the horses. Some of them moved restlessly as we approached them. If I could but find Red Lightning!

I had searched along one line almost the full length of the chamber and had started along a second when I heard a low nicker close by. It was he! Love of The Flag! It was like finding my own brother.

In the slovenly manner of the Kalkars the saddles and bridles lay in the dirt in the aisle behind the horses. Fortunately I found my own, more easily, of course, because it is unlike those of the Kalkars, and while I slipped them quietly upon Red Lightning the Or-tis, selecting a mount haphazard, was saddling and bridling it.

After a whispered consultation we led our horses to the rear of the room and mounted among the shadows, unobserved by the guard. Then we rode out from behind the picket lines and moved slowly toward the entrance, talking and laughing in what we hoped might appear an unconcerned manner, the Or-tis riding on the side nearer the guard and a little in advance, that Red Lightning might be hidden from them, for we thought that they might recognize him more quickly than they would us.

As they saw us coming they ceased their chatter and looked up, but we paid no attention to them, riding straight on for the aperture that led into the trail outside the structure. I think we might have passed them without question had there not suddenly burst from the doorway of what was, I judge, the guardroom, an excited figure who shouted lustily to all within hearing of his voice:

"Let no one leave! The Julian and the Or-tis have escaped!" he screamed.

The guards threw themselves across the entrance and at the same instant I put spurs to Red Lightning, whipped out my sword and bore down upon them, the Or-tis following my example. I cut at one upon my left front and Red Lightning bore down another beneath his iron hoofs.

We were out upon the trail and the Or-tis was beside us. Reining to the left we bore south a few yards and then turned west upon another trail, the shouts and curses of the Kalkars ringing in our ears.

With free rein we let our mounts out to far greater speed than the darkness and the littered trail gave warrant, and it was not until we had put a mile behind us that we drew in to a slower gait. The Or-tis spurred to my side.

"I had not thought it could be done, Julian," he said; "yet here we ride, as free as any men in all the country wide."

"But still within the shadow of The Butcher," I replied. "Listen! They are following hot-foot." The pounding of the hoofs of our pursuers' horses arose louder and louder behind us as we listened. Again we spurred on, but presently we came to a place where a ruined wall had fallen across the trail.

"May The Butcher get me!" cried the Or-tis! "that I should have forgotten that this trail is blocked. We should have turned north or south at the last crossing. Come, we must ride back, and quickly, too, if we are to reach it before they."

Wheeling, we put our mounts to the run back along the trail over which we had but just come. It was but a short distance to the cross trail, yet our case looked bad, for even in the darkness the pursuing Kalkars could now be seen, so close were they. It was a question as to which would reach the crossing first.

"You turn to the south," I cried to the Or-tis, "and I will turn to the north. In that way one of us may escape."

"Good!" he agreed. "There are too many of them for us to stand and fight."

He was right—the trail was packed with them, and we could hear others coming far behind the van. It was like a young army. I hugged the left hand side of the trail and Or-tis the right. We reached the crossing not a second in advance of the leaders of the pursuit, and Or-tis turned to the south and I to the north.

Into the blackness of the new trail I plunged and behind me came the Kalkars. I urged Red Lightning on and he responded, as I knew he would. It was madness to ride through the black night along a strange trail at such speed, yet it was my only hope.

Quickly, my fleet stallion drew away from the clumsy, ill-bred mounts of my pursuers. At the first crossing I turned again to the west, and although here I encountered a steep and winding hill it was fortunately but a short ride to the top and after that the way was along a rolling trail, but mostly downhill.

The structures of the ancients that remained standing became fewer and fewer as we proceeded, and in an hour they had entirely disappeared. The trail, however, was fairly well marked and after a single, short turn to the south it continued westward over rolling country in almost a straight line.

I had reduced my speed to conserve Red Lightning's strength, and as no sign of pursuit developed I jogged along at a running walk, a gait which Red Lightning could keep up for hours without fatigue. I had no idea where the trail was leading me, and at the time I did not even, know that it was bearing west, for the heavens were still overcast, although I judged that this must be the fact. My first thought was to put as much distance as possible between me and the Kalkar camp and at the first streak of dawn take to the hills and then work my way north and east in an attempt to rejoin my people.

And so I moved on, through country that was now level and now rolling, for the better part of three hours. A cool breeze sprang up and blew in my face. It had a damp freshness and a strange odor with which I was entirely unfamiliar. I was tired from my long exertions, from loss of sleep and from lack of food and water, yet this strange breeze revived me and filled me with new strength and life.

It had become very dark, although I knew that dawn must be near. I wondered how Red Lightning could pick his way through the utter blackness. This very thought was in my mind when he came to a sudden halt.

I could see nothing, yet I could tell that Red Lightning had some good reason for his action. I listened, and there came to my ears a strange, sullen roar—a deep pounding, such as I never had heard before. What could it be?

I dismounted to rest my beloved friend, while I listened and sought for an explanation of this monotonously reiterated sound. At length I determined to await dawn before continuing. With the bridle reins about my wrist I lay down, knowing that, if danger threatened, Red Lightning would warn me. In an instance I was asleep.

How long I slept I do not know—an hour, perhaps—but when I awoke it was daylight and the first thing that broke upon my sensibilities was the dull, monotonous booming, the pounding, pounding, pounding that had lulled me to sleep so quickly.

Never shall I forget the scene that burst upon my astonished eyes as I rose to my feet. Before me was a sheer cliff dropping straight away at my feet, upon the very verge of which Red Lightning had halted the previous night; and beyond, as far as the eye could reach, water—a vast expanse of water, stretching on and on and on—*the sea!* At last a Julian had looked upon it.

It rolled up on the sands below me, pounding, surging, booming. It rolled back again, resistless, restless; and, at once, terrifying and soothing—terrifying in its immensity and mystery, soothing in the majestic rhythm of its restlessness.

I had looked upon it—the goal of four hundred years of strife—and it gave to me renewed strength and determination to lead my people to it. There it lay, as it had always lain, unaltered, unalterable.

Along its shore line, sweeping away upon either hand toward distant haze dimmed headlands, was a faint scratch at the foot of its bold cliffs that may mark the man-made trail of the ancients, but of man or his works there is no other sign. In utter solitude its rolling waters break upon its sands, and there is no ear to hear.

To my right an old trail led down into a deep canyon that opened upon the beach. I mounted Red Lightning and followed its windings along the half obliterated trail of the ancients down among giant oaks and sycamores and along the canyon's bottom to the beach. I wanted to feel the cool waters and to quench my thirst.

Red Lightning must have been thirsty, too, but the great waves rolling in frightened him so that it was with difficulty that I urged him to the water's edge; but training and heredity are stronger than fear, and at last he walked out upon the sands until the waters, surging in, broke about his pasterns. Then I threw myself from him at full length upon the beach and as the next wave rolled in I buried my face in it and quaffed one deep drink.

One was enough. Sputtering, choking and gagging, I sprang to my feet. What poisoned liquid idled in this hellish cauldron? I became very sick. Never in my life had I experienced such ill sensations.

I thought that I was dying, and in my agony I saw Red Lightning dip his velvet muzzle into the treacherous liquid.

Red Lightning took one draught, as had I, and then, snorting, be leaped back from that vast pool of iniquity. For a moment he stood there wide-eyed, staring at the water, pained surprise in his eyes.

Then he fell to trembling as, upon wide spread feet, he swayed to and fro. He was dying—together we were dying at the foot of the goal we had achieved after four hundred years of battle and suffering.

I prayed that I might live even if it were only long enough for me to reach my people and warn them against this hideous monster lying in wait for them. Better that they flee back to their desert than trust themselves to his unknown world where even the fairest of waters held death.

But I did not die. Neither did Red Lightning die. I was very sick for an hour; but after that I rapidly recovered. It was a long time after before I learned the truth about sea water.

# SIX

# Saku the Nipon

Hungry and thirsty, Red Lightning and I set off up the canyon away from the sea, presently entering the first side-canyon* bearing in a northerly direction, for it was my desire to pass through these mountains in the hope of finding a valley running east and west which I could follow back in the direction of my people.

We had proceeded only a short distance up the side-canyon when I discovered a spring of pure water and around it an abundance of fine pasture. It was, nevertheless, with some feeling of trepidation that I sampled the liquid; but the first mouthful reassured me and a moment later Red Lightning and I were drinking avidly from the same pool. Then I removed his saddle and bridle and turned him loose to browse upon the lush grasses, while I removed my clothing and bathed my body, which was, by now, sorely in need of it.

I felt much refreshed, and could I have found food should soon have been myself again; but without bow and arrows my chances seemed slight unless I were to take the time to construct a snare and wait for prey.

This, however, I had no mind to do, since I argued that sooner or later I must run across human habitation, where, unless greatly outnumbered by armed men, I would obtain food.

For an hour I permitted Red Lightning to line his belly with nutritious grasses and then I called him to me, resaddled, and was on my way again up the wooded, winding canyon, following a well marked trail in which constantly appeared the spoor of coyote, wolf, hellhound, deer and lion, as well as the tracks of domestic animals and the sandaled feet of slaves, but I saw no signs of shod horses to indicate the presence of Kalkars. The

---

*Probably Rustic Canyon, which enters Santa Monica canyon a short distance above the sea.

imprints of sandals might mark only the passage of native hunters, or they might lead to a hidden camp. It was this latter that I hoped.

Throughout all the desert and mountain country the camps of the slaves are to be found, for they are not all attached to the service of the whites, there being many who live roving lives, following the game and the pasture and ever eluding the white man. It was the Kalkars who first gave them the name of slave, they say, but before that they were known to the ancients by the name of In-juns.

Among themselves they use only their various tribal names, such as Hopi, Navaho, Mojave, to mention the better known tribes with which we came in contact on the desert and in the mountains and forests to the east. With the exception of the Apache and the far Yaqui, and of the latter we knew little except by repute, they are a peaceful people and hospitable to friendly strangers. It was my hope, therefore, to discover a camp of these natives, where I was sure that I would be received in peace and given food.

I had wound upward for perhaps two or three miles when I came suddenly upon a little, open meadow and the realization of my wish, for there stood three of the pointed tents of slaves consisting of a number of poles leaning inward and lashed together at the top, the whole covered by a crazy patchwork consisting of the skins of animals sewn together. These tents, however, were peculiar, in that they were very small.

As I came in sight of the camp I was discovered by a horde of scrawny curs that came bristling and yapping toward me, apprising their masters of the presence of a stranger. A head appeared in the opening of one of the tents and was as quickly withdrawn.

I called aloud that I would speak with their chief and then I waited through a full minute of silence. Receiving no reply I called again, more peremptorily, for I am not accustomed to waiting long for obedience.

This time I received a reply. "Go away, Kalkar, "cried a man's voice. "This is our country. Go away or we will kill you."

Evidently these people dared voice their antagonism to the Kalkars, and from my knowledge of the reputation of the latter I knew this to be ~~the~~ most unusual in any country that they dominated. That they hated them I was not surprised—all people hate them. It was upon the assumption of this common hatred that I based my expectation of friendly assistance from any slave with whom I might come in contact in the Kalkar country.

"I am not a Kalkar," I therefore replied to the voice, whose owner still remained behind the skins of his diminutive tent, upon the floor of which he must have been sitting, since no man could stand upright in it.

"What are you?" asked the voice.

"I am a desert Yank," I replied, guessing that he would be more familiar with that word than American or Julian.

"You are a Kalkar," he insisted. "Do I not see your skin, even if your cloak and bonnet were not enough to prove you a Kalkar?"

"But I am not a Kalkar. I have but just escaped them and I have been long without food. I wish food and then I will go on, for I am in search of my own people who are fighting the Kalkars at the edge of their great camp to the east."

He stuck his head through the flap then and eyed me closely. His face was small and much wrinkled and he had a great shock of stiff, black hair that stuck out in all directions and was not confined by any band. I thought that he must still be sitting or squatting upon the ground, so low was his head, but a moment later, when, evidently having decided to investigate my claims more closely, he parted the flap and stepped out of the tent, I was startled to see a man little more than three feet tall standing before me.

He was stark naked and carried a bow in one hand and several arrows in the other. At first I thought he might be a child, but his old and wrinkled face as well as the well developed muscles moving beneath his brown skin belied that.

Behind him came two other men of about the same height and simultaneously from the other two tents appeared six or eight more of these diminutive warriors. They formed a semicircle about me, their weapons in readiness.

"From what country do you come?" demanded the little chief.

I pointed toward the east. "From the desert beyond your farthest mountains," I replied.

He shook his head. "We have never been beyond our own hills," he said.

It was most difficult to understand him, although I am familiar with the dialects of a score of tribes and the mongrel tongue that is employed by both the Kalkars and ourselves to communicate with the natives, yet we managed to make ourselves understood to one another.

I dismounted and approached them, my hand held out towards them as is the custom of my people in greeting friends, with whom we always clasp hands after an absence, or when meeting friendly strangers for the first time. They did not seem to understand my intentions and drew back, fitting arrows to their bows.

I did not know what to do. They were so small that to have attacked them would have seemed to me like putting children to the sword, and, too, I craved their friendship, for I believed that they might prove of inestimable value to me in discovering the shortest route back to my people, that was at the same time most free of Kalkar camps.

I dropped my hand and smiled, at a loss as to how best to reassure them. The smile must have done it, for immediately the old man's face broke into a grin.

"You are not a Kalkar," he said; "they never smile at us. He lowered his weapon, his example being followed by the others. "Tie your horse to a tree. We will give you food." He turned toward the tents and called to the women to come out and prepare food.

I dropped my reins to the ground, which is all the tying that Red Lightning requires, and advanced toward the little men, and when I had thrown aside my Kalkar coat and bonnet they crowded around me with questions and comment.

"No, he is not a Kalkar," said one. "His cloak and bonnet are Kalkar, but not his other garments."

"I was captured by the Kalkars," I explained, "and to escape I covered myself with this cloak which I had taken from a Kalkar that I killed."

A stream of women and children were now issuing from the tents, whose capacity must have been taxed beyond their limit. The children were like toys, so diminutive were they, and, like their fathers and mothers, quite naked, nor was there among them all the sign of an ornament or decoration of any nature.

They crowded around me, filled with good-natured curiosity, and I could see that they were a joyous, kindly little people; but even as I stood there encircled by them I could scarcely bring myself to believe in their existence, rather thinking that I was the victim of a capricious dream, for never had I seen or heard of such a race of tiny humans.

As I had this closer and better opportunity to study them I saw that they were not of the same race as the slaves, or In-juns; but were of a lighter shade of brown, with different shaped heads and slanting eyes. They were a handsome little people and there was about the children that which was at once laughable and appealing, so that one could not help but love them and laugh with them.

The women busied themselves making fire and bringing meat—a leg of venison and flour for bread, with fresh fruits such as apricots, strawberries and oranges. They chattered and laughed all the time, casting quick glances at me and then giggling behind their hands.

The children and the dogs were always under foot, but no one appeared to mind them and no one spoke a cross word, and often I saw the men snatch up a child and caress it. They seemed a very happy people—quite unlike any other peoples who have lived long in a Kalkar country. I mentioned this fact to the chief and asked him how they could be so happy under the cruel domination of the Kalkars.

"We do not live under their rule," he replied. "We are a free people. When they attempted to harass us, we made war upon them."

"You made war upon the Kalkars?" I demanded incredulously.

"Upon those who came into our hills," he replied. "We never leave the hills. We know every rock and tree and trail and cave, and being a very little people and accustomed to living always in the hills we can move rapidly from place to place.

"Long ago the Kalkars used to send warriors to kill us, but they could never find us, though first from one side and then from another our arrows fell among them, killing many. We were all about them, but they could not see us. Now they leave us alone. The hills are ours from the great Kalkar camp to the sea and up the sea for many marches. The hills furnish us with all that we require and we are happy."

"What do you call yourselves?" I asked. "From where do you come?"

"We are Nipons," he replied. "I am Saku, chief of this district. We have always been here in these hills. The first Nipon, our ancestor, was a most honorable giant who lived upon an island far, far out in the middle of the sea. His name was Mik-do. He lives there now. When we die we go there to live with him. That is all."

"The Kalkars no longer bother you?" I asked.

"Since the time of my father's father they have not come to fight with us," replied Saku. "We have no enemies other than Raban, the giant, who lives on the other side of the hills. He comes sometimes to hunt us with his dogs and his slaves. Those whom he kills or captures, he eats.

"He is a very terrible creature, is Raban. He rides a great horse and covers himself with iron so that our arrows and our spears do not harm him. He is three times as tall as we."

I assumed that, after the manner of the ignorant, he was referring to an imaginary personification of some greatly feared manifestation of natural forces—storm, fire or earthquake, perhaps—probably fire, though, since his reference to the devouring of his people by this giant suggested fire, and, so, dismissed the subject from my mind, along with Mik-do and the fabulous island in the sea.

How filled is the mind of the ignorant native with baseless beliefs and superstitions. He reminded me of our own slaves who told of the iron horses drawing tents of iron and of men flying through the air.

As I ate I questioned Saku concerning the trails leading back in the direction of my people. He told me that the trail upon which he was camped led to the summit of the hills, joining with another that led straight down into a great valley which he thought would lead me to my destination, but of that he was not sure, having only such knowledge of the extent of the valley as one might glean from viewing it from the summit of his loftiest hills.

Against this trail, however, he warned me explicitly, saying that I might use it in comparative safety only to the summit, for upon the other side it led straight down past the great, stone tent of Raban the giant.

"The safer way," he said, "is to follow the trail that winds along the summit of the hills, back toward the camp of the Kalkars—a great trail that was built in the time of Mik-do—and from which you can ride down into the valley along any one of many trails. Always you will be in danger of Raban until you have gone a day's march beyond his tent, for he rides far in search of prey; but at least you will be in less danger than were you to ride down the canyon in which he lives."

But Raban, the imaginary giant, did not worry me much and although I thanked Saku for his warnings, and let him believe that I would follow his advice, I was secretly determined to take the shortest route to the valley beyond the hills.

Having finished my meal I thanked my hosts and was preparing to depart when I saw the women and children pulling down the tents to an accompaniment of much laughter and squealing while several of the men started up the canyon voicing strange cries. I looked at Saku questioningly.

"We are moving up the canyon for deer," he explained, "and will go with you part of the way to the summit. There are many trees across the trail that would hinder you, and these we will move or show you a way around."

"Must you carry all this camp equipment?" I asked him, seeing the women struggling with the comparatively heavy hide tents, which they were rolling and tying into bundles, while others gathered the tent poles and bound them together.

"We will put them on our horses," he explained, pointing up the canyon.

I looked in the direction he indicated to see the strangest creatures I had ever looked upon—a string of tiny, woolly horses that were being driven toward camp by the men who had recently gone up the canyon after them. The little animals were scarce half the height of Red Lightning and they moved at so slow a pace that they seemed scarce to move at all. They had huge bellies and most enormous ears set upon great, uncouth heads. In appearance they seemed part sheep, part horse and a great deal of the long-eared rabbit of the desert.

They were most docile creatures and during the business of strapping the loads to them the children played about between their feet or were tossed to their backs, where they frolicked, while the sad-eyed, dejected creatures stood with drooping heads and waving ears. When we started on the march all the children were mounted upon these little horses, sometimes perched upon the top of a load, or again there would be three or four of them upon the back of a single beast.

It did not take me long to discover that Red Lightning and I had no place in this cavalcade, for if we went behind we were constantly trampling upon the heels of the slow moving little horses, and if we went ahead we lost them in a few yards, and so I explained to Saku that my haste made it necessary for me to go on, but that if I came to any obstacle I could not surmount alone I would wait there for them to overtake me.

I thanked him again for his kindness to me and we exchanged vows of friendship which I believe were as sincere upon his part as they were upon mine. They were a happy, lovable little people and I was sorry to leave them.

Pushing rapidly ahead I encountered no insuperable obstacles and after a couple of hours I came out upon a wide trail at the summit of the hills and saw spread before me a beautiful valley extending far to the east and to the west. At my feet was the trail leading down past the tent of the imaginary Raban and toward this I reined Red Lightning.

I had not yet crossed the old trail of the ancients when I heard the sound of the flying feet of horses approaching from the west. Here the trail winds upward and passes around the shoulder of a hill and as I looked I saw a running horse come into view and at its heel another in hot pursuit. The rider of the second horse was evidently a Kalkar warrior, as a red robe whipped in the wind behind him, and the figure upon the leading animal I could not identify at first, but as they drew rapidly nearer the streaming hair of its head suggested that it must be a woman.

A Kalkar up to his old tricks, I thought, as I sat watching them. So intent was the man upon his prey that he did not notice me until after he had seized the bridle rein of his quarry and brought both animals to a halt not a score of feet from me, then he looked up in surprise. His captive was looking at me, too.

She was a girl with wide, frightened eyes—appealing eyes that even while they appealed were dulled by hopelessness, for what aid might she expect from one Kalkar against another, and of course she must have believed me a Kalkar.

She was a Kalkar woman, but still she was a woman, and so I was bound to aid her. Even had I not felt thus obligated by her sex I should have killed her companion in any event, for was he not a stranger in addition to being a Kalkar?

I let my Kalkar cloak slip to the ground and I tossed my Kalkar bonnet after it.

"I am The Red Hawk!" I cried as I drew the sword from my belt and touched Red Lightning with my spurs. "Fight, Kalkar!"

The Kalkar tried to bring his spear into play, but it was slung across his back, and he couldn't unsling it in time; so he, too, drew a sword, and, to gain time, he reined his horse behind that of the girl. But she was master of her own mount now, and with a shake of her reins she had urged her horse forward, uncovering the Kalkar, and now he and I were face to face.

He towered above me and he had the protection of his iron vest and iron bonnet, while I was without even the protection of a shield; but whatever advantage these things might have seemed to give him, they were outweighed by the lightness and agility of Red Lightning and the freedom of my own muscles, unencumbered by heavy metal protections.

His big, clumsy horse was ill-mannered, and, on top of all else, the Kalkar's swordsmanship was so poor that it seemed ill-befitting a brave warrior to take his almost defenseless life; but he was a Kalkar, and there was no alternative. Had I found him naked and unarmed in bed and unconscious with fever, it would still have been my duty to dispatch him, although there had been no glory in it.

I could not, however, bring myself to the point of butchering him without appearing at least to give him a chance, and so I played with him, parrying his cuts and thrusts and tapping him now and then upon his metal bonnet and vest. This must have given him hope, for suddenly he drew off and then rushed me, his sword swinging high above his head. The Flag! What a chance he offered, blundering down upon me with chest and belly and groin exposed, for his iron shirt could never stop a Julian's point.

So wondrously awkward was his method of attack that I waited to see the nature of his weird technique before dispatching him. I was upon his left front, and when he was almost upon me he struck downward at me and to his left, but he could not think of two things at once—me and his horse—and as he did not strike quite far enough to the left his blade clove his mount's skull between the ears, and the poor brute, which was rushing forward at the time, fell squarely upon its face, and, turning completely over, pinioned its rider beneath its corpse.

I dismounted to put the man out of his misery, for I was sure he must be badly injured, but I found that he was stone dead. His knife and spear

I appropriated, as well as his heavy bow and arrows, although I was fearful as to my skill with the last weapons, so much lighter and shorter are the bows to which I am accustomed.

I had not concerned myself with the girl, thinking, of course, that during the duel she would take advantage of the opportunity to escape; but when I looked up from the corpse of the Kalkar she was still there, sitting her horse a few yards away and eying me intently.

# SEVEN

# Bethelda

"WELL!" I exclaimed. "Why have you not flown?"

"And where?" she demanded.

"Back to your Kalkar friends," I replied.

"It is because you are not a Kalkar that I did not fly," she said.

"How do you know that I am no Kalkar," I demanded, "and why, if I am not, should you not fly from me, who must be an enemy of your people?"

"You called him 'Kalkar' as you charged him;" she explained, "and one Kalkar does not call another Kalkar that. Neither am I a Kalkar."

I thought then of what the Or-tis had told me of the thousand Americans who had wished to desert the Kalkars and join themselves with us. This girl must be of them, then.

"Who are you?" I asked.

"My name is Bethelda," she replied. "And who are you?"

She looked me squarely in the eyes with a fearless frankness that was anything but Kalkarian. It was the first time that I had had a good look at her, and, by The Flag, she was not displeasing to look at! She had large, gray-green eyes and heavy lashes and a cheerful countenance that seemed even now to be upon the verge of laughter. There was something almost boyish about her, and yet she was all girl. I stood looking at her for so long a time without speaking that a frown of impatience clouded her brow.

"I asked you who you are," she reminded me.

"I am Julian 20th, The Red Hawk," I replied, and I thought for an instant that her eyes went a little wider and that she looked frightened; but I must have been mistaken, for I was to learn later that it took more than a name to frighten Bethelda.

"Tell me where you are going," I said, "and I will ride with you, lest you be again attacked."

"I do not know where to go," she replied, "for wherever I go I meet enemies."

"Where are your people?" I demanded.

"I fear that they are all slain," she told me, a quiver in her voice.

"But where were you going? You must have been going somewhere."

"I was looking for a place to hide," she said. "The Nipons would let me stay with them, if I could find them. My people were always kind to them. They would be kind to me."

"Your people were of the Kalkars, even though you say you are no Kalkar, and the Nipons hate them. They would not take you in."

"My people were Americans. They lived among the Kalkars, but they were not Kalkars. We lived at the foot of these hills for nearly a hundred years, and we often met the Nipons. They did not hate us, though they hated the Kalkars about us.

"Do you know Saku?" I asked.

"Since I was a little child I have known Saku the Chief," she replied.

"Come, then," I said; "I will take you to Saku."

"You know him? He is near?"

"Yes. Come!"

She followed me down the trail up which I had so recently come, and although I begrudged the time that it delayed me, I was glad that I might have her off my hands so easily and so quickly; for of a certainty I could not leave her alone and unprotected, nor could I take her upon my long journey with me, even could I have prevailed upon my people to accept her.

In less than an hour we came upon Saku's new camp, and the little people were surprised indeed to see me, and overjoyed when they discovered Bethelda, more than assuring me by their actions that the girl had been far from stating the real measure of the esteem in which the Nipons held her. When I would have turned to ride away they insisted that I remain until morning, pointing out to me that the day was already far gone, and that being unfamiliar with the trails I might easily become lost and thus lose more time than I would gain.

The girl stood listening to our conversation, and when I at last insisted that I must go because, having no knowledge of the trails anyhow, I would be as well off by night as by day, she offered to guide me.

"I know the valley from end to end," she said. "Tell me where you would go and I will lead you there as well by night as by day."

"But how would you return?" I asked.

"If you are going to your people perhaps they would let me remain, for am I not an American, too?"

I shook my head. "I am afraid that they would not," I told her. "We feel very bitterly toward all Americans that cast their lot with the Kalkars—even more bitterly than we feel toward the Kalkars themselves."

"I did not cast my lot with the Kalkars," she said proudly. "I have hated them always—since I was old enough to hate. If four hundred years ago my people chose to do a wicked thing, is it any fault of mine? I am as much an American as you, and I hate the Kalkars more because I know them better."

"My people would not reason that way," I said. "The women would set the hounds on you, and you would be torn to pieces."

She shivered. "You are as terrible as the Kalkars," she said bitterly.

"You forget the generations of humiliation and suffering that we have endured because of the renegade Americans who brought the Kalkar curse upon us," I reminded her.

"We have suffered, too," she said, "and we are as innocent as you," and then suddenly she looked me squarely in the eyes. "How do you feel about it? Do you, too, hate me worse than as though I were a Kalkar? You saved my life, perhaps, today. You could do that for one you hate?"

"You are a girl," I reminded her, "and I am an American—a Julian," I added, proudly.

"You saved me only because I am a girl?" she insisted.

I nodded.

"You are a strange people," she said, "that you could be so brave and generous to one you hate, and yet refuse the simpler kindness of forgiveness—forgiveness of a sin that we did not commit."

I recalled the Or-tis, who had spoken similarly, and I wondered if perhaps they might not be right; but we are a proud people and for generations before my day our pride had been ground beneath the heels of the victorious Kalkar. Even yet the wound was still raw. And we are a stubborn people—stubborn in our loves and our hatreds.

Already had I regretted my friendliness with the Or-tis, and now I was having amicable dealings with another Kalkar—it was difficult for me to think of them as other than Kalkars. I should be hating this one—I should have hated the Or-tis—but for some reason I found it not so easy to hate them.

Saku had been listening to our conversation, a portion of which at least he must have understood.

"Wait until morning," he said, "and then she can at least go with you as far as the top of the hills and point out the way for you; but you will be wise to take her with you. She knows every trail, and it will be better for her to go with you to your own people. She is not Kalkar, and if they catch her they will kill her.

"Were she Kalkar we would hate her and chase her away; but though she is welcome among us it would be hard for her to remain. We move camp often, and often our trails lead where one so large as she might have difficulty in following, nor would she have a man to hunt for her, and there are times when we have to go without food because we cannot find enough even for our own little people."

"I will wait until morning," I said; "but I cannot take her with me; my people would kill her."

I had two motives in remaining over the night. One was to go forth early in the morning and kill game for the little Nipons in payment for their hospitality, and the other was to avail myself of the girl's knowledge of the trails, which she could point out from some lofty hilltop. I had only a general idea of the direction in which to search for my people, and as I had seen from the summit that the valley beyond was entirely surrounded by hills I realized that I might gain time by waiting until morning, when the girl should be able to point out the route to the proper pass to my destination.

After the evening meal that night I kept up a fire for the girl, as the air was chill and she was not warmly clad. The little people had only their tents and a few skins for their own protection, nor was there room in the former for the girl, so already overcrowded were they. The Nipons retired to their rude shelters almost immediately after eating, leaving the girl and me alone. She huddled close to the fire and she looked very forlorn and alone. I could not help but feel sorry for her.

"Your people are all gone?" I asked.

"My own people—my father, my mother, my three brothers—all are dead, I think," she replied. "My mother and father I know are dead. She died when I was a little girl. Six months ago my father was killed by the Kalkars. My three brothers and I scattered, for we heard that they were coming to kill us also.

"I have heard that they captured my brothers; but I am not sure. They have been killing many in the valley lately, for here dwell nearly all the pure descendants of Americans; and those of us who were thought to favor the true Or-tis were marked for slaughter by the false Or-tis.

"I had been hiding in the home of a friend of my father, but I knew that if I were found there it would bring death to him and his family, and so I came away, hoping to find a place where I might be safe from them; but I guess there is no place for me—even my friends, the Nipons, though they would let me stay with them, admit that it would be a hardship to provide for me."

"What will you do?" I asked. Somehow I felt very sorry for her.

"I shall find some nearly inaccessible place in the hills and build myself a shelter," she replied.

"But you cannot live here in the hills alone," I remonstrated.

She shrugged her shoulders. "Where may I live, then?"

"For a little while, perhaps," I suggested, "until the Kalkars are driven into the sea."

"Who will drive them into the sea?" she asked.

"We," I replied proudly.

"And if you do, how much better off shall I be? Your people will set their hounds upon me—you have said so yourself. But you will not drive the Kalkars into the sea. You have no conception of their numbers. All up and down the coast, days' journeys north and south, wherever there is a fertile valley, they have bred like flies. For days they have been coming from all directions, marching toward The Capital. I do not know why they congregate now, nor why only the warriors come. Are they threatened, do you think?" A sudden thought seemed to burst upon her. "It cannot be," she exclaimed, "that the Yanks have attacked them! Have your people come out of the desert again?"

"Yes," I replied. "Yesterday we attacked their great camp; today my warriors must have eaten their evening meal in the stone tents of the Kalkars."

"You mean The Capital?"

"Yes."

"Your forces have reached The Capital? It seems incredible! Never before have you come so far. You have a great army?"

"Twenty-five thousand warriors marched down out of the desert beneath The Flag," I told her, "and we drove the Kalkars from the pass of the ancients back to The Capital as you call their great camp."

"You lost many warriors? You must have."

"Many fell," I replied; "thousands."

"Then you are not twenty-five thousand now, and the Kalkars are like ants. Kill them, and more will come. They will wear you down until your few survivors will be lucky if they can escape back to their desert."

"You do not know us," I told her. "We have brought our women, our children, our flocks and herds down into the orange groves of the Kalkars, and there we shall remain. If we cannot drive the Kalkars into the sea today, we shall have to wait until tomorrow. It has taken us three hundred years to drive them this far, but in all that time we have never given back a step that we have once gained; we have never retreated from any position to which we have brought our families and our stock."

"You have a large family?" she asked.

"I have no wife," I replied as I rose to add fuel to the fire. As I returned with a handful of sticks I saw that she hugged closer to the blaze and that she shivered with the cold. I removed my Kalkar robe and threw it across her shoulders.

"No," she cried, rising. "I cannot take it. You will be cold." She held it out towards me.

"Keep it," I said. "The night will be cold, and you cannot go until morning without covering."

She shook her head.

"No," she repeated. "I cannot accept favors from an enemy who hates me."

She stood there, holding the red robe out toward me. Her chin was high and her expression haughty.

I stepped forward and took the robe and as her hand dropped to her side I threw the woolen garment about her once more and held it there upon her slim figure. She tried to pull away from it, but my arm was about her, holding the robe in place, and as I guessed her intention I pressed the garment more closely around her, which drew her to me until we stood face to face, her body pressed against mine. As I looked down into her upturned face our eyes met, and for a moment we stood there as if turned to stone.

I do not know what happened. Her eyes, wide and half frightened, looked up into mine, her lips were parted, and she caught her breath once in what was almost a sob. Just for an instant we stood thus, and then her eyes dropped and she bent her head and turned it half away and at the same time her muscles relaxed and she went almost limp in my arms.

Very gently I lowered her to her seat beside the fire and adjusted the robe about her. Something had happened to me. I did not know what it was, but of a sudden nothing seemed to matter so much in all the world as the comfort and safety of Bethelda.

In silence I sat down opposite her and looked at her as though I never before had laid eyes upon her, and well might it have been that I had never; for, by The Flag, I had not seen her before, or else, like some of the tiny lizards of the desert, she had the power to change her appearance as they change their colors, for this was not the same girl to whom I had been talking a moment since; this was a new and wonderful creature of a loveliness beyond all compare.

No, I did not know what had happened, nor did I care. I just sat there and devoured her with my eyes. And then she looked up and spoke four words that froze my heart in my bosom.

She looked up and her eyes were dull and filled with pain. Something had happened to her, too—I could see it. She was changed.

"I am an Or-tis," she said, and dropped her head again.

I could not speak. I just sat there staring at the slender little figure of my blood enemy, sitting, dejected, in the firelight. After a long time she lay down beside the fire and slept, and I suppose that I must have slept, too, for once, when I opened my eyes, the fire was out, I was almost frozen, and the light of a new day was breaking over rugged hilltops to the east. I arose and rekindled the fire. After that I would get Red Lightning and ride away before she awakened; but when I had found him, feeding a short distance from the camp, I did not mount and ride away, but came back to the camp again. Why, I do not know. I did not want to see her again ever, yet something drew me to her.

She was awake and standing looking all about, up and down the canyon, when I first saw her, and I was sure that there was an expression of relief in her eyes when she discovered me.

She smiled wistfully, and I could not be hard, as I should have been to a blood enemy.

I was friendly with her brother, I thought—why should I not be friendly with her? Of course, I shall go away and not see her again; but at least I may be pleasant to her while I remain. Thus I argued, and thus I acted.

"Good morning," I said as I approached. "How are you?"

"Splendid," she replied. "And how are you?"

Her tones were rich and mellow and her eyes intoxicated me like old wine. Oh, why was she an enemy?

The Nipons came from their little tents. The naked children scampered around, playing with the dogs in an attempt to get warm. The women built the fires, around which the men huddled while their mates prepared the morning meal.

After we had eaten I took Red Lightning and started off down the canyon to hunt, and although I was dubious as to what results I should achieve with the heavy Kalkar bow, I did better than I had expected, for I got two bucks, although the chase carried me much farther from camp than I had intended going.

The morning must have been half spent as Red Lightning toiled up the canyon trail beneath the weight of the two carcasses and myself to the camp. I noticed that he seemed nervous as we approached, keeping his ears pricked forward and occasionally snorting, but I had no idea of the cause of his perturbation and was only the more on the alert myself, as I always am when warned by Red Lightning's actions that something may be amiss.

And when I came to the camp site I did not wonder that he had been aroused, for his keen nostrils had scented tragedy long before my dull senses could become aware of it. The happy, peaceful camp was no more. The little tents lay flat upon the ground and near them the corpses of two of my tiny friends—two little naked warriors. That was all. Silence and desolation brooded where there had been life and happiness a few short hours before. Only the dead remained.

Bethelda! What had become of her? What had happened? Who had done this cruel thing? There was but a single answer—the Kalkars must have discovered this little camp and rushed it. The Nipons that had not been killed doubtless escaped, and the Kalkars had carried Bethelda away a captive.

Suddenly I saw red. Casting the carcasses of the bucks to the ground, I put spurs to Red Lightning and set out up the trail where the fresh imprint of horses' hooves pointed the direction in which the murderers had gone. There were the tracks of several horses in the frail, and among them one huge imprint fully twice the size of the dainty imprint of Red Lightning's shoe. While the feet of all the Kalkar horses are large, this was the largest I had ever seen.

From the signs of the trail, I judged that not less than twenty horses were in the party, and while at first I had ridden impetuously in pursuit, presently my better judgment warned me that I could best serve Bethelda through strategy, if at all, since it was obvious that one man could not, single-handed, overthrow a score of warriors by force alone.

And now, therefore, I went more warily, though had I been of a mind to do so I doubt that I could have much abated my speed, for there was a force that drove me on, and if I let my mind dwell long on the possibility of the dangers confronting Bethelda I forgot strategy and cunning and all else save brute force and blood.

Vengeance! It is of my very marrow, bred into me through generations that have followed its emblem, The Flag, westward along its bloody trail toward the sea. Vengeance and The Flag and The Julian—they are one. And here was I, Lord of Vengeance, Great Chief of the Julians, Protector

Julian 20th and Red Lightning in Pursuit

of The Flag, riding hot-foot to save or avenge a daughter of the Or-tis! I should have flushed for shame, but I did not. Never had my blood surged so hot even to the call of The Flag. Could it be, then, that there was something greater than The Flag? No, that I could not admit; but possibly I had found something that imparted to The Flag a greater meaning for me.

# EIGHT

# Raban

I CAME TO the summit without overtaking them, but I could tell from the trail that they were not far ahead of me. The canyon trail is very winding and there is a great deal of brush, so that, oftentimes, a horseman a score of yards ahead of you is out of your sight and the noise of your own mount's passage drowns that of the others. For this reason I did not know, as long as I was in the canyon, how close I might be to them, but when I reached the summit it was different. Then I could see farther in all directions.

The murderers were not in sight upon the great highway of the ancients, and I rode swiftly to where the trail drops down upon the north side of the mountains to the great valley that I had seen the day before. There are fewer trees and lower brush upon this side, and below me I could see the trail at intervals as it wound downward, and as I looked I saw the first of a party of horsemen come into sight around the shoulder of a hill as they made their way down into the canyon.

To my right, a short distance, was a ridge leading from the summit downward and along the flank of the canyon into which the riders were descending. A single glance assured me that a few minutes of hard and rather rough riding would permit me to gain the canyon ahead of the riders and unseen by them, unless the brush proved heavier than it appeared or some impassable ravine intervened.

At least the venture was worth essaying, and so, not waiting for a longer inspection of the enemy, I wheeled and rode along the summit and out onto the ridge which I hoped would prove an avenue to such a position as I wished to attain, where I might carry out a species of warfare for which we are justly famous, in that we are adepts at it.

I found along the ridge a faint game trail and this I followed at reckless speed, putting Red Lightning down steep declivities in a manner that must have caused him to think me mad, so careful am I ordinarily of his legs, but today I was as inconsiderate of them as I was of my own life.

At one place the thing I most feared occurred—a deep ravine cut directly through the ridge, the side nearer me dropping almost sheer to the bottom. There was some slight footing, however, part way down, and Red Lightning never hesitated as I put him over the brink. Squatting on his haunches, his front legs stiff before him, he slid and stumbled downward, gaining momentum as he went, until, about twenty feet from the bottom, we went over a perpendicular dirt cliff together, landing in the soft sand at the foot of it a bit shaken, but unhurt.

There was no time even for an instant's breathing spell. Before us was the steep acclivity of the opposite side, and like a cat Red Lightning pawed and scrambled his way up, clinging motionless at times for an instant, his toes dug deep into the yielding earth, while I held my breath as Fate decided whether he should hold his own or slip back into the ravine; but at last we made it and once more were upon the summit of the ridge.

Now I had to go more carefully, for my trail and the trail of the enemy were converging and constantly the danger of apprehension increased. I rode now slightly below the brow of the ridge, hidden from whomever might be riding the trail along the opposite side, and presently I saw the mouth of the canyon to my right and below me and across it the trail along which the Kalkars must pass—that they had not already done so I was confident, for I had ridden hard and almost in a straight line, while they had been riding slowly when I saw them and the trail they were following wound back and forth down the canyon side at an easy grade.

Where the ridge ended in a steep declivity to the bottom of the canyon I drew rein and dismounted and, leaving Red Lightning hidden in the brush, made my way to the summit where, below me, the trail lay in full view for a distance of a hundred yards up the canyon and for half a mile below. In my left hand I carried the heavy Kalkar bow and in my right a bundle of arrows, while a score or more others protruded from my right boot. Fitting an arrow to my bow I waited.

Nor did I have long to wait. I heard the clank of accouterments, the thud of horses' feet, the voices of men, and a moment later the head of the little column appeared about the shoulder of a hill.

I had tried my Kalkar bow this morning upon the bucks, and I was surer of it now. It is a good bow, the principal objection to it being that it is too cumbersome for a mounted warrior. It is very powerful, though, and carries its heavy arrows accurately to a great distance. I knew now what I could do with it.

I waited until half a dozen riders had come into view, covering the spot at which they appeared, and as the next one presented himself I loosed my shaft. It caught the fellow in the groin and, coming from above, as it did, passed through and into his horse. The stricken animal reared and threw itself backward upon its rider; but that I only caught with the tail of my eye, for I was loosing another shaft at the man in front of him. He dropped with an arrow through his neck.

By now all was pandemonium. Yelling and cursing, the balance of the troop galloped into sight and with them I saw such a man as mortal eye may never have rested upon before this time and, let us pray, never may again. He sat on a huge horse, which I instantly recognized as the animal that had made the great imprints in the trail I had been following to the summit, and was himself a creature of such mighty size that he dwarfed the big Kalkars about him.

Instantly I saw in him the giant Raban, whom I had thought but the figment of Saku's imagination or superstition. On a horse at Raban's side rode Bethelda. For an instant I was so astonished by the size of Raban that I forgot my business upon the ridge, but only for an instant. I could not let drive at the giant for fear of hitting Bethelda, but I brought down in quick succession the man directly in front of him and one behind.

By now the Kalkars were riding around in circles looking for the foe, and they presented admirable targets, as I had known they would. By the blood of my fathers! But there is no greater sport than this form of warfare. Always outnumbered by the Kalkars, we have been forced to adopt tactics aimed to harass the enemy and wear him down a little at a time. By clinging constantly to his flanks, by giving him no rest, by cutting off detachments from his main body and annihilating them, by swooping down unexpectedly upon his isolated settlements, by roving the country about him and giving battle to every individual we met upon the trails we have driven him two thousand miles across the world to his last stand beside the sea.

As the Kalkars milled about in the canyon bottom I drove shaft after shaft among them, but never could I get a fair shot at Raban the Giant, for always he kept Bethelda between us after he had located me, guessing, evidently, that it was because of her that I had attacked his party. He roared like a bull as he sought to urge his men up the ridge to attack me, and some did make the attempt, half-heartedly, prompted no doubt by fear of their master—a fear that must have been a little greater than fear of the unknown enemy above them; but those who started up after me never came far, for they and I soon discovered that with their heavy bow I could drive their heavy arrows through their iron vests as if they had been wool.

Raban, seeing that the battle was going against him, suddenly put spurs to his great mount and went lumbering off down the canyon dragging Bethelda's horse after him, while those of his men who remained covered his retreat.

This did not suit me at all. I was not particularly interested in the Kalkars he was leaving behind, but in him and his captive, and so I ran to Red Lightning and mounted. As I reined down the flank of the ridge toward the canyon bottom I saw the Kalkars drawing off after Raban. There were but six of them left, and they were strung out along the trail.

As they rode they cast backward glances in my direction as if they were expecting to see a great force of warriors appear in pursuit. When they saw me they did not return to engage me, but continued after Raban.

I had reslung my bow beneath my right stirrup leather and replaced the few arrows in my quiver as Red Lightning descended the side of the ridge, and now I prepared my lance. Once upon the level trail of the canyon bottom I whispered a word into the pointed ear before me, couched my lance, and crouched in the saddle as the thirtieth descendent of the first Red Lightning flattened in swift charge.

The last Kalkar in the retreating column, rather than receive my spear through the small of his unprotected back, wheeled his horse, unslung his spear and awaited me in the middle of the trail. It was his undoing.

No man can meet the subtle tricks of a charging lancer from the back of a standing horse, for he cannot swerve to one side or the other with the celerity oft necessary to elude the point of his foe's lance, or take advantage of what opening the other may inadvertently leave him, and doubly true was this of the Kalkar upon his clumsy, splay-footed mount.

So awkward were the twain that they could scarcely have gotten out of their own way, much less mine, and so I took him where I would as I crashed into him, which was the chest, and my heavy lance passed through him, carrying him over his horse's rump, splintering the wood as he fell to earth. I cast the useless stump aside as I reined Red Lightning in and wheeled him about.

I saw the nearer Kalkar halted in the trail to watch the outcome of the battle, and now that he saw his companion go down to death and me without a lance he bore down upon me, and, I assume, he thought that he had me on the run, for Red Lightning was indeed racing away from him, back toward the fallen foe, but with a purpose in mind that one better versed in the niceties of combat might have sensed. As I passed the dead Kalkar I swung low from my saddle and picked his lance from where it lay in the dust beside him, and then, never reducing our speed, I circled and came back to meet the rash one riding to his doom.

We came together at terrific speed, and as we approached each other I saw the tactics that this new adversary was bent upon using to my destruction, and I may say that he used judgment far beyond the seeming capacity of his low forehead, for he kept his horse's head ever straight for Red Lightning's front with the intention of riding me down and overthrowing my mount, which, considering the disparity in their weights, he would certainly have accomplished had we met full on, but we did not.

My reins lay on Red Lightning's withers. With a touch of my left knee I swung the red stallion to the right and passed my spear to my left hand, all in a fraction of the time it takes to tell it, and as we met I had the Kalkar helpless, for he was not expecting me upon his left hand, his heavy horse could not swerve with the agility of Red Lightning, and so I had but to pick my target and put the fellow out of his misery—for it must be misery to be a low creature of a Kalkar.

In the throat my point caught him, for I had no mind to break another lance since I saw two more of the enemy riding toward me, and, being of tough wood, the weapon tore out through the flesh as the fellow tumbled backward into the dust of the trail.

There were four Kalkars remaining between me and the giant who, somewhere down the canyon and out of sight now, was bearing Bethelda off, I knew not where or to what fate. The four were strung out at intervals along the trail and appeared undecided as to whether to follow Raban or wait and argue matters out with me. Perhaps they hoped that I would realize the futility of pitting myself against their superior numbers, but when I lowered my lance and charged the nearer of them they must have realized that I was without discretion and must be ridden down and dispatched.

Fortunately for me they were separated by considerable intervals and I did not have to receive them all at once. The nearer, fortified by the sound of his companions' galloping approach, couched his lance and came halfway to meet me, but I think much of his enthusiasm must have been lost in contemplation of the fate that he had seen overtake the others that had pitted their crude skill against me, for certainly there were neither fire nor inspiration in his attack, which more closely resembled a huge senseless boulder rolling down a mountainside than a sentient creature of nerves and brain driven by lofty purposes of patriotism and honor.

Poor clod! An instant later the world was a better place in which to live, by at least one less Kalkar; but he cost me another lance and a flesh wound in the upper arm, and left me facing his three fellows, who were now so close upon me that there was no time in which to retrieve the lance fallen from his nerveless fingers.

There was recourse only to the sword, and, drawing, I met the next of them with only a blade against his long lance; but I eluded his point, closed with him and, while he sought to draw, clove him open from his shoulder to the center of his chest.

It took but an instant, yet that instant was my undoing, for the remaining two were already upon me. I turned in time to partially dodge the lance point of the foremost, but it caught me a glancing blow upon the head and that is the last that I remember of immediately ensuing events.

When next I opened my eyes I was jouncing along, lashed to a saddle, belly down across a horse. Within the circumscribed limits of my vision lay a constantly renewed circle of dusty trail and four monotonously moving, gray, shaggy legs. At least I was not on Red Lightning.

I had scarcely regained consciousness when the horse bearing me was brought to a stop and the two accompanying Kalkars dismounted and approached me. Removing the bonds that held me to the saddle they dragged me unceremoniously to the ground, and when I stood erect they were surprised to see that I was conscious.

"Dirty Yank!" cried one and struck me in the face with his open palm.

His companion laid a hand upon his arm. "Hold, Tav," he expostulated, "he put up a good fight against great odds." The speaker was a man of about my own height and might have passed as a full-blood Yank, though, as I thought at the time, doubtless he was a half-breed.

The other gestured his disgust. "A dirty Yank," he repeated. "Keep him here, Okonnor, while I find Raban and ask what to do with him." He turned and left us.

We had halted at the foot of a low hill upon which grew tremendous old trees and of such infinite variety that I marveled at them. There were pine, cypress, hemlock, sycamore and acacia that I recognized, and many others the like of which I never before had seen, and between the trees grew flowering shrubs. Where the ground was open it was carpeted with flowers—great masses of color; and there were little pools choked with lilies and countless birds and butterflies. Never had I looked upon a place of such wondrous beauty.

Through the trees I could see the outlines of the ruins of one of the stone tents of the ancients sitting upon the summit of the low hill. It was toward this ruined structure that he who was called Tav was departing from us.

"What place is this?" I asked the fellow guarding me, my curiosity overcoming my natural aversion to conversation with his kind.

"It is the tent of Raban," he replied. "Until recently it was the home of Or-tis the Jemadar—the true Or-tis. The false Or-tis dwells in the great tents of The Capital. He would not last long in this valley."

"What is this Raban?" I asked.

"He is a great robber. He preys upon all and to such an extent has he struck terror to the hearts of all who have heard of him that he takes toll as he will, and easily. They say that he eats the flesh of humans, but that I do not know—I have been with him but a short time. After the assassination of the true Or-tis I joined him because he preys upon the Kalkars.

"He lived long in the eastern end of the valley, where he could prey upon the outskirts of The Capital, and then he did not rob or murder the people of the valley; but with the death of Or-tis he came and took this place and now he preys upon my people as well as upon the Kalkars, but I remain with him since I must serve either him or the Kalkars."

"You are not a Kalkar?" I asked, and I could believe it because of his good old American name, Okonnor.

"I am a Yank, and you?"

"I am Julian 20th, The Red Hawk," I replied.

He raised his brows. "I have heard of you in the last few days," he said. "Your people are fighting mightily at the edge of The Capital, but they will be driven back—the Kalkars are too many. Raban will be glad of you if the stories they tell of him are true. One is that he eats the hearts of brave warriors that are unfortunate enough to fall into his hands."

I smiled. "What is the creature?" I asked again. "Where originates such a breed?"

"He is only a Kalkar," replied Okonnor, "but even a greater monstrosity than his fellows. He was born in The Capital of ordinary Kalkar parents, they say, and early developed a lust for blood that has increased with the passing years. He boasts yet of his first murder—he killed his mother when he was ten."

I shuddered. "And it is into the hands of such that a daughter of the Or-tis has fallen," I said, "and you, an American, aided in her capture."

He looked at me in startled surprise. "The daughter of an Or-tis?" he cried.

"Of *the* Or-tis," I repeated.

"I did not know," he said. "I was not close to her at any time and thought that she was but a Kalkar woman. Some of them are small, you know—the half-breeds."

"What are you going to do? Can you save her?" I demanded.

A white flame seemed to illumine his face. He drew his knife and cut the bonds that held my arms behind me.

"Hide here among the trees," he said, "and watch for Raban until I return. It will be after dark, but I will bring help. This valley is almost exclusively peopled by those who have refused to intermarry with the Kalkars and have brought down their strain unsullied from ancient times. There are almost a thousand fighting men of pure Yank blood within its confines. I should be able to gather enough to put an end to Raban for all time, and if the danger of a daughter of Or-tis cannot move them from their shame and cowardice they are hopeless indeed."

He mounted his horse. "Quick!" he cried. "Get among the trees."

"Where is my horse?" I called as he was riding away. "He was not killed?"

"No," he called back, "he ran off when you fell. We did not try to catch him." A moment later he disappeared around the west end of the hill and I entered the miniature forest that clothed it. Through the gloom of my sorrow broke one ray of happiness—Red Lightning lived.

About me grew ancient trees of enormous size with boles of five to six feet in diameter and their upper foliage waving a hundred and more feet above my head. Their branches excluded the sun where they grew thickest and beneath them baby trees struggled for existence in the wan light, or hoary monsters, long fallen, lay embedded in leaf mould marking the spot where some long dead ancient set out a tiny seedling that was to outlive all his kind.

It was a wonderful place in which to hide, although hiding is an accomplishment that we Julians have little training in and less stomach for. However, in this instance it was in a worthy cause—a Julian hiding from a Kalkar in the hope of aiding an Or-tis! Ghosts of nineteen Julians! To what had I, Julian 20th, brought my proud name?

And yet I could not be ashamed. There was something stubbornly waging war against all my inherited scruples and I knew that it was going to win—had already won. I would have sold my soul for this daughter of my enemy.

I made my way up the hill toward the ruined tent, but at the summit the shrubbery was so dense that I could see nothing. Rose bushes fifteen feet high and growing as thickly together as a wall hid everything from my sight. I could not even penetrate them.

Near me was a mighty tree with a strange, feathery foliage. It was such a tree as I had never seen before, but that fact did not interest me so much as the discovery that it might be climbed to a point that would permit me to see above the top of the rose bushes.

What I saw included two stone tents, not so badly ruined as most of those one comes across, and between them a pool of water—an artificial pool of straight lines. Some fallen columns of stone lay about it and the vines and creepers fell over its edge into the water, almost concealing the stone rim.

As I watched a group of men came from the ruin to the east through a great archway, the coping of which had fallen away. They were all Kalkars, and among them was Raban. I had my first opportunity to view him closely.

He was a most repulsive appearing creature. His great size might easily have struck with awe the boldest heart, for he stood a full nine feet in height and was very large in proportion about the shoulders, chest and limbs. His forehead was so retreating that one might with truth say he had none, his thick thatch of stiffly erect hair almost meeting his shaggy eyebrows.

His eyes were small and set close to a coarse nose, and all his countenance was bestial. I had not dreamed that a man's face could be so repulsive. His whiskers appeared to grow in all directions and proclaimed, at best, but hearsay evidence of combing.

He was speaking to that one of my captors who had left me at the foot of the hill to apprise Raban of my taking—that fellow who struck me in the face while my hands were bound and whose name was Tav. The giant spoke in a roaring, bull-like voice which I thought at the time was, like his swaggering walk and his braggadocio, but a pose to strike terror in those about him.

I could not look at the creature and believe that real courage lay within so vile a carcass. I have known many fearless men—The Vulture, The Wolf, The Rock and hundreds like them—and in each courageousness was reflected in some outward physical attribute of dignity and majesty.

"Fetch him!" he roared at Tav. "Fetch him! I will have his heart for my supper," and after Tav had gone to fetch me, the giant stood there with his other followers, roaring and bellowing, and always about himself and what he had done and what he would do. He seemed to me an exaggeration of a type I had seen before, wherein gestures simulate action, noise counterfeits courage, and wind passes for brains.

The only impressive thing about him was his tremendous bulk, and yet even that did not impress me greatly—I have known smaller men, whom I respected, that filled me with far greater awe. I did not fear him.

I think only the ignorant could have feared him at all, and I did not believe all the pother about his eating human flesh. I am of the opinion that a man who really intended eating the heart of another would say nothing about it.

Presently Tav came running back up the hill. He was much excited, as I had known be would be, even before he started off to fetch me.

"He is gone!" he cried to Raban. "They are both gone—Okonnor and the Yank. Look!" He held out the thongs that had fastened my wrists. "They have been cut. How could he cut them with his hands bound behind him? That is what I want to know. How could he have done it? He could not unless—"

"There must have been others with him," roared Raban. "They followed and set him free, taking Okonnor captive."

"There were no others," insisted Tav.

"Perhaps Okonnor freed him," suggested another.

So obvious an explanation could not have originated in the pea girth brain of Raban and so he said: "I knew it from the first—it was Okonnor. With my own hands I shall tear out his liver and eat it for breakfast."

Certain insects, toads and men make a lot of unnecessary noise, but the vast majority of other animals pass through life in dignified silence. It is our respect for these other animals that causes us to take their names. Whoever heard a red hawk screeching his intentions to the world? Silently he soars above the treetops and as silently he swoops and strikes.

# NINE

# Reunion

THROUGH THE conversation that I overheard between Raban and his minions I learned that Bethelda was imprisoned in the westerly ruin, but as Raban did not go thither during the afternoon I waited in the hope that fortune would favor me with a better opportunity after dark to attempt her liberation with less likelihood of interruption or discovery than would have been possible during the day, when men and women were constantly passing in and out of the easterly tent. There was the chance, too, that Okonnor might return with help and I did not want to do anything, while that hope remained, that might jeopardize Bethelda's chances for escape.

Night fell and yet there was no sign of Okonnor. Sounds of coarse laughter came from the main ruin, and I could imagine that Raban and his followers were at meat, washing down their food with the fiery liquor of the Kalkars. There was no one in sight and so I determined to come out of my concealment and investigate the structure in which I believed Bethelda was imprisoned. If I could release her well and good; if not I could but wait for the return of Okonnor.

As I was about to descend from the tree there came down with the wind from out of the canyon to the south a familiar sound—the nicker of a red stallion. It was music to my ears. I must answer it even though I chanced arousing the suspicions of the Kalkars.

Just once my answering whistle arose sharp and clear above the noises of the night. I do not think the Kalkars heard it—they were making too much noise of their own within doors—but the eager whinny that came thinly down the night wind told me that two fine, slim ears had caught the familiar summons.

Instead of going at once to the westerly ruin I made my way down the hill to meet Red Lightning, for I knew that he might mean, in the end, success or failure for me—freedom or death for Bethelda. Already, when I reached the foot of the declivity, I faintly heard the pounding of his hoofs and, steadily increasing in volume, the loved sound rolled swiftly out of the darkness toward me. The hoof beats of running horses, the rolling of the war drums! What sweeter music in all the world?

He saw me, of course, before I saw him, but he stopped in a cloud of dust a few yards from me and sniffed the air. I whispered his name and called him to me. Mincingly he came, stopping often, stretching his long neck forward, poised, always, ready for instant flight.

A horse depends much upon his eyes and ears and nostrils, but he is never so fully satisfied as when his soft, inquisitive muzzle has nosed an object of suspicion. He snorted now, and then he touched my cheek with his velvet lip and gave a great sigh and rubbed his head against me, satisfied. I hid him beneath the trees at the foot of the hill and bade him wait there in silence.

From the saddle I took the bow and some arrows and, following the route that Tav had taken to the top of the hill, I avoided the hedge of roses and came presently before the south archway of the ruin. Beyond was a small central court with windows and doors opening upon it. Light from flares burning in some of the rooms partly illuminated the court, but most of it was in shadow.

I passed beneath the arch and to the far end of the inclosure, where, at my right, I saw a window and a door opening into two rooms in which a number of Kalkars were eating and drinking at two long tables. I could not see them all. If Raban was there he was not within range of my vision.

It is always well to reconnoiter thoroughly before carrying out any plan of action, and with this idea in mind I left the court by the way I had entered and made my way to the east end of the structure, intending to pass entirely around it and along the north side to the westerly ruin, where I hoped to find Bethelda and devise means for her rescue.

At the southeast corner of the ruin are three gigantic cypress trees, growing so closely together as to almost resemble a single huge tree, and as I paused an instant behind them to see what lay before me, I saw a single Kalkar warrior come from the building and walk out into the rank grass that grew knee high on a level space before the structure.

I fitted an arrow to my bow. The fellow had that which I craved—a sword. Could I drop him noiselessly? If he would turn I was sure of it, and turn he did, as though impelled to it by my insistent wish. His back was toward me.

I drew the shaft far back. The cord twanged as I released it, but there was no other sound, except the muffled thud as the arrow entered its victim's spine at the base of the brain. Mute, he died. No other was around. I ran forward and removed his sword belt, to which were attached both sword and knife.

As I arose and buckled the weapons about me I glanced into the lighted room from which he had just come. It was the same that I had seen from the court upon the other side and directly adjoining it was the other room that I had seen. Now I could see all of them that I had not seen before.

Raban was not there. Where was he? A cold terror ran suddenly through me. Could it be that in the brief interval that had elapsed while I went down to meet Red Lightning he had left the feast and gone to the westerly ruin! I shuddered as I ran swiftly across the front of the house and along the north side toward the other structure.

I stopped before it and listened. I heard the sound of voices! From whence came they? This was a peculiar structure, built upon a downward sloping hill, with one floor on a level with the hilltop, another above that level and a third below and behind the others. Where the various entrances were and how to find the right one I did not know.

From my hiding place in the tree I had seen that the front chamber at the hilltop level was a single apartment with a cavernous entrance that stretched the full width of the ruin, while upon the south side and to the rear of this apartment were two doors, but where they led to I could not guess.

It seemed best, however, to try these first and so I ran immediately to them, and here the sounds of voices came more distinctly to me, and now I recognized the roaring, bull-tones of Raban.

I tried the nearer door. It swung open, and before me a flight of stairs descended and at the same time the voices came more loudly to my ears—I had opened the right door. A dim light flickered below as if coming from a chamber near the foot of the stairs.

These were but instantaneous impressions to which I gave no conscious heed at the time, for almost as they flashed upon me I was at the foot of the stairs looking into a large, high ceiled chamber in which burned a single flare that but diffused the gloom sufficiently for me to see the figure of Raban towering above that of Bethelda whom he was dragging toward the doorway by her hair.

"An Or-tis!" he was bellowing. "An Or-tis! Who would have thought that Raban would ever take the daughter of a Jemadar to be his woman? Ah, you do not like the idea, eh? You might do worse, if you had a choice, but you have none, for who is there to say no to Raban the Giant?"

"The Red Hawk!" I said, stepping into the chamber.

The fellow wheeled and in the flickering light of the dim flare I saw his red face go purple and from purple to white, or rather a blotchy semblance of dirty yellow. Blood of my Fathers! How he towered above me, a perfect mountain of flesh. I am six feet in height and Raban must have been half again as tall, a good nine feet; but I swear he appeared all of twenty and broad in proportion!

For a moment he stood in silence glaring at me as though overcome by surprise, and then he thrust Bethelda aside and drawing his sword advanced upon me, bellowing and roaring as was his wont for the purpose, I presume, of terrifying me and, also, I could not help but think, to attract the attention and the aid of his fellows.

I came to meet him then and he appeared a mountain, so high he loomed; but with all his size I did not feel the concern that I have when meeting men of my own stature whose honor and courage merited my respect. It is well that I had this attitude of mind to fortify me in the impending duel, for, by The Flag, I needed whatever of encouragement I might find in it.

The fellow's height and weight were sufficient to overcome a mighty warrior had Raban been entirely wanting in skill, which he by no means was. He wielded his great sword with a master hand, and because of the very cowardice which I attributed to him, he fought with a frenzy wrought by fear, as a cornered beast fights.

I needed all my skill and I doubt that that alone would have availed me had it not been upborne and multiplied by love and the necessity for protecting the object of my love. Ever was the presence of Bethelda the Or-tis a spur and an inspiration. What blows I struck I struck for her, what I parried it was as though I parried from her soft skin.

As we closed he swung mightily at me a cut that would have severed me in twain, but I parried and stooped beneath it at once. I found his great legs unguarded before me and ran my sword through a thigh. With a howl of pain, Raban leaped back, but I followed him with a jab of my point that caught him just beneath the bottom of his iron vest and punctured his belly.

At that he gave forth a horrible shriek, and although sorely wounded began to wield his blade with a skill I had not dreamed lay in him. It was with the utmost difficulty that I turned his heavy sword and I saved myself as many times by the quickness of my feet as by the facility of my blade.

And much do I owe, too, to the cleverness of Bethelda, who, shortly after we crossed swords, had run to the great fireplace and seized the flare from where it had reposed upon the stone shelf above, and ever after had kept just behind my shoulder with it, so that whatever advantage of light there

Julian 20th Fighting Raban the Giant

might be lay with me. Her position was a dangerous one and I begged her to put herself at a safe distance, but she would not, and no more would she take advantage of this opportunity to escape, although that, too, I urged upon her.

Momentarily, I had expected to see Raban's men rushing into the chamber, for I could not understand that his yells had not reached every ear within a mile or more, and so I fought the more desperately to be rid of him and on our way before they came. Raban, now panting for breath, had none left with which to yell and I could see that from exertion, terror and loss of blood he was weakening.

It was now that I heard the loud voices of men without and the tramp of running feet. They were coming! I redoubled my efforts and Raban his—I to kill, he to escape death until succor came. From a score of wounds was he bleeding and I was sure that the thrust in his abdomen alone must prove fatal; but still he clung to life tenaciously, and fought with a froth of blood upon his lips from a punctured throat.

He stumbled and went to one knee, and as he staggered to rise I thought that I had him, but then we heard the hurrying feet of men descending the stairs. Instantly Bethelda hurled the flare to the floor, leaving us in utter darkness.

"Come!" she whispered, laying a hand upon my arm. "There will be too many now—we must escape as they enter or we are both indeed lost."

The warriors were cursing at the doorway now and calling for lights.

"Who hides within?" shouted one. "Stand forth, a prisoner! We are a hundred blades."

Bethelda and I edged nearer the doorway, hoping to pass out among them before a light was made. From the center of the room came a deep groan from where I had left Raban, followed by a scuffling noise upon the floor and a strange gurgling. I came to the doorway, leading Bethelda by the hand. I found it impassable, choked with men.

"Aside!" I said. "I will fetch a light."

A sword point was shoved against my belly. "Back!" warned a voice behind the point. "We will have a look at you before you pass—another is bringing a light."

I stepped back and crossed my sword with his. Perhaps I could hew my way to freedom with Bethelda in the confusion of the darkness. It seemed our only hope, for to be caught by Raban's minions now after the hurts I had inflicted upon him would mean sure death for me and worse for Bethelda.

By the feel of our steel we fenced in the dark, but I could not reach him, nor he me, although I felt that he was a master swordsman. I thought that I was gaining an advantage when I saw the flicker of a light coming from the doorway at the head of the stairs. Some one was coming with a flare. I redoubled my efforts, but to no avail.

And then the light came and as it fell upon the warriors in the doorway I stepped back, astounded, and dropped my point. The light that revealed them illumined my own face and at sight of it my antagonist voiced a cry of joy.

"Red Hawk!" he cried; and seized me by the shoulder. It was The Vulture, my brother, and with him were The Rattlesnake and a hundred warriors of our own beloved clans. Other lights were brought and I saw Okonnor and a host of strange warriors in Kalkar trappings pushing down the stairway with my own, nor did they raise swords against one another.

Okonnor pointed toward the center of the chamber and we looked, and there lay Raban the Giant, dead.

"The Red Hawk, Julian 20th," he said, turning to those crowding into the chamber behind him, "Great Chief of the Tribe of Julians—our chief!"

"And Jemadar of all America!" cried another voice, and the warriors, crowding into the room, raised their swords and their hoarse voices in acclamation. And he who had named me thus pushed past them and faced me, and I saw that he was no other than the true Or-tis with whom I had been imprisoned in The Capital and with whom I had escaped. He saw Bethelda and rushed forward and took her in his arms, and for a moment I was jealous, forgetting that he was her brother.

"And how has all this happened," I asked, "that Or-tis and Julian come here together in peace?"

"Listen," said my brother, "before you pass judgment upon us. Long has run the feud between Julian and Or-tis for the crime of a man dead now hundreds of years. Few enough are the Americans of pure blood that they should be separated by hate when they would come together in friendship.

"Came the Or-tis to us after escaping the Kalkars and told of your escape and of the wish of his father that peace be made between us, and he offered to lead us against the Kalkars by ways that we did not know, and The Wolf took council with me and there was also The Rock, The Rattlesnake and The Coyote, with every other chief who was at the front, and in your absence I dissolved the feud that has lain between us and the chiefs applauded my decision.

"Then, guided by the Or-tis, we entered The Capital and drove the Kalkars before us. Great are their numbers, but they have not The Flag with them and eventually they must fall.

"Then," he continued, "came word, brought by the little Nipons of the hills, that you were in the mountains near the tent of Raban the Giant and we came to find you, and on the way we met Okonnor with many warriors and glad were they of the peace that had been made and we joined with them who were also riding against Raban to rescue the sister of the Or-tis. And we are here awaiting the word of The Great Chief. If it is for peace between the Julian and the Or-tis, we are glad; if it is for war our swords are ready."

"It is for peace, ever," I replied, and the Or-tis came and knelt at my feet and took my hand in his.

"Before my people," he said very simply, "I swear allegiance to Julian 20th, The Red Hawk, Jemadar of America."

# TEN

# Peace

THERE WAS still much fighting to be done, for although we had driven the Kalkars from The Capital they held the country to the south and west and we could not be satisfied until we had driven them into the sea, and so we prepared to ride to the front again that very night, but before we left I wanted a word with Bethelda who was to remain here with a proper retinue and a sufficient guard in the home of her people.

Leading Red Lightning, I searched about the grounds around the ruins and at last I came upon her beneath a great oak tree that grew at the northwest corner of the structure, its mighty limbs outspreading above the ruin. She was alone and I came and stood beside her.

"I am going now," I said, "to drive your enemies and mine into the sea. I have come to say good-by."

"Good-by, Julian." She held out her hand to me.

I had come full of brave words and a mighty resolve, but when I took that slim and tender hand in mine I could but stand there mute and trembling. I, Julian 20th, The Red Hawk, for the first time in all my life knew fear. A Julian quailed before an Or-tis!

For a full minute I stood there trying to speak and could not, and then I dropped to my knee at the feet of my enemy and with my lips against her fair hand I murmured what I had been too great a coward to look into her eyes and say: "I love you!"

She raised me to my feet then and lifted her lips to mine and I took her into my arms and covered her mouth with kisses; and thus ended the ancient feud between Julian and Or-tis, that had endured four hundred years and wrecked a world.

Two years later and we had driven the Kalkars into the sea, the remnants of them flying westward in great canoes which they had built and launched upon a beauteous bay a hundred miles or more south of The Capital.

The Rain Cloud said that if they were not overcome by storms and waves they might sail on and on around the world and come again to the eastern shores of America, but the rest of us knew that they would sail to the edge of the Earth and tumble off and that would be the end of them.

We live in such peace now that it is difficult to find an enemy upon whom to try one's lance, but I do not mind much, since my time is taken with the care of my flocks and herds, the business of my people and the training of Julian 21st, the son of a Julian and an Or-tis, who will one day be Jemadar of all America over which, once more, there flies but a single flag—The Flag.

RICHARD J. GOLSAN

# Afterword

I FIRST discovered the writings of Edgar Rice Burroughs on a family vacation to Folly Beach, South Carolina, when I was ten years old. The weather was unseasonably hot, so hot that in our cottage at night no one could sleep. One night around midnight, while my father rocked on the front porch waiting in vain for a cooling sea breeze, I flipped on the bedside lamp and began to read a book my mother had bought for me at a local newsstand. The book was *Swords of Mars*. Within a few pages of beginning the story I was not thinking about the heat (or the mosquitoes) of South Carolina, but instead was winging my way over the wastes of Mars in a flyer, my long and short swords and radium pistol rattling reassuringly at my side. I was John Carter, or at least I wanted very much to be, with Dejah Thoris waiting to be rescued at the end of my journey.

John Carter was everything I ever wanted to be: tall, handsome, a valiant warrior, and in love with a beautiful woman who adored him. In short, he was the ideal hero for me and most other adolescent boys. But Carter was also a Virginian and a "Southern gentleman," a term that had a special significance for me. Born and raised in Georgia, I had been told by my grandfather that I must always live up to the moral and ethical standards and embody the grace and gentility of a "gentleman." I must also struggle against evil and protect the downtrodden. Who better exemplified all these than John Carter, and what better place to test one's principles and mettle than on the dying and dangerous world of Barsoom?

That summer I was hooked, and over the next several years I devoured the Mars series and all of the Tarzan books (Lord Greystoke is simply a *British* gentleman!). I became an admirer of Carson Napier of Venus, and especially of the generations of the Julian family I read about in *The Moon Maid*. I was never disappointed that every one of the stories followed the same basic plot and involved the same stock characters; it didn't bother me that I could predict the story's twists and turns and final outcome before I opened the book. Invariably Burroughs's hero is plunged unexpectedly into a dangerous and forbidding world chock full of truly malevolent villains intent on destroying him. His first obligation is merely to survive, but along the way he encounters a beautiful, courageous, strong-willed, and sexually virtuous young woman with whom he will eventually fall desperately in love and who he will save from many dangers (including the lascivious attentions of the story's archvillain). The basic plot of a Burroughs story is often complicated by the inevitable ups and downs of the lovers' courtship, obstacles that are finally overcome though not always in a completely happy way. Dangers persist, catastrophes and calamities are always waiting around the corner. But of course this plot device is essential if the hero is to be able to launch into new adventures and vanquish new foes in the narrative's next installment.

It was only years later—and perhaps I was particularly naive at the time—that in reading the likes of William Faulkner I realized that a dark underside often exists within the ideal of the Southern gentleman (although for me Faulkner's Gavin Stevens later became a more realistic version of John Carter). It was also years later, in reading the romantic tragicomedies of seventeenth-century French dramatist Pierre Corneille, that I understood the romances in Burroughs's novels as not real but idealized ones. They are the romances of superior beings who recognize each other's superiority and whose love is inspired by mutual "estime," as Corneille would say. But one doesn't need to read Corneille to know that love rarely, if ever, works this way.

It was also years later, after rereading the Mars series when I gave them to my adolescent sons to read, that I recognized the existence of some perhaps troubling dimensions to Burroughs's vision of reality and society to which I had been oblivious in my youth. No doubt Burroughs certainly is, by contemporary standards, an elitist; his depiction of his heroes and the alien cultures and societies he imagines reflect that perspective. John Carter doesn't fall for a Martian waitress, he falls for a Martian princess. Dejah Thoris is a princess of Mars's red race which, as all fans of Barsoom know, is the planet's superior and most "civilized" race. Tarzan may be raised as a savage by apes, but his superiority to them is understood to emanate at least partially from his noble origins. In short, blood line counts.

At the same time, the worlds Burroughs creates are remarkably cruel and violent, and the hero succeeds somewhat through intelligence, but mostly by being a warrior fiercer than anyone he encounters. The friends he does make in these dangerous worlds are essentially comrades in arms, men of virtue like himself but also fierce and superior warriors. In Edgar Rice Burroughs's universe, male bonding is a privileged form of interaction.

Remarkable intelligence and genius are often inextricably linked with evil in Burroughs's novels. Nowhere is this more evident than in the first part of *The Moon Maid*. The calamity that eventually visits two worlds, a calamity that results in the destruction of Earth's civilization for hundreds of years, originated in the evil genius of Orthis. Are we to conclude that extraordinary intelligence is a vice and not a virtue?

Looking back on the history of the bloody twentieth century we are painfully aware of the terrible political and human damage that can be caused by an unwavering belief in notions like the superiority of particular peoples or races. We also understand the dangers inherent in an uncritical adulation of warrior virtues and extreme patriotism and devotion to the flag—certainly evident in the tales of Julian 9th and Julian 20th. Should we condemn Burroughs for espousing such things in his books?

Even in this age of "political correctness" I believe the answer is "no." First, the traits Burroughs invests in his heroes are basically an expression of the traditional American frontier virtues of self-reliance, physical courage, and healthy survival instincts. Second, the fantastic creatures encountered in beautiful and forbidding places are what form a frontier experience, something with which Burroughs was certainly familiar from his early days in the army of Arizona to his extended sojourns in Utah and Idaho. One wonders, in fact, if *Tarzan of the Apes* and *A Princess of Mars* were successful among American audiences early on because both books were in many ways simply of cowboys and Indians transported to far away continents and alien worlds. John Carter, remember, first gets transported to Mars after holing up and dying in an Arizona cave while hiding from Apache warriors.

But if Edgar Rice Burroughs's novels are comparable to pulp dime store novels of western adventure (of which Burroughs wrote several himself), then on occasion they are also cautionary and even visionary works that draw on recent historical events to imagine the potential for globally cataclysmic consequences of human folly and destructiveness. Consider the tale of Earth's dealings with the Moon over many generations, as recounted in this book. It is not surprising that the first installment of the tale, "The Moon Maid," was published in 1923, only five years after the conclusion of the World War I in Europe. The massive and horrific destruction of the Great War gave rise to the fervent hope in many quarters that the European conflagration of 1914 to 1918 would be the "war to end all wars." Efforts to preserve peace and resolve conflicts through the creation of the League of Nations gave way to an increasingly desperate attempt in the 1930s to preserve peace at all costs. In the United States disarmament and isolationism were the order of the day. The consequences of all this are well known. A policy of appeasement in dealing with Hitler's Nazis led to the disaster of the Munich Accords, and finally to a war which was in many ways more horrific than the first one.

In *The Moon Maid* the Great War ends not in 1918 but, finally, in 1967. Burroughs's extension of the date in this way is prophetic, because we now know that in crucial ways the conclusion and aftermath of World War I spawned World War II (so much so that in some quarters one now hears not of two conflicts but of one "Thirty Years' War"). Exhausted by bloodshed, the world of the Julians disarms almost to the man, with only the International Peace Fleet to deal with the occasional trouble spot. The story opens at the beginning of the twenty-first century, after peace and disarmament have been maintained for fifty years. When radio contact is established with Barsoom, a spaceship designed by Orthis and commanded by Julian 5th is launched for Earth, but due to the treachery of Orthis it is forced to land inside the Moon. There Julian meets Nah-ee-lah, Princess of Laythe (and of course, the Moon's superior race), while Orthis joins forces with the Kalkars, the Moon's evil race. After many adventures Nah-ee-lah and Julian 5th escape, and with the rest of the spaceship's crew they return to Earth. Orthis, meanwhile, builds an invasion fleet with the help of the Kalkars and returns to conquer a defenseless Earth. He succeeds.

The next tale, "The Moon Men," takes the reader to several generations later in the story. Julian 9th, a young man living modestly with his family outside the ruins of Chicago in a world totally subjugated by the Kalkars, who now bear a striking resemblance to the Bolsheviks of Soviet Russia. The Kalkars are ruled by a Central Committee of sorts, in Washington, D.C., but Julian 9th's main enemy is Brother-General Or-tis, the descendent of the original archvillain and equally evil. Julian 9th, inspired by the desire to protect the girl he loves and to defend and restore the honor of "the Flag," is fated to lead the initial revolt against the Kalkars and to die in the peoples' uprising. Resolution of the conflict will be left to Julian 20th in the third tale, "The Red Hawk." There we see the final demise of what is left of Kalkar hegemony, in a world that has reverted, by and large, to a jumble of roaming warrior tribes.

It is not difficult to see the implicit message of *The Moon Maid*. If the desire for peace becomes so strong that we allow ourselves to become defenseless, we risk not only losing our freedom but our civilization as well. Other nations who invade us—whether they be Kalkars or Nazis or Soviets—bring not peace but the destruction of our moral universe and the end of our way of life. In "The Moon Men" and "The Red Hawk," the Flag is not a symbol of excessive power and privilege but of simple freedoms and the right to live in peace and honor.

I may be reading too much into *The Moon Maid*, and those who think it is simply a good adventure may well smile. Whatever the case may be, the tale is a testimony to Edgar Rice Burroughs's imagination and his ability to create fascinatingly alien worlds that, ultimately, are not so different from our own.

PHILLIP R. BURGER

# Red Blood vs. the Red Flag

L ATE IN 1918, shortly after the conclusion of the Great War, Edgar
Rice Burroughs contemplated writing a story set two centuries in
the future depicting life following a worldwide adoption of communism.
The Bolshevik Revolution of the previous November was still fresh in the
minds of people throughout the world, and Burroughs thought such a
story "would be of value in setting people to thinking of the results which
must follow the continued dissemination of this type of propaganda."[1]
Unfortunately no magazine editor shared his sentiment. Written in 1919,
"Under the Red Flag" was rejected eleven times; Burroughs found the
reasons for rejection so flimsy that he might have thought a communist
conspiracy was afoot.[2]

In 1922 Burroughs spent one day rewriting "Under the Red Flag," changing the Bolsheviks to invading Kalkars from the Moon. The story sold
handily. Which just goes to show that science fiction is only escapist entertainment and really has no underlying meaning at all.

Of course Burroughs rigged the game by making his now-renamed
"The Moon Men" a sequel. A few months later Burroughs wrote "The
Moon Maid," wherein he laid the groundwork for his lunar invasion; in
1925 he wrapped up the saga with "The Red Hawk." In 1926 all three
were combined for book publication under the title *The Moon Maid*.[3]
Burroughs managed to take an unpublishable short novel and turn it into a
multigenerational family saga and elaborate future history. Plus it remains
a biting anti-communist tract—and so much more besides.

*The Moon Maid* was written in a time when the American worry over
the Red Menace became part of our national character. Worrying about
the communists was a great deal more complicated following the Great
War than it later became during the Cold War. To Americans of the time
Bolshevism was more than a hostile political ideology; it was a system of

government comprised of people who *by their very nature* were both inca-
pable of governing and inferior in every way to those they ruled. Many felt
that a Bolshevik uprising in this country would destroy the established—or
the "proper"—racial and class structure of American society. Equality for
all through communism would be achieved by dragging everyone down
to the lowest level. Class conflict would be eliminated through the simple
expedient of eliminating the social classes that contribute the most to civilization: intellectuals and the providers of capital, or, in more specific terms,
the Anglo-Saxon ruling elite. The Kalkars of *The Moon Maid* are more than
just evil "Commies"—they are a potent symbol of the fears that pressed on
white America at the time. For his trip into the far future Burroughs took
along plenty of cultural baggage.

"We have peace, but what shall we do with it?" asks the anonymous
narrator in the opening pages of *The Moon Maid*. His Great War had
concluded in 1967, resulting in "the absolute domination of the Anglo-
Saxon race over all the other races of the world." Burroughs neatly sums
up the country's postwar malaise while revealing the complicated racial lens
through which America viewed itself and the world. Government propaganda had emphasized the degraded and bestial aspects of the hated Hun:
during war bond drives through his Chicago neighborhood Burroughs had
cheerily baited those he considered unpatriotic by handing out "yellow
cards[,] each of which bore the name of some suspected German sympa-
thizer."[4] In addition, final victory during the war had only emphasized the
superiority of the Anglo-Saxon race over the Teutonic race and the assorted
"lesser" races that had allied with it. "Race," a somewhat freewheeling term
as it was used in the early twentieth century, denoted everything from skin
color to skull shape to language. A 1911 government report noted that there
were "45 races or peoples among immigrants coming to the United States";
some particularly studious souls could identify many more.[5]

Wartime patriotism and a strong dislike of anyone who might, in the
words of literary and drama critic Brander Matthews, "resent those aspects
of American civilization which we have been in the habit of calling 'Anglo-
Saxon,'" was carried over into the postwar years.[6] Current thinking had it
that a truly patriotic American upheld Anglo-Saxon ideals—in short, he or
she embraced unquestioningly the dominant culture. "After the war," wrote
Burl Noggle in his study of the period, "the crusade against Germany gradually but unmistakably turned toward a peculiar brand of conformity labeled '100% Americanism'—a brand with little tolerance for conscientious
objectors or for other groups who had opposed the war."[7] Throw the Bolshevik Revolution into the mix, along with extensive labor unrest through-

out the country, suddenly anyone with a critical thought was branded as un-American and a potential anarchist. An English journalist observed that the country had become "hag-ridden by the spectre of Bolshevism. It was like a sleeper in a nightmare . . . and the horrid name 'Radical' covered the most innocent departure from conventional thought with a suspicion of desperate purpose."[8] Bomb-throwing anarchists did pop up enough to feed the fear that an uprising was in the offing. Thus began the Red Scare and a witch hunt that would have set Joseph McCarthy's heart a-flutter.

Ray Long of *Blue Book* had rejected the original "Under the Red Flag" because, "In spite of all we know about what Bolshevism does and has done, it seems incredible that anything of this sort could happen to America."[9] Long may have been the voice of reason, but many others shared Burroughs's worry that Bolshevism was destined to spill beyond Russia's borders. "[T]he Department of Justice has warned the American people that there are at least 300,000 people in our country who hate the Republic, and are seeking to overthrow its free institutions," warned Newell Dwight Hillis, the pastor of Brooklyn's Plymouth Church.[10] Issuing warnings about an imminent Bolshevik-style uprising in America was a veritable cottage industry at the time. If Pastor Hillis's "facts" weren't enough to galvanize patriotic Americans, Seattle mayor Ole Hanson's description of what would happen should all these proto-Bolsheviks have their way added to the fear:

> [B]olshevism is the autocratic rule of the lowest, least intelligent, least able class who believe that by "direct action" and "force" they can terrorize our people into turning over to them the conduct, ownership, and control of everything . . . With [bolshevism] thrive murder, rape, pillage, arson, free love, poverty, want, starvation, filth, slavery, autocracy, suppression, sorrow and Hell on earth. It is a class government of the unable, the unfit, the untrained; of the scum, of the dregs, of the cruel, and of the failures.[11]

Hanson's vision is the future America Burroughs depicts in *The Moon Maid.* While the mayor's hysterical rhetoric today appears more amusing than alarming (where better would autocracy thrive than under autocratic rule?), his description does represent the tenor of the times and the corrosive atmosphere in which Burroughs penned his future history. Indeed, Burroughs shared Hanson's accusatory vocabulary, describing those earthmen who join the Kalkars as "the lazy, the inefficient, the defective, who ever place the blame for their failures upon the shoulders of the successful," that is, the sort most likely to find the Bolshevik message appealing.

For both Burroughs and Hanson these lazy, inefficient, and defective people were the members of the radical labor movement, in particular the Industrial Workers of the World (IWW), or "Wobblies." While never very powerful the IWW's members were nonetheless vocal, and as a result they came to be seen as the prime source of trouble in organized labor. (The IWW was even too radical for other radicals; the Socialist Party expelled it as a group in 1912). Because they advocated the use of "direct action" (sabotage and violence) to achieve their goals, patriotic Americans viewed the group as terrorists in their midst. The IWW had opposed the United States's entry into the war and so was doubly damned as un-American. "Wobbly talk of revolt and Wobbly scorn for church and flag as symbols of an unjust status quo stirred state and federal governments to frantic action. From 1905 until its virtual destruction as an effective force in the early Twenties, the IWW was a focal point for a drive to rid the nation of radicals." [12]

Burroughs's hometown of Chicago had a rich history of radical labor activities—and a corresponding distrust of the movement held by the city's well-to-do citizenry. The Haymarket Square bombing of 1886 resulted in all leftists being branded as anarchists; when the IWW was formed in Chicago in 1905 it was viewed as more of the same. Burroughs's dislike of organized labor was well seated, probably learned from his father, a minor industrialist who manufactured electric batteries and for whom Burroughs briefly worked. Burroughs took swipes at the Wobblies in *The Land That Time Forgot* (1918), *The Girl from Hollywood* (1922), and *Marcia of the Doorstep* (1924). He does not mention the IWW by name in *The Moon Maid*, but there was no need; IWW members were the most popular scapegoats of the day. In describing the period of the Kalkar invasion Burroughs says, "workmen were then permitted to labor only four hours a day, when they felt like it," a parody on the IWW's goal of a seemingly lazy four-hour workday. Burroughs, like so many others, may have been unaware that the purpose behind this goal was to ensure full employment (at a time when thousands were striking to achieve an eight-hour workday).

Burroughs was not totally unsympathetic to the plight of the working man; he had spent several years mired in poverty before his writing career flourished. In *The Moon Maid* he criticizes the "accursed income tax . . . [that] falls hardest on those least able to support it" (the federal income tax had been imposed in 1913), while elsewhere he takes to task "America's rich and powerful farming class . . . [that] had sought to throw the burden of taxation upon the city dwellers." But Burroughs defined his own period of poverty as "an indication of inefficiency, and nothing more." [13] He had finally achieved success and fortune all on his own and so had little tolerance of those who resorted to organized labor rather than old-fashioned sweat and toil to make something of themselves.

Burroughs became a popular (and well-paid) writer at a time when laborers across the country were losing many of their hard-won gains, and so he was quite ignorant of the sources of labor's grievances. "There was never a more prosperous or independent class of human beings than the American laboring man of the twentieth century," Burroughs declares through the character of Julian 8th, revealing that he was either uncaring or unaware that postwar inflation had doubled the cost of living for these supposedly prosperous laboring men. He believed that the working class never had it so good and its members should allow "the rich nonproducers" with their "intelligence and imagination" to provide the needed direction. Apparently this sensible setup is hereditary, as these rich nonproducers "could transmit to their offspring the qualities of mind that are essential to any culture, progress or happiness that the world ever may hope to attain." The Kalkars, being merely the "offspring of generations of menials and servants," and hence lacking these essential qualities of mind, will lead the world to galloping ruin should they or their like ever gain power.

Burroughs's class consciousness is both striking and typical of his times; it pervades *The Moon Maid* just as it pervaded American society. The Julians during the Kalkar reign are of the "rapidly diminishing intellectual class" who never allow "the pretty girls of our class" to be seen in public; Julian 9th is brought before a military tribunal upon which sits "no person of my class or race," while the Kalkars themselves are "the most burdensome class of parasites the world ever has endured." Julian 8th (of the intellectual class) and Jim Thompson (of the working class) engage in spirited debates about how each other's class is more responsible for the triumph of the Kalkars—discussions that take place two hundred years after the class structure has supposedly been eliminated. While the men are good friends each nonetheless is fully aware of his place in the class structure because it has been bred into him.

Class is defined by more than one's financial standing; it is defined by one's hereditary endowments. The Julians are a literal expression of this belief: each is a reincarnation of a previous Julian, making them a family of hereditary leaders. (Certainly Tarzan, Burroughs's most popular fictional creation, in large part owes his standing as lord of the jungle to his aristocratic heritage.) The Kalkars (or their earthly equivalents) have not been blessed with sufficient brainpan to be leaders; their attempts at lording it over those with better blood runs counter to the natural order of things. "[T]he social stratification which exists in modern industrial communities is positively correlated with a corresponding stratification of innate moral and intellectual quality," explained psychologist William McDougall, trying to apply a scientific justification to this well-entrenched class prejudice. For those persons with slightly smaller vocabularies (but not, one assumes, for every mouth-breathing rube out there), McDougall dumbed down his explanation a bit: "the upper social strata, as compared with the lower, contain a larger proportion of persons of superior natural endowments." [14] In the logic of social darwinism, members of the upper social strata are the fittest to rule because their kind has always done so. Those who objected to this sensible social order were thought to be advocating class warfare and were (naturally) labeled as Bolsheviks.

Julian 9th is cognizant of a time in American history when people "came from all other parts of the world to share our happiness and when they had won it they sought to overthrow it, and when the Kalkars came they helped them." By 1911 three-fifths of the working class were foreign born, and that growing multitude was dominated by immigrants from the perceived intellectual and economic backwaters of Europe: Russia, Poland, Italy (Sicily specifically), the Balkan states, and Greece. By contrast, nineteenth-century immigrants had come predominantly from northern Europe and had been, as Brander Matthew observed, "anxious to assert their solidarity with the older stock of Americans. They wanted to be like us . . . they shared our opinions and even our prejudices." [15] That last is a rather telling comment. Newer immigrants wanted to maintain their Old World customs and languages, which only emphasized their standing in Americans' eyes as outsiders. Worse still, the majority of these recent arrivals were penniless and unskilled, and so more likely to find appealing the left's propaganda—if they weren't practicing Bolsheviks already. "Why do we still allow the dregs of Southern and Eastern European nations to swarm into our community by the thousands every day," asked one desperate observer of the invasion, "when we know that there are hundreds of active or potential Bolshevists among them who may not be discovered under our hurried and superficial mental and literacy tests?" [16] The Socialists and Wobblies experienced a heavy influx of foreign-born members during the war, which meant that the mainstream's distrust of the radical left became married to a distrust of America's immigrant population.

The "dregs of Southern and Eastern Europe" were bringing the Bolshevik plague to America. Anyone who rallied to the banner of "100% Americanism" came "to distrust anything that was foreign, and this radicalism [was seen] as the spawn of long-haired Slavs and unwashed East-Side Jews." [17] Burroughs portrays the Kalkars as having the characteristics of these twin bearers of Bolshevism in postwar America. Consider his first full description of a Kalkar: "His eyes were close set upon either side of a prominent, hooked nose. They were watery, fishy, blue eyes, and the hair growing profusely above his low forehead was flaxen in color. His physique was admirable, except for a noticeable stoop. His feet were large and his gait awkward when he moved."

Kalkars are further identified as "a mongrel breed, comprising many divergent types," a potent description that emphasizes their blend of negative elements and basic impurity. Their low foreheads immediately tag them as being intellectually challenged, while their large feet and splendid build suggest low-class Slavic laborers. Kalkars do not care for water or bathing—raising the unpleasant stereotype of the "dirty Jew." Burroughs endowed the mixed-race Or-tis with "a thin, cruel upper lip and a full and sensuous lower," highlighting the Jew's supposedly cunning and lustful natures. [18]

Burroughs had few qualms about depicting racial and ethnic characters using stereotypes, his choices reflecting the stereotypes then current in the mainstream culture. Stereotypes are used by popular fiction writers to evoke an immediate response in the reader, thereby eliminating the need for elaborate (and in adventure fiction, usually dull) characterizations. Even supposedly scientific texts of the time (many of them anti-immigrant texts glossed with a scientific patina) fed into the fear of these foreign invaders, utilizing stereotypes to accentuate the otherness of the immigrants, these "hirsute, low-browed, big-faced persons of obviously low mentality . . . [t]hese oxlike men [who] are descendants of those *who always stayed behind*." [19] Burroughs utilized such imagery to direct his readers to respond in a particular way to characters he endowed with these unsavory traits.

The war and postwar years saw a resurgence in the stereotyping of Jews, some of it sparked by anti-Semitic feelings, some the result of plain ignorance. Dispassionate scientists argued over an "Anthropological Explanation of the Facial Aspect of the Jew" (a tract that read, "the cunning and shrewdness that is characteristic of all people who have to live by their wits; a shade of anger and resentment . . . the calculation, coldness and scanning . . . which we think is a result of long experience in financial operations"). [20] In a somewhat less dispassionate way sociologist Edward Alsworth Ross assessed the recent Jewish immigrants as "moral cripples, their souls warped and dwarfed by iron circumstance. The experience of Russian repression has made them haters of government and corrupters of the police." [21] Jews, perhaps more than any other group, were perceived as outsiders, a people with strange customs and even peculiar physiognomies (which led others to question if they were a separate race), a people loyal to a fabled homeland rather than to the United States. Jews were a convenient screen upon which "true blue" Americans could project their fears.

Burroughs has been rigorously attacked for being anti-Semitic, primarily because of his characterization of Adolph Bluber in *Tarzan and the Golden Lion* (1922). Yet he has been just as rigorously defended against charges of anti-Semitism, with his defenders pointing to the example of the Jewish tanner Moses Samuels in *The Moon Maid.* Richard Lupoff (quite rightly) asserts that Samuels is a "tragic, heroic figure, one of the most believable of all [Burroughs's] characters."[22] Samuels is a marvelous example of Burroughs's ability to achieve rich characterization when he put his mind to it. But Burroughs did not make Samuels a Jew simply to showcase his gift for characterization. That Samuels is identified by his religion contradicts the book's basic scenario in which Burroughs has set up a nation stripped of all religious identification. Samuels's Jewishness serves another purpose. The Kalkars are endowed with the beaked nose, the bulging eyes, the sensual lips, and the peculiar odor of the Jewish stereotype, yet Samuels is "one Jew who hates a Kalkar." In stressing Samuels's ethnicity and religious identity Burroughs shows that the character is, above all else, a model American.

Differentiating between types of Jews—between the American Jew Samuels and the Old World–styled Kalkars—may seem like ethnic hair-splitting, yet such was done by members of the Jewish American community themselves, at least at that time in Chicago. The German Jews who had migrated to the city during the nineteenth century were well assimilated within the dominant Anglo-American culture; they too looked upon the unassimilated Eastern European Jews as outsiders (probably to guarantee that their position within American culture would not be compromised).[23] American Jewish businessmen likewise shared Burroughs's aversion to the radical left, thus distancing themselves further from the radical-leaning newcomers. "The native Jewish worker, like the Average American, is an ardent sportsman. The radical catchwords have little fascination for him." Thus did John A. Dyche ("a Jew himself," we are told in the introduction to his book) highlight the Americanism of the native-born Jew. On the other hand, "The immigrant worker from the despotic countries of Eastern Europe generally is disappointed and discontented. . . . He hates the landlord. . . . He hates the government official who took his last penny away in taxes and who made him do military service."[24]

In contrast, Moses Samuels's ancestors fought side by side with the Julians in the Great War, a time of resurgent anti-Semitism; as Jews, Samuels's ancestors unequivocally sided with the dominant Anglo-Saxon culture. Such a family history emphasizes Samuels's status as an American and sets him apart from the ethnic hordes arriving from European backwaters. Samuels understands and accepts his position in the American cultural landscape; he knows his place, unlike the Jewish immigrants from eastern Europe. Samuels's torture and death at the hands of the Kalkars makes him, ironically, a martyr for the cause of 100 percent Americanism. This Jew, this perpetual outsider to all societies, becomes the symbol for a resurgent Anglo-American culture.

Now, having apparently cast Mr. Burroughs in a rather grim light, I feel compelled to pull him back from the abyss into which the PC police would like to consign him. In a time when the federal government arrested and deported thousands of alleged anarchists (while ignoring their civil rights); when science was warped to rank all humanity against an Anglo-Saxon ideal (and then found wanting); when supposedly nonbiased government commissions fit research to match preconceived notions about the inferiority of southern and eastern European immigrants (resulting in a highly restrictive, eugenically based quota system in 1924); that Burroughs expressed through his fiction the fears of his day should surprise no one. It would be more of a surprise had he not done so.

The Red Scare of 1919 and 1920 was an ugly period in American history—one of many ugly periods. The stories that comprise *The Moon Maid* reflect that ugliness. But the Red Scare passed, and although Burroughs maintained a hatred of Communism (fueled, in part, by Russian publishers who paid him no royalties), his class consciousness later diminished, and his patriotism became somewhat less rabid (at least until the next war began). Even the stereotypes Burroughs used have lost their currency. To modern readers the Kalkars are nothing more than unpleasant invaders from the Moon. Much of Burroughs's ire no longer resonates, but that doesn't really cause irreparable damage to his story. Because, after all, science fiction, *The Moon Maid* is only escapist entertainment and as such has no underlying meaning at all.

## NOTES

1. Letter of 4 December 1918 to the U.S. Department of Justice. Quoted in Irwin Porges, *Edgar Rice Burroughs: The Man Who Created Tarzan* (Provo UT: Brigham Young University Press, 1975), 313.

2. Some of the reasons for rejection (and Burroughs's reaction thereto) are covered in Porges, *Burroughs*, 313–14.

3. "The Moon Maid" was first serialized in the *Argosy All-Story Weekly* from 5 May to 2 June 1923; "The Moon Men" from 21 February to 15 March 1925; and

"The Red Hawk" from 5 to 19 September 1925. A. C. McClurg's 1926 hardback edition was substantially different from the magazine serials. All mass-market paperback editions printed "The Moon Maid" as a separate novel, while combining the longer magazine versions of "The Moon Men" and "The Red Hawk" under the former title. This one particular sequence of novels and their assorted versions has proved to be a bibliographic nightmare for Burroughs fans. See Alan Hanson, "On the Trail of the Real Moon Maid," *Burroughs Bulletin* New Series (spring 1998): 8–16; and Robert R. Barrett's rather onanistic followup, "The Real 'Moon Maid' Revealed!" *Burroughs Bulletin* New Series (spring 2001): 24–30.

4. Edgar Rice Burroughs, "Home Guarding for the Liberty Loan," quoted in Porges, *Burroughs*, 288. No publication or bibliographic information given for the original.

5. Dillingham Commission's Report on Immigration (1911), quoted in Matthew Frye Jacobson, *Whiteness of a Different Color: European Immigrants and the Alchemy of Race* (Cambridge MA: Harvard University Press, 1998), 78.

6. "Are We Still Anglo-Saxons?" *Literary Digest* 74 (9 September 1922): 31. The quote originally appeared in an unidentified issue of the *New York Times Book Review*.

7. Burl Noggle, *Into the Twenties: The United States from Armistice to Normalcy* (Urbana: University of Illinois Press, 1974), 87.

8. Robert K. Murray, *Red Scare: A Study in National Hysteria, 1919–1920* (Minneapolis: University of Minnesota Press, 1955), 16.

9. Letter of 2 July 1919, quoted in Porges, *Burroughs*, 314.

10. Newell Dwight Hillis, *Rebuilding Europe in the Face of World-Wide Bolshevism* (New York: Fleming H. Revell, 1920), 163–64.

11. Ole Hanson, *Americanism versus Bolshevism* (New York: Doubleday, Page, 1920), vii–viii.

12. Noggle, *Into the Twenties*, 87. The literature on the IWW is quite extensive, but a good modern source is the revised edition of Patrick Renshaw, *The Wobblies: The Story of the IWW and Syndicalism in the United States* (Chicago: Ivan R. Dee, [1967] 1999). For an inside opinion, see Fred Thompson's optimistically titled *The IWW: Its First Fifty Years, 1905–1955* (Chicago: Industrial Workers of the World, 1955).

13. Edgar Rice Burroughs, "Autobiography of Edgar Rice Burroughs," unpublished. Quoted in Porges, *Burroughs*, 106.

14. William McDougall, *Is America Safe for Democracy?* (New York: Charles Scribner's Sons, 1921), vii.

15. "Are We Still Anglo-Saxons?" 32.

16. Clinton Stoddard Burr, *America's Race Heritage* (New York: National Historical Society, 1922), 5.

17. Frederick Lewis Allen, *Only Yesterday: An Informal History of the Nineteen-Twenties* (New York: Harper and Row, 1931), 41.

18. Compare Burroughs's description of the Kalkars with the vivid newspaper descriptions of Leo Frank, a Jewish murder suspect, in Jacobson, *Whiteness of Different Color*, 65–67.

19. Edward Alsworth Ross, *The Old World in the New* (New York: Century, 1914), 285–86.

20. "Anthropological Explanation of the Facial Aspect of the Jew," *Current Opinion* 61 (September 1916): 178. Interestingly, so pervasive was the image of the Jewish "facial aspect" that nowhere in the article is this unique phenomenon actually described.

21. Alsworth, *Old World in the New*, 154. Across the Atlantic a similar distrust of Jews and Bolsheviks was in full swing. The opinions of British adventure writers Rudyard Kipling and H. Rider Haggard are summed up in Harry Ricketts, *Rudyard Kipling: A Life* (New York: Carroll and Graf, 1999), 350–53.

22. Richard Lupoff, *Edgar Rice Burroughs: Master of Adventure* (New York: Ace Books, rev. ed. 1968), 128.

23. Robert G. Spinney, *City of Big Shoulders: A History of Chicago* (DeKalb IL: Northern Illinois University Press, 2000), 136.

24. John A. Dyche, *Bolshevism in American Labor Unions: A Plea for Constructive Unionism* (New York: Boni and Liveright, 1926), vii.

# Glossary

## CAST OF CHARACTERS

Bethelda—Sister of the True Or-Tis, she was twice rescued by Julian 20th, who finally united the feuding clans when he took her as his mate.

Burroughs, Edgar Rice—A Bureau of Communications employee, he transcribed the story narrated by Julian 3rd, the tale of *The Moon Maid*.

Carter, John—Earthman mystically transported to Mars (Barsoom), where he rose to the rank of Warlord, ruling the powerful Helium empire.

Colby, Orrin—Chicago blacksmith and head of the underground ecumenical church (by dint of the fact that his great grandfather once was a Methodist minister). Colby's calm demeanor inspires confidence and hope in his parishioners.

Corrigan, Dennis—A Chicago Yank sentenced to ten years in the mine for trading at night.

The Coyote—Chieftain of one of the Julian clans.

Gapth—Kalkar who captured Julian 5th when the latter entered by mistake the tunnels of City 337.

Go-va-go—Chief of the No-van tribe of Va-gas, captors of Julian 5th, Orthis, and Nah-ee-lah.

Hoffmeyer—Surly agent of Pthav, the Kalkar coal baron.

James, Elizabeth—Julian 8th's mate and mother of Julian 9th.

Jarth—Jemadar of the United Teivos of America, whose goal was to craft America into a military oligarchy. Toward that end he and his henchmen like Or-Tis instituted rigid discipline in the Teivos.

Jay—A lieutenant on the ship *The Barsoom*.

Johansen, Peter—A lanky, stooped Yank traitor who spied on his neighbors, including the Julians, in order to curry favor with the Kalkars.

Ju-lan-fit—Julian 5th's name as pronounced by the Laytheans; he told them "Fit" was a title analogous to "prince," leading them to call him Ju-lan Javadar.

Julian 1st—First of the Julian line, he was born in 1896 and married in 1916. A West Point graduate who became a major by age twenty-two, establishing a family tradition of military service, he was killed in France on Armistance Day, 1918.

Julian 2nd—Born in 1917, he was killed in battle in Turkey in 1938.

Julian 3rd—Born in 1937, he rose through the military to the rank of Admiral of the Air and Commander of the International Peace Fleet. A reincarnation of Julian 1st, he died in 1992 in the line of duty.

Julian 5th—Commander of *The Barsoom*. He and his crew were stranded in Va-Nah. He escaped and returned to Earth with his bride, Nah-ee-lah, but died battling the lunar invasion led by Orthis.

Julian 6th—The son of Julian 5th and Nah-ee-lah, born in 2036.

Julian 8th—Father of Julian 9th. A large and powerful man and Chicago goat trader who aided his son in the rebellion against the Kalkars and was presumably killed in battle.

Julian 9th—A Chicago resident, he launched a human uprising against the Kalkars in 2122. Though martyred in the revolution, his descendents carried on the battle, eventually triumphing over the Moon Men in 2432.

Julian 15th—Drove the Western contingent of the Kalkars out of the Mojave Desert toward a final stand in southern California.

Julian 18th—Forcing his way nearly to the sea in 2048, he was mortally wounded by the Kalkars while battling to return to his Mojave Desert home. He briefly described the Western lands to his tribe before dying.

Julian 19th—Chief of Chiefs of the Julian clan, he was killed by the Or-Tis on his son's birthday, August 12, 2429.

Julian 20th—"The Red Hawk," leader of the united Julian clans in 2430, he began the final drive to exile the Kalkars from America by 2432.

Julian 21st—Son of Julian 20th and Bethelda.

Ko-tah—The most powerful noble of Laythe, who intended to usurp Sagroth and force a marriage with Nah-ee-lah to claim her hereditary throne as ruler.

Ko-vo—Kamadar and ally of Ko-Tah who greeted Julian 5th and Moh-goh upon their arrival in Laythe.

Levy, Nellie—American woman taken as a mate by a Kash Guardsman.

Mik-do—The god of the Nipons, presumably a bastardization of Emperor Mikado.

Moh-goh—A Laythean nobleman imprisoned with Julian 5th in City 337. He escaped with Julian and tried to encourage the Earthman to ally himself with Ko-tah.

Nah-ee-lah—Princess of Laythe, the only child of Jemadar Sagroth, and heiress to the throne of the city.

Nallah—A sister of Julian 20th (from Nah-ee-lah?).

Neeta—A sister of Julian 20th.

Norton—Seventeen-year-old ensign of *The Barsoom*. He cannily appeared to ally himself with Orthis so that he might learn Orthis's engineering secrets in order to repair and fly the ship.

Okonnor—Pure-blooded American follower of the true Or-Tis who briefly joined Raban's forces to prey on the Kalkars before freeing the imprisoned Julian 20th and allying himself with the Julians.

Orthis, Lieutenant Commander—Air school graduate and rival of Julian 5th. Brilliant and unscrupulous, Orthis allowed his deranged jealousy of Julian to overcome his judgment, which led him to vandalize *The Barsoom* and force a landing in the Moon. Orthis later allied himself with the evil Kalkar race, overthrowing the last remnants of the lunar U-ga civilization before moving to conquer the Earth.

Or-tis (false)—The son of a Kalkar woman and a renegade uncle of Or-Tis who assassinated the true Or-Tis and sought to exterminate his followers.

Or-Tis (5th)—The new Commandant of Chicago, appointed by Jarth, Jemadar of the United Teivos of America. Or-Tis was a fifth generation descendent of Orthis.

Or-Tis (16th)—The true descendent of Orthis and the leader of the tribe of Or-Tis. He sought peace between the feuding Earthmen bloodlines, allying himself with Julian 20th against the Kalkars.

Pthav—Kalkar merchant who owned the coal concession in the Teivos of Chicago.

Raban the Giant—A monstrous, nine-foot-tall Kalkar brigand who terrorized the West San Fernando Valley until Julian 9th ended his reign of terror.

The Rain Cloud—Julian 20th's sixteen-year-old brother. He was sensitive but a good warrior.

The Rattlesnake—Chieftain of one of the clans of Julian.

The Red Hawk—Julian 20th's nickname, taken from his family's totem (he wore a single hawk feather in his hair).

The Rock—One of the clan chieftains of the Julians.

Sagroth—Aging Jemadar of Laythe and father of Nah-ee-lah.

Saku—Chief of the Nipons.

Samuels, Moses—Elderly Jewish tanner and friend of the Julians. He was tortured to death by the Kalkars, exacting a vow of vengeance from Julian 9th.

Sheehan, Mollie—Jim Thompson's mate and neighbor of the Julians.

Soor—Cowardly tax collector in the Teivos of Chicago.

St. John, Juana—A former Oak Park resident rescued from Hellhounds and later married to Julian 9th. She escaped the slaughter of the Yank revolutionaries and bore Julian's son, Julian 10th.

Tav—A Kalkar henchman of Raban's who helped capture Julian 20th.

Thompson, Jim—With his mate, Mollie Sheehan, the Julians' neighbors and best friends. A large and powerful man who is a descendent of the American working class.

Vonbulen—A bull-like, mustachioed Chicagoan to whom Soor gave the Julians' marketplace stall. Julian 9th forcibly evicted Vonbulen.

The Vulture—Julian 20th's eighteen-year-old brother, a maturing warrior.

West—Senior Lieutenant on the ship *The Barsoom*.

White—U.S. Secretary of Commerce who sent Julian 3rd in search of the vacationing Burroughs to tender a promotion.

The Wolf—Chieftain of one of the clans of Julian, a seasoned fifty-year-old warrior.

Worth, Betty—Dennis Corrigan's mate, a friend of the Julians, and a member of the church congregation.

Wright, Andrew—A resident of the Teivos of Chicago. His woman bore twins, but the girl "died at birth" to preserve her from a life of harassment by the Kalkars.

## Peoples and Tribes

Apache—The warlike tribe of American Indians, who by 2430 have reasserted their claim to their ancestral lands.

Barsoomians—Inhabitants of Mars (in their own tongue).

Hopi—Descendents of the American Indian tribe, they continue to occupy their traditional homeland in the time of Julian 20th.

In-juns—The Julians' and Kalkars' term for the dark-skinned, native inhabitants of America.

Julians—One hundred human clans, led by the family of noble Julians, whose home in the twenty-fifth century is the Mojave Desert.

Kalkars—A "mongrel breed," this lunar race emerged from "The Thinkers," a secret society and political party consisting of the disenfranchised lower classes who overthrew the educated upper classes, devolving lunar society as a result. With the aid of Orthis the Kalkars were able to carry their revolution to Earth, conquering the world and bringing about a new Dark Age of feudalism and eventual nomadism among Earthmen. Kalkars resemble Earthly humans but tend to be more bovine in appearance, with prominent, hooked noses and hulking physiques.

Kolrados—A tribe presumably occupying the former region of Colorado. The tribe is renowned for the quality of their metals, which they trade peacefully with the Julians.

Lu-thans—A large and powerful Va-ga tribe that were attacked and decimated by Go-va-go's No-vans.

Mojave—Descendents of the American Indian tribe who continue to occupy their traditional homeland in the time of Julian 20th.

Moon Men—Kalkars.

Navaho—Descendents of the American Indian tribe who continue to occupy their homeland in the time of Julian 20th.

Nipon—A pygmy tribe dwelling in the wilds of the Santa Monica Mountains. Presumably of Japanese descent, they hate the Kalkars and consider the pure-blood Or-Tis their friends.

No-vans—The tribe of Va-gas, ruled by Go-va-go, who captured Julian 5th and Orthis, and later Nah-ee-lah.

Or-Tis—The twenty-fifth-century descendents of Orthis, who claim pure Earth bloodlines.

U-gas—The human race of Va-nah, distinguished by their glossy black hair and marble white skin.

Utaws—A trading tribe occupying the region of Utah whose metals are inferior to those of the Kolrados.

Va-gas—Warlike, cannibalistic humanoid quadrupeds who terrorize the rural areas of Va-nah. The size of a small pony, the Va-gas has a broad human face, wears a tunic and harness, and carries spears and daggers as weapons. They capture and eat the human U-gas race. The U-gas return the favor by breeding Va-gas for their flesh.

Yanks—The Kalkars' contemptuous term for native-born Earthmen of America, worn as a badge of pride by the Americans.

Yaqui—The warlike tribe of American Indians. By 2430 they have reasserted their claim to their ancestral lands.

## FLORA AND FAUNA

flowers—Lunar flowers are described as being "of highly complex form, of pale and delicate shades, of great size and rare beauty." Stalks are flesh-colored like that of mature lunar grass.

flying toad—Toadlike creatures with bat wings that flit about the Va-nah treetops, uttering plaintive cries. Their flesh is poisonous, but they are nonaggressive to humans.

fruit—Lunar forests bear fruit "of considerable size and of a variety of forms and colors."

grass—Pink lunar grasses that become flesh-colored at maturity.

hellhounds—Feral dogs grown large, bold, and aggressive, which terrorize the inhabitants of the United Teivos of America.

insects—Undescribed by the Earth adventurers, these creatures inhabit the lunar forests.

Lonay—Pack leader of the Julians' hounds, which guard their flocks.

nuts—Presumably similar to those found on Earth, they form part of the Va-ga diet.

Red Lightning—A previously intractible bay stallion that Julian 9th purchased from Hoffmeyer for one goat. After breaking the stallion it became a loyal mount and friend to Julian.

Red Lightning (2nd)—Julian 20th's bay stallion.

reptiles—Lunar reptiles, all venomous, include the rympth, the tor-ho, and the flying toad.

rympth—A lunar snake that is five feet long with four frog-like legs and a flat head with a single eye in the center of the forehead. The creature wriggles like a snake while the legs scramble to aid locomotion. Amphibious with poisonous flesh, the rympth is "considered the lowest and most disgusting creature of Va-nah," though it is nonaggressive to humans.

shrubs—Low shrubs which bear a berry-like fruit, grown in Va-nah forests.

snakes—*See* rympth.

tor-ho—A voracious reptilian carnivore about the size of an Earthly puma. The extremely rare creature has long fangs and poisonous claws resulting from its primary diet of rympths and winged toads.

vegetation—Va-nah is covered with rank vegetation in pale hues: lavenders, violets, pinks, and yellows predominate. The crew of *The Barsoom* also discovered vegetation on the external surface of the moon, apparently a fungus-like tree. Fast-growing enough to appear to be moving, the plants grow in "riotous profusion" in valleys and deep ravines. During a life cycle spanning twenty-seven days a tree develops from a spore to a mighty plant hundreds of feet high, with angular, grotesque branches and broad, thick leaves in all seven primary colors. When plants go into shadow during the moon's monthly lunar cycle they disintegrate into dust. Apparently small creatures dwell in the plants and eat the leaves.

## GEOGRAPHY

Arizona—The eastern boundary of the Julian holdings, a rich land that the Julians eschew inhabiting that they might keep the Kalkars at bay from a vantage point in the Mojave Desert.

Barsoom—The Martians' name for their home world.

Bear—A large mountain lake in California, presumably the former Big Bear Lake.

The Capitol—The former Los Angeles, ground zero of the Kalkar occupation of California.

City Number 337—Kalkar city in which Julian 5th is imprisoned. He later escapes with the Laythean nobleman Moh-goh.

Helium—Capital of Barsoom's greatest empire, ruled by transplanted Earthman John Carter, Warlord of Mars.

Laythe—Large, proud city of the U-gas, who have managed to retain their culture despite the loss of their technology, while staving off Kalkar overthrow. Ruled by the Jemadar Sagroth, his wife, and his daughter, Nah-ee-lah.

Va-nah—Moon-dwellers' term for their world, the lunar interior.

## Miscellaneous Terms

Admiral of the Air—Julian 3rd's title and rank after his promotion at the end of the Great War.

Air School—The training academy and alma mater of Julian 5th and Orthis.

*The Barsoom*—Interplanetary ship built by Earthmen and captained by Julian 5th, who was commissioned with the first manned flight to Mars.

Barsoomian Ray—The repulsive Eighth Ray of Mars.

Blue Room—The lounge in the transoceanic liner *The Harding* in which Edgar Rice Burroughs met Julian 3rd.

Bureau of Communications—Government agency whose employee Edgar Rice Burroughs met Julian 3rd and learned his tale.

"The Butcher"—Kalkar state executioner, so called because he slashes throats to conserve precious ammunition.

"By the Flag!"—Julian oath sworn on the sacred flag.

Chief of Chiefs—Head of all the hundred Julian clans of the West who swear allegiance. The title is held by the descendent of the original Julian line, Julian 20th, the Red Hawk.

Council Ring—Circular table at which the Julian tribesmen take their meals and engage in council.

Eighth Earthly Ray—The repulsive Eighth Ray of Earth.

Eighth Jovian Ray—The repulsive Eighth Ray of Jupiter.

Eighth Lunar Ray—The repulsive Eighth Ray of the Moon.

Eighth Mercurian Ray—The repulsive Eighth Ray of Mercury.

Eighth Ray—A repulsive force that renders gravity impotent. Long used for levitation by Barsoomian airships, the discovery of the Earth's Eighth Ray provided a means for interplanetary travel, first undertaken by *The Barsoom*.

Eighth Solar Ray—The repulsive Eighth Ray of the Sun.

Eighth Venusian Ray—The repulsive Eighth Ray of Venus.

The Flag—The deity of the Julians, "it has the power of life and death, and it brings the rains and the winds and the thunder." It is represented by a tattered relic of the American flag, which the Julians worship.

Flag of Argon—The full title of the Flag, the origin and meaning of which are lost in the mists of antiquity.

Great Chief—*See* Chief of Chiefs.

Great Feud—The historic enmity between Or-Tis and Julian.

Great War—World War I, which lasted from 1914 to 1967.

Gu-e-ho—Va-ga word which has at least twenty-seven different meanings, depending on the note in which each syllable is sung.

Harding—A transoceanic airship on which Edgar Rice Burroughs meets Julian 3rd, who relates the tale of his descendents.

Hoos—"Holes," lunar craters that pierce the hollow moon's crust and allow ingress to the world of Va-nah.

Imperial Guard—The personal bodyguard of Sagroth, Jemadar of Laythe.

International Peace Fleet—The international police force charged with keeping the peace of the world community following the abolishment of war in 1967.

javadar—"Prince" in the lunar language.

Jemadar of America—Julian 20th's title by proclamation, decreed upon the final defeat of the Kalkars.

Jemadar—"Emperor" in the lunar language.

Jemadav—"Empress" in the lunar language.

Kaisers—Yank term of disrespect for the Kalkars, obviously remembered from the Great War.

Kalkar Guard—Another term for the "Kash Guard."

kamadar—Lunar title analogous to the English title "Duke."

Kash Guard—Soldiers of the occupying Kalkar forces (denoting singular and plural).

keld—The lunar year, composed of ten ulas, approximately 272 days of Earth time.

Lord of Vengeance—One of Julian 20th's titles.

"Love of the Flag!"—A Julian oath, based on the deification of the American flag.

nonovar—"Princess" in the language of the U-gas.

ola—One hundreth of an ula, approximately six hours and thirty-two minutes in Earth time.

paladar—Lunar title analogous to the English title "Count."

Protector of the Flag—Another of Julian 20th's titles.

Teivos—"District" in the governing hierarchy of the Kalkars, as in "The United Teivos of America"; or the administrative body of that district.

Twentyfour—Kalkar municipal ruling committee.

ula—A sidereal month, measured by the U-gas by observing the lunar cycle as evidenced by the sunlight disseminating through the hoos.

United Teivos of America—The Kalkar appellation for America.

Zo-al—A great beast believed by the superstitious Va-gas to dwell in the depths of the lunar craters, from where it generates fierce storms when angry.

## Chronology of *The Moon Men*

| DATE | EVENT |
|---|---|
| 4 Mar. 1866 | John Carter is astrally transported to Mars. |
| 1896 | Julian 1st is born. |
| 1914–1959 | World War I (The Great War). |
| 1916 | Julian 1st is married. |
| 1917 | Julian 2nd is born. |
| 1918 | Julian 1st is killed in France on Armistance Day. |
| 1937 | Julian 3rd, a reincarnation of Julian 1st and the narrator of *The Moon Men*, is born. |
| 1938 | Julian 2nd is killed in battle in Turkey. |
| 1940 | Extraterrestrial radio waves are detected and determined to have originated on Mars. |
| 1945 | Apparatus to send messages to Barsoom is perfected. |
| 1953 | Julian 3rd enters the war at age sixteen. |
| 1959–1969 | Men make worldwide peace their goal. |
| Apr. 1967 | Victory Day—Worldwide peace is achieved. Julian 3rd is commissioned as Admiral of the Air and transferred to the International Peace Fleet. |
| 10 June 1967 | "Mars Day"—First decoded message from Barsoom is broadcast to the world. ERB meets Julian 3rd in the Blue Room of the *Harding*, and Julian recites the events of *The Moon Maid*. |
| Mar. 1969 | ERB, hunting polar bears in the Arctic, is rescued near death, and Julian 3rd recites the events of *The Moon Men* and *The Red Hawk*. |
| 1970 | Julian 4th is born (date of death unknown). |
| 1992 | Julian 3rd is killed in the line of duty. |
| 2000 | Julian 5th, a reincarnation of Julian 3rd, is born in Illinois. |
| 2015 | A Barsoomian spacecraft with a crew of five is launched for Earth and goes off course. |
| 2016 | Julian 5th graduates from Air School and joins the International Peace Fleet, the fifth generation of Julians in one hundred consecutive years to serve his country. |
| 2020 | Last message from the Barsoomian spacecraft is received—caught in the grip of Jupiter after narrowly avoiding a fiery death in the sun. |
| 2024 | Lieutenant Commander Orthis discovers the Eighth Solar Ray. |

| | |
|---|---|
| Two months later | Rays of the moon, Mercury, Venus, Earth, and Jupiter are discovered. |
| Late 2024 | Radio-operated prototype spaceship is completed and successfully tested on Earth. |
| 2025 | Eight months of work pass before *The Barsoom* is completed. |
| 24 Dec. 2025 | Elaborate White House Ball is given for the crew of *The Barsoom*. |
| 25 Dec. 2025 | *The Barsoom* casts off for Mars. |
| 6 Jan. 2026 | *The Barsoom*'s closest scheduled encounter with the Moon occurs. |
| 7 Jan. 2026 | A drunken Lieutenant Commander Orthis speaks insubordinately to Julian 5th; he is later found wrecking the auxiliary engine to force a landing on the moon. |
| 8 Jan. 2026 | *The Barsoom* discovers Va-nah at 11 A.M. after a twenty-six-hour descent into a lunar crater. |
| 2026–2036 | The lunar events of *The Moon Maid* transpire; after escaping the Va-Gas, Orthis ingratiates himself with the Kalkars and spreads propaganda. |
| 2036 | Julian 5th and *The Barsoom* return to Earth, with Nah-ee-lah, the Moon Maid, aboard. |
| 2036–2050 | The Kalkars, under the direction of Orthis, build fleets with which to attack the Earth. |
| 2050 | One thousand ships manned by one hundred thousand Kalkars and carrying one thousand Va-gas are led by Orthis against Earth. Orthis wipes out almost the entire International Peace Fleet within thirty days. |
| Late 2050 | Julian 5th goes into hiding, devising a counter-weapon which ultimately results in the deaths of Orthis and himself. |
| 1 Jan. 2100 | Julian 9th born in the Teivos of Chicago. |
| 2110 | A visiting Yank from the West tells of his experiences and the state of the rest of America, greatly impressing young Julian 9th. |
| 2117 | Jarth becomes Jemadar of the United Teivos of America; oppression worsens. |
| 2120–2122 | The events of *The Moon Men* take place. |
| 2122 | Julian 9th dies in the Yanks' uprising. |
| 2122–2309 | The Yanks, led by Julian's descendents, push the Kalkars back to both coasts of America. |
| 2309 | Julian 15th drives the Kalkars to a last stand along the California coastline. |

| | |
|---|---|
| 2330–2430 | The Yanks are stymied for one hundred years by the Kalkars entrenched in southern California, despite twenty warring sorties over the century. |
| 2408 | Julian 18th rides alone almost to the Pacific and is killed upon his return to the desert. |
| 12 Aug. 2409 | Julian 20th is born. |
| 2411 | The Vulture is born. |
| 2413 | Rain Cloud is born. |
| 2414–2419 | Julian 20th learns the history of the Julian clan, Or-Tis, and the Kalkars. |
| 12 Aug. 2429 | Julian 20th becomes a man. |
| 12 Aug. 2429 | Julian 19th dies in the Great Feud; Julian 20th becomes the Great Chief. |
| Jan. 2430 | Julian 20th plans the final drive. |
| Apr. 2430 | The Yanks move into the valley and renew hostilities; the further events of *The Red Hawk* transpire. |
| 2432 | The Kalkars are driven into the sea at the former site of San Diego (end of the Chronicles). |

# Alterations to the Text

## Silent Corrections

### CAPITALIZATION

Edgar Rice Burroughs's style on occasion is to capitalize certain key words that are not invariably considered proper nouns (for example, Moon, Earth, Father, Mother) and also to capitalize the direct article of titles (for example, The Red Hawk, *The Barsoom*, The Capital). Such capitalization preferences, found in the book version and inconsistently in the serialization, have been adopted and standardized in this edition. Those occasional words capitalized in the serialization but not in the book version (for example, hellhound, teivos), have been rendered in lowercase.

### INCORRECT AND INCONSISTENT SPELLINGS

Misspelled words have been corrected. Words that were inconsistently spelled in the three serial installments have been standardized to follow the book version (for example, The TwentyFour appeared as "The TwentyFour" in the serial *Moon Maid* and as "the Twenty-Four" in the serial *Moon Men*). Burroughs's preferences for hyphenating adjectives (for example, well-armed) and nouns (such as clan-sign), as set forth in the book version, have been adopted in this edition.

### THE MOON MAID

The chapter titles that appear in the serialization of this tale were changed for the book version; the latter headings are used in this edition. The original serial chapter titles are noted below.

1 The serial chapter title is "Prologue."

7 Following the format established for Parts II and III ("The Moon Men" and "The Red Hawk") in the book version, "The Moon Maid" is labeled in this edition "Part 1," and is accompanied by the tagline "Being the Story of Julian 5th."

9 The serial chapter title is "An Adventure in Space."

22 The serial chapter title is "The Secret of the Moon."

31 The serial chapter title is "Animals or Men?"

40 The serial chapter title is "Captured."

49 The serial chapter title is "Out of the Storm."

58 The serial chapter title is "The Moon Maid."

70 The serial chapter title is "A Fight and a Chance."

78 The serial chapter title is "A Fight with a Tor-ho."

88 The serial chapter title is "An Attack by Kalkars."

96 The serial chapter title is "The City of Kalkars."

108 The serial chapter title is "A Meeting with Ko-tah."

116 The serial chapter title is "Growing Danger."

126 The serial chapter title is "Death Within and Without!"

136 The serial chapter title is "The Barsoom!"


## THE MOON MEN

Because chapter 1 of the serialization is considered a prologue in the book edition, the chapter numbers differ by one between the serialization and book edition—chapter 2 in the serialization is chapter 1 in the book edition, and so forth. This edition follows the chapter titles and arrangement of the book edition.

149 Following the book edition, "The Moon Men" is labeled "Part II" and is accompanied by the tagline "Being the Story of Julian 9th."

151 The serial chapter title is "A Strange Meeting."

151–54 The account of the second meeting between Julian 3rd and the narrator is represented differently in the book edition, which eliminates the polar journey: "It was two years after I had first met him abroad the liner *Harding* that I came across him again. I had just been appointed Secretary of Commerce. He came to my office in Washington on official business during March, 1969. I invited him to my home for dinner and it was later in the evening that I importuned him for the promised story of Julian 9th" (207).

155 Added from the book edition (207): "radio communication for *seventy* years."

160 Substituted from the book edition (213): "*may* only remain conjecture" rather than "*can* only remain conjecture."

160 Substituted from the book edition (213): "Elements *who* had been discontented" rather than "Elements *which* had been discontented."

160 Added from the book edition (213): "labor and capital *each* saw."

160 Added from the book edition (214): "Nah-ee-lah, his *Moon Maid* mother."

161 The serial chapter title is "Soor, the Tax Collector."

161 Added from the book edition (215): "who ruled *us.*"

168 When describing the hellhounds, Burroughs used the present tense in the book version (217), and that tense is adopted here.

168 This chapter finishes in the serialization at the end of the paragraph that concludes with "we call them the hellhounds." The book version extends this chapter for a few more pages (217–23); that organization is followed in this edition.

168 Burroughs's description of Jim Thompson and Mollie—Sheehan is cast in the present tense in the book version (217), and so that tense is adopted here.

169 The book edition eliminates the castigation of Jim by Julian 8th and the ensuing spirited dispute between them instead adds these sentences (219):

Father placed his hand upon Jim's shoulder.

"We must not weaken, my friend," he said. "I often feel the same way," and then he walked quickly across the room to the fireplace.

These sentences are not included in this edition because in tone and content they are out of place in the narrative if the deleted serialization passages are retained.

172 Added from the book edition (222): "and worldly wise *and so I knew what I had not known as a little child.*"

172 Added from the book edition (222): "I knew who it was *who* owned the face."

172–73 The book edition ends chapter I with the sentence "we prepared for bed" (223) and commences the next chapter (224) with the paragraph beginning "I had just slipped off my tunic." Two and one half descriptive paragraphs are interposed between these sentences in the serialization of "The Moon Men," material that was cut from the book edition. Those deleted sentences are retained in this edition in their original place in the narrative, and so begin chapter II.

174  Added from the book edition (224): "screams of the woman, *which were repeated twice.*"

174  Added from the book edition (224): "and ran off *before I reached them; but not far.*"

176  The book edition (227) casts in the present tense the mention of the Kalkars drinking to excess, and so that preference is adopted here.

177  Added from the book edition (227): "Two only *of the hellhounds* returned to the attack."

178  Substituted from the book edition (229): "the common *garmenture*" rather than "the common garb."

185  Substituted from the book edition (238): "The foundation *and the walls* above the ground" rather than "The foundation walls and above the ground."

187  Added from the book edition (240): "moved to Juana, where she stood just behind my shoulder at the far side of the room."

187  Substituted from the book edition (241): "'*Mm-m,*'" rather than "'H-m!'"

188  Substituted from the book edition (242): "her scorn of the *man*" rather than "her scorn of the Kalkar."

189  The serial chapter title is "The Fight on Market Day."

189  Substituted from the book edition (244): "she *bade* me good night" rather than "she bid me good night."

191  Substituted from the book edition (244): "*The Flag* had been removed" rather than "it had been removed."

196  Substituted from the book edition (249): "with *soft hog dung*" rather than "smeared with dirt."

200  Added from the book edition (254): "broad entranceway, *facing toward the west.*"

200  Added from the book edition (254): "*I was soon to find out.* Or-tis asked who appeared."

201  Added from the book edition (255): "until I died *and I laughed in their faces.*"

204  Added from the book edition (259): "in my arms *and tossed her to the ceiling.*"

205  Added from the book edition (261): "and *she was* seemingly very glad to see me."

205  Added from the book edition (261): "threaten them—*each has plenty of his own.*"

205  Substituted from the book edition (261): "*opposite* shore" rather than "other shore."

206 Added from the book edition (262): "if there had been any passers-by, *which except upon rare occasions there were not.*"

206 Added from the book edition (262): "guess at its age—*it had been there longer than they could recall.*"

208 Added from the book edition (265): "bright spots in our drab existence *that helped to make life bearable.*"

210 Added from the book edition (266): "hour later, *after the rest had gone,* we started out."

211 Substituted from the book edition (266): "half an hour *after* we reached" rather than "half an hour before we reached."

212 Added from the book edition (268): "persecuted us of late—*rather they had left us alone*—a respite."

213 Added from the book edition (270): "Is my man, *my Julian,* less brave than he?"

215 Substituted from the book edition (271): "who knows but that *he already has been ordained!*" rather than "who knows but that He already has done so."

215 Added from the book edition (272–273): "beasts of the forest. *When his friends come he serves them food and drink and—me! Ugh!* I could kill him."

217 Added from the book edition (274): "a rough niche was built *in,* containing a few shelves."

217 Added from the book edition (274): "to its former place, *being careful to see that it fitted tightly.*"

217 Added from the book edition (274): "in the *stygian* darkness of the tunnel."

217 Added from the book edition (274): "life this *and push it aside.*"

217 Added from the book edition (274): "the men scattered in different directions, *each taking his woman with him.*"

224 Added from the book edition (277): "had to applaud *my horsemanship.*"

224 Substituted from the book edition (279): "*The latter consists* of a high stockade" rather than "It consisted of a high stockade."

225 Substituted from the book edition (279): "a detention camp *where they hold those who are* awaiting trial" rather than "a detention camp to hold those awaiting trial."

225 Added from the book edition (279): "and those *who have been* sentenced to the mines."

225 The description of the military prison is rendered in the present tense in the book edition (279) and in this edition. Two additional

descriptive paragraphs (beginning with "They marched them" and "Though men were sometimes sentenced") were cut from the book edition. For consistency and readability, those passages also have been cast in the present tense.

225 Substituted from the book edition (279): "speak *with* Julian 8th" rather than "speak to Julian 8th."

228 The book edition (283) contains a snippet of additional text: "there would surely be enough of us to overthrow those who remained loyal *to The Flag.*" This change has not been incorporated in this edition because it renders meaningless the sentence. Julian 9th and others are in fact themselves "loyal to The Flag" and want "to overthrow" those loyal to the Kalkars.

229 Added from the book edition (283): " . . . fight him off; *but he was forcing her slowly toward her bedroom, for* he was a large."

230 Added from the book edition (285): "he was spreading *alarm and* consternation among the people."

234 Substituted from the book edition (289): "I could best succeed in *any* plan" rather than "I could best succeed in my plan."

235 Added from the book edition (290): "upon his face—*his head crushed to a pulp.* He never knew."

236 Added from the book edition (291): "I was *as* much at home in that liquid element."

236 Added from the book edition (291): "came to the surface. *When I was sure that no one was directly above me* I swam farther."

236 Added from the book edition (292): "we caught *up* Red Lightning."

237 Added from the book edition (292): "who had been as close to her as her own *people*; but she was as brave."

237 Added from the book edition (293): "mines lie about fifty miles away—*those to which our people are sent*—and west of south."

238 Added from the book edition (293): "the remnants of clearings *that must once have been farms* which were not yet."

238 Added from the book edition (294): "rich and powerful farming class—*those people of olden times whose selfishness had sought to throw the burden of taxation upon the city dwellers where the ignorant foreign classes were most numerous and had thus added their bit to fomenting the discontent that had worked the downfall of a glorious nation. They themselves suffered much before they died, but nothing by comparison with the humiliation and degradation of their descendants—an illiterate, degraded, starving race.*"

240 Substituted from the book edition (297): "I leaped *for them* and caught *them, and* then I scrambled up" rather than "I leaped and caught hold. Then I scrambled up."

240 Added from the book edition (297): "I took his *bayonetted* rifle."

240 Substituted from the book edition (297): "I saw coming *upon the next*" rather than "I saw coming up."

240 Substituted from the book edition (297): "what was going on *fifty feet* away" rather than "what was going on a few feet away."

241 Substituted from the book edition (298): "upon them like wild *bees* upon a foe" rather than "upon then like wild beasts upon a foe."

241 Added from the book edition (298): "to follow on foot—*on* to Chicago."

241 The book edition (298) reads that "The very thought of the feared Kalkars and their Kash Guards took the marrow from the hearts of many." In the serialization, "bones" appears instead of "hearts," and, since that metaphoric usage is less disjunctive, it is incorporated in this edition.

245 Added from the book edition (304): "they had led—*they and their mothers before them.*"

247 Added from the book edition (306): "they would wait for me outside and *so* we parted."

249 Substituted from the book edition (310): "all of that *incarnation*" rather than "all of that re-incarnation."

249 Substituted from the book edition (310): "'another?' I *insisted*" rather than "'another? I persisted."

## THE RED HAWK

251 Following the book edition, "The Red Hawk" is labeled "Part III" and is accompanied by the tagline "Being the Story of Julian 20th."

253 The serial chapter title is "The Flag."

253 Substituted from the book edition (313): "I reined Red Lightning in *upon* the summit" rather than "I reined Red Lightning in at the summit."

253 Added from the book edition (313): "since the Moon Men *had* swept down upon us."

253 Substituted from the book edition (313): "their side of the gashes they *have* built forts" rather than "their side of the gashes they had built forts."

253 Substituted from the book edition (314): "That was *over* three hundred years ago" rather than "That was more than three hundred years ago."

255 Substituted from the book edition (315): "His breeches, wide *below* the hips" rather than "His breeches, wide about the hips."

255 Added from the book edition (315–316): "sewn to the hide in various *manners of design*" not "sewn to the hide in various designs."

256 Substituted from the book edition (317): "upon the world's western edge, *a few* Kalkars are making" rather than "upon the world's western edge, the Kalkars are making."

257 Substituted from the book edition (319): "Then we *went in to* our women" rather than "Then we greeted our women."

258 Added from the book edition (320): "her voice heard in The Council Ring."

259 Substituted from the book edition (322): "from father to son for *over* a hundred years" rather than "from father to son for more than a hundred years."

259 Substituted from the book edition (322): "She was silent some time before *replying*" rather than "She was silent some time before making a reply."

260 Added from the book edition (323): "eating might begin. *Before each warrior was an earthenware vessel containing beer and another filled with wine, and there were slaves whose duty it was to keep these filled, which was no small task, for we are hearty men and great drinkers, though there is no drunkenness among us as there is among the Kalkars.*"

260 Added from the book edition (323): "*Other* slaves brought meat and vegetables."

260 Substituted from the book edition (324): "each warrior he *rose* and leaning" rather than "each warrior he arose and leaning."

260 Substituted from the book edition (324): "behind the warriors were *two or three score* shaggy hounds" rather than "behind the warriors were twoscore shaggy hounds."

261 Added from the book edition (324): "gall the soul of *The* Red Hawk least of all."

263 Substituted from the book edition (326): "all are *here*—some fifty thousand" rather than "all are there—some fifty thousand."

266 Added from the book edition (328): "For horsemen alone it would have been *but* a hard march."

269 Added from the book edition (329): "the heaviest toll, *fully ten thousand head*, mostly lambs."

269 Substituted from the book edition (329): "legends of our slaves *say*" rather than "legends of our slaves tell us."

269 Added from the book edition (330): "The herds were gathered *in* and held."

270 Substituted from the book edition (332): "a few minutes later I *brought Red Lightning to a halt*" rather than "a few minutes later I reined in Red Lightning."

270 Added from the book edition (332): "dotted with *the glowing embers of a thousand* dying camp fires."

272 Substituted from the book edition (334): "during the *past* hundred years" rather than "during the last hundred years."

273 Substituted from the book edition (334): "savage throats *rose* the awful cries" rather than "savage throats arose the awful cries."

273 The book edition (334) contains the phrase "the cursing, shrieking mob that fled before them only to be ridden down and trampled by *their* horses' feet," which differs from the serialization: "the cursing, shrieking mob that fled before them only to be ridden down and trampled by *our* horses' feet." The phrase as rendered in the serial version is clearer in meaning—it is the Americans' horses, not the Kalkars', that are trampling the "shrieking mob" of Kalkars—and so it is retained in this edition.

273 Substituted from the book edition (335): "the wild, *hoarse* war-cries of battle-maddened men" rather than "the wild, raucous war cries of battle-maddened men."

274 Substituted from the book edition (336): "did this fellow, with his *great bulk* and his little" rather than "did this fellow, with his black whiskers and his little."

274 Added from the book edition (336): "even though the reins hung loose *upon his withers.*"

275 Substituted from the book edition (337): "I was able only *to partially* parry" rather than "I was able only partly to parry."

282 Punctuated incorporated from the book edition (345) in order to clarify the interrogative: "for had I not accomplished what my people had been striving after for a hundred years—a foothold on the western coast?"

284 Added from the book edition (347): "they may have all of the country east *and southeast* of a straight line drawn from the pass of the ancients south to the sea; we will occupy the country to the west *and northwest* of that line."

288 Substituted from the book edition (351): "remaining buildings had

been *gutted* by flame" rather than "remaining buildings have been eaten by flame."

290 Added from the book edition (354): "I told him as much. *He shrugged his shoulders.*"

293 Substituted from the book edition (359): "I *like to have slipped and fallen* twice in that distance" rather than "I came close to slipping and falling twice in that distance."

295 Added from the book edition (359): "as we crept *forward* toward a doorway."

295 Substituted from the book edition (359): "either by the fires that have *gutted* most of the buildings" rather than "either by the fires that have destroyed the interiors of most of the buildings."

295 Substituted from the book edition (360): "It cast a pallid *luminance* beneath it" rather than "It cast a pallid luminescence beneath it."

295 Substituted from the book edition (360): "the Or-tis riding on the side *nearer* the guard" rather than "the Or-tis riding on the side nearest the guard."

296 Added from the book edition (362): "leaders of the pursuit *and Or-tis turned to the south and I to the north.*"

297 Substituted from the book edition (363): "I dismounted to rest my beloved *friend* while I listened" rather than "I dismounted to rest my beloved mount while I listened."

297 Substituted from the book edition (363): "In *an instance* I was asleep" rather than "In another minute I was asleep."

298 Substituted from the book edition (364): "as far as the eye could reach, water" rather than "as far as the eye could reach, was water."

300 Substituted from the book edition (366): "as well as *the tracks* of domestic animals" rather than "as well as those of domestic animals."

301 Added from the book edition (366): "wound upward for perhaps *two or* three miles."

302 Substituted from the book edition (367): "make ourselves understood to *one another*" rather than "make ourselves understood to each other."

304 Substituted from the book edition (370): "probably fire, *though,* since his reference" rather than "probably fire, since his reference."

306 Substituted from the book edition (373): "A Kalkar up to *his* old tricks" rather than "A Kalkar up to their old tricks."

307 Substituted from the book edition (374): "whatever advantage these things might have *seemed to give* him" rather than "whatever advantage these things might have given him."

307 Added from the book edition (374): "high above his head. *The Flag!* What a chance."

307 Substituted from the book edition (374–75): "two things at once—*me and his horse*—and as he did" rather than "two things at once—his horse and his opponent—and as he did."

308 Substituted from the book edition (375): "I was *fearful* as to my skill" rather than "I was distrustful as to my skill."

311 Substituted from the book edition (379): "hate me worse than *as though* I were a Kalkar?" rather than "hate me worse than if I were a Kalkar?"

311 Added from the book edition (379): "'a Julian,' I added, *proudly.*"

311 Substituted from the book edition (379): "Already *had I* regretted" rather than "Already I had regretted."

312 Added from the book edition (381): "she looked very forlorn and alone. *I could not help but feel sorry for her.*"

313 Substituted and added from the book edition (382): "'You lost many warriors? *You must have.*'" rather than "'You have lost many warriors?'"

314 Substituted from the book edition (383): "I replied as I *rose* to add fuel" rather than "I replied as I arose to add fuel."

314 Added from the book edition (383): "'will be cold.' *She held it out towards me.*"

315 Added from the book edition (384): "I could see it. *She was changed.*"

316 Substituted from the book edition (386): "There *were the tracks* of several horses" rather than "There was the spoor of several horses."

318 Added from the book edition (387): "could not admit; but *possibly* I had found."

318 Substituted from the book edition (387): "a greater meaning *for* me" rather than "a greater meaning to me."

319 Substituted from the book edition (388): "I could tell from the *trail* that they" rather than "I could tell from the spoor that they."

319 Substituted from the book edition (388): "Then I could see *farther* in all directions" rather than "Then I could see further in all directions."

319 Substituted from the book edition (388): "A single glance *assured* me" rather than "A single glance determined me."

320 Added from the book edition (389): "constantly the danger *of apprehension* increased."

320 Substituted from the book edition (390): "the thud of horses' *feet*" rather than "the thud of horses' hoofs."

321 Substituted from the book edition (392): "prompted no doubt by *fear*

of their master" rather than "prompted no doubt by the fear of their master."

322 Substituted from the book edition (392): "never came far, for they *and I* soon discovered that with *their* heavy bow I could drive *their heavy* arrows" rather than "never came far, for they soon discovered that with my heavy bow I could drive arrows."

322 Substituted from the book edition (392): "crouched in the saddle as the *thirtieth descendant of the first Red Lightning* flattened" rather than "crouched in the saddle as the splendid animal flattened."

323 Substituted from the book edition (394): "for certainly there *were* neither fire nor inspiration" rather than "for certainly there was neither fire nor inspiration."

324 Substituted from the book edition (395): "I turned in time to *partially* dodge" rather than "I turned in time to partly dodge."

327 Substituted from the book edition (400): "bellowing, and *always about* himself and what he had done" rather than "bellowing, and it always was about himself and what he had done."

327 Substituted from the book edition (400): "and *wind* passes for brains" rather than "and craft passes for brains."

328 Added from the book edition (400): "as I had known that he would be, *even before he started off to fetch me.*"

330 Substituted from the book edition (402): "the nicker of *a* red stallion" rather than "the nicker of my red stallion."

330 Substituted from the book edition (404): "so closely together as *to almost* resemble a single" rather than "so closely together as almost to resemble a single."

332 Substituted from the book edition (406): "glaring at me as *though* overcome by surprise" rather than "glaring at me as if overcome by surprise."

334 Substituted from the book edition (408): "as he staggered to *rise* I thought" rather than "as he staggered to arise I thought."